Whistling Women and Crowing

"Melora Fern has written a totally original and psychologically complex novel about her appealing young heroine Birdie's coming of age as a "whistling woman" in an all-girl musical group with the famed Chautauqua Circuit as they travel the country on tour. Sexy, smart, and irresistible, this is historical fiction of a very high order—I literally could not put it down! Highly recommended."

NY Times best-selling author, Lee Smith

* * *

"*Whistling Women and Crowing Hens* is a thoroughly immersive and uplifting tale, deftly exploring female ambition in the riotous 1920s. Birdie Stauffer is a winsome heroine, and readers will cheer for her to succeed both on-stage and off. As Birdie wrestles with learning to trust herself, a gripping love triangle and an entertaining cast of side characters impact her in unforeseen ways. Fern's vivid details bring the historical time period and charming characters to life."

—Heather Bell Adams, author of *Maranatha Road*
and *The Good Luck Stone*

* * *

"*Whistling Women and Crowing Hens* is an immersive read set in the Chautauqua circuit of the 1920s. Talented whistler and trombonist Birdie Stauffer finds herself a member of a quintet performing throughout the northeast. When small-town Birdie steps into the wider world, she discovers aspects of herself she never knew existed. Increasingly at odds with societal and sisterly expectations, she must choose between following her truth and disappointing the most important people in her life.

Melora Fern's debut novel offers an unconventional coming of age story set against the backdrop of a nation doing the same. As the propriety of the Victorian era gives way to the anything-goes roaring twenties, women find themselves newly enfranchised and empowered, yet still traditional expectations endure.

Fern's attention to detail and a cast of unforgettable characters make this book hard to put down. Full of the drama and humor that come from five women sharing close quarters for weeks at a time, *Whistling Women and Crowing Hens* is at times raucous, tragic, and uplifting. At its heart, this book is about finding one's voice and singing (or whistling) it loud."

—Culley Holderfield, author of *Hemlock Hollow*

*   *   *

"I'm drawn to stories of women's self-discovery and the challenges they face, and Melora Fern's *Whistling Women and Crowing Hens* is a true gem. Set in the Roaring Twenties as women defied societal norms, Birdie Stauffer enters the Chautauqua arts movement and discovers her extraordinary talent as a concert whistler. Although the Golden Age of musical whistling is past, this historical novel captured my heart as Birdie finds her voice and explores the world, love, and her unique path as a woman. Between her two suitors, a domineering sister, and her fellow choir members, Birdie must forge her own path in an era of newfound freedoms, all while remaining a heroine we admire. Melora Fern's historical novel resonates with Prohibition-era nostalgia and warmth."

—Julia Park Tracey, author of *The Bereaved* and *I've Got Some Lovin' to Do*

*   *   *

"Settle into your armchair, because you won't want to leave until the end of this whistlestop tour of the Roaring Twenties. When Birdie Stauffer leaves the nest to join the all-woman Versatile Quintet on the Chautauqua Circuit, she finds her wings and learns to soar. From the boarding house to the stage, from the hinterlands to the big city, Melora Fern's *Whistling Women and Crowing Hens* will take you on an extraordinary journey of music, adventure, friendship and unexpected love."

—Mimi Herman, author of *The Kudzu Queen*

Whistling Women and Crowing Hens

A Novel

Melora Fern

Sibylline
DIGITAL FIRST

Sibylline Press
Copyright © 2025 by Melora Fern
All Rights Reserved.

Published in the United States by Sibylline Digital First,
an imprint of All Things Book LLC, California.

Sibylline Press is dedicated to publishing the brilliant work
of women authors ages 50 and older.

www.sibyllinepress.com

Sibylline Digital First Edition

ISBN ebook: 9781960573643
Print ISBN: 9781960573803
Library of Congress Control Number: 2025931532

Cover Design: Alicia Feltman
Book Production: Leo Baquero

To all my Birdies

"Whistling women and crowing hens
Always come to some bad ends."

—*American folk saying*

"Girls who whistle and hens that crow
Will make their way wherever they go."

—*Agnes Woodward*

CHAPTER 1

West Chester, Pennsylvania, March 1924

Birdie Stauffer emptied the valve by blowing spit onto a rag she'd tossed on the floor. She worked the trombone's slide back and forth as her sister Lydia took one more bow. The stuffy room filled with polite applause that evolved into the comfortable sound of female chatter.

Lydia winced. "Bertha. I've told you to do that in the privacy of our home." She swiped the pages of sheet music from their ornate music stand then placed them in her satchel.

"Yes, ma'am." Birdie tucked the rag and offensive instrument snug in its worn case.

For the past five years Birdie and Lydia had entertained at local ladies' luncheons because as Lydia often said, it was their duty to bring sophisticated culture to their community. Birdie went along with Lydia's creative crusade, just like she did with most of Lydia's ideas. It made everyone's life easier. She snapped the trombone case shut and gave herself a little hug before she faced Lydia.

"You played Sousa perfectly today." Lydia beamed. "At last, you're ready to perform with me at the Pocono Manor Resort."

Birdie had Lydia's Shakespearean monologues memorized; she could mimic each dramatic pause and theatrical gesture. Birdie surveyed today's audience, noting the many yawns and nodding heads.

She questioned if she wanted to impress the West Chester Auxiliary Women's Club crowd like her older sister.

"Pardon me." An elegant woman tapped their music stand with her folded fan.

"Ah, Mrs. Wilcox." Lydia extended her gloved hand, nudging Birdie aside.

"We enjoyed your little show." She motioned to the slender young woman who stood beside her. "I'd like you to meet my niece, Helen Wilcox, first in her class at Curtis Music Institute. She's quite impressed with your sister's talent."

A slight frown passed before Lydia's face turned broad then fixed, as if performing again. "Is that so?"

Helen stepped around Lydia to extend her hand in front of Birdie. "Delighted to meet you."

Birdie wasn't sure what to do, so she shook Helen's hand once while she admired Helen's audacity plus her unique brooch with two intertwined swallows.

"Join me for some punch?" Helen's emerald drop-waist dress and traveling cloak matched her lively eyes. She looked as if she had stepped out of one of Birdie's taboo *Vogue* magazines. Oh, to own a modern outfit like that.

"Thank you, but Bertha has obligations with me." Lydia placed a hand on Birdie's shoulder.

"I do however." Birdie faced her sister. "I'll only be gone a few minutes and will return with some punch for you as well." Birdie's stomach fluttered. Most days she accepted doting on Lydia, especially considering her older sister's delicate condition. What made her challenge Lydia today?

"Be quick about it." Lydia removed her hand from Birdie as she narrowed her eyes at Helen for a brief second. "There are several ladies you need to greet."

Helen eased them away from the growing cluster of elderly women surrounding Lydia. She reminded Birdie of someone but couldn't place who.

"I believe your sister will be well attended." Helen ladled pink punch into two crystal cups then handed one to Birdie. "She appears to enjoy the limelight." Helen's laugh resonated like glass wind chimes.

Birdie sipped the maraschino cherry punch, admiring Helen's Marcel-waved haircut. Helen must suspect Birdie was stuck in the medieval times with her long hair twisted up in a low bun.

"What about you? Do you like the stage as well?" Helen popped an entire deviled egg into her mouth.

"I guess I do." Birdie nodded towards Lydia. "I'm obviously not as talented as my sister."

"I think you're better." Helen shielded her mouth with her hand. "I adored your arrangement of Sousa's 'The White Rose.' Who taught you the trombone?"

"My Uncle Bert. He thought it would be hilarious if a young lady played trombone." Birdie tucked one worn button-up boot behind the other as she glanced down at Helen's T-strapped pumps. "Little did he realize I'd take to it so."

"You're a natural on the stage."

Birdie spooned salted almonds into her palm from a pedestal dish. Several tumbled on the lace tablecloth. "Ah, where's your Music Institute?"

"Philly. I'm studying classical piano and composition." Helen scooped the wayward almonds into her hand then ate them. Birdie almost choked. Helen had manners that would make Lydia gasp.

"That must be exciting. I adore Philadelphia," Birdie said after she got her voice back.

"Philly's where I was raised. But I've got bigger plans for this summer." Helen's eyes widened a bit. "I'm auditioning for the Westdale Chautauqua circuit next week."

"Glory be." Westdale Chautauqua was the most discriminating of all the traveling circuits.

"You should audition too."

"Me?" It felt like an almond had lodged in Birdie's throat.

"To be on the level, I've seen several of your variety act performances."

"Oh." Birdie tilted her head.

"I asked my aunt to introduce us so I could encourage you to audition." Helen pushed some hair behind her right ear.

Traveling with a Chautauqua circuit could be the ticket Birdie needed to leave Lydia and Gerald's home. Recently they had become infatuated with introducing her to every single man they knew—each dreadful bachelor a bigger dolt than the one before. Birdie wished for something other than marriage to a stuffy Pennsylvanian businessman and performing at ladies' luncheons. She finished her punch. Lydia wouldn't like the idea of auditioning. "I doubt if I'm qualified to perform with Westdale."

"A pretty blonde who has mastered the trombone would be quite the cat's meow. Do you have other musical talents?"

Birdie hadn't been called pretty for years. "Uh, I also perform monologues, play piano, sing, and ..."

"What?"

Birdie lowered her voice. "... imitate bird songs and calls. I know many."

"I knew it." Helen clapped once. "You are uniquely talented. Let's hear one."

"I can't here." Birdie shuddered at the thought. "My sister would faint from embarrassment."

"Let's go outside then."

"I should bring Lydia her punch." Birdie looked over her shoulder, Lydia basked in the middle of her circle of admirers.

"I'm certain one of her entourage will serve her." Helen led the way around the long buffet table and pushed the double wooden doors open with both arms. A crisp breeze welcomed them.

Birdie snickered; they were two schoolgirls sneaking away from the principal.

Helen pulled a felt blue Musketeer hat from one sleeve then slipped her arms inside her cloak. She placed the hat at an angle and gently pulled the two corners down.

"The fresh air is delightful."

Birdie turned around to stare at the building behind them. "I forgot my hat; do you think I'll be scolded by the ladies?" She meant Lydia, who would disapprove if she saw Birdie outside without her beret. Birdie pined for a trendy hat like Helen's. Lydia seemed determined to keep Birdie in pinafores and hair bows even though she had turned nineteen.

"Never mind them."

They walked along a path to a little garden. Birdie lowered her eyes. The Mount Gretna Chautauqua stage complete with the row of lime lights, the upright piano, and the hollow wooden platform formed in her mind. She could smell the straw that covered the ground, buttered popcorn, and the musky canvas tent. She saw rows of chairs filled with a rapt audience. Lydia had favored the theatre production on the last day, Gerald liked the lectures, but Birdie preferred the variety of musical acts. The opening act of a trio of women fiddlers playing Sousa's "The Liberty Bell" had been her favorite. Once a harpist mesmerized her with long black hair that brushed the stage when she swayed as her fingers plucked the strings. Birdie pictured herself next to the piano, trombone poised to play Scott Joplin's "Maple Leaf Rag," a tune that would surely make Lydia and her matron friends frown.

Helen tugged at Birdie's elbow. "Hey, you."

"Oh. Sorry. I got lost in my thoughts." Birdie scrunched her nose. "Lydia complains that my mind wanders like a chicken in search of its head."

"It sounds like your sister and my aunt were raised together." Helen relaxed on a sunlit bench and patted the wooden slats in invitation. "Nickel for those wandering thoughts?"

Birdie tucked her skirt under her legs as she eased onto the bench. A slight breeze freed strands loose from her bun. "Mount Gretna is where we first saw the three-day Chautauqua circuit show years ago." She tucked the wisps behind her ear. "I was, well, dreaming of that stage."

"Atta girl." Helen clapped her on the back. "Now, let's hear one of your bird calls."

Birdie scooted to the edge with her back straight. She detected a cardinal's chirp off in the distance. She wet her lips, puckered up and whistled one of the Northern Cardinal's songs, a string of clear down-slurred notes ending in a trill. First a red flash then the male cardinal landed on a branch in a budding mulberry tree across from them. He echoed her call.

Helen clasped her hands. "Oh. Do that again."

Birdie whistled identical to his notes. The cardinal tilted his head and repeated his song.

"You are the bee's knees, Bertha. You matched that bird in perfect pitch."

A giggle bubbled out before she could stop it. "Please, call me Birdie, it's been my nickname forever."

"It's fitting." Gold flecks speckled in Helen's green eyes. "Audition with me next week, Birdie."

The idea of auditioning nibbled at Birdie. *All's well that ends well: still fine's the crown; Whate'er the course, the end is the renown.* Birdie mouthed the memorized lines of Lydia's Shakespearean free verse. She dreaded a summer filled with luncheon monologues and mediocre bachelors. The only bright note was Lydia's pregnancy. Birdie relished the idea of being an aunt. The baby wasn't due until late autumn; surely the circuit would be finished by then.

"Bertha," Lydia called, drawing out her beckoning to match the wide sweep of her arm. "I've been looking all over for you." She stood just outside the double doors dressed in an outdated beige wool cloak with matching wide-brimmed hat.

Birdie sprinted towards her sister. "You'll never believe this." She stopped catching her breath. "Helen suggested I audition for the Westdale Chautauqua Circuit."

"That's nonsense." Lydia waved the idea away. "Those circuit performers travel far and wide." She turned towards the building. "Where's your hat? Gerald's waiting by the entrance."

Birdie's shoulders sagged. If it wasn't Lydia's idea, it couldn't be a good one. Helen had stepped so close Birdie caught her citrus scent. When Birdie felt Helen's slim fingers squeeze her arm, it emboldened her. Lifting her chin, Birdie cleared her throat.

"But Lydia." Birdie reached towards her sister. "I'd like to audition." Blood pumped loud in her chest.

Lydia turned, her left eyebrow arched and twitched at the edge. Birdie squared her shoulders. Last time she had received that look was when she had asked to wear her stockings rolled below her knees.

"Come with me." Lydia pulled Birdie's arm away from Helen. "We'll discuss this at home."

"It was something to meet you, Lydia." Helen gave a slight bow. She slid the audition flier into Birdie's hand and winked before she turned back towards the sunlit bench.

Lydia harrumphed at Helen. "Now, Bertha."

Catching Helen's gaze, Birdie nodded her thanks with crossed fingers. Pebbles scattered on the path when she turned. Birdie glanced upwards for inspiration on how to convince Lydia to let her audition. Two swallows dipped and danced before the thin white clouds. They made her think of Helen's exquisite brooch. If she could finagle ways to avoid boring bachelors, Birdie would find a way to win Lydia's approval.

CHAPTER 2

343 Walnut Street, West Chester, Pennsylvania

Birdie backed out of the screen door as she carried a silver tray stacked with cups of steaming coffee, cream, sugar, and a plate topped with raspberry scones. She lowered the heavy tray to the wicker table where Lydia and her husband, Gerald sat opposite in matching chairs.

"I would have helped with that if you had asked." Lydia straightened her crocheted blanket over her lap.

"Oh no. You shouldn't do heavy lifting."

Birdie scanned the spacious front porch of 343 Walnut Street, her home the past several years. This was where she had become fascinated with Uncle Bert's trombone and had practiced her bird songs with Edwin. She had suggested the porch for today's morning coffee knowing it would give her added courage. Birdie picked up one delicate cup with saucer and handed it to Lydia. She reached for the second cup and knocked it over, spilling hot coffee onto the saucer, plate of scones, and the tray.

"Goodness sakes, Bertha." Lydia pushed her blanket aside and started to rise.

"It's nothing." Gerald blotted the spilled coffee with a tea towel then handed the remaining cup and saucer to Birdie. "I've already had my two cups this morning."

Birdie accepted the coffee with a steady hand. She lowered herself onto the cushioned chair and listened for songbirds perched in the bare dogwood trees. She added two sugar cubes and a splash of cream to her coffee while confirming four different bird calls. She resisted the urge to join in their morning conversation to avoid irritating Lydia any further.

"We have a new copywriter starting today." Gerald eased back into his chair with a wink at Birdie. "His name is James Becker and he's from Lancaster. I hear he's quite the dapper dresser."

"You should invite him to supper this week." Lydia sipped her black coffee. "Poor soul doesn't know anyone in West Chester."

"You two aren't fooling me." Birdie placed a coffee-soaked scone on the edge of her saucer. "I know what you're up to." All the more reason to audition. This matchmaking had gotten out of hand since her recent birthday.

"And what's wrong with meeting an educated young man?" Lydia reached for a scone, drawing back once she saw all had been splattered with coffee. "I'd say I made an excellent choice." Her eyes shone on Gerald for a brief unfiltered moment.

"Nothing." Birdie took a tiny bite and swallowed. She could do this. She appealed to God for the correct words. "It's just that I'm ready to meet people from beyond Chester County."

"Now that sounds adventurous." Gerald broke off a generous portion of his scone.

"That's one of the reasons auditioning for Westdale Chautauqua Circuit makes good sense." Birdie leaned forward to count her extended fingers. "Another reason—"

"Just a minute, young lady." Gerald cocked his head. "What are you talking about? This is news to me."

"Some flapper put a harebrained idea into Bertha's head yesterday at the ladies' luncheon." Lydia brushed invisible lint off Gerald's vest.

"Helen is not some flapper. She's Mrs. Wilcox's niece. She's training to be a classical pianist at Curtis Music Institute in Philadelphia." Birdie faced Gerald. "Westdale Chautauqua is holding auditions for their Versatile Quartet next week. I'd like to audition." Birdie told herself 'Atta girl' and felt Helen's presence in the morning breeze.

"Please, tell us more." Gerald had become Birdie's advocate since her older brother Edwin had passed five years ago. Gerald wasn't as adept at persuading Lydia, but he was all Birdie had. For the umpteenth time, the hollowness her favorite sibling left made her wish she could change fate. Birdie shifted in her chair, refocusing her attention.

She smoothed out the flier Helen had slipped her. Birdie had it memorized but knew reading facts held more sway.

"The Versatile Quartet audition is next Tuesday at Westdale College at nine a.m. sharp." She glanced up at Gerald who sat with his hands formed in an open steeple. Lydia's attention had been captured by the neighbor's tomcat, who crouched on the bottom step eyeing the robins.

Birdie sprang from her chair and clapped her hands loudly to shoo away the intrusive cat. "We're to have two pieces prepared that showcase our unique talent and six copies of our résumé." Birdie scooped up the flier and eased back into her wicker chair. "It sounds exciting, doesn't it?"

"It does." Gerald rubbed his chin while he watched Lydia out of the corner of his eye. "Does it say anything about the time commitment or pay?"

"That's the best part. If selected, I'm paid sixty dollars a week." Birdie knew that would sell Gerald. "And they travel this summer all over eastern United States, even to Canada." Birdie sat so far forward she almost fell off her chair. She inched back to brace herself for Lydia's response.

Lydia pinched her lips as if holding three silver hat pins before attaching her favorite ostrich feather. It took most of Birdie's composure to wait for Lydia to speak. If she had a penny for every time Lydia quoted 'Patience is a virtue,' Birdie could have afforded a modern dress, cloak, and cloche. She held her face calm and stopped her toes from tapping against the cement porch floor.

Gerald finally broke the silence. "Well, dear, will I hear what you think of Bertha's idea before I leave for the office?" He stood, tucking his folded newspaper under his arm. "Or are you going to make me wait 'til supper?" He put a hand on the back of Birdie's chair.

"It appears as if you two have already made up my mind for me." Lydia tugged at the top button of her lace collar.

"Quite the contrary." Gerald removed his hand. "However, I trust you'll listen to the complete list of Bertha's reasons before dismissing her idea." He went inside and came out wearing his gray Homburg. "Perhaps you sisters can work out an arrangement where both my girls will be happy."

Leaning over, he kissed Lydia's cheek, patted Birdie's shoulder, then took off down the steps. Just like Gerald, offering a morsel of help before dashing off. Birdie watched his frame become smaller as he passed the brick houses that lined their neighborhood block. Continued patience was her best tactic now that she was alone with Lydia. The diminishing bird chatter seemed to agree.

"Perhaps we should move to the kitchen. Every one of these scones is ruined." Lydia pushed her chair back.

Not the kitchen. That was Lydia's domain. Birdie reached over and moved the top scones aside. "Here's a perfect one. Not soggy in the least." She placed it on one of the saucers and offered it to Lydia.

"So, tell me these brilliant reasons you think you should be traipsing across the country this summer." She inspected the scone and broke off a piece with her fork.

Taking a breath of the fragrant spring air, Birdie cleared her throat before listing her well-rehearsed reasons. "One, Westdale Chautauqua is United Methodist based. Two, it's only for the summer, I'll be home in plenty of time to welcome our newest family member." A shot of guilt ran through her body, but she continued. "Three, Chautauquas spread culture and enrichment to rural America, just as we do for the West Chester ladies." She continued counting each reason on her fingers as she had practiced. "Four, working with other talented artists will make me a better musician. Five, a circuit Chautauqua experience enhances my résumé. And six, I will save every cent I earn." She closed her hands hoping six reasons were enough.

Lydia pushed her half-eaten scone aside and dabbed the corners of her mouth with her napkin. Birdie sighed. She might as well have asked to go to a speakeasy with her girlfriends; the same negative response must be coming.

"Bertha, as you know, I've been responsible for you since our parents met their early demise, God rest their souls." Lydia clasped her hands over her heart and looked to the ceiling. "I take my obligation quite seriously."

Uh-oh, one of Lydia's virtue lectures. Birdie had been ten when her mother then her father passed due to consumption. Their mother had been called a saint—kind and encouraging to everyone. Lydia, nine years older, had the conviction she'd always been Birdie's mother. Birdie plastered on her most congenial expression.

"I am well aware that there are times you don't agree with my decisions, but I do care what's best for you as a proper lady." Lydia draped her hands over her mid-section. "As you have remarked, Gerald and I believe it's time you found a husband and started your own family. It's our duty to see that you wed a responsible, employed man. Do you honestly believe you'll meet an educated suitable spouse on your travels with Chautauqua?"

Lydia's abrupt question caught Birdie off guard. Her usual lectures continued for over five minutes. Maybe pregnancy softened her manner.

"I do, Lydia." Birdie took a minute to gather her convoluted thoughts. The potential weight of her answer made her shoulders ache. "The managers, workers, and most of the talent are college educated. You've been to Mount Gretna Chautauqua and seen for yourself that it's a high-brow operation." Birdie tried not to show her eagerness, but she felt a small crack forming in Lydia's resolve.

Lydia settled back into her cushioned chair. "What are the exact dates?"

"April twenty-first through October thirty-first."

"You'd miss both the Memorial Day and Labor Day family reunions."

"That disappoints me too, but it's just this one time." Birdie ran her hands up and down her arms to calm herself. "And of course, I'd be home well before your date of confinement in November." She cast up another silent prayer.

Lydia remained still. Birdie couldn't decipher the thoughts behind Lydia's eyes. She concentrated on the words of the 'Don't Quit' poem her mother had embroidered years ago. The framed sampler hung over her bed.

"Perhaps it wouldn't hurt to let you audition. We don't even know if you'll make it."

"Oh, thank you." Birdie jumped up to give Lydia a hug.

Lydia held up her hands. "Now don't get overexcited. Have you even thought about your audition pieces?"

"Oh yes. I could start with my 'Miss Congeniality' monologue, which you have already helped me perfect." It took most of Birdie's willpower not to twirl in joyous circles around the porch.

"Let me see that flier," Lydia beseeched with her outstretched fingers. Birdie handed her the wrinkled paper. She could have recited it word for word.

"Everyone is to sing two verses of 'America the Beautiful' for the vocal audition." The corners of Lydia's lips turned down. Did she have something against that patriotic song?

"'Down by the Old Millstream' for my trombone piece?"

"No." Lydia dismissed that as if flicking away a fly. Now that Lydia had acquiesced to the idea of auditioning, she would take over. Birdie's easiest response meant letting Lydia select her audition pieces.

"'Stars and Stripes' would be better suited to impress the judges." Lydia nodded her head as if to confirm her own brilliance.

"What if I whistled some of my bird calls too?" Birdie figured with Edwin's heavenly influence she might pass the audition. She whistled the rhythmic pattern of an American Robin greeting the day.

"Whistling women and crowing hens never come to a good end." Lydia scolded Birdie. "Act your age, you are not the young whistling prodigy that mother promoted."

Lydia had made it clear that she didn't appreciate Birdie's whistling, yet never before with that depressing saying. She had especially frowned when their mother had encouraged Birdie's whistling of hymns at church. Birdie wouldn't allow herself to care what Lydia thought of whistling. She focused on the unfathomable fact that she had convinced Lydia auditioning for the Westdale Chautauqua Circuit made sense. She wished she could let Helen know.

Lydia stood up and straightened the cups on the tray. "You'd best get practicing; Tuesday is not that far away."

"Of course." Birdie broke up the remainder of Lydia's scone and sprinkled the crumbs along the half wall of the porch for her birds. "Thank you." Birdie whispered towards the sky as she hefted the silver tray with both arms.

"One more thing, Bertha." Lydia turned just inside the screen door. "You must promise to choose one of our suitors by Christmas. No more fabricated reasons for why each bachelor is incompatible." Her left eyebrow arched and twitched.

Birdie almost dropped the tray. She should have known Lydia saw through her ruse and wouldn't give in so completely. Birdie abhorred the idea of marrying one of Gerald's stuffy employees. Her determination to travel with Chautauqua became more profound.

"All right Lydia. I promise." She would figure out how to deal with bachelors later.

CHAPTER 3

Swarthmore, Pennsylvania

Birdie sauntered along the outside platform of the Swarthmore station after her train had continued on to Philadelphia. The caboose wound its way around the track then disappeared behind a grove of trees. Lydia had grumbled when Birdie asked to take the earliest train from West Chester. She only agreed once Birdie explained it would help calm her nerves and Gerald offered to drive Birdie to the station.

Staring at the empty track, Birdie crossed fingers with both hands. The westbound train from Philadelphia was due in ten minutes. She imagined Helen dressed in a long jacket belted over a slim skirt or a tailored dress trimmed along the collar like the models from Birdie's fashion magazines. She wished Lydia had let her buy a drop waist dress or at least a cloche for the audition. Birdie set down her trombone case to tug at her wool skirt, straighten her beret, and scold herself. At least she was here for the Westdale Chautauqua Circuit audition and that alone was quite an accomplishment.

After what seemed like an hour, a train pulled into the simple clapboard station, filling the platform with steam. Birdie tried to appear nonchalant as she watched each passenger exit the train cars. A green cloak and a blue Musketeer hat confirmed her hopes. Helen walked straight towards Birdie as if she had no doubt Birdie would be right there waiting.

"Tell me how you convinced Lydia." Helen's musical laughter accompanied her greeting.

"Much persuasion, some acquiescing, and promised pastries." Birdie picked up her trombone and hurried to match Helen's confident stride.

"Atta girl." Helen crossed Chester Road and walked towards a cluster of stately buildings partially hidden by tall pine trees.

An entrance arch built from grey stones welcomed them to Swarthmore College. The campus grounds reminded Birdie of an arboretum. Budding trees, lush bushes, and a meticulously manicured lawn lined the walking path. The morning chatter of songbirds disrupted the peaceful surroundings and wrought iron benches along the path seemed to offer invitations for harried students.

"We've got time to catch our breath before going inside." Helen nodded towards the large white building with four columns along a broad entrance. The bronze sign spelling out 'Parrish Hall' caused Birdie's fist to tighten around her satchel.

"I could use a breather." Birdie sank to one of the benches and stood her trombone upright. "Are your insides as twisted as mine?"

"Not now." Helen eased next to Birdie. "I knew you had it in you to persuade Lydia, I just didn't know if she could bend."

"I'm quite surprised myself." Birdie tucked her button-up boots under the bench. "What piece are you playing?"

"'Chopin's Etude, Opus No 4.' You?"

"An arrangement from 'Stars and Stripes Forever.' Lydia chose it."

"You play Sousa very well." Helen turned towards Birdie and straightened her back. "Shall we warm up our voices?"

"Here?" Lydia claimed singing outdoors would deepen your voice.

Helen started humming the C scale up and down two octaves.

Birdie sat taller. It wasn't that cold today. She hummed along with Helen and then changed to the solfège syllables as Lydia had taught her.

Helen switched to singing their required verses of 'America the

Beautiful' waving her arms as if conducting an exuberant orchestra. Birdie matched Helen's gaiety and their harmonizing antics caused three other women to salute as they scurried past.

"I'd say we're perfect for the Versatile Quartet." Helen placed a hand on Birdie's shoulder. "Now all we need to do is convince the judges."

"Where do they get these judges?" Birdie's queasy stomach returned.

"Last year's circuit managers or the Lyceum I imagine."

A petite woman holding a violin case pushed the doors open and Helen stood to follow. Birdie picked up her trombone case and allowed herself one last look around the park before stepping over the threshold.

Thirty or more women filled wooden benches that lined both sides of the hallway, all in proper dress, waiting their turns. Helen had saved her a corner seat.

Birdie settled into a bench that took her back to the West Chester United Methodist Church. Except looking down the pew, a range of modern shoes from the popular T-straps to Oxfords tapped their pinched toes on the marble floor. Birdie pulled her outdated churchy shoes under the bench. Helen swayed, eyes closed, slender fingers playing her Chopin audition piece across her lap. When the large wooden door opened, all heads turned to the short man in a wrinkled gray suit with pants that spilled over his shoes.

"Ladies."

The hall became as quiet as a congregation right before the benediction.

He motioned to a young woman who had followed him out of the audition room. "This is Miss Adelle Rowley who performed with the Versatile Quartet last season. She's finished her audition and graciously offered to assist today."

Miss Rowley raised her chin causing the ends of her cropped black hair to swing back. She wore a simple navy suit with a straight skirt and held a folded newspaper under her arm.

"Now to continue. You will be called in the order you registered." He ran a finger down his clipboard. "Helen. Marie. Wilcox." He announced her name with staccato precision.

"Here, sir." Helen nodded to the gentleman as she rubbed the back of her neck. She looked a bit pale as she strode towards the open door. She fiddled with the wings on her brooch.

"Good luck," Birdie whispered. Even Helen got nervous.

Helen looked over her shoulder to half-smile at Birdie.

As soon as the doors closed, Miss Rowley addressed the remaining girls. "Be quiet during the auditions. Miss Florence Armstrong, you're next."

A tall girl with a reddish-blond bob moved closer to Miss Rowley, leaning in to say something. Miss Rowley frowned and shook her head. She opened her newspaper holding it like a shield. The tall girl tucked a silver cigarette holder behind her ear as she arched a perfectly plucked eyebrow in exaggerated irritation.

Birdie shrugged at the tall girl who could be a model. Dust particles sprinkled the morning sunlight that streaked across the hallway. She searched in her leather satchel for the roll of peppermint Life Savers Lydia had insisted she bring, popping one in her mouth to relieve her scratchy throat. She rested her head against the cool plaster wall, careful not to muss her Grecian knot.

Oh Lydia. Birdie had used judicious persuasion tactics to secure Lydia's approval but hated the promise she had made. First, Birdie had to pass the audition. She'd worry about Lydia's expectations later. Once swayed, Lydia became the force Birdie had grown up with. She selected the Sousa arrangement for Birdie and demanded hours of practice until Birdie's arms ached from working the trombone slide. They added new gestures and intonations to her monologue. Lydia found the best arrangement for "America the Beautiful" that featured Birdie's singing range. Lydia demanded perfection.

The muffled sounds of Helen's piano playing came through the heavy wooden door. Birdie glanced up and down the nearby benches at the other girls, then smoothed her long wool skirt to hide her button up boots. She closed her eyes and took deep breaths. A slight hint of cigarettes punctuated the stale air mixed in with her melting mint. Maybe Lydia was right. She couldn't be as talented as Helen or these other girls who lined the benches of Parrish Hall. She focused on the soothing words of the old needlepoint sampler hanging above her bed, "don't quit when things go wrong ..."

Helen sauntered out the wooden door from her audition and slid down next to Birdie. Miss Rowley gave a sharp nod to the tall girl with the reddish-blonde bob. She checked her list and called another name. The petite blonde with the violin and dressed similarly to Birdie acknowledged her name with a blushed wave.

"How was it?" Birdie asked.

"Nerve-racking and easy at the same time." Helen's color had returned.

"What were the judges like?"

"A row of seriousness."

The girls snickered together in nervous solidarity. Miss Rowley scowled towards them, tapping her folded newspaper on the clipboard. Several other girls squeezed close to Helen, mouthing questions about her audition. Birdie had to concentrate to hear Helen's muted replies.

"Miss Bertha Stauffer." Miss Rowley announced. "Are you here?" When Birdie stood, Miss Rowley remarked, "I called twice. Be ready, you're next."

"Yes, ma'am." Birdie's nerves tightened. She reached for her trombone case with quivering hands.

"You're going to do absolutely terrific." Helen leaned close to her ear. "Just picture the judges wearing clown hats."

"Bertha. Hintz. Stauffer," announced the man in the wrinkled suit gesturing towards the opening.

Birdie showed Helen her crossed fingers and stepped towards the imposing doors. She mouthed a quick prayer.

"Atta girl," Helen loud-whispered.

The wooden door swung shut behind Birdie, hitting the end of her trombone case. She stumbled forward as a row of four gentlemen seated in tall wooden chairs watched her. They wore similar dark suits, matching vests, starched white shirts with thin ties, and pointed black shoes. Tall paned windows lined up behind them, equal in uniform and formidable size.

Birdie walked to the upright piano situated in the center of the room. She laid her trombone case on the piano bench, pulled her sheet music and résumés from her satchel. As she passed out her résumés, she had to stifle a snicker, picturing each man topped with colorful cone-shaped hats. The striking young man with a brown bow tie standing at the end of the table unnerved her. Birdie had been expecting stuffy college professors, not someone so young with such straight teeth.

"Good morning, gentlemen." She returned to the piano. "Shall I begin with my vocal audition?"

The youngest judge with the bow tie nodded as he sat down in line with the others. Birdie played middle C on the piano. She matched the pitch, then sang two verses of "'America the Beautiful" in her mezzo soprano voice.

The bow-tied judge shifted in his seat and tipped his head up so his chestnut hair gleamed from the sunlit windows. He seemed to be in charge, which puzzled Birdie.

"Your instrumental piece next, please." He looked directly at her with soft brown eyes.

Birdie bent to pry open the clasps, lifted her trombone from its velvet-lined case and turned away to tighten the mouthpiece while buzzing her lips. She faced the row of somber judges.

"I'll be performing an arrangement of the trio from John Phillip

Sousa's 'Stars and Stripes Forever.'" She raised the long brass instrument to her mouth. Soon Sousa's patriotism filled the room. A couple of the judges straightened in their chairs and one widened his eyes as she played. She punctuated the end of the song with the slide extended then turned to empty the spit into a spittoon behind the piano. Wiping the slide with an embroidered handkerchief she returned the trombone to its worn cocoon, the clasps echoing in the rigid room.

"Now my monologue."

Lydia had chosen "Miss Congeniality" for Birdie knowing that her precise diction brought to life its hidden humor and passionate story. Birdie had been performing it since secondary school so each dramatic gesture had purpose. Once she finished, she tilted her chin towards the young attractive judge to indicate she was done.

"Thank you, Miss Stauffer." He seemed distracted as he opened and closed his pocket watch while he skimmed her résumé.

The wrinkled man ushered Birdie back through the heavy door. She found Helen curled up on the bench farthest from the audition room whispering to a couple of girls. Helen seemed to attract followers; these girls were captivated by her. Birdie secretly hoped none of these girls would pass this audition. When Helen noticed Birdie, her face brightened and she stopped mid-sentence, then stood to guide Birdie down the hall away from the others and Miss Rowley.

"I'm sure I bored the judges with my monologue. It felt stale."

"Not your trombone piece. Everyone marched along Parrish Hall."

"Really?"

"No, you sap." Helen side-hugged her. "I'm certain you did fine."

"Did you notice that one judge that seemed younger?" Birdie glanced to see Helen's reaction.

"They all looked stiff to me." Helen put her hand on Birdie's back. "Let's get some fresh air."

"What if the auditions finish and they can't find us?" Birdie leaned to look down the long hall lined with wooden benches.

"I'm certain Miss 'Killjoy' Rowley is watching where we go. Besides there's several more girls waiting to audition." Helen's comment about Miss Rowley made Birdie cringe and chuckle at the same time.

Helen charged out the double doors. Rain pelted the tin porch roof with the accuracy of snare drums. Helen put her hands on her hips as if to scold the skies. Birdie found a crate leaning against the far wall of the porch and pulled it behind Helen. They sat, back-to-back, watching the rain.

Helen raised her voice. "Can you teach me to whistle like a bird?"

"What's your favorite songbird?"

"I'm partial to the cardinal. Like you first whistled for me."

"Listen close." Birdie licked her lips and whistled the first pattern of the clear song with slow, precise chirps.

Helen mimicked the pattern, but her pitch went flat. She wiped her lips with the back of her hand and tried again. It sounded similar but not right.

"Try matching me note for note." Birdie whistled the first note. Helen whistled but the note was sharp.

"It's no use. My pitch is off." Helen sighed. "Do you realize what a gift your perfect pitch is?"

"My brother Edwin first pointed it out. We'd sit under our back-yard apple tree and he'd have me mimic every bird song we heard." Birdie stared at her shoes. Edwin had been her champion. He knew how to make her feel special with something simple like the used *Birdcraft* field book he saved for her. He had been the only one who could counter Lydia without letting her twitching eyebrow irk him. That unwelcome emptiness returned.

"He sounds like someone I'd like to meet." Helen shifted on the crate to be alongside Birdie.

Lowering her head, Birdie rested her hands in her lap.

"What?"

"He died from the Spanish flu in October of 1919." Birdie looked up at Helen. "He managed to survive the Great War as a captain of the Third Balloon Squadron," Birdie slowed, "yet singing in the choir of the First United Methodist Church of Pittsburgh proved more dangerous." She curled her fingernails into her palm pushing her sadness back inside. Edwin would have encouraged Birdie to whistle for her audition instead of dismissing her as Lydia had with her absurd quote about crowing hens meeting a bad end.

Helen draped her arm across Birdie's shoulders. "I'm sorry."

Birdie surveyed the tall pine trees clouded with gray mist. "The Northern Cardinal was one of his favorites, too."

"Then I'm going to learn that whistle." Helen rubbed her lips as if that would make them work better. "Start again."

A flicker of light on Helen's lapel sidetracked Birdie. "Your swallow brooch is so unique." Birdie wanted to trace her finger along the crystals set in one of the wings. "I've never seen one with two birds flying together."

"Miss Briarwood, my piano teacher, gave it to me." Helen stood and shook moisture from the sleeves of her coat. "We'd better get back inside."

"So soon?"

Helen's quick brush-off of her pin proved more curious than its craftmanship. Birdie followed Helen inside. Miss Rowley lowered her newspaper but not her stare once they had situated themselves among the other girls in the bench-lined hallway.

After the last few finished their auditions the air became taut. Clipped chatter replaced the reverent silence from before. It felt like hours later when the handsome judge opened the wooden doors. The wrinkled man came out with his clipboard tucked under his arm and clapped his hands.

"Ladies. We've selected the performers for the Versatile Quartet of Westdale Chautauqua this season." Helen reached over to squeeze

Birdie's hand. "If your name is not called, thank you for your time. The following ladies please come with me:

Florence. Eleanor. Armstrong,

Mary. Elizabeth. Brewer,

Adelle. Clara. Rowley,

Helen. Marie. Wilcox."

Helen covered her mouth with her hands and her dark eyes connected with Birdie. As she stood, she patted Birdie's shoulder and whispered, "We'll see about this."

The four chosen women followed the handsome judge and the wrinkled man down the hall. His staccato voice resonated in Birdie's ears. She willed him to come back to call the names again, this time with hers first. Shock blurred Birdie's vision as Helen signaled for her to wait just as she turned into another room. Birdie swallowed her distress several times.

A few of the remaining girls said quiet goodbyes and walked away, disappointed footfalls on the marbled floor. Birdie sat numb as she waited for Helen. Lydia had been right. Maybe Gerald knew some bachelor who appreciated whistling women. She squeezed her eyes shut, but tears dotted her eyelashes. She breathed in stale cigarette mingled with dust. "It's when things seem worst that you must not quit," she shook her head to clear out the aggravating poem. Once home the first thing she'd do was hide that needlepoint in the bottom drawer of her bureau.

A sudden flurry of activity caught her attention. The handsome judge with the bow tie hustled from the room where the girls had gone. He glanced her way while turning back into the audition room. Birdie blotted the corners of her eyes with her handkerchief. Deep voices, then a slap on the table was followed by muted laughter. He walked back out and greeted her with a dimpled smile that implied he knew a secret.

"Miss Stauffer, please follow me." He held the wooden door open.

Birdie stood, checked her bun, and inched into the audition room. She tightened her grip of her satchel and her trombone case handle.

Three judges stood off by the windows smoking, another sat on the piano bench, and the handsome judge stood in front of the others straightening his bow tie.

"Miss Stauffer has an additional musical talent." He held up a slim finger and whispered to Birdie. "Whistle some of your most impressive bird songs."

"My bird songs?" Her breath quickened.

"I've been told you can imitate birds in perfect pitch."

Birdie wet her lips, puckered up and only a sad slur with a buzz came out. Heat flowered across her bowed face. Looking up she glanced around and took encouragement from the younger judge's discreet nod. She imagined she was on the porch having a morning conversation with her feathered friends. Birdie pushed her shoulders back and wiped her lips. She buzzed her lips then the Northern Cardinal's song, a string of two-parted notes speeding up to a vibrato filled the room. Two judges turned towards her. The handsome one urged her to continue by tilting his head, causing his thick hair to fall across his forehead.

"Um, this is the Baltimore Oriole." Birdie whistled the sweet short series of high-pitched notes in her full flute-like tone, "And this is one of my favorites, the American Robin greeting the day." Her confidence grew as she whistled the procession of notes that said *cheerily, cheer up* as she did almost every morning.

"How many birds can you mimic?" asked a judge by the window.

"Forty or so."

"What about a canary?"

The canary's song was familiar to almost everyone, especially since the Victory Canary Songster toy whistle had become so popular. Birdie filled her lungs and whistled the lifting trill followed by a succession of rapid chirps, a gliding drawn-out note, and ending with three tight high-pitched chirps. She wiped her lips with the back of her hand.

"Beautiful, so perfect," said a judge as he moved closer.

"Can you whistle arias or other selections?" another asked.

Birdie nodded. "I can whistle hymns and familiar tunes. And, I'm a quick learner."

The men gathered, murmured together then one of them clapped the young handsome one on his back.

"Looks like you have a quintet this year, Hugo. Get her a contract."

With that, the wrinkled man steered Birdie down the hall into a small room. The handsome judge at her heels. He reached into his worn leather briefcase, pulled out a multi-page paper, and rolled it into his typewriter. He looked at her with glowing brown eyes.

"Well done. I'm Hugo Shubert, one of the Westdale Chautauqua circuit managers." His chiseled cheekbones drew her to him. "Please spell your full name."

"How did you know I could whistle bird calls?"

"Let's just say you have a persuasive friend who has the musical credentials to back up her request." He nodded to the chair beside his desk. "Please, sit."

CHAPTER 4

Philadelphia Broad Street Station

The red brick row houses melted away as Birdie gazed out the backseat window of Gerald's new Model T touring automobile. He turned on Market Street and passed Mosteller's Department store while Birdie looked at the display of modern hats in the front window. As he passed Marshall Square Park she took in a sharp breath. In the distance, huge clouds of locomotive steam climbed into the sky. Gerald parked in front of the signs marked for horse-drawn carriages at the entrance to West Chester's train station. Birdie winced at her brother-in-law's audacity. He stepped around the car with grace and simultaneously opened the doors for both her and Lydia. He set Birdie's new cardboard Daisy suitcase next to her beat-up trombone case on the sidewalk.

"Today's the day you fly the coop." Gerald wrapped Birdie with both arms and kissed her cheek.

"Oh, I'm going to miss you, Gerald." Birdie nudged him with her elbow. She took a deep breath to commit to memory his distinct scent of black Cavendish tobacco mixed with Brilliantine.

"It's just for the summer." Lydia reached over and straightened Birdie's beret. "I'm still a bit flabbergasted that you passed the audition." A little snort escaped as she turned away.

Evading Lydia's persistent questions around the audition had become Birdie's unwanted pastime the past few weeks. The typed contract, the official letter with the schedule, and practicing the new sheet music still hadn't quelled Lydia's suspicions. Birdie feared if she explained how she had whistled at the audition, Lydia might refuse to let her go. She wished her sister could acknowledge that Birdie had made it on her own merit. Lydia had always been able to magnify Birdie's doubts.

"Did you remember the extra handkerchiefs I laid out?" Lydia asked. "They'll come in handy on the dusty train."

"Yes." Birdie's lips tightened. "And the Life Savers and lunch are safely stowed in my satchel." She nodded towards Lydia. "Take care of this little one and yourself." That familiar wave of guilt coursed through Birdie again. "Follow the doctor's orders."

Lydia's last two pregnancies had both ended prematurely. Birdie sent up a pleading prayer. God had to protect Lydia's baby this time.

"Of course." Lydia gave Birdie a quick hug. "Don't dawdle or your train will depart without you."

Birdie's insides squeezed. She would miss Lydia despite her bossy ways. "Thank you both for, well, everything." Birdie blinked several times as she picked up her suitcase and trombone. She found comfort when Gerald moved to stand behind Lydia, his arms crossed over at her waist.

Birdie entered the brick station alone. When the eastbound train to Philadelphia arrived, she strolled the aisle to claim the first available window seat. Birdie concentrated on the clackity-clack of the train to ease her nervousness until thoughts of leaving West Chester and Lydia crowded in. Out the window tall silos stood over wooden barns at the base of green meandering hills. Birdie had never travelled so far by herself. She turned her delicate wristwatch's black face upwards. It had been their mother's. Edwin had insisted that Birdie should have it despite Lydia's protests. Birdie traced the silver filagree pattern with her finger. When they passed bed sheets clipped to a clothesline that fluttered as if to say goodbye, Birdie turned her contemplations to the circuit.

The day she received her thick packet from the Westdale Lyceum felt more exciting than any birthday. She'd read through the Westdale Chautauqua Handbook several times at home but now searched in her satchel for it. Smoothing the crisp booklet open, she skimmed the "Introduction" that explained the origin of Westdale Chautauqua Association, marveling again on page six where it said, "In 1922 we had over 800 Chautauqua towns on four rotating circuits." She couldn't believe she was a part of something with so much influence.

Birdie turned to page twelve, where the sixteen Westdale Chautauqua Talent Guidelines were listed like the Ten Commandments. Number eight puzzled her; they were to be dignified in greeting others because they were idolized by the communities at all times. Who are the others? Her finger stopped at Number thirteen, "Remember, you are professionals. Under no circumstance may the talent consort with management, crew, or townspeople. Common consideration for decorum prompts such a regulation." Good thing Lydia hadn't read the entire booklet. Birdie tapped her toes as she recalled how Mr. Hugo Shubert, that handsome judge, had looked up at her while he typed her name on her contract. He had such long eyelashes.

Setting her satchel and the booklet aside, Birdie buzzed her lips like she did before playing the trombone. Lydia had read over the music arrangements for the Patriotic Medley, "Blue Bells of Scotland," her trombone solo, and the music for their finale, "Come Where the Lilies Bloom" as if she was proofreading for one of Gerald's magazines. Once she had penciled in some minor changes, Lydia tested Birdie's knowledge of the required Versatile Quintet's music until Birdie could play each song flawlessly wearing a blindfold and standing on her head. Birdie tucked a loose strand of hair behind her ear. Well, not headstands, but Lydia *had* tied a silk scarf over her eyes to ensure she wasn't peeking.

Bits of conversation between a mother and her young daughter across the aisle interrupted Birdie's musings. The daughter shared a story about an upsetting playground incident while the mother patted her hand. Birdie turned away to watch as the rounded hills turned into rectangular houses. Once her mother hugged her just for whistling "How Great Thou Art" while she washed dishes. Edwin had inherited their mother's enthusiasm, he always encouraged Birdie to whistle just for fun. The train started to slow. Birdie directed her thoughts to how Lydia had orchestrated shopping at Mosteller's, favorite homecooked meals, and visits with Aunt Edith and Uncle Bert before she left. Now Birdie sat in a new linen skirt and rose-colored blouse on this train, riding away from everything familiar.

Once inside the Broad Street Station, she wandered around the unusual brick and terra cotta lobby in search of the placard that announced train departures. She double-checked her acceptance letter from the Westdale Lyceum, and it still said to take the 9:15 to Red Bank, New Jersey. The stench of coal smoke, wheels scraping steel, and too many travelers burned her throat. There were sixteen different train platforms, some in makeshift track sheds. Why weren't the train departures announced louder? Piercing train whistles, calls from conductors, and that consistent hubbub only found in crowded places made her head hurt.

Birdie clutched her things as people rushed past her like whipped branches of the orchard in a spring storm. She squinted her eyes as she slowed her breathing. Lydia had taught her to calm her mind first then tackle the problem. Birdie opened her eyes, took a big step towards the ticket booth, and walked straight into a well-dressed man with a blue bow tie.

"Miss Stauffer?"

"Oh my." Heat raced up her neck. Soon her cheeks would be pink splatters. Just her misfortune to bump into Mr. Hugo Shubert, now one of her new bosses.

"Are you all right?" He steadied her with a firm hold of her right elbow.

"I didn't see you, Mr. Schubert." Warmth flared again as she uttered his name. His dimple peeked out as he pushed back his thick wavy hair. He could pass for one of the male models in her magazines.

"It's difficult to see with your eyes shut." She thought she saw a twinkle in his brown eyes as he glanced at his pocket watch. "Come, we're departing from Platform eleven—and please call me Hugo."

He tucked her suitcase under his arm and strode through the crowd. She followed, trying to keep her wayward trombone from bumping strangers. They made it to the platform as the conductor blew the first warning whistle. Helen stood on the train's highest step, one hand clamping her blue Musketeer hat, her green cloak blowing behind her. She looked like a sea captain scanning the crowd. Birdie whistled the high pitch song of a Northern Cardinal, what she considered their private calling card.

"Birdie." Helen waved her forward. "There you are."

"Please take this." Hugo handed Birdie's suitcase up to Helen.

"Oh, hello, Mr. Shubert." The widening of Helen's eyes revealed that she suspected there might be something behind the giddiness Birdie felt.

"Time to get aboard ladies." Hugo handed the conductor tickets from his breast pocket then boarded the first-class car. Birdie bounded up the steps past Helen, ignoring her questioning look, put the trombone case on the luggage rack, then selected the seat next to the window. Helen stood in the aisle with a hand on her hip.

"I'm sorry I was late—I couldn't find Platform eleven." Birdie didn't understand her own reactions to Mr. Hugo Shubert, let alone offer any kind of explanation to Helen.

"You had me worried." Helen sank into the aisle seat next to her.

The train jolted forward. Birdie turned to Helen.

"Can you tell me about the other Versatile Quintet members?"

"Florence plays the harp; she comes across a bit brash but is very talented. Mary is so sweet and she plays violin like a maestro." Helen crossed her legs. "And you've met Miss Adelle Rowley. She plays banjo."

Seeing Hugo and hearing Helen made Birdie think that the other members may resent how she made them the Versatile Quintet instead of a quartet. They might be upset with less individual performance time or the logistical problems a fifth person caused. She needed to perform her absolute best to prove that Hugo had made the right decision. Scrunching her eyebrows together, Birdie held her breath. A whiff of Earl Gray mixed with jasmine turned her head.

"Penny for your thoughts?" Helen uncrossed her legs to lean forward. "Or a quarter, with that look of panic on your face."

Of course, Helen had no worries, she had sailed through the audition. She played the piano like no one Birdie had ever heard, even Lydia. "Oh, it's just—"

"Nothing to fret about." Helen scattered Birdie's doubts away with a robust pat on her leg. "We're off on the adventure of our lives and I'm starving."

Birdie removed a sandwich wrapped in brown wax paper from the depths of her satchel. She offered half to Helen.

"Lebanon bologna with spicy brown mustard."

"Why thank you." Helen held the sandwich aloft.

Next, Birdie brought out a tin can of Goods potato chips, an apple, and a thermos.

"What else is in that bag?" Helen peered over Birdie's lap. "All I brought is a bran muffin."

"Hershey chocolate bars and Life Savers. Lydia said be prepared for anything and everything."

"Oh, praise God for Sister Lydia."

CHAPTER 5

Red Bank, New Jersey

B irdie's jitters returned as they pulled into the Red Bank Station. Grabbing her suitcase and trombone from the overhead rack she followed Helen off the train. Horses snorted and stomped their hooves as they waited in line for men to load their hitched wagons at the far edge of the platform. Hugo instructed the young college men unloading the huge poles, canvas tents, trunks, and even an upright piano off the freight car as if directing a choir. A group of townsfolk watched and pointed at the commotion. With the sun bright above, Birdie squinted towards the banner that hung from one of the wagons announcing in bold maroon letters "Westdale Chautauqua This Week." It gave her goosebumps.

A lanky young man stood just outside of the train station with a hand-held cart full of luggage, instrument cases, and a tall reddish blonde who sat on the edge. Birdie recognized her from auditions as the one Miss Rowley had scolded. Helen walked right up to them.

"Hello, Florence, and you must be Mr. Zimmerman." She shook his hand. "I'm Helen Wilcox and this is our fifth member, Bertha Stauffer."

Miss Rowley, holding her familiar scowl and another woman whose blonde hair poked out from under a pink cloche walked closer.

"I'm honored to be here." Birdie nodded to each. "And please call me Birdie." Sweat tickled down her back. She tried not to fidget in front of these professionals; it felt as if she could hear Lydia whispering, "First impressions last."

"Pleased to meet you, Miss Stauffer and Miss Wilcox." Mr. Zimmerman removed his newsboy cap, tucked it under his arm and offered each a brief handshake. "I'm assistant circuit manager. It's my job to manage the first day talent." He shifted from one foot to the other as if he was embarrassed to be surrounded by all these pretty young women.

"I'm Flo." Florence rose from the cart into a sweeping bow. Her height matched Mr. Zimmerman's. "I for one am glad we're a quintet. It makes us that much more versatile."

Birdie couldn't tell if Flo's comment was a compliment or joke. She tried to show little reaction.

"Where're you from?"

"West Chester," Birdie answered.

"New York?" Flo twirled around the cart. "I'm a hoofer from Brooklyn, myself."

"Oh, no, West Chester, Pennsylvania." Birdie took a step back.

"Hello, I'm Mary," the petite blonde said as she gave a little curtsey. She glanced at Mr. Zimmerman from under her eyelashes. "I hail from Sewickley, northwest of Pittsburgh, so we're fellow Pennsyltuckians."

Birdie shrugged giving Mary an unconvincing nod. She'd have to ask Helen what Mary meant later.

"Adelle." Miss Rowley folded her arms across her chest.

"Now that we're all chums, lead us to our swanky hotel, Mr. Assistant CM." Flo stepped off the curb.

"No official titles for me, I go by Teddy." He reached for Birdie's trombone case, put it in the cart then pushed the heavy cart forward as if it were a baby buggy.

The girls looked nothing like the seasoned performers a professional quintet would suggest as they followed Teddy. Helen called out the street sign names read from directions she had in her hand. Mary kept her head down, dodging puddles to protect her shiny black patent T-strap heels. Adelle kept looking back as if she needed to avoid someone and Flo darted between each of them making comments and snorting with laughter. Birdie brought up the rear, watching the spectacle of the Versatile Quintet's arrival with apprehension.

They walked up Chestnut Street, took a right on Broad Avenue, and stopped in front of a large clapboard home. Once it might have been majestic, but now the faded paint was peeling, a shutter was missing, and the cement steps had huge cracks.

"Holy Moly, Teddy." Flo walked up the steps and as she reached for the handrail the decorative knob came off in her hand. She set it back on with a smack.

"Mr. Schubert gets the credit." Teddy held a screen door open for the girls. "Westdale Chautauqua talent has stayed here before."

A woman, dressed in an outdated long dress, came from behind a counter. As she started up the narrow steps she indicated to the group. "Welcome to Miss Pettit's Boarding House." The lobby reeked of Clorox, a new cleaner Lydia had recently discovered. The scent burned Birdie's nostrils. "Follow me, girls."

"The name doesn't fit the dame." Flo leaned towards Mary. Helen shot Flo a 'keep quiet' look. Adelle brought up the rear of the group, her arms crossed tight. They crowded together at the top landing.

Miss Pettit pointed to an open door. "This is the room with the extra bed. Towels are in the bottom drawer of the dresser." She unlocked another door across the hall with a large brass key and stale air rolled into Birdie's face. "Here's the other room with twin beds. The lavatory is at that end." All eyes followed her gesture down the narrow hallway.

She pushed passed the girls then turned back at the top of the stairs. "House rules: Breakfast from six to eight a.m., quiet hour starts ten p.m., front door locked by eleven, no male callers in your rooms." She glared at Teddy who had lined up three suitcases at the bottom of the stairs. "And no fraternizing in the parlor neither." Miss Pettit continued down the stairs, each step accentuated with the clunk of her buttoned-up boots. "Make yourselves at home."

"Is this a boarding house or a prison?" Flo put one hand at her narrow waist.

"Not the newer accommodations I was promised." Adelle frowned. "Hugo's going to hear about this."

"At least it's clean." Mary squeezed her nose. "Almost too clean."

Helen stepped past Birdie into the room with the twin beds. "Birdie and I'll take this one."

"That's not fair." Adelle peeked in the other room. "That means one of us has to sleep on a lumpy rollaway."

"We'll take turns, Adelle." Helen set her suitcase in the room. "We're in a different place almost every night so it will all work out."

"I don't know who made you the boss." Adelle charged towards the other room.

"I'm fine with whatever." Mary followed Adelle.

Flo made little waves with one hand to Helen and Birdie as she backed into the other bedroom.

Helen shook her head after she closed their door. "I sensed Miss 'Killjoy' Rowley had an attitude during the auditions."

"She's probably just tired from the train travel." Birdie set her suitcase on the end of one of the beds. "I know I am." She ran her fingers along the bumpy surface of the crocheted bedspread. It reminded her of Lydia's. "But I'm glad we're together for this first night. I'm so nervous."

"I've got a bit of stage fright myself." Helen poured clear water from the blue and cream porcelain pitcher on the washstand and splashed her face.

"Oh." Birdie stood beside Helen pointing to the pitcher and basin. "This is the same forget-me-not pattern in my room at Lydia's house." Her amber Tiffany lamp, the hand-quilted bedspread, and her favorite overstuffed reading chair with books tucked into the sides of the wide cushion formed in her mind. Her mother's needlepoint sampler hung over her bed. She squeezed her hands together.

"It must be nice to see something familiar. Nothing in this old place makes me think of home." Helen shook out wrinkles from her blue chiffon dress then hung it in the wardrobe.

"You said you were raised in Philly. Where exactly?"

"Northwest of downtown, it's called Mount Airy. We lived upstairs of my dad's office in a Greek Revival home." Helen laughed at Birdie's open mouth. "My dad's an architect. I grew up walking neighborhoods and he'd quiz me on the styles."

"I doubt I'd recognize a Greek Revival if I saw one."

"I'll be sure to point one out to you. It's such useless knowledge."

"Oh, well, I think it's fascinating." Birdie hung up her lavender blouse next to Helen's drop waist dress. She didn't like the contrast. Maybe she'd ask Helen to help her select a new dress with her first week's wages.

"What's a Pennsyltuckian?"

"No idea. You'll have to ask Mary."

"I have so much to learn." Birdie smoothed her skirt and adjusted her blouse.

"And how. Walk with me to where they're setting up the tents. I'd like to see the platform's layout before this afternoon's rehearsal." Helen checked herself in the mirror as she arranged her blue hat.

"I'd love to see how they raise those tents. It must be remarkable." Birdie followed Helen down the stairs. Miss Pettit stood behind the large wooden counter centered just below the stairs writing notes in a ledger.

"Remember girls, front door locked at eleven o'clock sharp." She kept her head bent as her pen scrawled along. "You Chautauqua talent always run late."

"Not the Versatile Quintet, Miss Pettit." Birdie stopped right in front of the counter. "We respect your rules."

"We'll see about that." Miss Petit looked up. "Don't let the door slam."

Helen held open the screen door. "Hope to see you at our show tonight, Miss Pettit."

Birdie stepped out on the porch to find Flo peeling a thin strip of paint from the railing, shaking her head. "What's with being so chummy with the house broad?"

"It can't hurt." Helen held the screen door until it closed.

"Join us, Flo." Birdie skipped down the steps. "We're going to the Chautauqua tents."

"Should we wait for Mary and Adelle?" Helen looked back at the aging boarding house.

"Only if you want to turn into a pumpkin." Flo shook her head which caused her auburn hair to shimmer. "Adelle's in the lavatory and Mary is writing a slew of letters."

"We'll see them at rehearsal then." Helen took off down the sidewalk.

"This place is a prune pit." Flo put on a sage cloche hat that she fit low, almost to her meticulous black eyebrows. "It reminds me of my great-grandmother's."

Helen checked the cross-street name then strode down Broad Avenue. "It's a bit drab, but quite clean. We can endure one night."

"Nice beret you're sporting, Birdie." Flo caught up with Helen to whisper something to her.

Birdie bristled, certain that Flo gossiped with Helen about Birdie's outdated style. When they were at Mosteller's Department store she had asked Lydia for a more modern cloche, but Lydia had insisted a beret suited her. Birdie knew that felt berets were for young ladies, not modern women. Birdie had never thought of Lydia's home as old fashioned, but Flo's sharp remarks made her wonder. Most of Lydia's furnishings were from their parents' home. It was the practical thing to do. The high-pitched bubbly song of a House Finch was a welcome distraction. She whistled its song back, matching chirp for chirp as she searched for the reddish-brown plumage in nearby maple trees.

Flo turned to stare at Birdie. "Now that's just the elephant's adenoids. I'd heard you could tootle, but I had no idea."

"I'm afraid it's what made us a quintet." Birdie looked up, admiring Flo's high cheekbones and perfect nose. Flo had a model's features but didn't sound like one.

"You copied that bird eggs-actly." Flo angled her chin as if to give Birdie a view of her best side.

"It's my hobby."

"Birdie whistles in perfect pitch." Helen waited for them to catch up. "We're going to add it to our act."

"Lydia insists proper women don't whistle." Lydia's quote about meeting her end played over in Birdie's head like a crowing hen.

"I don't know Lydia, but she's all wet." Flo pirouetted in a wide circle. "This could make the Versatile Quintet's act really swell."

"You could accompany her on your harp. That would add the sophistication Chautauqua requires." Helen tilted her head for several seconds. "How about an arrangement of Mendelssohn's 'Spring Song' where Birdie adds in a variety of bird songs?"

"That's the berries." Flo blew a kiss to Helen.

Helen continued walking. "There's the big tent."

The khaki tip of the tent pierced the blue sky. Birdie hurried down the street until she had an unobstructed view. Several men pulled on thick ropes attached to tall poles to steady the gigantic canvas tent. Others struck iron tent stakes to secure the ropes with large mallets. They shouted as they heaved the ropes and stretched the canvas until it snapped when hoisted. The tent covered most of the park. As soon as the big tent stood erect, another group of men started to set up a another one behind it.

Flo covered her ears with both hands. "Oh, the racket of the Anvil Choir."

"It's magical." Tingles raced down Birdie's arms.

A crowd gathered to watch as the men raised the circuit tents. Birdie waved to Teddy as he hefted a mallet longer than his arms over his head. Several men struggled to ease the upright piano off a wagon onto a flat cart with wheels. A line of townspeople curved around the horses, wagons, and trunks at the ticket-seller's booth. Birdie scanned the throng then picked out Hugo whose shirt sleeves were rolled up and his chestnut hair slicked back. He seemed to look directly at her when he straightened.

"Look at all these fellas flexing their muscles." Flo sashayed towards the tent. A few stopped mid heft to gawk at her.

"Oh Flo, you're going to be the cause of the tent's collapse." Helen watched the spectacle with Birdie right beside her.

"Flo knows how to capture attention." Birdie wished she could be so bold. Several young men's gazes followed Flo into the tent. She bowed before she ducked behind the big tent's door flap.

"Seems like Hugo had his eyes on you," Helen said.

"I didn't notice." Birdie tucked loose hair behind her ear. "Besides, we're not to fraternize with the management. Rule Number thirteen in the Westdale Chautauqua's Handbook." She tried to mimic Adelle's stern scowl.

"Of course you memorized the rule book." Helen shook her head as she stepped over a thick heavy rope. She offered Birdie a hand. The men had gone back to their work. "It looks like they've got the stage almost set. I'm going to tune the piano."

"You can tune a piano?"

"Miss Briarwood insisted it be part of my lessons. She encouraged me to learn whatever I wanted." Helen's collar shifted so her swallow brooch seemed to wink at Birdie. "I went to my first suffragette march with her."

"You surprise me." Life would have been much different if Lydia had been more like this Miss Briarwood.

Helen leapt onto the wooden stage to the piano then played the C scale. She pulled out three odd-shaped tuning tools from her cloak pocket, opened the top of the piano and adjusted something. She played the scale again.

"Sounds off to me." Flo stepped out from behind a side tent flap. "Right, Birdie?"

"The A key is flat?" Helen tipped her head seeking Birdie's confirmation.

"Very." Birdie nodded as she dodged two men who centered a podium on stage right as she strolled across the large platform. Two young men installed lime lights in front of the stage and another brought in a shiny metal microphone attached to a tall stand. The notes of the C scale bounced off the canvas walls.

"That's better," Birdie called.

Helen began playing an improvised version of "The Entertainer." Several of the men stopped to clap along. Walter Grantham, the seasoned lecturer who was featured after the Versatile Quintet's act, heaved himself onto the platform. He tapped the microphone next to the podium which forced Helen to stop playing. His rich voice filled the tent making Birdie think the audience was lucky to hear his predictions of world economics.

She'd no idea all the work and people it took to set up Chautauqua circuit when she had auditioned. To think that the Versatile Quintet kicked off Chautauqua Days in every town as the opening act. Other talent, lecturers, and the theatre troupe performed on the following days but it was up to them to start it all. Birdie leaned against the edge of the platform saying a silent prayer, thankful for Helen, Flo, Mary, and Adelle. And Hugo, orchestrating the unloading of the train, his sinewy arms visible through his rolled-up shirt sleeves. He must be very smart and capable. He organized different tent teams, several acts, ticket sales, and local volunteers. There might be something about Hugo that could encourage her to ignore Rule Number thirteen.

An out-of-tune Northern Cardinal's whistle interrupted her musings. Birdie followed the sound to Helen standing at the opening to the small side tent.

"Where were you wandering this time?" Helen turned towards open canvas flap. "It's lunch time."

Birdie caught up with Helen. "Thinking about tonight and making myself nervous."

"You've memorized all the music pieces, right?"

"Yes, but—"

"There's rehearsal this afternoon." Helen clasped her hands behind her back. "I'm certain you'll do great."

"Do you really think we should add my whistling bird calls to our act?"

"Ab-so-lute-ly." Helen turned to her. "It's what got you here, Birdie."

Birdie nodded but the queasiness in her stomach disagreed. "Well, we should run the idea past Hugo, since he's the circuit manager."

"He's one of them but I'm certain he'll say yes to you."

Birdie rubbed her arms. "We'll see."

Helen might be right about whistling bird songs for the Chautauqua circuit yet Birdie didn't like it. Helen's hinting about Hugo meant Birdie needed to tone down her attraction to him. Modern women didn't have schoolgirl crushes.

Helen walked along the narrow canvas corridor to the smaller tent so Birdie followed. She was greeted with robust conversations and the smell of garlic. It looked like a cowboy's diner with a serving line complete with metal trays, bowls, and simmering pots just to the right of the opening. Several of the Anvil Choir men sat at makeshift tables made from flat sheets of wood balanced between two sawhorses with crates for chairs. Helen went into what looked like a small room made with canvas walls along the left side. Flo beckoned to Birdie from her center spot among the others at one of the tables.

Birdie chatted briefly with the man in an apron serving mine-strone soup, who reminded her of Uncle Bert, as she added two slices of Wonder Bread to her tray. The family style dinner made her melancholy for the Stauffer family reunions at Willow Glen.

"You should hear her, Mary." Flo nodded towards Birdie. "We're going to add her bird whistling to our act."

"I heard a whistler perform at our church variety show." Mary scooted over to make room for Birdie. "The congregation got so quiet once he started. It gave me chills."

"You can't add new songs; we haven't even rehearsed yet." Adelle lifted her spoon, picked out a chunk of tomato and tucked it into her napkin.

"I agree, Adelle. I'm nervous too." Birdie stirred her soup.

Adelle pushed her unfinished soup away. "It makes sense that you'd be anxious since you finagled your way into our act."

Helen set her tray on the table and pressed in next to Birdie, across from Adelle. "What are you implying, Adelle?"

"Just that I wonder how *Miss Stauffer* got added to our act after we had already signed our contracts as a quartet, right Mary?" Adelle leaned forward.

Mary wiped the corners of her mouth with her napkin and cleared her throat. "I like the addition of Birdie. Having a trombone player will add a unique finesse to our musical pieces, especially the Sousa medley."

"But is a woman playing trombone dignified?" Adelle stared directly at Birdie, who felt her face getting hot.

"Applesauce, Adelle." Flo waved her hand as if pushing Adelle's words back. "You've got some strange bees in your bonnet."

"Is what dignified?" Hugo joined them standing behind Adelle.

"Oh, we were just discussing the cover of the latest *Vogue* maga-zine." Helen glared at Adelle. Mary nodded in agreement, but Birdie focused on the straw covered dirt floor.

Hugo glanced from Birdie to Adelle to the others then shook his head. "Yes, well, you ladies need to try on your costumes and then be on stage in …" He pulled out his pocket watch. "… fifteen minutes." He snapped the case closed.

"I hung up all our costumes." Flo raised herself by pushing against the table. Several of the young men in the tent looked up from their meals.

"Did the seamstress include Birdie's?" Adelle flicked her black hair back.

"Of course. There are five of each costume." Hugo raised his hand at someone near the entrance to the tent. "And I don't think you should call Bertha 'Birdie' just because she whistles." He tapped on the gold casing of his pocket watch as if he was annoyed.

"It's, it's been a nickname since I was little." Birdie hoped the others didn't notice how Hugo made her jittery.

"All right then." Hugo waved towards the back of the tent again. "Be ready to rehearse at 3:00 sharp." He strode past the lunch tables towards a small group of townsmen that had gathered just inside the tent. Adelle curled her lips just a bit then caught up with Hugo.

Birdie couldn't be as sophisticated as the other girls. She might trip onstage with her trombone. She'd already forgotten the order of their songs.

"Don't let Adelle get in your head, Birdie." Helen patted her hand.

"Helen's right. Adelle seems to be a bit spiteful today." Mary sighed. "Who knows why."

"Maybe it's those bees buzzing around in her head," Flo offered.

"We'll all feel better after our rehearsal." Mary playfully thumped Flo's sleeve.

"Thank you," Birdie said. "Lunch was just what I needed. That soup tasted like home."

"I'm sure Art would appreciate your compliments." Flo waved to the man standing behind the food table wearing his stained apron.

"How do you already know everyone's names?" Birdie asked.

"I have my ways." Flo strutted towards the canvas room which was their dressing area; her hips sway made it clear she knew every man in the tent watched her.

Birdie turned to Mary. "What's a Pennsyltuckian? I've lived in PA all my life and never heard that one."

"Oh," Mary chuckled, "it's a silly term my kin use to describe those of us who live outside the two biggest cities."

"Well, I'm delighted to be your Pennsyltucky cousin." Birdie felt better already. "How many siblings do you have?"

"Four sisters, I'm the middle." Mary held up five fingers, wiggling her middle one.

Teddy walked up to their table. "You're to be dressed and at the platform in eight minutes." He shook his head as he picked up Adelle's abandoned tray and stacked it with his. "Go on, ladies." He reached for Mary's tray.

Mary handed the tray to him, holding on until he looked at her. "Thank you, Teddy, I do appreciate a gentleman's kindness."

Birdie admired Mary's subtle spunk.

CHAPTER 6

Red Bank, New Jersey

B irdie followed the others into the canvas room on the left side of the small tent. A muslin cloth hung across a rope strung between two canvas walls. Dressed in black pants adorned with a gold stripe down each leg, a white shirt, and braided golden belt, Flo leaned against the army trunk that was centered in the room. Birdie had seen a sketch of this costume when the seamstress had taken her measurements right after the audition. It reminded her of a military band uniform.

"Close the curtain across the entire doorway, Birdie." Adelle, in just her slip, hung an empty hanger on the wooden clothes rack that held five coral-colored dresses and one remaining band uniform. The dress's skirts had several layers of lace. They looked more elegant than any dress Birdie had ever worn.

Mary slipped her legs into a pair of the black pants. "These are marked with my name but they seem too long?" She turned around in front of the stand-alone mirror at the end of the canvas room.

Birdie clutched her band uniform searching for a private place to undress.

Flo placed the tall hat on her head. "Maybe your legs shrunk?" She stretched the strap but it wouldn't fit under her chin.

"Where do we change?" Birdie whispered towards Helen who was tucking the tails of her band shirt into her pants.

"Here." Helen nodded towards one end of the trunk.

"In the open?"

"It is the *dressing* room." Adelle huffed. "And wear the strap under your nose, Flo. Like me." She nudged Mary aside to adjust her band hat in front of the mirror.

Birdie unbuttoned her rose-colored blouse with hesitant fingers. She had only undressed in front of Lydia. She slipped her band pants on under her linen skirt and then inched the skirt off. Turning her back to the others she dropped her blouse and slipped her arms into the cotton sleeves of the white band shirt.

"No time for modesty." Helen handed Birdie her gold belt and black hat. "It'll become second nature soon." She went to pin a poster with the order of their acts to the curtain.

Birdie picked up her clothes and piled them on top of the trunk.

"Line up over here." Adelle pointed to the canvas wall across from the muslin curtained door. "Birdie, buckle your belt." She sized them up like a general inspecting her troops. "Mary, you were to get one and a half inch heels not those flats." She shook her head at Mary's new shoes. "You'll have to make do for now."

"I thought Miss Minnie was our seamstress." Flo ran her hands down the legs of her pants.

"She missed her train so Hugo asked me to evaluate the costumes." Adelle made some notes in a small notebook.

"Five minutes till you're to be on stage, ladies." Teddy called from right outside the canvas walls which made Birdie jump back.

Adelle clapped her hands. "Everyone must dress faster tonight." She pushed the curtain open.

The girls scurried through the empty dining area through a canvas flap to the side of the big platform. The violin, banjo, and trombone cases were lined up just short of the opening. Flo's gold painted harp and stool looked refined next to the worn upright piano on stage left.

Hugo stood at the podium, tapping his pocket watch. Walter Grantham sat with each arm spread across a chairback in the front row as several of the Anvil Choir men unloaded and set up more chairs.

"Ladies." Hugo strolled towards them.

"The patriotic costumes are good." Adelle closed her notebook. "Mary needs new shoes and the others still need to try on the lacy costumes."

"Or her pants could be hemmed." Helen's look challenged Adelle.

"Oh. Well, come onto the platform for now." He stood in front of them. "You're to wait off stage until either I or one of the other circuit managers introduces you."

He walked across the stage gesturing with his hands. "Then you'll file in and stand in an even line with Flo's harp. Helen you move to the piano and give the cue to start the patriotic medley."

"I have a suggestion." Helen stepped forward.

"Uh, all right." Hugo ran a hand through his hair, making it stand up a bit in the front. He had such an unblemished forehead.

"Flo and I could slip onstage and situate ourselves at the piano and harp while you're greeting the audience." She motioned towards the piano. "Then Birdie can lead the others marching onto the stage at my cue."

"Can each of you march while playing?" Hugo asked.

"Yes." Adelle crossed her arms.

"Sure." Mary did a little two-step.

"I think so." Birdie inched closer to Mary.

"I like it—it's spiffier." Hugo moved over to the podium and tapped the microphone.

"What if Birdie trips?" Adelle asked.

Birdie's toes curled inside her black performance shoes. What was it that Helen called Adelle?

"But don't walk in during the greeting. Wait till it's finished," Hugo added.

"Line up." Adelle shooed the others off stage as if they were crows feeding on a cornfield.

Birdie didn't have time to be nervous. Adelle barked at them to tune their instruments. She played a middle C on her tuning fork and the sounds of the odd assortment of instruments bounced off the canvas walls. Birdie's hat strap kept slipping off her upper lip so it interfered when she raised her trombone's mouthpiece to her lips. She inched the strap up by wiggling her nose. Helen hid a grin behind her hand as she headed to the front of the line. Flo waited next, pulling at her hat strap, then Birdie with her trombone poised to play. Adelle had her banjo attached to a wide strap over her shoulder and Mary pulled at her pants leg while holding her violin and bow.

Hugo nodded to Helen then startled them with his announcer's voice booming into the near empty tent. "Good evening, ladies and gentlemen of Red Bank." He swept his arm wide. "You are in for an educational and entertaining treat as Westdale Chautauqua's finest performers, lecturers, and theatre actors are in town for three glorious days." His face brightened as he greeted the pretend audience. "Tonight, let me introduce the talented, beautiful, and very popular Versatile Quartet, I mean, Quintet for our opening act."

Helen and Flo walked onto the stage with their heads tipped back to counter the hat straps. Birdie stood poised with her trombone raised, ready to start. Helen played the opening stanza then raised her left hand so Birdie took a high step out onto the platform. No one had instructed her what to do after she had marched across to stage left so she circled the piano then lined up with Flo. Her hat fell off and rolled towards the piano. Adelle followed but couldn't march very high without hitting her banjo. Mary marched on her tiptoes and hardly played a note until she stopped behind Flo. The Versatile Quintet sounded surprisingly good once they were standing still as they played parts of Sousa marches and bits of patriotic songs from The Great War. The medley ended with all five singing several verses of "America the Beautiful" acapella. A couple of the Anvil Choir men stopped setting up chairs to applaud.

"Not bad for the first time." Hugo announced over the microphone. "Birdie, tonight make a figure eight across both sides of the platform when you march in."

"And you girls stand semi-circle around the harp player instead of in line." Mr. Grantham added with authority.

"You should have pinned your hat." Adelle tried to sound official.

"The strap interferes with blowing my horn." Birdie picked up her hat from the floor.

"I'll help you adjust it, if you'll help me sew my pants later." Mary bent to fold up the hem of each pants leg.

"All right." Hugo looked at his clipboard. "Helen's piano solo is next so the rest of you should march off stage once the patriotic medley is finished. Mary, you'll lead."

The rest of the dress rehearsal continued in this same manner with Hugo half-heartedly going through their acts, Helen making better suggestions, and Adelle ordering them around. Flo surprised Birdie when she played her Lucio di Lammermoor solo, she became a different person while holding her harp. Mary, the tiniest of their group, played her violin with such confidence and energy. Birdie had expected the rehearsal to be more formal yet each musician proved their professionalism by knowing their parts well and working together. She'd have to thank Lydia for being so tough on her about memorizing the music. They ran through their two group numbers, the patriotic medley and their closing song, "Come Where the Lilies Bloom" several times.

"That's it then." Hugo nodded to the girls. He turned to Walter. "What introduction do you want for this lecture?" As the two men talked over Walter's notes Teddy carried in their cases so the girls could put their instruments away.

"Teddy, can you fix the stage left lime light?" Helen re-ordered her sheet music on the piano's music shelf. "It's blinking off and on."

"I'll look into it. Anything else?" Teddy placed the instrument cases by the side entrance.

"The platform should be swept; there's straw all over it. And I need a chair for our duet." Adelle brushed her hands as if dismissing Teddy. "It was included in the show notes."

"I won't forget again." Teddy almost saluted Adelle but ran his hand through his bristled hair.

"When and where should we tune our instruments before each performance?" Birdie asked.

Adelle rolled her eyes. "Everyone tunes with me." She tapped her hand with the tuning fork. "And I always keep my banjo tuned."

Birdie took a small step forward. "Well, then your banjo needs some adjusting."

"The dame has perfect pitch," Flo called to Adelle. "You best listen to her."

Adelle pushed away the side-tent flap and then turned. "Each of you needs to try on your lacy costumes. Now."

Teddy walked away, shaking his head. Flo and Mary followed Adelle to the dressing room.

"Was I too bold?" Birdie asked Helen.

"You nailed her." Helen's musical laughter surrounded Birdie. "We should be tuning to the piano before each performance, not to Miss Killjoy's banjo or tuning fork." She linked her arm through Birdie's and they walked together through the empty dining area.

Flo was adjusting Mary's feathered headband when they entered the dressing tent. Birdie would have to learn how to dress as quickly as the others. She got hers and Helen's lacy costumes off the rack and laid them on the trunk. Once she slipped the dress over her head she felt as if she had transformed into a modern woman. Except her bun had become loose and messy. She turned to the mirror to adjust it. She'd have to remember more hairpins for tonight.

"When do we change into these dresses?" Mary stood by the list of their acts pinned to the muslin curtain.

"It's different for each of us." Helen strode next to Mary. "I'll change after my piano solo. Flo, Adelle, and you will change right after the patriotic medley. Birdie will wait until after her trombone solo." Helen marked an initial next to each of the songs.

"This is too short." Adelle pulled on Flo's dress as if she could stretch it longer.

"Git your mitts off." Flo batted at Adelle's hand. "I don't mind showing off my gams."

"We do." Mary snickered.

"Each hem was to be exactly five inches above our ankles." Adelle wrote some notes in her notebook.

"Excuse me. May I enter?" Hugo called from the curtained doorway.

"Yes." The girls answered in chorus.

Hugo pushed the curtain aside. "I have more notes for tonight and tomorrow." His tanned finger moved along the clipboard as he spoke. "Tonight's first call is at six-thirty sharp so you need to be in the dressing room at or before six o'clock." He shifted his weight. "Furthermore, keep very quiet while changing after your performance, these are canvas walls, after all." Flo half-snorted half-laughed and Adelle shushed her. "Tomorrow, your train to Millville departs at 9:05 a.m. so everyone be at the station by eight-thirty. Teddy will travel with you and ..." He traced a line on his paper. "... Mr. Derr will be your circuit manager when you arrive." He looked up from his clipboard. "Rehearsal went well but I expect you to perform much better tonight." As he turned to leave, he looked over his shoulder, his long lashes framing his brown eyes. "And re-read the Talent Rules section of the Westdale Handbook—The Lyceum expects you to behave accordingly." He reached to close the curtain. "Any questions?"

The girls looked at each other yet no one spoke.

"All right." Hugo stepped out of the dressing tent. "See you tonight."

"Well, that's just the bee's nose." Flo balanced her feathered head-piece on top of the mirror.

"We have a different circuit manger in each town?" Birdie asked.

"It's simple." Adelle sighed. "Hugo is manager for Circuit A. Charlie Derr for Circuit B. And so forth. It's all on the schedule they sent us."

"I read it and it's still not simple to me." Mary hung up her lacy dress then bent to remove her stockings.

"Westdale Chautauqua has four working circuits, A through D. Each circuit has a different manager, tents, ticket seller, and junior girl leader." Helen explained. "We are the opening act for every circuit, A through D. When we arrive at Millville, the tent might already be set up by Circuit B's team."

"I had no idea it was such a complicated operation." Birdie leaned against the trunk.

"What's a junior girl? Someone who's training to be a woman?" Flo twirled a silver cigarette holder between her fingers.

"She leads activities for the town's children." Birdie adjusted the waistband of her linen skirt. "I loved playing the clever hopscotch game one taught us at Mount Gretna Chautauqua years ago."

"We don't have to know all the onions; we just have to show up." Flo put her lacy costume back on the clothing rack.

Birdie nodded. Was she the only one confused by some of Flo's words?

"So, when do we get to see the other talent?" Mary smoothed her slip. "I can't wait to meet Lillian Shattuck. She's half the reason I auditioned."

"You won't," Adelle stated then scolded. "Birdie, don't lounge around in your costume."

Heat spread across Birdie's collar bone as she turned to remove her lacy dress.

"I won't ever see Lillian Shattuck?" Mary's mouth hung open a bit.

"Not unless the schedule has us staying around for day two." Helen patted Mary's arm. "I heard her play with the Philly symphony. She's truly a gifted violinist."

"We have about an hour before we're due back." Helen put her dress's hanger on the rack. "I'm going to review the music and make sure the piano stayed tuned."

"I need to fix my band hat." Birdie snapped the strap.

"Flo, will you pin the hem on these?" Mary had put her band pants back on.

"Use my tuning fork." Adelle extended it to Helen who tucked it under her arm.

"I'll pin them but I'm no seamstress." Flo knelt down to reach Mary's pant leg.

"I can hem them, Mary." Birdie reached for her satchel. "I know I put a sewing kit in here."

"If you hem Mary, I'll fetch some sodas from Art." Flo stretched her arms high after pinning the pantlegs. "I'm parched."

"How can I make this work?" Birdie looked into the mirror, trying the strap in different positions. "Putting the strap under my nose doesn't work when I'm playing my 'bone."

"What if you took the strap off and just used hairpins to hold the hat in place?" Mary stood next to her.

"Then I'd be different from everyone else." Birdie put the strap under her chin. "I'm going to try it like this tonight."

"That's how I've seen these hats worn by real marching bands." Mary handed Birdie her pants. "Thanks for hemming these. I can't afford another pair of new shoes right now."

"I'm happy to help."

Birdie laid the pants across the trunk. She used the whip stich to quickly hem each. Another task that Lydia had insisted she know became useful on the circuit. Birdie would be sure to thank Lydia for everything in her next letter home. She hung her lace dress, stockings, and headpiece back on the wooden clothes rack. She turned around in the now quiet dressing room. Her imagined circuit life hadn't created this level of female chatter and companionship. She stood on her tiptoes to reach Flo's abandoned headpiece then placed it over the correct hanger before she left the canvas room.

Helen had her arm inside the top of the piano when Birdie strolled into the main tent.

"Can I help?"

"Thanks. Play the notes while I'm adjusting it." Helen's voice echoed from inside the piano.

Birdie scooted the tuning fork over and pulled the piano bench closer. She played several octaves of the C scale. "This A key is flat again." She pressed the sticking key several times.

"It's as good as we can get it tonight." Helen removed her arm from inside the piano and closed the lid. She rolled her three tools into a felt cloth and tied it with an attached ribbon.

"We're quite a versatile group of women." Birdie played a few stanzas of Beethoven's fifth.

"Are you still nervous about tonight?" Helen sat next to Birdie facing away.

"Not as much." Birdie put her hands in her lap "Lydia always says a few nerves make you more alert on stage."

"Does Lydia have an anecdote for everything?" Helen swiveled around to face the keys.

"Almost." Birdie felt lighter. "How do you already know so much about the circuit?"

"I met with Hugo and some of the other circuit managers after our auditions." Helen rubbed her slender fingers along several black keys.

"Oh." Birdie tilted her head. "For what?" She hoped Helen hadn't had to do more convincing about hiring Birdie.

"To assist with music and other selections for our act."

"Who wrote the patriotic medley? Our assortment of instruments is unusual to state the obvious." Birdie faced Helen.

"It wasn't evident to Hugo." Helen looked back at Birdie then away. "I wrote the arrangements."

"Every piece?"

"Yes ma'am." Helen began playing the chords for their closing number, "Come Where the Lilies Bloom."

"You are beyond the bee's knees."

CHAPTER 7

Red Bank to Georgetown to Bel Air

B irdie had been exhausted after their first night's performance yet found it hard to fall asleep once she climbed under the crocheted bedspread. Not Helen, she snored lightly most of the night. After an hour of tossing around, Birdie slipped out of her twin bed and quietly reached into her satchel for her stationary kit. Maybe writing about the show would calm her excited nerves.

Dearest Lydia and Gerald,

Believe it or not, the Versatile Quintet's first performance was well received – many in the audience stood as they applauded us!

Birdie dipped her pen into the ink jar and lightly tapped the quill on the glass rim. She wanted to impress Lydia.

Mr. Hugo Schubert introduced us with much enthusiasm, You'd like him, Gerald. I started the VQ off by marching onto the platform while playing our Patriotic medley. I didn't even trip! It gave me chicken skin to hear the crowd clapping and singing along. Next Helen played her Chopin piece - perfectly. My trombone solo came next - I had to do the quickest costume change I've ever done! Adelle and Mary played a rousing banjo and violin duo of Handel's 'Aylesford Gavotte'. They blend their instruments seamlessly; both are very talented.

A chill ran down Birdie's back. Maybe performing with the circuit was her calling—she had never felt this exhilarated after her luncheon shows with Lydia.

Next Helen performed the most hilarious rendition of 'A Matter of Husbands' monologue – I laughed aloud back stage. And Flo mesmerized the audience and me when she played her harp solo from Donizetti's opera. Our finale is an instrumental/cappella arrangement of 'Come Where the Lilies Bloom.'. It's quite the crowd pleaser. And guess what? Helen wrote all the arrangements for our show!

Birdie considered scratching that line—would it make Lydia more jealous of Helen? A yawn decided it for her.

I can't thank you enough, dear Lydia, for all you've done to prepare me for my summer adventure. I've already hemmed pants, shared Lifesavers, and feel as talented as the other VQ musicians. Thank you!

I wish you could come see the VQ perform but know that's too much to ask in your condition. I hope you are resting and following your doctor's orders.

Love and miss you,

Bertha

Birdie glanced over at Helen. Only the very top of her curled blonde hair showed from under the covers. Birdie sighed with contentment as she sealed the envelope. She couldn't wait for their next performance.

*   *   *

At 8:10 a.m. the Versatile Quintet walked together carrying their suitcases from Miss Pettit's Boarding House to the train station.

"Birdie, you started us off with such confidence. You make it look easy." Mary mimicked marching with one arm straight and the other curved.

"Thank you. Can either of you give me advice about making my solo more entertaining?" Birdie slowed to walk between Mary and Flo. "Right now, I just stand there as I play."

"I'll teach you subtle choreography." Flo looked sleepy.

"You know subtle?" Helen turned back to wink at Flo.

"Oh, I know it all." Flo brightened as if challenged.

"It isn't professional to dance with your instrument." Adelle took long strides to pass Helen. She trotted up the steps to the Red Bank Train Station.

It pleased Birdie that they all had arrived earlier than requested. The girls stood in a loosely formed semi-circle on the shaded platform with their suitcases at their feet.

"Your Handel duet had the audience in awe." Birdie stood closer to Mary. "I don't think they knew classical music could be played on a violin and banjo by modern women."

"Rural crowds are easily entertained." Adelle adjusted her red cloche hat. "The next stop will be the same."

Birdie shielded her eyes from the morning sun. Adelle had unusual ways of accepting compliments. "And Flo, your harp solo from Donizetti's opera—absolutely the bee's best."

"Aren't we the mutual admiration society?" Flo tapped each of them with her empty silver cigarette holder. "I think Helen's 'Husband Monologue' was the caterpillar's kimono. That broad with the pink turban in the front row couldn't stop laughing."

"I'll take that as a compliment," Helen said.

"Good day, ladies." Hugo strolled up to them. "I appreciate that you arrived early." The sunlight made his wavy hair shine. His skin appeared almost golden. Birdie stopped herself from staring.

"I thought only Teddy traveled with the first day talent." Adelle eyed Hugo.

Hugo put his hand in his pocket, jiggling his watch chain. "I'm here to make sure everything's jake."

Birdie wondered how well Adelle and Hugo knew each other from last season. They seemed to have a complicated rapport.

"I wish I had a camera to capture the charming Versatile Quintet at this moment." Mary stepped back as if surveying the group.

"Teddy has a camera." Hugo waved to Teddy who had just arrived with his cart loaded with their instruments and the costume trunk. "Gather together, ladies."

"You too, Hugo." Adelle motioned to him. Hugo gave Teddy instructions, then dabbed his face with his handkerchief as he joined Flo in the back row. Helen's green traveling cloak ballooned off to the side.

Teddy held the boxy Kodak Brownie at his waist to aim it, calling out, "Smile for the camera." They made quite a picture with Flo, Hugo, and Helen in the back and Adelle, Mary, Birdie, and an assortment of suitcases in the front.

"Thanks Teddy." Mary stepped over the suitcases to pick up her violin from the cart. "You should be in the next picture."

The whistle announcing the train's arrival drowned out Teddy's reply but the way he gripped the large camera made Birdie think Mary's coy remarks reached him. Wind caused by the incoming train engine blew Birdie's beret off. She chased it around and around until a man stepped on it with the pointed toe of his loafer, stopping it from blowing onto the tracks. Birdie's eyes followed the creased pants leg to Hugo's brown eyes. She froze. Her stomach felt like it had dropped to the train tracks.

"Sorry about flattening it, Birdie. I was afraid it was a goner." Hugo dusted off her beret before handing it back to her.

"Uh, thanks." Part of her wished the old beret had blown away. She reshaped the felt hat. "I hope to get a more modern one soon."

"You should get a bob to go with your new hat." Flo stood next to Birdie as they waited to board.

"Oh, I can't afford a beautician and a hat in the same week." Birdie tapped her low bun. She felt old-fashioned around Flo.

"I've given many broads haircuts." Flo started up the metal steps of the train. She looked back at Birdie. "I could bob yours too."

Birdie picked up her suitcase and trombone, following Flo inside the train. "I'll think about it."

"You should." Mary was right behind her. "Your oval shaped face is perfect for a soft bob."

Today the Versatile Quintet had a compartment to itself, which surprised Birdie. She had never known there to be a compartment in second class. She hoisted her things to the brass shelf above the bench. Birdie surveyed the enclosed paneled space with identical red leather benches facing each other and chose a spot between the window and Helen. Hugo helped Teddy unload the things from the cart into the cargo car then Teddy jumped aboard. Hugo waved as the train pulled away.

The others continued to chatter about hairstyles, their performance, and cameras. After the audition, when Birdie hinted that a bob might be in order, Lydia had insisted long hair was easier to style for the costume changes. Birdie had envied the models in her *Vogue* magazines for years. She thought only high fashioned women in New York City or Philadelphia wore bobs, not normal women like her new friends.

Birdie glanced at each—Adelle, Mary, Flo, and Helen—as they settled into the rhythm of the moving train and realized that she was the only one without a modern haircut. Maybe Flo could style her hair. She'd dreamed of Marcel waves well before joining the circuit. Lydia might not approve, but she wasn't on this adventure. Birdie turned to see Helen watching her.

"You and your thoughts." Helen removed her hat, scratching the crown of her head.

"I do get lost." Birdie tapped her finger on the cool glass of the window. She leaned towards Helen, lowering her voice. "Do you think I should bob my hair?" Birdie had never seen eyes like Helen's. Gold flecks expressed gaiety yet they could become dark and serious.

"I like you as you are."

"Maybe I'm ready to be more modern." Birdie folded her beret and shoved it in her coat pocket.

"Suit yourself." Helen yawned covering her mouth with the back of her hand.

Birdie yawned too taking in the comforting scent of light jasmine mixed with Earl Grey. She faced Helen. "What is your perfume?"

Helen mumbled something as she opened a wax paper bag.

"It's Emeraude by Coty." Flo's cigarette holder was tucked behind her ear, like a pencil. "I prefer No. 5, but wear Coty when I run out of samples."

"You filch department store samples?" Helen shook her head in mock surprise.

"Of course." Flo snapped fingers with both hands as if playing castanets then pushed her bob back exposing her cigarette holder.

Birdie nodded towards Flo's ear. "Are you trying to quit?"

Flo removed the thin silver holder and twirled it across her fingers. "Hugo said smoking isn't proper for Chautauqua ladies." She gave a little snort. "The entire Anvil Choir puffs gaspers behind the tents, but it's forbidden for the female talent."

"The next women's rights principle we need to tackle." Helen offered a bite of a flaky cheese Danish to both.

Flo took a pretend puff from her cigarette holder as she shook her head no. "I'd just like to take a drag before our performances. You know it calms the nerves." She slid it back behind her ear. "Why are you dolls so tired?"

"I couldn't sleep last night." Birdie straightened her shoulders. "The excitement of our first performance kept me awake."

"Looks like those two had the same problem." Flo gestured towards Mary who had her head against the compartment side wall and Adelle who had hers against Mary's shoulder. Both sound asleep.

Flo crossed her arms, tipping her hat forward so it covered her eyes. "The train does make one drowsy."

"Not me." Birdie gazed out the window as catty-nine tails and other tall marsh grasses whirred by. She thought she could smell the oystery scent of the shore. Changing scenery had always encouraged her imagination.

"Has our piano maestro written the harp and bird tweeting music of 'Spring Song' yet?" Flo's body sank lower into the leather bench.

Birdie hoped Helen would wait a bit longer before writing her newest arrangement.

"I'm working on it." Helen tapped her toe as she finished her pastry. "But masterpieces take time."

"Nifty," Flo murmured.

*   *   *

Birdie couldn't contain her eagerness. Mary had promised they would shop together for new hats once they arrived in Georgetown, Delaware. They had received their first pay envelopes from the Lyceum cashier yesterday. Even after being on the road for ten days Birdie still couldn't believe she was getting paid to perform with the Westdale Chautauqua circuit.

"I've never been to Delaware." Mary wrote some words in her journal. "Someday I'll visit all forty-eight states."

"That's an empty goal." Adelle put a folded newspaper in her satchel. "Mine's to have performed in all forty-eight."

"I've got you both beat." Flo straightened her cloche as the train slowed. "I'm breaking hearts in all forty-eight and then some."

"Who's keeping tabs?" Helen clapped Flo on her shoulder and the girls snickered together.

"Looks like we've got fans in Georgetown." Birdie nodded out the window to the crowd of townspeople dressed in reds, whites, and blues lining the train station platform.

"I hope we're not expected to ride in the back of a wagon again." Adelle pulled her suitcase from the brass overhead shelf.

"I hear a band." Birdie's voice rose. "They're almost in tune."

The Versatile Quintet lined up along the aisle so they could exit together. Teddy ran from the cargo car to guide them through the crowd. He spoke to one of the townsmen who seemed to be in charge before assisting Flo off the train.

"Ladies and gentlemen, may I present the Versatile Quintet, Westdale Chautauqua's finest," the bearded townsman announced. The girls stepped off the train one by one to clapping and cheering. Even Adelle had to get goosebumps from this reception.

"And here's the esteemed lecturer, Walter Grantham." The bearded man turned to greet Walter who stood at the top stair of the first-class car. The crowd seemed to cheer even louder.

The townspeople parted and they were led outside of the quaint train station. Two young men held a banner on a rod announcing "Chautauqua This Week" with a row of girls dressed in colonial costumes lined up behind them. The bearded man indicated that the Versatile Quintet was to follow them. They paraded down the street with the marching band behind them playing Sousa's "Liberty Bell." The girls waved to the townspeople lined along their path. They turned onto a wider road named Market Street that had street lampposts adorned with patriotic ribbons and flags. The groups stopped in front of an impressive brick building with four large white columns. Walter stepped out of the black Model T he had ridden in and stood behind the Versatile Quintet. A few others from the Westdale D Circuit crew joined them. The bearded man motioned for quiet.

"Ladies and gentlemen, Westdale Chautauqua Week has officially begun." A loud cheer erupted from the gathering crowd so he had to hush them again. "If you don't already have your season pass, you can purchase tickets at the tent in Kimmey Park. Children, you may now follow the Junior Leaders." He gestured to the two young women wearing sashes with Westdale Chautauqua across the front. They did their best to corral the excited children.

The man then shook each of the Versatile Quintet's hands and a line of other townspeople followed him. They spent almost a half hour shaking hands, patting heads, and signing programs.

"Hoopty-doo. That greeting was absolutely the gazelle's hoofs." Flo bent over to touch her toes.

"Has anyone seen Teddy?" Mary looked around as the crowd dissipated. "I'd like to get to our boarding house and take a bath."

"Shouldn't we go shopping first?" Birdie felt worn out too but the cash in her satchel made buying a modern hat more urgent.

"Maybe tomorrow?" Mary asked.

"I'll go with you if afterwards we stop by that bakery we passed." Helen moved between Birdie and Mary.

"Of course." Birdie's excitement returned.

"There's Teddy." Adelle pointed to a figure pushing a handheld cart up Market Street. They walked over to Teddy who stood wiping his brow.

"Anyone else care to join us?" Birdie asked.

The others shook their heads as Helen got the boarding house address from Teddy.

"You can put your suitcases in the cart," Teddy said. "And remember first call is at six o'clock sharp."

"Yes, sir." Birdie did a little curtsy. "And thank you."

She caught up with Helen. They strolled around the circle roadway to a street that had shops and other businesses on both sides. They passed several before they came to Lou & Lily Milliner, a narrow shop with a window display overrun with colorful hats on stands, forms, and shelves. As Helen held the door open for Birdie, a little bell rang.

A trim saleslady with a short bob stepped from the back room. "May I help you?"

"I'd like to purchase a cloche." Birdie stood in awe of the different hat fabrics and jars of embellishments that surrounded her. She pushed her beret into her coat pocket.

"I'm happy to help." The saleslady stepped around the counter. "Which fabric and what color?"

"Uh, what do you think, Helen?"

"It's your hat." Helen patted her arm. "Take your time."

"I think felt and definitely blue." Birdie nodded.

"Atta girl."

"Let me measure your head." The saleslady took a measuring tape from around her neck. "Do you plan to cut your hair?"

"No. Not yet." Birdie looked at Helen, who shrugged.

"It'll need to be a tad bigger to accommodate your bun." The saleslady wrapped the tape around Birdie's head, over it and around it at a different angles, making notes between each measurement. "Just a moment." She disappeared into the back room then several moments later came out carrying four boxes. Birdie tried the first three that were nice but not what she wanted. Then the saleslady opened the last box. She lifted out an egg-shell blue cloche with tiny rose flowers sewed to one side. Birdie gasped and covered her mouth as the saleslady placed the hat on her head.

"It's just what I imagined." Birdie turned her head from side to side.

"It's you." Helen patted Birdie's shoulder.

"You'll want to use several hairpins to hold it and your bun in place." The saleslady stepped behind the counter. "Anything else?"

"No, thank you." Birdie kept admiring her modern hat in the large oval mirror.

"That'll be two dollars and forty-nine cents."

Birdie opened her satchel and lifted out her coin purse. So much for saving every penny she made, as she had promised Lydia.

* * *

Another week went by and now Birdie was just as quick at changing as the others. She even perfected hanging up her clothes as she undressed, to be more efficient. She'd only seen Hugo a couple of times but last night he had asked her to walk with him while he checked the tent stakes, after their performance. Walter Grantham's voice bellowed through the canvas walls. She felt giddy as they shared pleasantries. Raised in Harrisburg, Hugo then graduated from Swarthmore College and had worked the circuit for three years. After he had walked Birdie to their boarding house and said goodnight, she was still curious about his intentions. She couldn't sleep because Lydia appeared in her dreams reading Rule Number thirteen over and over.

Today the Versatile Quintet wasn't scheduled to depart until 11:45 then they changed trains in Aberdeen, Maryland before finishing their journey to Oxford, Pennsylvania. Helen had asked Birdie and Flo for an early morning practice so she could finish the arrangement of their harp and whistling duet or "Spring tweeting strings" as Flo called it. Birdie hoped she might run into Hugo after their rehearsal.

"Let me play through the music first." Helen sat at the piano. Birdie and Flo stood beside her. "Think of which of your bird songs might fit, Birdie."

Mary sat in the first row of chairs, writing a letter home while she listened. Helen played the first sixteen measures or so and then paused. "Something cheery here." She swayed with the music, her slender fingers barely brushing each key like they were floating apple blossoms. She played and paused, indicating where she planned for Birdie to whistle. There were over eight stops. Mendelssohn had written such a perfect score to add in bird songs. Birdie's worries about whistling on stage seemed silly now that she heard Helen's arrangement.

"I think we should start with the Rose-breasted Grosbeak then the Eastern Meadowlark or should it be the Carolina Wren next?" Birdie paced around the piano. "Perhaps we should end with the American Robin or maybe the Wood Thrush with its high-pitched complex trill?"

"Whoa. Now that makes a worm wiggle." Flo wriggled her hips back and forth. Mary looked up and shook her head.

"Flo, sit next to me so you can read the music." Helen scooted over. "Birdie, you whistle whatever you think fits and we'll let you know if we agree." She raised her hands and then played until the first pause.

Birdie whistled the operatic sweet notes of the Rose-breasted Grosbeak and added several variants to fill the pause. Both Helen and Flo nodded then Helen continued to play. Birdie chose to whistle the short liquid song of a Baltimore Oriole next. Helen stopped playing.

"I think that one would be better closer to the end." She raised her hands as if to start again. "How about the cardinal?"

"Even I can recognize that one." Flo leaned back. "Or at least I can now that you two whistle it all the time."

"Sounds good to me." Birdie put both hands on top of the piano and looked at Helen. Her face glowed when she worked out musical arrangements. They continued the remainder of the song and by the end Birdie would whistle nine bird songs. Now Flo needed to memorize the music on her harp.

"Do you think I should mention the name of the bird I whistle?" Birdie asked as Flo and Helen put away their sheet music.

"It would make it a better learning experience for the audience." Helen jumped off the platform.

"It might ruin the beauty of the song." Flo twirled around on the platform before stepping off.

"Try it next time you practice," Mary offered.

The four friends walked outside the main tent towards the Bel Air, Maryland train station. Adelle and Hugo were ahead of them, heads bent in deep discussion. Birdie would have to wait until the next A Circuit to visit with Hugo again. She wondered if Adelle would interrupt her plans then too.

CHAPTER 8

Mount Carmel, Pennsylvania

It only took a few weeks for the grueling travel schedule and late-night performances to take a toll on the Versatile Quintet. Everyone arrived at the train stations later and later each morning. Except Birdie. She cherished greeting her birds at dawn. She arrived at the Doylestown train station thirty minutes before their seven-thirty departure. The morning's breeze brought a freshness she craved. She sprinkled pieces of toast she had slipped in her pocket from the Morris Rooming House along the dirt path.

Each town's train station had a personality of its own. Some were brick with sharp corners and green awnings, others were painted clapboard walls and open-air platforms. And many, like the Doylestown one, were made from stones quarried nearby. Birdie ducked behind one of the cobbled gray stone pillars to avoid the gusts of wind that were growing stronger. She looked up at the pointed wood ceiling and wondered if Helen could name its architectural style. She whistled a greeting to the house sparrows lined along the rafters.

The red-bricked West Chester train station from her childhood stood in stark contrast. She thought of Lydia and Gerald less often as she traveled to these new and exciting places. She kept writing letters home, since Lydia made it clear in her last note that Birdie was missed.

Holding tight to her bird's-egg-blue cloche hat, Birdie hoped to find Helen at the train station early too, for a different reason; Helen rarely missed her breakfast pastries. Birdie had looked for her in the break-fast room but when she saw that the only option was Muffet's Shredded Wheat cereal, she figured Helen had gone in search of a local bakery.

"Cheerio," Birdie called from top of the train platform.

"Not in the mood this morning." Flo held her chiffon skirt down against the wind as she trudged up the steps.

"Oh." Birdie waved to Adelle and Mary as they followed Flo up to the platform.

"Goodness, Birdie. Do you ever sleep in?" Mary pulled her wool traveling cloak closed. "I didn't sleep a wink last night on account of this wind rattling the windows."

Adelle moved closer to Mary. "I made Hugo promise he'd find nicer accommodations in Mount Carmel."

"When do you find time to complain to Hugo?" Mary asked.

"I have my ways." Adelle stuck this week's local newspaper in her coat pocket.

"Tell him to scold Walter a good what-for."

"What did he do this time, Flo?" Mary pulled Birdie into their huddle.

"What do you mean?" asked Birdie.

"I wish I was as naive," Flo sighed. "He sneaks in a peck or a squeeze anytime he catches me alone."

"What? When?" Birdie watched the stairs. Where was Helen? She had to hear this.

"He cornered me just last night right before he went on stage." Flo kicked a rock off the platform and onto the tracks. "He's a disgusting heel."

"But Walter's a renowned lecturer and a deacon in the Methodist Church." Birdie hugged her cloak tighter. "He's married."

"You're a dumb Dora if you think that makes him decent." Adelle yelled over the roar of the incoming train.

"Who are you calling names now, Adelle?" Helen joined the group with her palm centered on top of her hat.

"Birdie's clueless, once again." Adelle crossed her arms.

"Where have you been Helen?" Mary patted Birdie's arm. "We missed you at breakfast."

"I had business to discuss with the circuit manager." Helen tipped her head towards Flo. "And Birdie's just a Pollyanna. We all benefit from her positive thinking." Helen ushered the others forward. "Let's get aboard and out of this wind."

Birdie boarded the train last though she wanted to talk with Helen. When she reached the pairs of seats, Flo and Helen huddled together in close conversation. Adelle and Mary had settled into the row behind them. Birdie found a coveted window seat a few rows back. She watched as the wind first whipped the town's flags, then roiled the fields and bent limber tree branches. It figured that she wasn't the only one who relied on Helen's calming friendship. It would be easier if she and Helen just shared a room every night. Helen's room rotation plan was almost too fair.

The rhythm of the tracks soon lulled other passengers to sleep, but Birdie remained awake, a tangle of concerns unraveled in her mind. Did Hugo like Adelle? If she had a crush on him, it could explain her prickliness towards Birdie. Yet Adelle was a cactus to everyone. The last time Birdie had seen Hugo, he had spent much of the afternoon with her in Oxford's park listening to her mimic bird songs. He had even bought them both Hires Root Beer in ice cold bottles. Birdie sighed, perhaps he was leading her on and Adelle was right, she was just a dumb Dora.

And poor Flo. Maybe she unwittingly invited Walter's vulgar attentions. Birdie would try to be a lookout for Flo. She leaned her forehead against the train window's cool glass.

And her whistling. Just thinking about it made the insides of her mouth dry. Could she whistle on stage in front of an audience? They'd find out tonight. The circuit managers had approved adding Helen's arrangement of "Spring Song" to the middle of the Versatile Quintet's act.

And was she a Pollyanna? Birdie crossed her ankles and stretched her arms above her head. Helen thought Birdie made everyone feel better. If only she could be as confident as Helen. Then none of them would have names for her other than Birdie.

Soon the engine filled the depot with steam as it pulled alongside the single-story train station in Mount Carmel. Birdie wiped the window and squinted, then blinked. Gerald, smoking his cigar, stood on the platform. Birdie grabbed her suitcase, hurried off the train while the other passengers were just stirring, and leapt onto the platform. "Gerald?"

"Surprise." He wrapped her in a one-armed bear hug.

"Is Lydia all right? What are you doing here?"

"Calm down, dear." He held her at arm's length. "All is good. Lydia decided it was time for us to see the Versatile Quintet perform."

"She has her doctor's permission to travel?"

"Of course."

"Birdie, introduce us to your Big Cheese." Flo's gawk went from Gerald's Homburg to his three-piece suit and polished wingtips. She and the other girls gathered around him like fans flocking a talkies star.

"Girls, this is my brother-in-law, Gerald." Birdie went around the circle. "Flo plays the harp, Mary's a fellow Pennsyltuckian, and Adelle is in her second year with the circuit. And this is Helen, who Lydia met at the Ladies' Auxiliary Luncheon. Birdie swept her hand before the group. "The famous Versatile Quintet."

"My honor." Gerald bowed his head. "Bertha's letters have been filled with your adventures."

"Well, she didn't tell us you were such a billboard." Flo's brashness continued to surprise Birdie.

"What Flo means is—we've heard charming stories about you and Lydia as well." Helen nudged Flo.

"Lydia and I are looking forward to the performance tonight." Gerald had an astute glint in his eyes. Birdie knew he'd appreciate her new friends. "That said, I must get back to the Marble Hall Hotel and report to Lydia."

"I-I want to come, too," Birdie's laugh became high pitched. "I can't believe you and Lydia are here."

"You have to have prior approval." Adelle stepped away from the cluster.

Helen scanned the crowd that had gathered to watch the unloading of the Chautauqua tents. "Go ask Hugo, he's the circuit manager tonight."

"I wish we were staying at the Marble Hall," Mary sighed. "I hear it's ritzy."

Birdie dashed to the front of the train where the Anvil Choir were unloading the long poles, tents, and trunks. Hugo stood in the middle giving commands and directing traffic. She stepped in front of him.

"Birdie. Watch out," Hugo yelled.

"I've got a question for you."

"Teddy, take over." Hugo handed Teddy his clipboard and led Birdie from the fray, where she shared about Gerald and Lydia and asked if she could join them.

"I'd like to meet Gerald." He had changed to his theatre voice.

As they walked towards Gerald and the girls, Birdie practically skipped. Hugo guided her at the small of her back. Birdie nestled into the warmth of his hand.

"Gerald, this our circuit manager, Mr. Hugo Schubert." The men shook hands then sized each other up as men do.

"Pleased to meet you, sir." Hugo straightened his bow tie.

"Bertha's shared how well you organize this circuit." Gerald stuck his cigar in the corner of his mouth. "Why don't you stop by the Marble Hall Hotel later?"

"I'd like that." Hugo fiddled with the chain of his pocket watch as he looked back at the unloading process. "Miss Stauffer, I'll allow this one exception. Enjoy your family." He motioned to Helen. "The rest of you ladies, please get on to the boarding house." He tipped his hat towards Gerald.

"Thank you, Hugo, uh, Mr. Shubert." Birdie glanced at the girls. Adelle screwed up her mouth as if she had just eaten a handful of green gooseberries. Mary gave Birdie an encouraging half-smile.

Hugo jogged back towards the Anvil Choir, calling out, "Wait for me before you lift that center pole."

Birdie hugged Gerald again before they turned on Market Street towards downtown. "You two are exactly what I need."

"Lydia is eager to see you too."

"She is all right, isn't she?"

"As right as always." Gerald held her elbow as they crossed the street. Brick buildings and shops with red awnings lined the sidewalk. They passed a large park sprinkled with iron benches, streetlamps, and blooming spring trees. A finch's bubbling chirp made Birdie remember her new whistling piece tonight. What would Lydia think?

At last, the impressive four-story Marble Hall Hotel came into view, the smooth white marble and tall arched windows gleaming in the sunlight. Birdie felt common in her new dusty rose drop-waist dress. A doorman invited them into the white and black marbled lobby.

"Have a seat." Gerald indicated to one of the upholstered chairs. "I'll bring Lydia."

Birdie considered removing her cloche hat, so Lydia wouldn't have a chance to comment on Birdie's frivolity. It sat just on top of her low bun—Mary must have used twenty hair pins so Birdie decided best to leave it. Birdie paced from the chair to the front windows. She'd also just decided to save her whistling in "Spring tweeting strings" song as a surprise for tonight's performance.

The brass elevator doors opened, and Lydia stepped out wearing a maroon wrap dress, which elegantly disguised that she was with child. Birdie knew of the taboo public rules for expectant women which made their traveling to see her perform all the more meaningful. She cherished how gingerly Gerald guided Lydia through the lobby.

Birdie greeted Lydia in a full embrace, whiffs of Lydia's lilac scented talcum powder made Birdie feel back at home. Lydia tolerated a longer hug than usual which brought tears to the corners of Birdie's eyes.

"Are you trying to be stylish?" Lydia held Birdie by the shoulder.

"You like it?" Birdie turned her head from side to side so Lydia could admire the full effect of the flowered embellishments on the light blue hat. "Please sit." Birdie motioned to the cushioned chair she had just vacated. "You must be worn out from your long automobile ride."

"I'm just fine." Lydia adjusted her belt then situated herself in the chair offered.

"I'll order some lemonades." Gerald strode purposely across the marbled floor to the large walnut front desk.

"Gerald tells me he met the others at the train station." Lydia rested her hands at the top of her waist.

"They'll get to meet you tonight. I can't believe you're actually here." Birdie scooted to the edge of her chair. "How did you manage?"

"Gerald has his ways." Lydia's shoulders dropped a bit. "Your face looks grey. Performing has taken its toll."

Birdie smoothed out her dress. "Some of the boarding houses can be mediocre but all have been clean and comfortable. It's the excitement after each performance that keeps me awake." She tucked her shoes under her chair. "I love the stage even more."

"Is that so?"

"The encouragement from the large audiences is exhilarating." Birdie's heart raced just thinking about it. "And the other girls are so talented. I'm learning new things every day."

"I see." Lydia settled back. She was the one who looked tired.

"I can hardly wait for you to see and hear Helen play; her fingers barely touch the keys." Birdie breathed a little prayer that Lydia would like Helen. "And she's the one who wrote the arrangements for all our pieces."

"Mrs. Wilcox rattles on about Helen's musical accomplishments at every luncheon."

"And Flo is entertaining. She's tall like a model but when she plays the harp, you'd think you were in Carnegie Hall. She's modern with the funniest sayings, all the guys adore her."

"She must be loose."

"Oh no. Just beautiful." Birdie held her hands in a steeple, matching her favorite of Gerald's gestures. "And Mary is the sweetest person I've ever met. She styled my hair today. She plays the violin like a virtuoso."

A waiter came over with three goblets on a silver tray. Birdie had never had lemonade served in a gold rimmed glass.

"Adelle was in the circuit last year, so she has the most experience. She plays the banjo so intricately and fast during their duet it always brings the crowd to its feet."

Lydia sipped her lemonade then set it on the marble-topped side table. "Westdale considers banjo playing sophisticated?"

"Ab-so-lute-ly." The modern word slipped out and seemed to hover over Lydia like a tiny hummingbird.

Birdie reached for a goblet with both hands. Lydia certainly hadn't changed. Bringing girlfriends home from school had resulted in similar snide remarks.

Gerald led a tuxedoed waiter who held a plate of various finger sandwiches. "I knew my girls would be hungry." He pulled up a third chair and spread a napkin across his lap. "Tell us Bertha, how's life on the road?"

With Gerald, she enjoyed sharing her stories of the train travels, the different towns, and the tent raising. Maybe being apart made it more obvious or maybe she had forgotten how much she had been on the defensive when sharing anything new with Lydia.

"In Collingswood they had banners announcing Chautauqua hanging from every storefront of their main street. And in Wilmington we rode in the back of several automobiles. A celebration of children ran alongside us, clapping." Birdie chuckled behind her hand. "Flo stood up from the jump seat, hooting and the kids joined in."

"Sounds like quite a greeting." Gerald finished off his fourth finger sandwich which looked like child's food in his hands.

"Sounds like a circus to me." Lydia pushed her half-eaten chicken salad sandwich to the side. It made Birdie worry. When she was expecting last time, the doctor had gone against common practice and encouraged Lydia to eat more.

"Tell us about your opening act." Gerald sat back in his chair.

"It's much more than the music I learned at home." Birdie scooted forward in her chair. "Each of us has a solo, there are a couple of duets and one monologue." Birdie continued with detailed descriptions.

"I'd like to freshen up before we see your big performance for ourselves." Lydia set her napkin aside.

Birdie wrapped a few sandwiches in the unused napkin. "Take these with you for later." She offered the packet to Lydia.

Lydia gripped the arms of her chair. "That's neither proper nor necessary, Bertha."

Birdie frowned. She should have expected Lydia to scold her for breaking old fashioned etiquette rules. Gerald helped Lydia to her feet then slipped an arm around her waist.

"I'll reserve seats for you in the front row." Birdie rose. Part of her wanted to hug Lydia again and part of her wished she'd the nerve to press the sandwiches back into her hands.

"We're looking forward to it." Gerald ushered Lydia towards the elevators.

CHAPTER 9

Mount Carmel, Pennsylvania

Birdie tripped over one of the thick ropes holding up the tent and received a grimace but also a hand from Teddy. She desperately wanted this performance to be perfect to make the strain between her and Lydia disappear. She pulled at a loose thread on the cuff to her band costume. Nothing had cooperated with Birdie's wish for the perfect evening, especially not the weather. Even the tent drooped. Inside the khaki canvas it was steamy and sticky. Sweat trickled down Birdie's back sticking her cotton shirt to her ribs.

"It's hotter than Dutch love in harvest." Mary fanned herself with a leftover program.

"That's ab-so-lute-ly the dumbest saying." Flo flicked sweat that had collected under her bangs. "My fingers are going to slip right off the strings."

"Oh, but we all have to perform our best tonight. 'Don't quit, remember, when things go wrong ...'"

The other girls groaned in unison. Adelle stormed away as if she couldn't hear the poem again.

"Not now, Birdie," Helen said. "It's too hot for your poem." She offered Birdie a drink of her water but Birdie shook her head.

"We'll do our best." Mary blotted her temples with a handkerchief. "Let's not waste energy talking about it."

Cupping a black puff of fur, Adelle came back into the dressing tent. "Look what the cook found nosing around the garbage."

"Ooooh." Mary rushed to pet the kitten.

"Now that's the kipper's knickers. I believe Art has found our mascot."

"I'd prefer a different one," Birdie said.

"Why?" Flo and Mary asked.

"Kittens become cats. Cats catch songbirds." Birdie glanced at Helen who wiped an amused smile off her lips with her handkerchief.

"Who'd have thought Miss Perfect Pitch hated kittens."

"All right, Adelle." Helen snapped her handkerchief causing the kitten to jump and dart behind the costume trunk.

Mary bent down, peering around the trunk. "She doesn't hate cats; she just likes birds better." She stood up, her cheeks flushed from bending over.

"You girls are on in five minutes." Teddy stuck his head inside the tent flap and locked eyes with Mary.

That made Birdie forget the heat, the kitten, and Lydia for a second. She followed the others along the canvas hallway. As Birdie screwed her trombone together she glanced through the tent flap. Every chair was filled with people waving their programs. A large mechanical fan had been installed in the back, blowing around the smells of straw, canvas, and body odor. All the movement made Birdie restless. Walter Grantham stood in the shadows across the stage obviously ogling Flo, who stood behind her. Birdie closed the flap. Maybe she had overestimated Walter.

The main tent quieted as Hugo stood before the podium. "Good evening, Mount Carmel." He swept his arm across the crowd. "Welcome to the engaging world of Westdale Chautauqua. I don't know who ordered this heat, but you all are in for a treat."

"Good luck," Mary whispered as Birdie raised her trombone poised to lead the Versatile Quintet, marching onto the stage. Soon the girls were performing their patriotic medley with contrived gusto. Lydia's silhouette stood out on the first row. Birdie brightened when the audience clapped along with the familiar songs. Her mood slumped when Helen's performance of her usually humorous monologue, "A Matter of Husbands" drew little laughter.

"Do your best, girls," Birdie encouraged Adelle and Mary right before their banjo and violin duet. "I'm afraid the audience has been dulled by the heat."

Adelle responded with a less than rousing performance. Mary mouthed 'sorry' as she passed Birdie off stage. Before she knew it, Birdie stood middle stage whistling her bird songs with Flo beside her playing Helen's arrangement of "Spring Song" on her harp. Birdie took in a big breath to finish with the Bluebird's warble. Her head felt fuzzy and white specks appeared before her eyes. She swayed a bit, then she was falling out of their old apple tree in the back yard of Willow Glenn. Birdie sensed movement beside her as Flo tipped over her harp attempting to catch Birdie before she fell. There was a gasp from the audience as she landed on the stage like a deflated balloon alongside Flo's upended harp.

Birdie became aware of sounds and commotion. Something kept brushing her face and tickling her nose. Was it that kitten? Was she at Willow Glenn? She felt cool fingers on her forehead and breathed a faint whiff of citrus. That's Helen—oh dear. Could she still be on the Chautauqua stage? She blinked. Flashes of Lydia nudging others aside came through her heavy eyelids. Lydia pushed her ostrich fan into Teddy's hands signaling for him to keep it moving.

"What happened?" Birdie unfolded her legs and tried to prop herself up. Several hands kept her flat.

"Give Bertha room to breathe," Lydia ordered and everyone stepped back. Birdie's thoughts were muffled, as if she was coming out of a springtime storm cloud.

"I'm sorry. You told me not to climb that tree," Birdie murmured.

Awkward laughter scattered throughout.

"Our songbird fell," Flo said.

"Let's get her outside." Hugo bent down to help Birdie upright. He patted her forehead with his damp handkerchief.

"But the audience," Birdie moaned.

"I've given everyone a ten-minute break." Hugo and Helen helped Birdie stand. She leaned into Hugo, breathed in an unpleasant musk, so turned her face away.

The outside air wasn't much cooler, but it was lighter, with a slight draft coming off the creek. Hugo gently leaned Birdie against a stack of pallets. She looked around from Hugo to Helen to Lydia and the other concerned faces. She could feel Teddy behind her moving the air with Lydia's ostrich feather fan. Gerald strode up with an armful of bottled seltzer waters and handed them out.

"So much for the flawless performance of the Versatile Quintet," Birdie said.

"If ever there was a time I wanted to quote 'Don't Quit' back to you, this is it." Helen pressed closer.

Lydia frowned. "Everyone except this young man fanning, give Bertha space."

"Oh Lydia, I'm fine now."

Birdie swept her arm to include the group. "Might as well introduce my dear gang. Adelle, Florence, Mary, Teddy, and Hugo. And you've met Helen." She nodded to Lydia. "This beautiful lady is my sister, Lydia."

"Where's Bertha?" quipped Flo.

"Oh Flo, you know I'm Bertha to Lydia."

"It's nice to meet you, Lydia." Hugo stepped away "Now that we know Bird-, ah I mean Bertha is all right, I need to get the crowd gathered back for Mr. Grantham's lecture." He motioned to Teddy. "You're needed too."

Teddy continued waving the ostrich feather as he started to step away.

"Here, young man. Give me that." Lydia reached for the fan. "Thank you for helping Bertha."

Adelle walked alongside Teddy as they followed Hugo towards the main tent.

"We should go too. Hugo may want us to entertain the crowd before Walter's lecture." Helen's face softened when she looked at Birdie. "It appears you're in good hands."

"I need to come too." Birdie rose from the pallet with a slight sway.

"No," Helen and Lydia said in unison.

"You rest," Helen finished. "We can be the Versatile Quartet for one evening." She, Flo, and Mary each hugged Birdie then scooted back towards the main tent.

A black paw batted at Birdie from under the pallets. "Scram."

"What's that, Bertha?"

"It's a kitten." Birdie stared past the dark slats of the pallets.

Lydia turned to Gerald. "She needs to be taken to our hotel. I think she's delusional."

"I wonder why I fainted." Birdie leaned on Gerald's offered arm. "You're the one with child."

"This oppressive weather had something to do with it." Lydia wrapped her arm around Birdie's waist. "And you've always let your emotions overwhelm you."

*   *   *

Sunlight filtered through lace curtains, creating an intricate pattern of shadows on Birdie's sheet and the rosette wallpaper across the room. She sank deeper into the plush down bedding filling her nose with the crisp lavender scented sheets. This was paradise. A big yawn followed her thoughts. She might never be able to sleep in another musty boarding house again.

Birdie leaned on one elbow, turning her silver wristwatch so she could see the face. She sat upright and shook her arm. It said almost ten o'clock. Pushing back the sheets she strode across the dense Oriental carpet to gather her clothes and thoughts. A thick page stuck out from under the hotel room door.

Bertha,

Good morning. Once you're finally awake, join me in room 407 – I've ordered room service. Gerald is meeting Hugo for breakfast. We've arranged for you to take a later train to Clearfield.

Lydia

Birdie tried to get dressed faster than the questions filling her head. What did Lydia mean she arranged a later train? She wrangled her blouse over her head. And why would Gerald entertain Hugo for breakfast? She struggled with the buttons on her skirt. Where were the others now? She pulled hard on her silk stocking; a thin run started from her big toe. How would she explain both sleeping at the Marble Hall Hotel and catching a later train? Adelle and the others would be more than envious. She stepped into her T-strap shoes and pushed her heels down. And what would Lydia say now that Birdie had slept so late? Birdie was convinced Lydia had invented the saying "the early bird eats the worm." She fingered her hair into a loose knot at the back of her neck, sticking in several random hairpins. And speaking of birds, Lydia had not commented about her whistling as part of the act last night.

She felt discombobulated. Too many questions and too rushed. Birdie charged out of the room, turned left and walked past several rooms before noting the room numbers. She turned around, trotted down the hall past several gilded mirrors, marble inlays, and paisley wallpaper with only a glance. She hesitated before the paneled door to room 407. Intuition told her to gird herself for the "Lydia lecture."

Birdie knocked.

Lydia's "Enter" was muted. She waited in an upholstered Queen Anne's chair with remnants of some pastry, toast, and a soft-boiled egg on a gold rimmed plate beside her. She set a newspaper aside.

"Good morning." Birdie strolled across the hotel room to calm her nerves. She stopped at the double windows overlooking the back garden. "My, what a beautiful view."

"Your breakfast is here but cold." Lydia gestured to the covered dish sitting on a tray.

"Thank you. I'm not hungry." Birdie watched birds flitting from the grass to the trees. Uncomfortable silence signaled a change. Months ago, she had wanted to chatter away with Lydia, proof that she knew the latest news or some local gossip. Now that Birdie had traveled with her new friends, impressing Lydia no longer mattered.

"You need to eat something." Lydia lifted the silver cover off the plate, revealing another egg and dry toast. "I must say, Gerald and I are quite taken with your Hugo." Birdie felt even more befuddled. Lydia hadn't started into one of her usual lectures.

"He's not *my* Hugo."

"Well, I sense he would be if you let him."

Lydia strode over to the windows to stand behind Birdie. "What's more interesting out there?"

"Nothing." Birdie turned from the windows facing her older sister. This morning Lydia's low waisted floral dress highlighted her pregnancy. "How are you feeling?"

"Fine. Dr. Williams says everything is progressing normally."

"Are you eating enough as he instructed?"

"Of course." Lydia straightened a pillow on an otherwise perfectly made bed. "Hugo told Gerald he was raised in Harrisburg."

"Why are we discussing Hugo?" Birdie sat on the edge of the Queen Anne's chair, her back rigid.

"You're exhausted, that's why you're not listening. He's a wonderful catch, Bertha."

"I slept in this morning."

Lydia's comments perplexed Birdie. Where was the scolding for slothfulness? The lecture on inappropriate bird calls?

"You need to give Hugo more attention. Charm him." Lydia walked over to the vanity and patted the small bench. "Come here. Your hair is a disgrace."

Birdie hesitated then moved to the bench. Lydia pulled out hairpins and brushed Birdie's hair with long strokes, yanking when she hit a tangle. Birdie winced. Lydia had often brushed out her frustrations in Birdie's hair. Lydia brushed, caught a tangle, and pulled again. Birdie covered her head with her arms.

"Enough. That hurts."

"You've never complained before." Lydia's eyes narrowed at her younger sister in the mirror. "Let me work out all the tangles." She picked up the brush, starting at the top of Birdie's head.

"Flo's going to cut it for me anyhow."

"She will not. You don't want that floozy touching your long hair."

"Flo is my friend. All the girls agree I'd look better with a soft bob."

Lydia picked up the hairpins. When Birdie rose, Lydia pushed her back down, twisted her hair into a Grecian style bun and pinned it.

"There. Now you look refreshed, maybe enough to entice Hugo," Lydia said, her hands still on Birdie's shoulders.

Birdie stared again at their reflections. The opaque glass blurred their faces just enough to soften the tension.

"What did you mean, I can take a later train?"

"Gerald assured Hugo we'd put you on the 12:45." Lydia's pursed her lips. "You'll arrive in plenty of time for your next show."

But the others had left on the 9:45. Birdie turned around on the bench, away from the mirror. "Did you like what you did see of our performance?" She might as well hear Lydia's rant about whistling now.

"Gerald may offer Hugo a job once the circuit season is over."

"What?"

"Don't get in a tizzy. Gerald agrees it's an excellent idea." Lydia straightened the brush, comb, and bottles of cream on the dresser. "Hugo would be nearby all winter." Birdie thought she heard the word *propose* whispered at the end of Lydia's harebrained comment.

"Lydia. This is insane. I'm not permitted to date Hugo." Birdie practically leapt towards the door. "The Lyceum rules explicitly state that the talent cannot consort with the management." The realization hit her as if she had slapped her own forehead. Lydia hadn't planned lectures on sleeping late or bird calls. Her only focus was matchmaking between Birdie and Hugo. And to think Lydia said Birdie wouldn't meet any educated bachelors on the circuit. She sure had changed her tune.

"You'll see. I'm right." Lydia patted Birdie's arm, as if she were a little girl again. "Go gather the rest of your things. I'll order a box lunch for the train."

"This talk of Hugo is over as far as I'm concerned." Birdie's insides fired up. She stalked out of the room, her head high.

"Be in the lobby in fifteen minutes, Bertha." Lydia banged the door closed.

Birdie paused in the hotel hall, the room numbers going in and out of focus. After a moment she removed a hairpin. Then another. She pulled out each hairpin, one by one and dropped them in front of the door to room 407. Birdie shook her head, enjoying her hair sweeping freely against her back as she took long strides down the hallway to her room.

CHAPTER 10

Clearfield, Pennsylvania

Hunkered down on a back facing seat, Birdie sat on the 12:45 train, trying to hide that her long hair was stuffed up under her cloche. Dropping all her hairpins had seemed like such a good idea earlier this morning, but as the train lurched forward, it felt juvenile.

Lydia hadn't made any snide remarks about Birdie's hair when they'd said their stiff goodbyes from the Mount Carmel platform. Birdie knew better, even if Lydia had been preoccupied, she noticed. Seeing Lydia's hands perched on her pregnant belly emphasized that both sisters were experiencing changes.

"Traveling alone?" asked the elderly gentleman sitting directly across from Birdie.

"Yes sir." She didn't want to make small talk.

"All the way to Buffalo?" His wife adjusted her toque.

"No ma'am. I'm getting off at Clearfield." Birdie stared outside as the buildings blurred into countryside, hoping to dissuade any further conversation.

"We're visiting kinfolk in Buffalo," remarked the man. "You?"

Birdie slowly faced the couple. It wasn't their fault Lydia infuriated her.

"I'm with Westdale Chautauqua circuit. We're performing in Clearfield tonight."

"Well, I'll be." The women leaned forward studying Birdie's face. "Are you the one that fainted?"

Birdie gave them a slight nod. "Yes ma'am."

"We've been season ticket holders for Chautauqua for over three years and never saw the likes of that." The lady turned to her husband. "I told you the caliber of Chautauqua has decreased."

Birdie closed her eyes. Fainting hadn't been in her plans either. She recalled how Hugo's eyes crinkled with concern. Their mutual attraction, if it could be called that, had just started. Now that Lydia had made Hugo the chosen bachelor, it almost caused Birdie to abandon her own romantic musings about him. She sighed. She needed to hear Hugo's side of this morning's breakfast discussion with Gerald. No telling what mortifying stories Gerald had shared.

Worries that the other girls might resent her for staying overnight at the Marble Hall Hotel kept Birdie alert. She searched for ideas of how to make it up to them tenfold. Loud snoring interrupted her brooding. The man had his head on his wife's shoulder, and she had her head against the back of the seat, her mouth slightly askew. Birdie shouldn't let their comments sting, yet they did.

Birdie stretched her legs, leaned against the window, and gave the countryside her attention. The vivid summer fields breezing by brought Helen's unusual green eyes to mind. She yearned to share all of this with Helen. Birdie crossed her ankles and tugged her cloche down. Helen wouldn't care if she stayed at a fancy hotel. Birdie twisted loose strands of hair back inside her felt helmet. Of her list of things to do, the most important remained to take Flo up on her offer to bob her hair.

Birdie opened the hotel's box lunch Lydia had shoved into her satchel. Unwrapping the wax paper revealed thin sliced white bread spread with cream cheese, and a slice of turkey. She took in the wood paneling of the train, worn leather seats, brass luggage racks, and wide glass windows. She thrived in this new world, with these new friends.

Just the idea of not knowing what the next town looked like, what the next audience would bring, and what adventures were out there made her heart sing. The train soothed the turmoil chugging through her mind, each sway bringing relief that she was returning to her new life.

She wrapped the other half of sandwich for later. Turkey was no match for Lebanon bologna. She couldn't wait to share the hair pin incident with Helen. Lydia might not have even noticed them scattered outside her hotel room door, but Birdie doubted it. Not much got past Lydia.

As the train slowed into the Clearfield station, Birdie's right foot tapped repeatedly against the wooden floor. She had to find Flo and get her hair bobbed. Then she'd be ready to tackle her other problems. Birdie sprang from her seat before the train came to a complete stop. When it did, she stumbled halfway into the gentlemen's lap. After profuse apologies, Birdie grabbed her Daisy cardboard suitcase from the metal rack and hurried off the train.

The cream-colored banner with *Westdale Chautauqua–THIS WEEK* in navy letters strung across the entrance to the Clearfield station gave Birdie a sense of coming home, even though she'd never been here. She reached into the pocket of her satchel and squinted at the crumpled paper. Hugo needed penmanship lessons. She tried to decipher the hurried scribbles into a readable address. It maybe said Greene's boarding house, thirty-one something Fourth Street. First streets normally started at the train station. Maybe that would lead her to Fourth Street.

Birdie flicked her wrist to push back her sleeve, thirty minutes past four. Gracious sakes. First staying overnight at the Marble Hall Hotel and then arriving so late. She was certain the other girls would be over-the-moon jealous. She didn't blame them.

This was all Lydia's fault. Best head to the tents instead. She scanned the horizon looking for the peaks of canvas. A cluster of brick buildings with green tiled roofs signaled downtown, complete with a white plaster church and steeple pointing towards the sky. Gray clouds formed rolled Marcel waves as if God was trying to mock her. Standing on her tiptoes she searched past the buildings, barely making out trees along a river with the massive tent silhouette off to the far side.

Birdie walked briskly, avoiding a trio of boys throwing a ball back and forth across the street. She passed the wide plate glass window of Eastern Drug Store. Inside, Mary spun on a red covered stool next to Teddy. His eyes shone as he leaned forward to sip the last bit from his cone shaped soda glass. Mary twirled a strand of hair around her pointer finger. Birdie chose not to interrupt their interlude, instead she fantasized that it was Hugo sitting next to her on a stool. Honks of geese flying overhead broke her reverie. She didn't have time to daydream about Hugo. Lydia might be right about one thing, Birdie did dawdle.

She hurried past the rest of the quaint shops and clapboard homes at an almost jog. If she was lucky, she'd find Flo before the performance. Removing her cloche, her hair unfurled into long strands billowing behind her. She shook her head and laughed loud enough that the trio of boys echoed with their own hoots.

Birdie burst into the side tent. She spotted Flo surrounded by several of the young college men from the Anvil Choir. Flo attracted men like hens to scattered feed. Birdie rushed to the edge of the table, self-conscious about her disheveled hair.

"What's eating you?" Flo shooed the guys away.

Adelle sauntered up to Birdie, tugging a strand of her hair. "Looks like a cat dragged you in."

"I want to take you up on your offer," Birdie said in a rush, still catching her breath. "You said you could bob hair better than a beautician, right?"

"Ab-so-lute-ly." Flo reached for a handful of hair that fell in uneven strands to the middle of Birdie's back. "Are you sure? This is longer than I thought."

"Yes. Pos-i-tive-ly."

"Let's hop to it." Flo called to Mary who had just ducked into the tent. "Our poor little bunny wants her hair bobbed."

Birdie would have preferred just Flo, but the girls scurried her to the dressing room. Mary had her sit on the edge of the trunk. Flo pulled long, thin silver scissors from her vanity case snipping them open and closed. Adelle turned the mirror towards the canvas wall, away from Birdie.

"Wait. I want to watch too." Birdie squeaked the words out as if a question.

"Trust me. You don't," Adelle said.

"Adelle's right, it's better this way, for your first cut." Mary started to brush Birdie's hair with short gentle strokes. "Your hair is so fine."

"Why now?" Adelle stood too close. The heat of the small canvas tent became oppressive. Birdie started having second thoughts.

"I just, well, I'm ready to be modern too." Birdie braced herself on the trunk's edge. She eased as Mary worked through a tangle with her fingers. The contrast to Lydia yanking her head yesterday was comforting. Birdie released her shoulders. These were friends she could trust. "Where's Helen?"

"You're going to look spiffy in no time." Flo stood right behind Birdie. "Now sit very still."

Flo picked up a section, metal sliced against hair, and a long curl of honey blond hair fell to the dirt floor. Birdie squeezed her eyes shut as more and more snips came. The scissors brushed her neck. Adelle gasped. Birdie should have discussed bob styles with Flo before she let her start. Flo snipped some more, brushed Birdie's hair with her fingers and clipped again. And again. Birdie felt the brush bristles on the back of her neck and reached up to touch her skin.

"Jeez." Flo flicked Birdie's hand. "I could have sheared off your finger."

"Sorry."

Flo rubbed pomade in, cooling Birdie's scalp.

"It already feels lighter."

"Of course, it does." Adelle snickered. "There's more hair on the ground than on your head."

Birdie's eyes flew open. Adelle was right. Mounds of Birdie's hair surrounded the trunk. She had more than second thoughts now. Maybe it hadn't been such a good idea after all.

Flo stepped back admiring her work. She adjusted different curls, clipped here and there, then laid the scissors down on the trunk.

"Birdie, you look air-tight." Flo stood even taller.

"The cat's meow." Mary giggled.

"Unrecognizable," Adelle said.

"Can I see too?" Birdie raised herself off the trunk on wobbly legs. Mary and Adelle turned the mirror around. The turkey sandwich boiled in her stomach.

A slender woman with large hazel eyes, slight shoulders and extremely short, bobbed hair stared back at her. Flo had cut her hair in the Eton crop style, close to her head, parted on one side, accented with pomade. Birdie had only seen this style on models or movie stars, not on a real woman, certainly not one from West Chester, Pennsylvania. She stared at her reflection. The silence in the tent became as obvious as the piles of her cut hair on the dirt floor.

"Has anyone seen Birdie?" Teddy pushed open the muslin curtain. "Hugo said she should have arrived before five and it's ..." His mouth hung open. "Who's—" Teddy rubbed the back of his head. "Is that you, Birdie?"

"Isn't she ritzy?" Flo brushed her hands like a professional beautician. "Honest engine, this one's the best cut I've done." Flo stood behind Birdie beaming at their reflection.

"I, I guess so." Birdie couldn't stop touching her hair, the back of her exposed neck.

"What do you think?" Mary elbowed Teddy in that way that said he needed to say something.

"You look short, I mean smart." Teddy backed out of the dressing room. "First call in half hour."

"Don't cast a kitten, hair grows back." Adelle brushed past Birdie and left.

"She's just envious." Mary swept up clumps of hair, emptying the dustpan in a barrel by the door. "The cut is so striking on you. I wish I could pull off such a dramatic bob." Mary eased out of the dressing tent.

"I don't know what to say." Birdie looked away from the mirror. She had wanted a modern cut but this was too short. She bowed her head to hide her eyes.

"Thank you would be swell." Flo waited for Birdie.

"Um, I ..." Birdie choked on her words. "It's so dramatic."

"Says you." Flo's long strides took her past Birdie and out of the dressing tent.

Birdie raised her eyes to the mirror again. She didn't know if she liked the new modern woman staring back at her. She wasn't ready for what this Eton cut represented. She stepped closer to the mirror and took in the carefully crafted layers, combed part, and finger curls. There wasn't even enough hair on her head to Marcel wave. She wished Helen had been here. She ran her hands up and down her arms. She couldn't help but wonder if Flo's intention was to embarrass her with a such a short bob. She backed away, mesmerized by the unknown woman watching her leave.

*   *   *

After that night's performance, Birdie tried to repair the tension she had created with her friends. Between her night at a fancy hotel or her lack of appreciation of Flo's handiwork, it was hard to know where to begin.

"Thank goodness I didn't faint during tonight's whistling act." Birdie held open the curtain to the dressing tent. Adelle bumped her as she walked towards the mirror. "I think my new haircut gave me extra confidence."

Flo sauntered past, whispering with Mary. Neither acknowledged Birdie.

"Your whistling was right on pitch as usual." Helen glanced at Birdie and then away. "Did Hugo tell anyone else the latest news?"

"What?" Birdie and the other girls circled Helen in various stages of undress.

"The Lyceum let Miss Minnie go. We're to clean and mend our own costumes for the rest of the season."

"That's baloney." Flo stepped out of her lacy dress.

"Teddy says it may get worse if ticket sales don't increase." Mary placed her headband inside the trunk. "See you later at the boarding house. I'm helping him with the stage lights tonight."

"This never happened last year." Adelle picked up her vanity case, glaring directly at Birdie as if she had caused the firing of Miss Minnie.

"Flo and I've got things to discuss with Hugo." Helen turned so Birdie could button the back of her dress.

"I'll put the costumes away. It's the least I can do since I arrived so late." Birdie offered.

"Thanks. The boarding house is nearby," Helen said. "Wait till after Walter's lecture and one of us will take you there." She and Flo were gone before Birdie could answer.

"Make sure everything's folded nicely." Adelle stood by the mirror, applying lipstick. "And check for stains. Art has seltzer water if needed." She followed the others.

Birdie picked up a pair of discarded band pants and folded them in thirds. Everyone's treatment of her during the performance had been cool. Helen had not reacted to her haircut as Birdie had hoped. She shook out Helen's lacy dress, causing Emeraude perfume to surround her. Whenever Birdie had glanced at Helen, she had stared back in an odd way. Birdie looked at herself in the mirror again. Even after a rousing performance, her hair had stayed styled.

She pulled on one of the curls. At least Hugo had appreciated her new look. He had kept close to her backstage, whispering back and forth about his breakfast with Gerald, his ripe breath tickling the back of her exposed ear. Hugo assured her that Gerald had only talked business. He seemed quite impressed with Gerald's publishing business. Gerald had that way about him.

Alone in the dressing tent, Birdie placed the band costumes into the trunk and several blonde hairs shimmered from the dirt floor. She caught herself in the mirror, still uncertain whose reflection she saw. She did look more modern and felt more sophisticated too. She shimmied her shoulders, then twirled around in a circle while watching her new bob shake and move. She blew a kiss to the stylish young woman in the mirror. Could a haircut change a person?

CHAPTER 11

Galeton, Pennsylvania

A palette of pinks spread out over the horizon and the rising sun briefly showed its face before disappearing into the thick cloud cover. Birdie stretched her arms high to fill her lungs with the dawn air as she strode towards the tents. She whistled her morning greeting to the robins scattered under the trees with more gusto than she had in days. She turned on the lights then ducked into the dressing room, satisfied with her plan. The town of Galeton earned its name today as the wind caused the tent to buckle and groan.

After a week Birdie had become accustomed to and even enjoyed her new look, except for the cowlick that wouldn't lay like Flo had styled it that first night. Their "Spring tweeting strings" duet becoming quite a crowd pleaser was the easiest thing between them right now. The tent whooshed as if it confirmed her guilt. Not that she hadn't tried to soothe Flo's ego about the haircut multiple times.

Birdie had convinced herself that the other girls resented her. She sensed it on the train rides, during the performances, and especially nights in their shared boarding rooms. It was the little things that they didn't say or their side conversations, even her champion, Helen, had grown cold.

Convincing the baker to open early felt impolite but the fifty-cent tip had changed his tune. Her new haircut had emboldened her. She counted on Helen, the earliest riser, to find the warm bacon muffins, Hershey bars, and Birdie's note on the counter of the boarding house kitchen. Lydia had been right, bringing local Pennsylvanian chocolate had come in handy. A loose tent flap slapped against the canvas startling her.

She inspected Mary's coral lace costume for rips then pulled out her needle and thread from her satchel. Thanks to Lydia's insistence, she had learned to mend anything. She hummed bits of "Blue Bells of Scotland," her trombone solo, as she restitched the torn lace. She hoped they all loved bacon muffins and chocolate bars as much as she did. Another gust buckled the canvas sides causing the ropes to squeal.

She worked through the stack of band pants, making sure each had a secure stripe and buttons. Adelle's persistent comparison of everything to last year was about as grating as when she sang off pitch. Mending all their costumes should quiet Adelle's moans about losing Miss Minnie. Birdie reattached feathers to Flo's hairband while whistling "Stars and Stripes." Each inhale comforted her with the now familiar scents of straw, canvas, and popcorn.

"Is that you, Birdie?" A voice called from the main tent.

"In here." She picked up Adelle's lacy costume and examined the loose hem. The wind rattled the sides of the dressing room tent like a row of drummers.

Teddy pushed the curtain aside. "Why are you here so early?"

"Pretending to be Miss Minnie." She patted the stack of band pants.

"I've been looking all over for you." Teddy fished a folded telegram from his overalls pocket.

"Oh." Birdie reached for the manilla envelope. A sudden breeze blew across the back of her neck.

"I have to double check all the tie downs." Teddy tramped off, holding his large mallet like a baseball bat. "I never heard of bacon muffins," he called over his shoulder. "But those you left were de-licious."

Birdie's fingers quivered as she stuck the needle into the dress.

Telegrams only brought bad news. She tore open the envelope scanning the typed message. Tears made everything blurry and surreal. She smoothed out the fragile paper trying to focus on the blue block letters.

LYDIA LOST BABY<stop>

WE NEED YOU AT HOME<stop>

GERALD<stop>

She dropped what she was doing and went searching for Helen, for Hugo, for anyone. As she scanned the dark clouds, Birdie found herself mouthing a prayer for Lydia. She stumbled up the path towards town, thoughts darting in and out of her mind like the forceful wind. She needed to go home, be with Lydia—this was her third miscarriage. But performing gave Birdie purpose—she had found her people. But her sister needed her. She'd be forced to quit the circuit. Family was family and she should put Lydia first.

"Yoo-hoo," Helen called through cupped hands.

Birdie ran towards Helen; the wind lashed and pushed her along.

"What's wrong?"

Birdie started to speak but choked on her words. She handed Helen the crumpled telegram instead. Helen's eyes darkened as she read. She wrapped Birdie with a full hug that blocked her from the wind.

Birdie cleared her throat. "I have to go home."

"I'm so sorry." Helen wiped a tear from the side of Birdie's nose.

"Lydia needs me." Birdie stared at the bits of grass blowing across her shoes.

"My heart breaks for Lydia." Helen lifted Birdie's chin with her finger. "But what do *you* want to do?"

Birdie hiccupped, catching her breath. "What I want is different from what I should do."

Round raindrops began to fall. Helen gently steered Birdie back towards the tent, then followed her inside.

"Do you want to talk through your options?" Helen leaned on the edge of their costume trunk, pushing the stack of band pants aside.

Birdie knew the decision was hers to make but she willed Helen to make it for her. "I only see two." Birdie paced the room. "Go and comfort Lydia or stay and disappoint Lydia."

"Lydia's not the only one affected by your decision."

"I know. I'd be letting down the other girls. And Hugo." Birdie turned around at the mirror. Helen's reflection crossed her arms and looked away.

"And yourself." Helen brooded for a moment and then added. "What you want counts too."

Birdie took two steps towards her. "You always know what you want, and you take action." Birdie had missed talking with Helen the last few days. She eased next to Helen on the trunk. "Can you just make my decision?"

"No." Helen turned towards Birdie. "I'm perplexed, what can you being home do to change Lydia's tragic situation?"

Birdie considered Helen's candid question. She was right. Birdie couldn't make the fact that Lydia had miscarried again go away. How could she explain the strong family ties that bound her to Lydia when she didn't understand them herself?

"After our parents and then Edwin died, it left only us sisters. We take care of each other." She rubbed her arms down and back up then let her fingers rest on the exposed back of her neck. "She has Gerald, and he's very caring but our extended family is tight knit and opinionated." The catch in Birdie's stomach got stuck in her throat. "My aunts, uncles, cousins, and even our neighbors will expect me to be there for her."

"I guess I've never experienced that kind of family binding." Helen gripped the edge of the trunk. "It doesn't seem fair to you." Helen tapped her fingers against the trunk. "What if you asked Hugo for a brief leave? Gerald's telegram didn't ask you to stay."

"Our contract is clear about family emergencies. I've already over-extended Hugo's generosity."

"I doubt that. He wants to impress you. And Gerald." Helen stood up. "It's worth a try." So, Helen had noticed Hugo's interest in Gerald too. She didn't miss a thing.

"What would the other girls think? I've already tried their patience with staying overnight at the Marble Hall Hotel."

"Oh, no one cares about that."

"Wait. Did you say the others don't care that I stayed in a fancy hotel?"

"A lot has happened since then." Helen turned to face her. "We have other worries than where you stayed with Gerald and Lydia for one night." Helen pushed the curtain aside. "Let's find Hugo."

Birdie wondered if Helen was right or just didn't notice the other's feelings. Either way she was still glad she had delivered muffins and mended costumes.

"You haven't said what you think of Flo's handiwork." Birdie turned her head from side to side. Her timing was all wrong, but she might not have another chance to ask and needed Helen's approval.

Helen swallowed. "You look like Leatrice Joy."

The hair on Birdie's arms stood up like an upside-down centipede.

"So, you didn't just avoid me because you thought my bob was friv-olous?" Birdie squeezed past the opening bumping Helen's side.

"I told you; I've been talking with Hugo and every other circuit manager." Helen playfully bumped Birdie back. The rain pattered on the canvas walls. "I want them to do something about Walter's behavior." She raised her head higher. "If Walter persists on taking unwelcome liberties with Flo, I'm going to, well, it's better left unsaid."

"Walter is ghastly. And Hugo and the others should do something." Birdie poked overhead on the sagging canvas to splash out collected rainwater. "But should you get involved?"

Helen stopped. "Of course. We should all get involved."

"Then I'll say something to Hugo, too."

"Atta girl." Helen gave Birdie a robust pat, just as she had when they first met.

"I'm not sure why you put up with me." Birdie feigned a dramatic sigh, but her insides warmed.

"I have my reasons." Helen looked sideways at Birdie. "An unlimited supply of Hershey chocolate may be one of them." She put an arm across Birdie's shoulder. "Let's unearth Hugo. We'll find a way you can help Lydia and stay on the circuit."

The rain had slowed but Hugo proved as elusive as the sunshine. Helen searched inside and Birdie looked all around the main tent. They ran into Teddy and other Anvil Choir boys, who had been tightening all the tie-downs. Teddy threw up his hands when they asked if he'd seen Hugo.

The girls checked Schmidt's Boarding house next. Flo was enjoying the last crumbs of a bacon muffin. Birdie took a quick moment to gush about how well her haircut had survived the wind. Flo ruffled Birdie's hair then sauntered upstairs.

Adelle was a different story. She didn't like bacon. She wouldn't eat Hershey chocolate because it was too bittersweet. And she pretended she knew Hugo's whereabouts but kept coy about the details. Helen cajoled, pleaded, even tried praise but finally resorted to sarcasm, which made Adelle mad. She remained as tight lipped as a turtle. Adelle marched upstairs and slammed her room door so hard, the coffee cups rattled on the walnut sideboard. Mary had just been coming down the stairs and shrugged at Adelle's antics.

"Maybe Hugo's already at the train station." Mary slipped two chocolate bars into her purse. "He might have extra arrangements to make since we're off to Canada soon."

"I should have thought of that." Helen started up the stairs. "Let's get packed and head there next."

"I need to reply to Gerald." The telegram felt heavy in Birdie's pocket.

"You can telephone him from the station." Helen called from the top of the stairs.

"Did something happen?" Mary asked.

Birdie didn't want to blurt her sister's business to everyone, but she knew Mary would find out soon enough. "My sister lost her baby."

"Oh dear." Mary covered her mouth. "I'm so sorry."

"I don't know what to do." Birdie sank into a wooden kitchen chair. "Gerald asked that I come home."

"But you'd have to—"

"I know, quit the circuit." Birdie rested her chin on her hands with her elbows on the table.

"It makes sense she wants you there. You two remind me of my sisters, we're best friends." Mary offered Birdie one of the muffins.

"Lydia and I best friends?" Birdie shook her head.

Mary sipped her coffee. "Well, she was very protective when you fainted. It's obvious she cares for you."

"She does." Birdie's insides caved in. Lydia had always been there for her. Now here Birdie was, trying to wheedle a way to only see Lydia for a short visit or not at all. She didn't need to find Hugo to ask a favor. She needed to get to the train station and purchase a ticket to West Chester.

Helen came back downstairs, suitcase in hand. "Ready?"

"Give me one minute." Birdie took the stairs two at a time. She came back downstairs with her Daisy suitcase and her mind made up.

As they walked to the Galeton train station the wind-blown mist felt like stabbing hatpins. Birdie figured she deserved it, like a heavenly form of punishment. The windy rain also made it impossible to talk, which was a relief for Birdie. How would she tell Helen she was leaving the circuit? They scooted inside the brick station and Helen stood to the side, brushing the rain off her cloak sleeves. Birdie went straightaway towards the ticket office, slipping a bit on the wet tiled floor. Her suitcase bumped the elbow of a man coming around the corner.

"Pardon me." Birdie looked into familiar brown eyes. "Hugo."

"We've got to quit meeting like this, babe. One of us is going to get hurt." He rubbed his elbow.

Hugo had just started calling her babe. Since meeting Gerald and Lydia, he had paid more attention to her. She wanted to think it was her new look. She didn't like his nickname for her, but now wasn't the time to tell him.

"We've been looking for you." She set her things down. She clutched the telegram in her pocket. "I've got to—"

"We've got a favor to ask." Helen stepped in front of Birdie grasping Hugo's coat sleeve.

"One at a time, ladies." Hugo's face fixed into his opening night look.

"I have to quit the circuit," Birdie blurted, surprising herself.

"What?" Helen looked like someone had slapped her.

"Nonsense," said Hugo.

The normal noises of the station stopped. Everyone stared at Birdie.

"I received a telegram from Gerald. Lydia lost her baby." Birdie said it in monotone, slowing down with each word. "I need to return home to West Chester."

"But babe." Hugo put his arm around Birdie's sagging shoulders. "Let's try to work this out." He guided her to a bench. Birdie could see Helen turning away out of the corner of her eye.

"Helen, I'm sorry," Birdie called to her with a hoarse voice and received her retreating back in reply.

Hugo took off his felt hat to run his fingers through his hair. "Did Gerald ask you to come home?"

Birdie handed him the telegram.

"I see." He sat with his hands on his knees, holding the telegram. He started to talk several times but stopped himself.

"I don't have a choice, Hugo," Birdie finally said for him. "My contract is clear, no breaks for family emergencies."

"And you are determined you need to go home?" He rubbed his face. His eyes seemed red rimmed, as if he had been crying too.

"Yes. Lydia needs me." Birdie felt more convinced since her talk with Mary.

"Does Gerald realize what he's asking of you?" Hugo took her hands in his and the telegram fluttered to the floor.

"I, I don't know." Birdie hadn't thought of that. Would Gerald have asked if he knew she had to quit? She had shown him the contract but had directed him to the line about her weekly pay, not the small print below that line.

"How about I call Gerald before you purchase your train ticket home?"

"I guess so." She saw compassion in his face. "But be sure he knows this was your idea. That I'm ready to come home." She liked the idea of letting Hugo make the call for her.

"Absolutely." He squeezed her hands and went towards the office of the train station.

Standing on her tiptoes Birdie couldn't see Helen anywhere. She wanted to find her but was afraid to leave the bench before Hugo returned. She picked up the telegram, put it in her pocket, and sat down to wait. She checked her wristwatch's time against the two-sided wrought-iron clock that stood in the center of the station. Only 11:03.

Hugo strode back to her. He tried to appear somber, but she could read triumph all over his rugged face.

"I had a good chat with Gerald. And of course, he doesn't expect you to quit. He had no idea or wouldn't have asked." He opened and closed his pocket watch; each click a verification of his accomplishment.

Birdie didn't know how to react. She wished she had gone with Hugo to hear it from Gerald herself. It was a mistake to sit idle while

Hugo did the talking for her. And she could have talked with Lydia too. So much for the idea that her new haircut emboldened her.

"Are you certain?"

"Yes." Hugo pulled her to standing holding both hands. "I wouldn't lead you astray."

She should be feeling relief, but she just felt empty.

"He asked that you call Lydia once you get settled in Oswego. She was napping when I rang."

"Of course."

"Everything jake?" He cocked his head in concern, but the way the corners of his lips curved up revealed he was quite proud of himself. "I've got to get back to the tents."

"Thank you."

"I'm still getting used to your flapper haircut, but I like what I see." He winked.

Birdie sank down on the slatted wooden bench. She should go look for Helen. She should write a letter to Lydia. Rain pounded on the tiled roof like hammers of the Anvil Choir. She might as well wait here. Their train departed in little over an hour. Birdie leaned her head against the plaster wall behind the bench and started humming "What A Friend We Have in Jesus" as another prayer for Lydia and maybe herself, too.

CHAPTER 12

Oswego, New York

The pelting rain had stopped by the time the Versatile Quintet boarded the 12:15 train to Oswego, New York. Birdie searched for Helen but stopped when Mary invited her to sit next to her with a pat on the aisle seat. Just as Birdie had settled next to Mary, Helen walked past with only a curt nod, selecting a seat several rows back beside Flo. Adelle boarded last and situated herself in an empty row across from Helen and Flo.

The pink sunrise and Birdie's carefully laid plans seemed like they had happened weeks ago, not just this morning. Mary chattered away about antics with her sisters. Birdie nodded at the appropriate pauses but only heard Mary's drone.

Helen and Flo seemed to be in cahoots. They whispered to each other behind curved hands. Adelle kept flicking the newspaper each time she turned the pages as if announcing that she was the only one who kept up with current events. Other passengers nodded in sleep.

Birdie wished the rhythm of the train's wheels along the tracks would lull her. All she heard with each click was a scolding "you should've." She should've found Helen and explained everything. She should've called Gerald herself. She should've bought a ticket to West Chester. Quite some time passed before Birdie realized Mary had stopped talking. She leaned against the window which blocked Birdie's outside view.

Closing her eyes, Birdie tried to feign sleep. She couldn't shake the dread of Lydia's loss. Even the deep breathing tricks Lydia had taught her did nothing to bring peace. The train click-clacked along, made several stops, and seemed to take its time to pull into Oswego.

Birdie couldn't wait to get to the boarding house. She wanted to call Lydia right away. Teddy announced that he needed to get to the tents immediately since their train had arrived later than expected. For the first time, the Versatile Quintet was responsible for unloading their instruments and costume trunk at the tents then finding their lodging. Birdie's trusty wristwatch confirmed that they only had an hour and half before curtain call.

"It's not right that we have to carry our things all the way to the tents." Adelle crumpled up her newspaper and stuffed the ball into a trash can. "Surely Teddy could let one of the guys help us."

"They let several of the college boys go after they fired Miss Minnie." Helen looked around the platform. "We need a cart."

"Don't get all lathered up, Adelle." Flo whipped out her cigarette holder. "There's plenty of bozos that can do our bidding." She sauntered over to one of the railroad workers. Flo managed to get a light and a rolling cart in no time. The railroad hand followed her to the train's cargo car.

Birdie picked up two suitcases along with hers. Helen had jogged ahead to help direct Flo and her new "bozo."

Mary walked beside Birdie. "Teddy said Hugo had to cut costs."

"It was never this bad last year." Adelle shot a sideways smirk at Birdie then picked up her pace until she was several yards ahead.

Did Hugo regret that he added her to the talent costs? Adelle's remark stung. Knowing that Miss Minnie and some of the Anvil Choir had been let go made Birdie choke. The extra train tickets, the extra bed, and the extra meals could add up.

"I try to give Adelle grace, but she has been a nudnik lately." Mary put her hand on Birdie's back. "Don't give her comments another thought."

"Thanks. Adelle does take extra patience." Birdie let out her held breath.

Helen, Flo, and the railway hand had managed to wrangle the costume trunk onto the cart. Flo hoisted her harp case next to the trunk. Birdie wedged her trombone case between the two and Mary piled on the violin and banjo. The conductor called for the railway man. He left with kisses on both cheeks from Flo and fifty cents from Helen.

Flo and Helen pushed the cart towards the train station but it had a janky wheel and kept veering towards the tracks. Birdie placed the two suitcases on top of the trunk to guide the cart from the front. When the cart hit the threshold into the station, the suitcases fell off.

"Glory be," Birdie said but Flo's "Dad-burned effing cart" outshouted her.

Mary picked up both suitcases and lugged them along with hers. Adelle meandered behind them all, carrying only her own suitcase and satchel. It took all of Birdie's willpower to not call Adelle one of Flo's colorful names.

"Who wants to stay with the cart while the others check into our lodgings?" Helen asked.

"Me," Adelle answered first.

"Me too." Flo flexed her arm muscle. "Pushing a cart is the bullfrog's beard but I could use a break."

Helen surveyed the three girls who had collapsed on a long bench under one of the ceiling fans. "Birdie and I will take the suitcases and get us checked in. Then we'll go to the tents together."

"Your reward will be an ice-cold soda when you return." Flo patted her pocketbook. "My treat."

"Why you're just the duck's quack," Mary said with a forced giggle.

"The pig's wings," Flo snorted.

Adelle opened a newspaper that she had retrieved from the bench and turned away from the cackling girls.

Helen picked up three suitcases and soon her heels clicked on the tile towards the station's doors. Birdie walked away with made-up sayings echoing in her ears. She took long strides, swinging the two suitcases as if to propel her to catch Helen. Once outside several trolley cars passed them as they trudged along First Street.

Helen called out. "We're staying at the Penfield Rooming House on Fifth Street." She crossed the street. Birdie followed with flying steps.

"It's only a few more blocks that way." Helen turned and Birdie who had managed to catch up, knocked Helen's elbow with one of the swinging suitcases.

"Sorry, Helen."

"You bump into everyone these days."

Birdie struggled with what to say to Helen. "Are you mad that Hugo figured out a way for me to stay on the circuit?"

Helen turned around and continued walking. They covered the next block in heated silence. Birdie certainly wouldn't share that Hugo had called Gerald for her. Birdie gripped the suitcase handles tighter. Helen's silence burned in her ears as well as Birdie's stomach.

Helen stopped in front of a two-story home with four round columns across the wide front porch. Each column had big curlicues at the ceiling, and everything was painted a bright white. She dropped the suitcases. It clearly wasn't the Penfield Rooming House. It was too nice.

"This is a Greek Revival." Helen pointed to the house.

"Okay?"

"The architectural style. Greek Revival—a temple-styled entrance with at least four columns." Helen shielded her eyes from the bright sun. "Like my home. In Philly."

Birdie stood on the sidewalk gawking up at the building's façade, trying to decipher what had just transpired between them. Just when she got the nerve to ask, Helen spun away and dashed across the street. Birdie's eyes followed her up the stairs to a sagging clapboard home.

Birdie got a fresh grip on her suitcases, raised her shoulders, and hiked up to the Penfield Rooming House.

Helen stood at the front desk talking with an older man, the proprietor. He handed her two keys. Birdie hung back.

"Let's put these suitcases in the rooms then return to the station." Helen held out one of the keys.

"I need to make a quick call to Lydia."

"You didn't talk with her at the Galeton station?"

"She was napping."

"Go ahead. I'll take these up." Helen put a suitcase under each arm, one in her left hand and tried to pick up two in her right hand. All the suitcases clattered to the floor.

"Miss." The proprietor turned around from the desk. "My son will carry your cases if you will be the least bit patient."

"Yes sir." Helen nodded to Birdie. "Make your call."

Birdie asked if she could use the house phone. The man directed her to a tiny closet behind his desk. The padded navy velvet bench had rips at the seams and dust particles fell from the matching curtain when he closed it after her. Kneading her neck, she collected her thoughts. She picked up the earphone then jiggled the cradle to call the operator.

"343 Walnut Street in West Chester, please."

"Just a moment."

Birdie heard three clicks and then a buzz.

"No such number. Did you say Westchester, New York?

"No ma'am, West. Chester. Pennsylvania."

"Hrumpf."

It took many clicks, numerous buzzes and several minutes before Birdie heard a faint voice that resembled Lydia.

"Hello?" Lydia sounded as if she were in a cave.

"It's me." Birdie leaned forward to speak into the candlestick mouthpiece. "How are you?"

"Fine." The scratching on the line echoed her.

"I'm so sorry." Birdie pressed the black earphone closer so she could hear.

"What?"

"I said, I'm sad." Birdie gripped the candlestick tighter. Another "should have" clicked with the static on the line. She should have written to Lydia back at the Galeton train station.

"Yes, well."

"I miss you," Birdie shouted.

The proprietor poked his head through the velvet curtain with his pointer finger pushed against his thin lips. He swiped the curtain closed again. Dust particles filled the room. The entire world scolded her.

"What?" A buzz whined just as Lydia spoke.

"I. Love. You," Birdie said as clear as she could. When was the last time she had said those words to Lydia?

"Goodbye, dear."

"I'll try to come home soon," Birdie said to the buzzing line.

She replaced the earphone to its hook and eased back the heavy curtain. The proprietor stood right outside; palm outstretched. She asked him to put the phone bill on her room tab. Helen stopped her pacing when she saw Birdie. She opened the front door without a word.

"Wait." Birdie skipped down the steps and caught up with Helen. "I'm sorry. I should have told you I had changed my mind about going home."

"Why does Hugo call you babe?"

"Um, he … just does." Birdie held out her hands in apology. "But I don't like it."

"Then tell him to stop." Helen's eyes flashed dark green then she strode ahead.

Birdie didn't have the energy left to chase Helen.

When she reached the station, Adelle had moved over to a small chair near the conductor's office. Flo and Mary were sipping from soda bottles, still volleying sayings to each other.

"You're just the lizard's lips," Mary chortled.

Helen took a swig from her orange soda. "All right you two loopy dames, let's get to the tents."

"Aren't you a bossy baboon?" Flo held out the last bottle to Birdie.

The cold soda soothed Birdie's scratchy throat. She tried to join the camaraderie. "Thanks. You're a dog's breath."

"You're not up to speed with your quips." Helen's musical laughter echoed in the station. Birdie would have to figure other ways to get back in Helen's graces but at least here was an opening. They stood at opposite corners at the front of the cart.

Together the four of them heaved the cart forward past Adelle. She rose from her chair, tucking this newspaper into her satchel.

"None of you would believe what I just read."

"We don't want to hear anything from a walrus's wet blanket." Flo grunted as she pushed on the cart alongside Mary. "We'd rather you get a wiggle and help us."

"I wasn't going to share it with you anyhow." Adelle maneuvered herself several feet in front of the cart. "This news is for Hugo." Still carrying just her banjo and satchel, Adelle led the way down the sidewalk towards the Lake Ontario shoreline where they could see the tips of the tents.

"Wonder what she read?" Birdie did her best to keep Mary's violin case on top of the trunk as she and Helen guided the cart along the bumpy sidewalk.

"Most likely local gossip about the circuit." Helen's mood sobered.

"It makes me sad that Miss Minnie was fired." Mary said from behind the cart.

"She was the real cat's meow," Flo said.

"The bear's hug." Birdie added. She hadn't even known to say goodbye. Hugo was going to hear about this. Right after she told him to quit calling her babe.

The girls pushed the cart the remaining three blocks to the tent with little conversation. Once close to the tents Teddy ran up and took over.

"You girls look worn out."

"And how." Flo gave the cart one last push towards Teddy.

"Hopefully we can muster enough energy to perform well tonight." Mary walked alongside Teddy.

"As we've all heard from a little bird, 'Rest if you must, but I'll be dammed if you quit.'" Flo rubbed her lower back, her eyebrow raised at Birdie.

"You should embroider a banner of your version, Flo." Helen stretched her arms above her head. The excursion had brightened her cheeks. It delighted Birdie to see flecks of gold in Helen's eyes again. She fought the urge to wrap her arms around Helen's narrow waist.

"I can't sew." Flo nodded to Birdie. "Our new seamstress can start on it as soon as she finishes mending our costumes."

"Like hell," Birdie said.

Helen, Flo, and Mary hooted out loud.

Teddy looked back and forth between the four. "I'm going to have you girls load your own cart more often."

"Noooo." They cried in unison. Mary hit him with a playful swat as they turned towards the tent.

Birdie held back. The different emotions she experienced in one day felt like a symphony made from a variety of songbirds. Cardinal's chirps as simple amends towards her friends, a Blue Jay's squawk from her first argument with Helen, a loon's sorrowful calls from failing to comfort Lydia, the finch's bubbling tweets over a loaded cart, and the Mourning Dove's coos over lost workmates. She wrapped her arms around herself as she ducked past the open flap.

CHAPTER 13

Picton, Ontario

The following morning Teddy told the Versatile Quintet they'd be taking the last train out of Fort Bend that night right after their act. When Helen questioned the late-night departure one too many times Teddy snapped.

"I'm merely following orders, Helen. Back off." He held up his hands in frustration.

Birdie and Mary watched in fearful silence while Adelle mouthed something about telling Hugo. For the first time, Flo didn't add a quip or comment. The tension showed in their act, it felt forced. Teddy had the cart loaded and hurried them to the station as Walter started his lecture.

They arrived at the Picton, Ontario, Canada train station well after midnight. To Birdie the schedule change allowed them a chance to sleep in. She'd have an entire day to figure out ways to reconnect with Lydia and Helen, the latter who vacillated between irritation and delight. At the most inopportune times Birdie wanted to quit and go home to West Chester. Everyone seemed off kilter. Maybe Canada would give the Versatile Quintet a boost.

The darkness added eeriness to the unfamiliar buildings and empty streets. Teddy prodded them along. Flo and Mary were giddy with sleep deprivation so Adelle kept hushing them. She reminded Birdie of a stern schoolmarm on many occasions but even outdid herself tonight. Helen lagged behind so Teddy cajoled her on the most.

Teddy stopped his cart on the corner of a block of stately homes and tilted his clipboard towards the solitary streetlamp. He approached the only one that had its porch light on out front and a muted glow behind the closed drapes. He double checked the address then retrieved a key from his pocket. Birdie remained on the street clutching Helen's arm. Even Mary, Flo, and Adelle became still.

"What are you doing, Teddy?" Helen hissed. She clambered the steps to the porch.

"This is the Maple-Leaf Boarding house." He fumbled with the key. "I was told we should let ourselves in." The key turned so Teddy pushed the front door open. He held the door open wide and nodded to the girls indicating they should go inside. No one moved.

"It doesn't feel right," Helen said.

"But it is. See the sign?" He gestured to his clipboard and pointed to a hand painted sign affixed to the left side of the front door. It had a big red maple leaf with the name painted in bold white letters. He held his arm towards the open door as if pointing to the light from the foyer.

"I'm not going to argue." Adelle lugged her suitcase inside. The others followed one after the other into an entryway appointed with a brocade settee and hardwood floors. Three keys with numbered tassels rested atop the knotted bureau. The room smelled of baked bread mixed with lemon scented cleaner. A handwritten sign with 'Welcome Chautauqua' in curlicue script was propped against the beanpot lamp.

"You girls take rooms numbered four and six. I'll take the attic room," Teddy said nodding towards the keys. "I'll bring the trunk and instruments inside for tonight."

"Where's the proprietor?" Helen moved an embroidered pillow aside to ease onto the settee.

"They said she'd have turned in by the time we arrive." Teddy stepped out on the porch as he held the door. "So be quiet."

"The one night we're without a fire extinguisher and we arrive after midnight?" Flo took off her hat and shook her head.

"What, Flo?" Birdie scanned the room for a fire.

"A chaperone, you sap." Flo did a little shimmy. "Sometimes you're such a rube, Birdie."

"Give it a rest, Flo." Helen moved hers and Birdie's suitcases to the base of the stairs. "We're all tired."

"I just hope the beds are clean and comfy." Mary held the front door wide as Teddy made another trip inside carrying the trombone, violin, and banjo and went outside again.

"I bet you and your sheik will get more than cozy." Flo wrapped her arms around herself as if necking.

Mary went to swat Flo and let the door shut. Helen sank to the bottom step holding her head in her hands. Teddy knocked on the door. Twice. Birdie whistled to Mary, but she had covered her ears to block Flo's smooching sounds. Adelle shushed so loud she spit across the room. By the time Helen heaved the door open, Teddy was pounding, with one arm wrapped around the harp. Helen clapped twice. The lobby went from ruckus to quiet in seconds. Upstairs they heard a door open and then close. Adelle pursed her lips, grabbed the keys, and marched partway up the carpeted stairs.

"You just woke up the entire place," she huffed. "Who's going to explain this fiasco?" She tramped the rest of the way.

"To your rooms, girls," Teddy said with as much authority as he could muster. "You may have a morning of luxury, but I have to help raise the tents at dawn."

Flo, Mary, and Birdie started up the steps. Helen followed behind Birdie. When they got to the top landing, Adelle came out of one of the rooms.

"There's a problem." She indicated towards both open doors. "Each room only has two beds." She glared directly at Birdie.

"Perhaps Mary will be bunking with Teddy after all," Flo whispered. Mary covered her face with her hands.

"Helen, Flo, and I can take one room. We'll push the beds together and sleep longways across them for one night." Birdie looked from Helen to Flo.

"Fine with me." Adelle backed into the room.

"Thank you, Birdie." Mary pushed past Flo, closed the door, and locked it.

"Well, that's just horse feathers." Flo looped her arm through Birdie's, and they made an unbalanced pair meandering down the hall.

Helen latched the door once Flo and Birdie had entered. They set their suitcases down and it became obvious Birdie's plan for sleeping three across the beds wouldn't work. Each twin bed had four spindle bed posts, held together by planked frames. There would be a wide gap even if shoved together. The other furniture in the room consisted of a narrow bureau, a hat rack, and a small chair whose caned base appeared unstable. The hardwood floor had an oval rag rug between the beds.

"This is a pickle." Flo looked under each bed searching for a hidden rollaway.

"Not quite as I had envisioned." Birdie dropped her arms to her sides.

"I'll tell Mary we weren't kidding about her bedding with Teddy," Flo said.

"Don't do that." Birdie moved to the edge of the chair and rubbed her foot. "Your teasing was a bit much for Mary."

"Is that so?" Flo flung her cloche towards the hat rack. It caught itself on a lower hook. "And what do you know about romance?"

"Never mind." Helen yanked the quilt coverlet off one of the twins. "I'll make a pallet on the floor and you each can have a bed."

"Oh, you don't need to sleep on the floor, Helen." Birdie tugged at the other twin's quilt. "I will."

"I've slept on many floors." Helen creased the quilt longways and plopped it on top of the rug.

"It was my idea for the three of us to sleep here." Birdie sighed. "I couldn't endure another of Adelle's accusatory glares tonight."

"She can be a wet blanket. But I'm not arguing about sleeping on the floor. I'll take this bed." Flo placed her suitcase on the bed farthest from the door and removed her silk Billie Burk pajamas from within. She began to undress with her back to Helen and Birdie. "I think Hugo's keen on Adelle."

A hot prickle singed inside Birdie's chest. "What makes you think that?" She folded the other quilt in half, flattened it with her fists and folded it again.

"I've seen them cozying up backstage." Flo shook out her dress. She stepped into her pajama pants and turned around as she finished buttoning her shirt.

Birdie sensed Helen watching her. She smoothed out the quilt on the pallet and arranged the pillow at the top. Hugo had been the first to admire her Eaton haircut. He nicknamed her babe. She ran her palm from her neck to her collar. Maybe Flo was teasing or even worse, testing her.

"I can't imagine he sees anything in Adelle." Helen picked up their suitcases and handed Birdie hers with a sideways smile.

"Oh, I bet he's seeing a lot of Adelle." Flo made a motion with her hands like the shape of an hourglass.

Birdie unlocked her suitcase with two loud pops as she flipped open the clasps. She grabbed her night shirt. "It's late."

"You're forever the gossip, Flo." Helen removed her dress. She motioned towards Birdie with a tilt of her head.

"I assume the lavatory is down the hall." Flo opened the door and strode into the quiet hallway.

"Why does she do that?" Birdie slipped off her dress and pulled on her nightshirt. She missed the opening for her head and got stuck with one arm up, the other trapped and her face tangled in the thick cotton. "Helen, help."

Birdie felt Helen's hands wrenching at the stubborn material. "Wiggle your arms."

"I am, silly." Birdie squirmed and twisted. Helen pulled at the nightshirt and finally Birdie's head popped through. Helen's nose was less than an inch from Birdie's. One hand still held the hem of Birdie's shirt taunt. Helen wore only her slip. Her neck and shoulders exposed. Birdie had a sudden urge to tickle Helen. She reached up and lightly poked Helen under her arms.

Helen squeezed her arms to her sides holding her lips tightly closed. This made Birdie try even harder. She reached for Helen's waist, playfully tickling as if Helen were a child. Helen tried to get away but laughed despite herself. Flo walked in just as Helen retaliated, her hands on either side of Birdie's middle. Their faces were flush, each breathless.

"Me-ow." Flo stood with one hand on the doorknob and the other at the top of the frame.

Helen jerked away. She grabbed her vanity case, whispered something to Flo in short phrases and left. Flo looked down at her bare feet.

"I don't know what came over me." Birdie slumped onto the bed. "I'm so exhausted I'm loopy." She had perturbed Helen. Again. That seemed to be happening more often.

"None of us knows what we're doing sometimes." Flo pulled back the sheet from her twin bed. "I'm sorry if what I said about Adelle and Hugo upset you."

Birdie snuck a puzzled look. Flo had never offered Birdie an apology. She thrived on teasing, flirting, and attention. Maybe there was more to Flo than Birdie had imagined.

"It's all right. You meant no harm."

"Thanks."

"I've been meaning to ask. Does Walter still ah, bother you?"

"Recently he's backed off."

"That's a relief. I'm glad Hugo warned him."

"It was Helen who scared him." Flo curled up on her side under the blanket. "She's a bearcat."

"Really? You think Helen threatened him?" Birdie recalled their conversation on the day she had received Gerald's telegram. She wondered if Helen had persuaded Hugo to get Walter to stop or if she'd intimidated Walter herself.

Birdie picked up her leather beauty box and headed out the door towards the lavatory. She passed Helen and neither looked directly at the other. Why did she act so immature around Helen? Birdie regretted her stupid tickle attack. Helen was one of the few people who seemed to understand her.

When Birdie returned, the lamp had been turned off. The air felt tight and suspended. She sensed Helen and Flo had stopped mid-chat when she opened the door. She climbed under the mussed covers of her bed. She lay on her side, with her head resting on her curved arms. Her gaze went to Helen, who was staring at the ceiling while huddled in her quilt cocoon on the floor. Birdie bit her lip.

"What were you two talking about?" Birdie whispered as loud as she dared.

"You don't have to whisper," Flo mumbled. "We're still awake."

"Nothing important." Helen closed her eyes. Silence stretched over the three of them like pulled taffy. Enough time passed that Birdie thought the others had given in to sleep.

"I'm about to burst with a secret." Flo's voice echoed against the quiet. "I think Hugo is planning something shifty."

Birdie clenched her fingers. "Why would you think that?" The surprises Flo had shared about Hugo tonight were curious. She began to wonder if what Flo said could be trusted.

"He rearranged the schedule so he's the circuit manager in Picton with us tomorrow instead of Derr." Flo propped up on her elbow. "He's the one who insisted we arrive so late tonight." She pulled a loose thread from the edge of her sheet. "Have you noticed that when he is with us, he holds mysterious meetings away from the tents?"

Helen sat up and hugged her knees. "That could explain why he's always hard to find."

"But Hugo's not the shady type." Birdie only saw silhouettes of the others faces. The darkness of the room made what Flo implied even more sinister.

"He could be." Flo tapped the wood bedframe with her fingernails. "He's run this circuit for years. He knows the ins and outs."

"But that means he also knows the rules." Birdie rolled to her back. "Besides, what could he be doing that's questionable?"

Helen exaggerated her yawn. "We really should get some sleep, girls."

"He's craftier than he lets on." Flo copy-yawned.

"Oh goodness." Birdie laid back down. "How will I ever fall asleep?"

"Count birds landing on a wire," Flo turned towards the wall.

Helen tweaked Birdie's dangling fingers. "Try to shoo away your wayward thoughts. Things will look better in the morning."

"Right." Birdie doubted she could sleep. Flo had stirred up worries of Hugo and Adelle, that added to Birdie's concerns for Lydia. But after a few deep breaths, she nestled into sheets smelling of fresh air mixed with Ivory soap, and let exhausted sleep come.

*   *   *

So much for sleeping in, Birdie woke at dawn after a restless night. She dreamt that Lydia chased Adelle with a knife she kept under her Edwardian hat. A flurry of newspapers followed Adelle as if they were a protective flock of printed birds. Then Hugo married Flo and they had a baby who arrived dressed like a miniature flapper. The baby even had Hugo's thick hair formed into miniature Marcel waves.

Birdie stretched her arms over her head, noting Flo still heavy with sleep. She looked down and could barely make out the crown of Helen's hair under the layers of quilt. She slipped on her dusty-rose drop waist dress which made her recall the struggle she had getting into her night-shirt last night with a silent snort. She managed to sneak out of the room without waking Flo or Helen.

The stairs creaked as she descended to the foyer. Teddy must have left earlier with the instruments, trunk, and his cart. There was a flat rustic basket filled with an assortment of pastries sitting on the bureau. She chose one topped with creamy icing. It tasted like pancakes slathered in maple syrup; she licked her fingers and considered eating another so counted them. She sighed. Just enough for the others.

She poured herself a mug of steaming coffee from a ceramic lidded pitcher that hid under a handmade embroidered cozy. Lydia used cozies like this when they had coffee on the porch in autumn. She must find a special notecard for Lydia and maybe something else as a souvenir from Canada. She wished she could mail a maple pastry to her. Lydia was partial to baked sweets. So was Helen, Birdie realized with a laugh. Those two women couldn't be more different in every other way.

When Birdie stepped outside, morning light transformed the gloomy houses from last night into elegant homes. She strolled past the brick and wooden buildings along Main Street then was drawn to a unique large two-story building not far from the tents.

The cross shaped building was painted olive green with rows of connected windows on both levels and every side. It had a steep roof but Birdie was drawn to all the glass. Maybe it was a resort because there were both horse-drawn carriages and automobiles parked on the surrounding lawn. As she got closer, it became evident that it was a grand hall of some sort with white painted arches inside. The surrounding scenery reflected in the windows made the building meld with its surroundings. Even Lake Ontario was mirrored in a wavy way on the one side. Damp marshy air filled her lungs as she stood with hands clasped behind her back, counting the windows.

"It's called the Crystal Palace of Picton." Hugo walked up from behind her.

Birdie jerked away. "Oh. What are you doing here?"

"Admiring the view." He brought his gaze to her. "How many windows?"

Birdie cleared her throat. "You interrupted me at 128."

"Ah. I'll save you getting a crick in your neck. There's over 400." He extended his arm towards the building as if he had built it himself. "It's modeled after the Crystal Palace in England."

Birdie nudged long blades of grass with her the toe of her shoe. Everything Flo had revealed last night swirled in her mind.

"When did you arrive to Picton?" Birdie looked at her wristwatch. It was just half past nine.

Hugo offered her his arm. "Walk with me to the tents?"

"I'd like to get a souvenir card to mail Lydia." She took a step back. "I believe I saw a dry goods store back on Main Street."

"I can allow a few extra minutes to escort you there." He wiggled the crook of his arm. "Babe?" He squinted as he faced the sun behind her head.

"I need you to be frank with me." She smoothed her dress several times. "What's going on between you and Adelle?" She pressed her lips, holding her face steady.

"Me and Adelle?" He scrunched his brows together. "Nothing." His arm fell to his side. "What did she say?"

Birdie remained tense. What if Flo had been tricking her? "Someone suggested that you are keen on her."

"Well, whoever told you is full of malarkey." He removed his hat to rake his hand through his hair.

The sunlight in his hair coupled with his model-like features made her question what she was doing.

"Adelle corners me with complaints or half-baked ideas after every performance. But believe me, I wouldn't risk my job with Chautauqua for the likes of her."

That comment made Birdie flinch. "Are you risking your job?"

"Not for her." His answer raised more questions. He placed his hand at the small of her back to steer her away from the Crystal Palace.

The sounds of people, carriages, and a few autos made their shared silence louder. Maybe she shouldn't have expected so much of Hugo. They weren't going steady after all. He'd call her babe but then be gone for days. He'd share stories with her one night then flirt with Adelle the next time he was circuit manager. Birdie glanced at his profile. He appeared lost in his thoughts. He stopped even with a row of cottonwood saplings and cocked his head.

"Name that one."

"What?"

"Listen."

The three-note pattern was a version of a bird call Birdie recognized. "Black Capped Chickadee." She whistled the song back.

"It sounds like you're calling him your sweetie."

"Maybe I am."

"That could be our song." Hugo looked away.

Once again, he seemed to struggle to put words together, like he had at the Galeton train station. "When Gerald asked if I had good intentions, of course I answered yes." He directed her off the street to the shaded side of a large brick building.

She leaned against the wall. He stood in front of her with one hand on the wall near her ear. "But you have to understand the risk I'm taking even talking to you." He ducked his head then raised his eyes to meet hers. His long dark eyelashes blinked slowly.

"Gerald asked about your intentions towards me?"

Hugo held up both palms in defense. "During our breakfast."

"You assured me you two only talked business." Birdie pulled away from the building.

"It was just as he was leaving."

That sounded like something Gerald might do. "But what risk?"

He pulled her closer. "It's complicated, babe."

"Because the Chautauqua Lyceum forbids fraternizing with the talent." She raised her head towards him. "But there's more, isn't there?"

His offensive smell reminded Birdie how it unsettled her after she had fainted. It was sweet almost like Lydia's apple butter but with more vinegar.

He twisted one of her tiny curls between his fingers, wry amusement causing his lips to curl. "Your flapper look makes me goofy and reckless." He bent his head down and kissed her lightly. She gasped and he kissed her again, letting his lips linger on hers. Birdie stepped away, her hand touching her lips. Her first real kiss.

"We can't do this now, babe." He placed his hat on his head.

"I'm not the one who kissed me." She surprised herself. Last night she had vowed to stay away from Hugo. "And please stop calling me babe."

"What?" He squeezed her elbow.

"I'm not going to be the reason you lose your job." She looked away.

His hand slid down her arm and gripped her hand. "What's wrong with babe?"

"I'd prefer you call me Birdie. Like everyone else." She saw hurt behind his eyes. "I'm sorry, I—" She couldn't make sense of her own feelings.

Hugo glanced at his pocket watch then snapped the case closed. "As much as I hate to leave, I've got an appointment in five minutes." He cupped her chin, his mischievous twinkle returned. "But I promise we'll continue this after tonight's performance."

CHAPTER 14

Picton, Ontario

B irdie stood on the sidewalk as Hugo quickly retreated, more perplexed by her own feelings than before. Men irritated her. She let out her held breath and traipsed up the steps to the West End Dry Goods store. Well, not all men. Mostly Hugo. She stepped inside the old-fashioned store filled with all sorts of items from stacks of canned goods to straw hats. She found several souvenir postcards of the Crystal Palace on a small display rack near the newspapers and magazines. She chose a white framed postcard that included a reflection of the sunset that she thought Lydia would like. According to the description on the back, the Picton Crystal Palace was a built for the Agricultural Society for county fair exhibits.

Birdie flipped through the latest *Vogue* and saw that the Eton bob was now quite popular. Perhaps Flo hadn't undermined her after all. She tucked the magazine under her arm, meandered the aisles noting the difference between this store and ones back home. The elderly man behind the wood counter wore an apron over his chambray shirt, sleeves rolled up to his elbows. He absently chewed on the edges of his graying mustache.

"That'll be all, miss?" His tenor voice appealed to her. She hadn't heard an accent like his before.

"What's this area known for?"

He raised a bushy eyebrow.

"I want to purchase a special souvenir for my sister." Birdie searched the shelves behind his head.

"Depends who you talk to." He twirled the end of his mustache. "Several would say the canned goods that come from Wellington." His vivid blue eyes reminded her of Helen's when she was tickled. "But I prefer these glass trinkets." He pointed to several bracelets made from silver and smooth glass on a tin tray next to the cash register. "I'm partial because my wife makes 'em."

"May I see?"

He moved the small tray to the center of the counter. Each bracelet was unique with either brown, green, or cloudy white pieces of glass set in hammered silver. They had an exquisite style but the opaque glass gave them a rustic feel.

"Are you in town for Chautauqua week?" he asked.

"I'm part of the Versatile Quintet for opening night." Birdie held a bracelet with green pieces against her wrist thinking of Helen. "Where does your wife get the glass?"

"Worn smooth from the sandy shores of Lake Ontario. Nature's way of turning trash to treasure." He straightened one which held iridescent white pieces.

"How much?"

"For a pretty, talented lady, two dollars each."

Birdie got out her pocketbook before she could change her mind— she had just spent less than that on her new two-toned shoes. She had to have the green one for Helen, it suited her. She touched the other bracelets thinking about Lydia's reaction. She'd call it extravagant yet unrefined. The postcard was best for Lydia. Birdie opened the clasp of her coin purse.

"Oh goodness. Do you accept American dollars?"

"Good as gold here." He wrapped the bracelet in onionskin paper and tied it with a piece of twine. "With the postcard and magazine, that's two twenty-five."

She counted out two singles and the change. "Will I see you in the audience tonight?"

"Haven't missed a Chautauqua week in six years."

Birdie strolled outside under puffy clouds piled in the morning sky like the icing on her morning pastry. She should have asked that clerk for directions to the post office. Standing on the steps, she looked up and down Main Street, which was filling up with all sorts of people. When she looked to her right, she saw a familiar blue hat. Helen. She skipped down the steps and embraced her friend.

"Good morning to you, too." Helen's dimples accented her smooth cheeks.

"Did you devour one of those pastries like I did?" Birdie was delighted. Now they could talk.

"Don't tell the others, I ate two." Helen looked around. "I wonder if we'll have a small crowd tonight."

"There's more to this place than its first impression." Birdie pulled Helen along. "I want to show you quite the architectural wonder." She had seen some benches on the grounds surrounding the Crystal Palace. She could give Helen her present there.

"What makes you so chipper this morning?"

"A charming encounter with the shop clerk." Birdie liked that it was Helen who had to match her fast pace this time. "And quite honestly, I'm happy to be with you." She glanced at Helen. "Just us two."

"Our roommate rotation does get frustrating." Helen slipped her hand through the crook of Birdie's arm. "I left a note requesting a third bed for tonight."

"Here." Birdie stopped so Helen could appreciate the Crystal Palace from a distance. The morning sunlight sparked off the windows making the glass brighter.

"Wow-ey." Helen clasped her hands then took slow steps towards the massive building. "It mimics Edwin Paxton's design with a four-structure outlay but not the gabled roof." Helen stared as she strode around the building. Birdie held on to her elbow to keep Helen clear of the parked autos and snorting horses. "Why would they construct this in rural Canada?"

"It was built for exhibits during the county fair." Birdie enjoyed watching Helen. "Hugo told me it was designed after the Crystal Palace in London, so I thought of you."

Helen stopped to face Birdie. "You met Hugo here this morning?"

"He ran into me on my morning walk."

"Running into Hugo so often is becoming suspect." Helen deflated. "Why was he here?"

"I don't know." Birdie hadn't thought to ask him. Now that Helen mentioned it, it did seem odd, Hugo's showing up.

"What *did* you two discuss?" Helen had turned away from the Crystal Palace and led them towards the water. The edges were lined with cat-o'-nine tails and tall reeds.

Birdie hesitated. "Well, I asked if he was keen on Adelle." The breeze off the harbor stopped.

Helen walked near the water's edge as if looking for something. "What line did he give you?"

Birdie didn't like this conversation. She wanted it to return to light and happy. "Ah, well, he said Adelle cornered him." Birdie recalled their conversation. At the time it hadn't sounded like another story coming from Hugo. "He said he wouldn't risk his job for the likes of her." Sharing his words with Helen made them sound pretentious. Birdie sighed. "It doesn't matter. He told me it's all complicated." The vision of them hiding in the shadows of the dry good store passed.

"Your face tells me he said or did more."

"He did." Birdie's voice dropped. "He kissed me." Why did she blurt that out?

"Did you like it?"

Having Helen ask that, she realized what she most recalled was his odor and well, that was it. His lips felt soft and warm but there was no tingle or yearning like she had read about in her magazines.

"He didn't force himself on you, did he?"

"No." Birdie felt certain Helen would understand. "He has this distinct smell." Birdie nervously giggled at the ridiculousness of her statement. "I wish he'd change his cologne."

Helen's sharp laugh pierced the marshy air. "Oh, Pollyanna." Her cheeks turned a faint pink. Birdie hadn't seen Helen blush. "It's because he's hungover, Birdie." Helen's eyes darkened making Birdie realize Helen wasn't embarrassed, she was mad. "He's a rummy."

"That's harsh." It was illegal to drink alcohol and Hugo would never break Westdale Chautauqua rules or the law. "Why don't you like Hugo?"

"He can't be trusted." Helen sank onto a wooden bench that faced the Picton Harbor. The breeze returned to blow wisps of her hair against her blue hat. "Believe me, Teddy is who makes the circuit work when Hugo is the circuit manager."

"I've never seen him with a flask." Birdie stood beside the bench and stared at the ripples on the water.

Helen rested her elbows on her knees to hold her head. "He's careful around you." Birdie thought Helen murmured something else about Gerald.

"What else are you saying?"

"Just that Hugo's trying to impress Gerald, too." Helen straightened. "I don't want Hugo to hurt you."

"What makes you so certain he drinks hootch?" Birdie crossed her arms.

"His red rimmed eyes. His nose runs. His stink. Ask any of the others. It's not just me who sees it. Remember what Flo said last night?" Helen patted the bench. "Forget it for now. Let's not waste this gorgeous day arguing about Hugo."

"I need to find the post office and mail a postcard to Lydia."

"I'll join you." Helen leaned forward as if to stand.

"I'd rather be alone." Birdie turned and her heel made a scratching sound in the sand. She noticed a tiny piece of the smooth green glass on the ground. Just like the bracelet she had bought and not given to Helen.

"Don't be mad at *me*." Helen absently fiddled with her swallow pin.

"Hmmmm."

"Ask Mary. Or Teddy. They see it, too."

"Sounds like you're setting me up to be the Versatile fool." Birdie turned away. "I'm not that much of a sap," she said over her shoulder.

What had gotten into her? Part of Birdie wanted to run back to apologize. Instead, she sprinted away from the Crystal Palace and Helen. She found a small rowboat pulled up on the shore. No one was nearby so she eased herself inside and gingerly sat on the wooden seat. As her breathing slowed, she heard several bird songs she couldn't identify. Deep inside she knew Helen was right about Hugo. She rooted around in her satchel and brought out the postcard, a pen, and a Hershey bar. So why did she run away instead of admitting Helen was right?

Birdie shifted on the hard bench rocking the boat a little in the marshy ground. She picked up the postcard for Lydia then set it aside after wiping chocolate smudges away from the edges. She paged through the *Vogue* magazine instead.

Her new haircut had done nothing to hide who she really was. She hadn't gone home to comfort her sister. She flirted with Hugo. She'd been unkind to her best friend, Helen. She wasn't even an essential part of the Versatile Quintet. She was a fake. The chocolate settled heavy and sticky in her stomach.

*   *   *

Birdie was greeted with a scowl from Teddy when she rushed into the canvas hallway at twenty minutes to seven.

"Call is at half past six." Teddy brushed past her with his clipboard in his hand and a pencil tucked behind his ear.

"Sorry, Teddy."

"I've got enough to worry about, leastwise you." He strode away.

Birdie had spent the rest of the afternoon sitting in that rowboat, trying to imitate the local birds, and berating herself. She kept going over her argument with Helen then finding ways to deny the truth about Hugo. She'd run to the post office to mail Lydia's postcard and then hurried to the dressing tent. She patted the bracelet in her pocket as she pushed the muslin cloth aside, grateful for Flo and Mary's laughter.

"And I said that American girls prefer gin." Flo waved her feather headband as if it was a fan.

"Whose heart are you breaking tonight, Flo?" Birdie found her band costume and began to get dressed.

"A university fella." Flo twittered. "You should see him, he's something to whistle at."

Birdie fluffed her hair, picking out the floating bits of cat-o'-nine tails.

"Why were you late, Birdie? We never saw you in town or at the boarding house." Mary adjusted her band hat.

"Has anyone seen Hugo?" Helen leaned into the opening. She looked at each girl and lowered her gaze when she saw Birdie. "Teddy can't find him."

The room filled with "nos."

Adelle, dressed in her band costume, sauntered in past Helen. "I spent most of the day with him here at the tents." She glanced from Birdie to Helen. "He had an appointment with someone at three."

"On stage in ten minutes." Teddy walked by.

His eyes searched Helen's and she shook her head no.

"Goldarn it," Teddy said through clenched teeth.

"I hope nothing's happened to him." Birdie pinned her band hat in place. "He's never missed before."

"What's Teddy to do?" Mary bit the side of her fingernail.

Minutes later they heard Walter's gravelly voice greeting the audience. He lacked Hugo's charisma, but he had volume. They lined up in their places. Birdie stood off to the side, trombone raised, waiting for her cue.

It started with Walter introducing them as the "Volatile" Quintet. Flo giggled so much that she hiccupped when she sat down at her harp. Then Birdie tripped on a stray rope partway across the platform and blurted a hard honk through her trombone. The piano had arrived late so it wasn't tuned properly and Helen had to skip over the worst keys. They hadn't thought ahead to realize that no one in the Canadian crowd would sing along with their patriotic medley. And Flo was so busy flipping her hair at her college fella that she missed several chords during their "Spring tweeting strings" duet. Only Adelle seemed oblivious to it all, pulling them together for a rousing ending of "Come Where the Lilies Bloom" on her banjo. When Walter returned to the podium to deliver his lecture, some people began to trickle out.

Back in the dressing room Adelle became judge in her own court.

"Every one of you should be ashamed." She took off her feathered headband and tossed it towards the open trunk. "Believe me, Hugo will hear about you nudniks."

"Tell it to Sweeny, Adelle." Flo stood in front of the mirror applying rich plum lipstick which made her mouth look like a perfect bow. "I'm taking advantage of Hugo's absence and going to a swanky joint with my Joe Brooks." Dressed in a pink silk sleeveless gown, Flo looked like a talkies star. She wore a sequined netted hair piece that framed her face, accenting her high cheekbones.

"You look so elegant." Birdie couldn't keep her eyes off Flo.

"More like a tomato to me." Adelle left the dressing room.

"Join us, Birdie. My Joe Brooks has air-tight friends." Flo put her silver cigarette holder into a beaded evening bag.

"Not tonight." Birdie placed her trombone in its case. She looked towards Helen. "I'm ah, worried about Hugo."

"Suit yourself." She winked at Mary then shook her head. "I'd invite you, but I figure you have plans with some rube from around here. And Helen, I'm not even going to ask." Flo guffawed.

"Don't be a night owl." Helen folded up her band costume.

"You're all wet blankets." Flo sashayed out of the dressing tent.

Teddy passed by the opening. Mary slipped out to catch him. Their hushed whispers bounced off the canvas walls.

Birdie picked up Flo's discarded band pants and pulled the legs right-side out. She reached for the shirt, shaking it out while Helen retrieved Flo's feather headband from the top of the mirror.

"I don't know what got into me this morning," Birdie said. "I was out of sorts."

Helen looked at Birdie, her eyes soft. "I wish we could start today over."

"Me too." Birdie felt lighter. "Let's do it. We could have our own dinner down by the Crystal Palace."

"That would be nice." Helen surveyed the dressing room. "But aren't you worried about Hugo?"

Birdie wondered about Hugo's whereabouts but wanted to make-up with Helen more. "Why would he miss a performance?"

"Let's see what Teddy knows."

Walter was nearing the end of his speech, with the usual crescendo of his voice followed by his moniker hand slap to the podium. Teddy and Mary were outside the main tent with one of the older Anvil Choir boys. They stopped talking as soon as they saw Birdie and Helen.

"Any news?" Helen asked Mary.

"Uh, no." Mary glanced at Birdie then away.

"Should we search for him?" Birdie asked. Hugo had promised her they'd finish their "conversation" after the performance.

"He's jake." Teddy's smile was forced. "I'm sure something important came up."

Helen made the slightest nod to Teddy as if they had some unspoken secret. She tugged Birdie's arm. "Let's find something to eat. Your stomach's been growling."

Birdie was hungry, yet her unease overrode her appetite. It was clear the others knew something they weren't sharing. "But what about Hugo?"

"He's fine, right Teddy?" Helen said with a tight voice.

"Sure. There's nothing we can do right now." Teddy looked everywhere except at Birdie.

Birdie paused, wondering if she should push this Hugo business further. "Join us for dinner, Mary?"

"Not this time. I'm helping clean up." Mary reached for Teddy's hand.

"See you both back at the Maple Leaf then." Helen turned to leave.

The main tent resonated with applause. Birdie could see Flo standing next to several well-dressed young men through the open tent flap. Walter muscled his way through the departing crowd towards Flo and blocked Birdie's view of the group. She could barely see Flo's crossed arms and strained expression. Helen whistled something resembling a cardinal's song, her own version of their signature calling.

"Helen." Birdie responded by nodding to the inside of the main tent. "Flo may need our help."

Helen followed Birdie's sightline and they both could see Walter confronting Flo. Only one tall young man remained and Flo had both arms wrapped firmly around one of his. Her "Joe Brooks" looked like a wind-blown sapling next to Walter. Helen took off towards them. Birdie struggled to keep up.

"You know the rules." Walter half-shouted at Flo, his spittle speckling the dusty air. "Don't make me—"

"Walter." Helen maneuvered between him and Flo. "Can you tell us where Hugo is?"

"I have no idea." He puffed up his chest and started to step around her towards Flo. Birdie blocked his path.

"We all know you're in cahoots with the Chautauqua management." Helen put her hands on her hips with her elbows wide, her legs braced. "Why are you covering for Hugo?"

Flo and her new beau slunk away. Flo mouthed "thank you" to Birdie.

"I did no such thing." Walter's eyes tracked Flo. "What are you implying?" He redirected his scowl to Helen.

"Well, you made the introduction tonight. What were we to think?" Helen shrugged her shoulders, stepping back.

"You're paid to make music, not think." He pulled his hat down on his head. "Excuse me." He stormed outside in the same direction as the crowds and Flo.

"You are a bearcat." Birdie wasn't sure if she was impressed or terrified.

"Where did you hear that?"

"Flo, of course." Birdie gripped Helen's arm. "Do you think she'll be all right?"

"She can take care of herself with a college boy." Helen started towards the tent exit. "Walter won't do anything in front of anyone else. He's got his reputation to protect."

"What a night." Birdie walked alongside Helen.

"Now I'm hungry. Let's find something to eat." Helen draped her arm across Birdie's shoulders.

They managed to find a small café just off Main Street, people mingling inside by the high counter and outside at wooden tables. Birdie sank to a slatted chair near a round table for two and they both ordered fish chowder, a favorite with the locals. Soon the waiter returned with two steaming ceramic bowls, filled with white fish, parsnips, and other vegetables plus large slices of brown bread. Birdie thought she might hug him. Helen ordered two lagers. They ate without saying much.

Birdie sipped the drink and made a face. "Ugh. That's the worst cider I've ever had."

Helen finished a long swallow and wiped her lips with the back of her hand. "Oh, Birdie, don't tell me you're a teetotaler?"

"No. Of course not." Birdie took another sip. The drink wasn't sweet like cider. It had a grassy, almost malted flavor. She drank a big swallow which burned her throat making her cough.

"Do you know what a lager is?"

Birdie's shoulders dropped. Helen knew her too well. "No."

"It's a beer."

"Isn't that against the law?"

"Not in Canada."

Birdie tried the beer again. It was refreshing in a way. "I like it." Helen always knew just what to do in situations like this. There was so much of Helen's world that Birdie wanted to learn.

"We'll have to watch you. I imagine Lydia would pop her girdle if she found out you like beer."

"It'll be our secret." Birdie watched Helen over the thick rim of her glass. She remembered when she first met Helen at the West Chester ladies' luncheon only months ago. She felt as if they'd been best friends their entire lives.

"Speaking of secrets, what's really going on with Hugo?" Birdie set her glass down.

"It's nothing." Helen tore off a chunk of bread and dipped it in her soup.

"Why don't you tell me?" Birdie stirred the last bit of soup. "I'm not the Pollyanna you think I am."

"You're right." Helen chewed on another big bite of the bread. "Teddy has suspicions about Hugo's whereabouts, but he doesn't feel he can betray his boss." Helen wiped her bowl clean with her bread. "Like what Flo shared earlier, Hugo is acting shifty."

"And you don't want to tell me because you think I'm sweet on him and will get angry again."

"Something like that."

"Well, you don't have to hide things from me about Hugo. I've learned he's trouble."

"But Lydia and Gerald are impressed with him." Helen sat back in her chair and finished her drink.

"They were impressed by Velma Meyer's son, too."

"Who?"

"Nobody. What I mean is, they are easily impressed by any eligible bachelor." Birdie tried to finish her drink like Helen had but ended up choking. She cleared her throat. "But not me."

"Perhaps you've had enough lager for tonight." They paid their bill and left the charming café.

"Let's stroll by the Crystal Palace to see if it's lit up." Birdie turned towards the water.

Picton was alive that night. It must be because of Chautauqua week. She had seen this same thing happen in other towns that they had visited. Quiet and charming when they arrived, bustling, and crowded when they left.

Ambling along from the café, Birdie stubbed her toe and tripped forward. Helen caught her by the elbow and guided them towards a bench. Birdie felt aflutter as if a chickadee flapped its tiny wings inside her head.

"I feel a bit lightheaded."

"I don't doubt that."

"The Crystal Palace looks like a giant's chandelier." Birdie stared at the building. The lights inside reflected off the panes of glass, playing tricks on her eyes. She blinked several times and slowly turned her head away. Helen watched, her dimples turning into a lopsided grin.

"Remind me to order a lager for you every night." Helen stretched her arm behind Birdie on the back of the bench.

"I have something for you." Birdie rummaged in the pocket of her coat. She brought out the onionskin packet and placed it to Helen's open palm.

"What's this?" Helen tugged at the string and folded open the package. When she held up the bracelet, the obscure green glass caught the lights of the Crystal Palace. "It's stunningly unique." She placed her wrist on her lap and draped the bracelet over.

"Let me help." Birdie reached over and lightly touched the inside of Helen's smooth wrist. Birdie bit her lip, concentrating on clasping the bracelet.

"Thank you, but why?" Helen leaned close. Birdie breathed in her now favorite scent, Emeraude but tonight mixed with the harbor smells.

"I, well, I thought it would complement your pin and your eyes." Birdie straightened Helen's collar, so the swallow pin lay straight. She shivered again. "I wanted to thank you for being such a swell friend."

The gold flecks in Helen's eyes sparkled brighter in the lights. She turned the bracelet around on her wrist.

"It's made from bits of glass that have been worn by the sand and the lake. The store clerk claimed, 'nature turning trash to treasure.'" Birdie's voice sounded childish and high pitched in her head.

Helen touched the bracelet then her brooch. "A lovely reminder of you wrapped around my wrist."

"Tell me more about your pin."

"There's not much more to tell." The look in Helen's eyes turned inward for a brief instant. "Miss Briarwood was a close friend and mentor. It's special because of her."

"You're special too." Birdie deepened her voice. The sensations running through her body bewildered her. She crossed her ankles.

"Some would beg to differ." Helen squeezed both of Birdie's hands. She paused as if she had something more to say but then said, "Thank you." She looked past the Crystal Palace and towards downtown. "We should head back. We've got an early departure tomorrow."

"Another town. Same show," Birdie said. "I hope we perform better tomorrow night."

Helen pulled Birdie up by both hands so their faces almost touched. Birdie stared at her shoes. The cool night breeze swirled around them and when Birdie looked up, Helen had stepped away.

CHAPTER 15

Picton, Ontario to Susquehanna, Pennsylvania

Just as Birdie and Helen turned off Main onto a smaller street, they saw a bulky figure dash away from the main tent. Birdie squeezed Helen's arm as they watched the figure run in and out of the night shadows. Birdie ran towards the tents. Helen caught up and they arrived breathless at the entrance.

"Hugo?" Birdie yelled into the dark, empty canvas.

Helen pulled the string attached to a single light bulb. Birdie scanned the shadows and, far as she could tell, saw nothing unusual. Helen's short breaths brought up goosebumps on Birdie's arms. There was no wind, nor other sounds, just the hovering stench of canvas, straw, and sweat. Birdie called again. Helen leapt onto the platform, turned on another light to search behind the piano, around the platform, and side stage areas. She jerked her head towards the dressing room and motioned for Birdie to follow.

The muslin curtain stood half-way closed. Birdie heard moaning and could barely make out a rose-hued heap near the costume trunk. Helen rushed to the heap, gently rolling it over. It was Flo.

"Get a cloth and some water." Helen sank to the ground and moved Flo's head to her lap. Flo's left eyelid was swollen with a purple welt forming just below it. Birdie's entire body shook. Flo's dress was torn at one shoulder. There were bits of straw with dirt stuck to the delicate material.

"Now, Birdie." Helen's demand was harsh.

Birdie forced herself to the makeshift kitchen. She returned with damp cloths and bottled seltzer water. Birdie reached to comfort Flo, but words stuck in her throat. She handed one cloth to Helen and used another to wipe dirt from Flo's exposed shoulder.

"Who did this to you?" Helen growled.

Flo turned her face away.

"Be gentle. She must be scared." Birdie soothed Flo with murmurs and soft strokes.

Flo moaned, curling her legs into herself.

Birdie knelt closer, tears blurring her vision. Helen shifted Flo's head to Birdie's lap.

"What happened, Flo?" Helen stood up.

Birdie gulped, sucking in the close air. "We need to call a doctor."

"First we need Flo to name the culprit."

"We don't. It doesn't matter right now who did this." Birdie stared at Helen, her eyes pleading.

Helen paced the small dressing room.

"We're here now, Flo." Birdie stroked her hair. Flo raised her hand to cover her eyes. Birdie dabbed at the little bit of dried blood from the corner of Flo's mouth. "You're going to be okay."

Helen dug through the trunk then covered Flo with a wool blanket. "He's going to pay for this."

"Who?" Birdie whispered. She looked up at Helen. Even in the dim light, Birdie could see Helen's green eyes darken.

"Walter. I'm certain it was him running away." Helen resumed her pacing.

"We don't know that." Birdie's gaze dropped to Flo, her shoulders shaking. "It could have been that college boy." Birdie tucked Flo's hair behind her ear. "Flo's comfort is our priority right now."

"That's why I need to know who hurt her." Helen stopped pacing. "I'm going to call the cops."

Flo moaned. "No buttons." She shifted and tried to sit up.

"Be still, Flo." Birdie gently kept her laying down. Birdie glared at Helen and put her finger to her lips.

"Was it Walter?" Helen asked. She was relentless.

Flo covered her ears with both hands.

"I knew it." Helen slammed her palm on the top of the trunk. Both Birdie and Flo flinched.

"Jeez, Helen." Birdie frowned. She bent down close to Flo's ear and whispered, "May I call a doctor?"

"No, please. No," Flo said in a quiet pleading voice.

"I'll fetch Mary and Teddy." Helen started for the door.

"No." Flo pushed herself to a somewhat seated position. She eased back against the trunk to use Birdie as support. With her left eye swollen shut, a dark purple bruise covering her cheek, Flo curled her legs underneath like a small child. "No one else."

"How can we help?" Birdie tugged the blanket up around Flo's shoulders.

"I'll track down Walter at the train station." Helen looked out towards the main tent. "I'm sure no trains are leaving this late."

"No." Flo's voice was hoarse but strong. "Help me to the boarding house."

Helen sighed but after a few seconds she seemed resigned. "All right." She bent down to lift Flo's arm. "I'll deal with Walter tomorrow."

Helen and Birdie combined their strength to heave Flo to her feet. It was as if she couldn't lift herself. She leaned on Birdie's shoulder and Helen wrapped her arm around Flo's waist. They edged towards half open curtain when Birdie stopped. A small stain showed through the back of Flo's pink gown.

"Wait." Birdie motioned to Flo's dress. She rushed out and came back with one of Art's aprons. She made a bow with the apron strings at Flo's waist.

Flo started weeping. She leaned against Helen as Birdie checked the dressing tent. Flo's sparkly head piece sat off to the side of the trunk, smashed and ruined, the tiny bright triangles pushed into the dirt. Birdie closed the curtain completely.

With Flo propped between them, Birdie and Helen took slow steps down the empty and dark streets. Flo became heavier as they moved forward, her height made walking together difficult. She winced every time one of them shifted. The roads leading to the Maple Leaf seemed endless. Birdie wished Helen had gone for Mary or Teddy despite Flo's protests.

Finally, they stopped outside the boarding house, Flo held onto Birdie. Helen ran up the steps and turned the handle. The door was locked. She banged several times yet no one came. Time had stopped back at the tent, but Birdie reasoned it must be well after one o'clock. Helen stepped back in the yard to shout up at the windows. A dog startled from its sleep started barking.

"Mary. Adelle. Let us in."

A voice across the street yelled, "Shut up."

Helen ran back to the porch and raised her fist to bang again. Teddy opened the door.

"Quiet," Teddy scolded. "You'll wake the whole, what the—?"

Teddy charged past Helen, catching Flo as she started sinking from Birdie's grip. He hoisted her in his arms and staggered up the steps while Helen ran to catch the door. His frantic eyes searched both their faces as Helen and Birdie held the door open wide. Flo screamed something as she pushed away from Teddy. He almost dropped her but maneuvered them both into the foyer. Flo collapsed onto the brocade settee. Mary had stopped partway down the stairs. She ran the rest of the way and held Flo's shaking shoulders. Flo's unintelligible words mixed with sobs.

Birdie closed the front door and latched the lock. She leaned her head back against the foyer's wall. Helen spoke to Teddy and Mary in sharp whispers. Birdie didn't hear much but recognized Walter's name in Helen's tirade.

"We have to get Flo to bed," Birdie said with confidence she didn't know she had.

"Yes. Of course." Mary spoke softly. "Flo. It's Mary. Teddy and I are going to help you up the stairs."

"Not him," Flo said.

Teddy stepped back. Mary and Helen pulled Flo off the small couch using both her arms.

"You're going to have to help us, Flo," Helen whispered.

Flo shook her head. "I want Birdie." Helen arched her eyebrow, stepping away.

Birdie moved to Flo's right side and wrapped an arm around her waist. "We can do this together."

They inched up the stairs, with Birdie using the wall and Flo the banister. Flo murmured or moaned with each step. Helen and Mary followed. Teddy paced in the small foyer muttering to himself with his hands in his pockets. Once Birdie and Flo got to the top landing Mary moved to Flo's other side and the three of them worked their way towards the lavatory at the end of the hall.

"I'm going to talk with Teddy," Helen whispered.

As they passed room number six, Adelle peeked out through a slim crack in the open door. Once inside the lavatory, Birdie eased Flo's grip from Mary's arm, untied the apron all while using soft words to explain each move. As Flo's vacant eyes watched the warm water fill the tub, she went from incoherent sobs to silence.

Together, Birdie and Mary helped Flo settle into the soothing water. Small bruises dotted her upper back and shoulders. Flo lowered her head near her bent knees. Lavender soap masked the acrid smell of blood, washed away the dirt, but did nothing to ease the shame. Mary signaled that she'd retrieve Flo's nightclothes. Birdie wrapped her arm around Flo, her own tears mingling with the steam as she gently drew the washcloth down Flo's back.

Mary returned with two towels and Flo's silk Billie Burke pajamas. Birdie released the drain, and Flo seemed mesmerized by the brownish-pink water swirling away. After patting Flo dry, they struggled to dress her. Flo touched her bruised cheek before Birdie could tug her away from the clouded mirror.

Helen stood in room number eight veiled by the glow of a single lamp. Birdie helped Flo to the far twin bed. Flo curled into a fetal ball as Birdie tucked the pastel patchwork quilt around her. No one spoke as Birdie caressed Flo's back in gentle figure eights. Mary balanced on the other twin with clasped hands. It creaked when Helen joined her, opening and closing her fists. Flo's tremors soon slowed, but there was still no sign of Adelle. Birdie sighed, looking from Mary to Helen to a rollaway bed that had been crammed in the corner of the room.

"What now?" Mary whispered.

Helen motioned by walking her fingers towards the hall.

Birdie leaned over Flo. Her uninjured eye was closed too. Birdie nodded, easing herself from Flo's twin bed without a squeak.

"Stay, Birdie," Flo moaned to the wall.

Relieved to let others handle what to do next, Birdie waved Helen and Mary out. She began singing Brahms's lullaby in a low voice. Struggling to remember all the words, she hummed the tune. Her mother had sung this to her during summer thunderstorms. Birdie lay down matching the curve of Flo's body.

*　　*　　*

Sunlight seeped around the curtains. Birdie woke next to Flo with a stiff shoulder, cramped calves, and a neck crick. She caught herself just before falling to the rug. Dressing silently by the other bed Helen mouthed, "meet in hall." Dark crescents underlined her green eyes.

Birdie flattened the wrinkles in her dress and followed Helen, leaving the door cracked in case Flo woke up.

"Still no sign of Hugo." Helen's lips were tight. "And Teddy says Walter's missing too." She ran her hand through her hair causing bits to stand up at odd angles.

"Should we still catch the ten-fifteen?" Birdie slid her watch around on her wrist. It was just after eight.

Helen crossed her arms. "If you think Flo can travel."

"We can ask." Birdie smoothed down some of the wayward strands of Helen's bob. "Flo slept a little."

"She cried out several times. Each time you'd calm her by rubbing her back."

"I don't know what else to do."

"She obviously needs you right now." Helen's arms fell to her sides.

Birdie touched Helen's shoulder. "You're doing what you do best and I'm doing what I do. We're Flo's team."

Helen's dimples appeared for an instant.

"What's with Adelle?" Birdie glanced back to the closed door of room number six.

Helen shrugged. "It's strange. Mary said that after she shared everything that happened to Flo, Adelle closed her eyes."

"She makes me so mad." Birdie widened her stance.

"Birdie?" Flo groaned.

Birdie hurried into the room. "I'm here.." She knelt alongside the twin bed patting Flo's shoulders through the quilt. Helen stood in the doorway.

"I'm thirsty."

Birdie handed Flo a seltzer water bottle. Flo leaned on her elbow, winced, and drank several swallows. She laid back down. And said nothing. No quips or "Flo-isms."

"Our train departs in under two hours." Helen stood at the foot of the bed. "Do you think you can be ready by then?"

After several moments, Flo nodded her head.

"I'll bring up coffee and pastries. Birdie will help you get dressed and packed." Helen waited for a reply.

Birdie shooed Helen on her way. She sensed Flo didn't want Helen in the room.

Flo rolled onto her back exposing her tear-stained pillow. Birdie used the corner of the sheet to dab new ones away. The left side of Flo's face had become a swollen purple welt.

"I want a bath." Flo sounded like a little girl.

"Mary and I bathed you last night."

Flo recoiled.

"But of course, you can bathe again." Birdie folded back the quilt.

Flo took several more minutes until she eased off the bed, unsteady as she held onto the spindly bedpost.

Birdie gathered towels and Flo's vanity case. She rummaged around in Flo's suitcase searching for a suitable dress. Birdie lifted a colorful striped drop waist dress. Flo shook her head. Birdie held up the navy chiffon one. Flo nodded.

As she clutched Birdie's arm, Flo balanced along the wall to make it to the lavatory. While Flo hovered at the edge of the tub avoiding the mirror, Birdie ran the bath water. When Birdie handed Flo her Lux soap, she stared at the wisps of steam as if it held her in a trance.

"Can you bathe yourself?" Birdie silently willed Flo to say yes.

"Uh-huh, but …" Flo watched the water. "Will you stay right outside the door?"

"Of course."

"Don't leave."

"Pinky promise."

Birdie eased the door shut. She spoke through the painted wood. "I'm right here." She soon heard swishing water. She leaned her forehead against the door, kneading the ache in her neck. Footsteps padded towards her. Birdie lifted her head. Adelle. Her face drawn tight with eyes red rimmed. Adelle stopped when she saw Birdie, spun around, and ducked back into her room. If Birdie hadn't promised Flo she'd stay right there, she would have charged after her.

With perseverance, they made it to the Picton train station well before the train. Teddy had insisted on carrying everything. Several times he glanced at Flo, shaking his head with his knuckles squeezed white. Mary lent Flo a wide brimmed hat she fastened with a scarf tied under Flo's chin, which helped to hide most of her bruised face. Flo never let go of Birdie's arm and several times Birdie almost tripped over their combined feet. Neither Helen nor Adelle were at the station when they arrived.

Birdie, Flo, and Mary rested on a bench under the awning, observing the bustling people. Teddy stacked their instrument cases, suitcases, and the trunk at the end of the platform. The sun shone bright, the air dry and cool. On any other morning Birdie would have listened for bird calls. Today all she wanted to hear was the train whistle, signaling that they were leaving Canada.

The train screeched into the station, filling the air with such caustic smelling steam that Birdie and Mary covered their mouths and noses. Not Flo. She tipped her head up to take a deep breath which caused her to cough. People stepped off the train with cheerful greetings that made Flo squeeze Birdie's hand whenever someone shouted or laughed.

Teddy and one of the Anvil Choir boys started to load the costume trunk. Birdie turned her gaze towards the opposite end of the train. The sunlight reflection from a stack of shiny instrument cases made her pause. She looked back as Eddy hoisted Flo's black harp case into the baggage car. Then she turned back to the first-class car as someone wearing a suit helped a baggage handler load a trombone case, then a harp case into the reserved cargo space. She shielded her eyes as the men shook hands. Why were there duplicate instrument cases? Dread crawled up her arms as Hugo sauntered from the first-class car whistling bits of their patriotic medley.

"Cheerio ladies." Hugo tipped his hat. His usually tan face looked gray. His greeting sounded forced.

"You bastard." Helen charged down the platform swinging her cardboard suitcase. It hit Hugo on his palms raised in defense. She hoisted it again but he covered his head with his arms as he dodged away.

"Whoa!"

"Where were you last night?" Helen held her bearcat stance, breathing heavy. Several people stared as they scurried past.

"It's not your concern." He glanced from the passing strangers to Helen to the trio sitting on the bench and shrugged his shoulders.

"You owe us more than one of your lame excuses." She yanked his elbow, pulling him away.

Helen's voice bounced off the stone walls. Hugo first crossed his arms, then changed to running his fingers through his hair and settled with his hands in his pockets. Teddy joined their conversation but Birdie couldn't hear either of the men's voices. Birdie leaned past Flo to catch Mary's attention but Adelle had slipped in behind Mary's end of the bench. Birdie's questions for Mary would have to wait.

The conductor's whistle interrupted her quandary. Just after Birdie hoisted Flo to her feet, Hugo appeared before them. He jiggled the chain to his pocket watch.

"I'm sorry to hear what er, happened. You may take a day off if you'd like."

"No," Flo said to his scuffed wingtips.

Birdie would have swung her own suitcase at Hugo if she hadn't been supporting a fragile Flo.

"If you change your mind, just let Teddy know." Hugo wiped his nose with his handkerchief then glanced at Birdie with pleading bloodshot eyes. Birdie looked away. With a guilty looking nod, Hugo strode off towards the back of the train.

Teddy told Mary that he had reserved compartment 144A for

them. Mary led the way onto the train with Birdie and Flo right behind. Once Mary slid the door to the compartment open, Flo eased onto the forward-facing bench while Birdie settled next to the window. After putting their suitcases away, Mary sank onto the opposite bench. Helen stood in the center of the compartment, wiping her forehead with her handkerchief. Adelle slipped in and huddled towards the wall next to Flo. Teddy appeared and stretched his long legs across the doorway as if to defend the compartment.

The train lurched to a start which knocked Helen almost on Mary's lap then she inched over to the window seat across from Birdie, nursing a banged elbow. Flo kept her head down holding tight to Birdie's arm and Adelle lost herself in the local newspaper. Only Mary and Teddy spoke to each other in clipped whispers.

Birdie turned to the window willing the Canadian countryside to rush by. It took all of her willpower not to ask her questions aloud but Birdie felt protective around Flo, who hadn't spoken about the attack since last night. Birdie kneaded the crick in her neck with frustrated fingers. After some time, the others had closed their eyes but the tension inside the compartment confirmed that everyone feigned sleep.

When they pulled into the Susquehanna train station, townspeople lined the platform, clapping and cheering. A large "Chautauqua This Week" banner blew against the long brick structure. Teddy went to the window. He instructed them to stay put then jumped off the car before it came to a complete stop. Minutes later he returned, his face cringing.

"Hugo just remembered that there's a parade today." He twisted his cap in his hands. "The Versatile Quintet is supposed to ride in the back of two breezers down Main Street."

"Of all days." Helen straightened her Musketeer hat while Adelle frowned at Teddy then writhed around him to exit the train. Mary retied Flo's hat, spreading the scarf, so it covered most of the purple welt.

"You don't have to do this," Birdie whispered to Flo. "We can tell them you're ill."

"It's expected." Flo raised her head. "Stay next to me."

"Of course." Birdie maneuvered them off the train. They followed a bearded gentleman to the front of the train station. Two open-air Model T's stood waiting, each decorated with banners, American flags, and streamers. Climbing to the back jump seat of the first automobile, Birdie and Mary flanked Flo. A small youth band led with off-pitch Sousa marches. The bright day made it almost perfect, and any other time the girls, especially Flo, would have reveled in the cheering towns-people lining the street and children chasing alongside. Flo kept her head bowed and braced herself between Birdie and Mary.

This wasn't what Chautauqua had promised to be.

CHAPTER 16

Susquehanna, Pennsylvania

That evening Flo had insisted she felt well enough to perform, pleading that she had to honor her contract. Mary begged Flo to skip the performance to rest at the boarding house. Helen tried her best to convince Flo they could perform without her. Birdie listened to everyone and then realized that Flo must be afraid to stay alone at the boarding house so relented. She helped Flo change into her band uniform. Flo carried a handkerchief to cover her face until she sat at her harp stool, which Teddy had scooted back into the darker part of the stage.

The Versatile Quintet came out wearing different hats with their lacy costumes so what Flo's hat covered wouldn't be so obvious. But during her harp solo, she stopped playing several times eyes darting into the crowd. Helen finished Flo's song with an improvised piano solo. Both Birdie and Flo were off during their "Spring tweeting strings" duet because Birdie focused more on Flo than her whistling. And then when Walter appeared side stage, it caused the entire Versatile Quintet to misstep during the finale.

Teddy ushered them offstage, standing guard outside the muslin door. Everyone flinched each time Walter's voice boomed, even Adelle. Helen must have told all of them that she suspected Walter to be Flo's attacker. The girls changed out of their costumes the fastest they ever had. Birdie assisted Flo with her dressing while Adelle actually helped

Mary fold the costumes into the trunk. Helen paced the dressing tent, wearing a path through the straw to the dirt. Flo continued to cling to Birdie as if they were pinned together.

"Why is Walter even on stage?" Helen asked Teddy when she opened the muslin curtain.

Teddy shrugged, looking away. He guided the girls outside through a side flap.

"Hugo's a cad, letting Walter lecture tonight." Helen's eyes had become their darkest green. Birdie feared she'd charge the stage and tackle Walter during his lecture.

"Flo, join me for some supper?" Mary reached her arm around Flo's waist. "Teddy says this boarding house's special is stew." She eased Flo away from the Birdie.

"Birdie, can you come too?" Flo asked softly.

"I'll be with you in a few minutes." Birdie needed to help calm Helen and would have to thank Mary later.

They had barely left when Helen kicked the stack of wooden pallets. "I can't wait to get my hands on Walter."

"Be reasonable," Birdie sighed. "You can't punch Walter."

"You'd be surprised."

"Let's ask our circuit manager. Who is it tonight?"

Helen pointed at Birdie. "It figures you'd want to involve Hugo."

"He's tonight's circuit manager?" Birdie arranged her cloche hat. That didn't make any sense, the circuit managers rotated.

"Along with Mr. Derr." Helen shrugged. "For some reason we have two circuit managers tonight."

"Well, we need to talk with them."

"She's right." Adelle's words startled Birdie, she hadn't noticed that Adelle hadn't left with Mary and Flo.

"I don't like it." Helen pushed her hat down.

"Hugo's one of our bosses. Not you." Adelle made her words prick. She strode past Helen nodding at Birdie.

Birdie followed Adelle, perplexed by her unexpected solidarity. She tugged Helen's sleeve and whispered, "Take a deep breath to calm down. Your anger isn't going to help Flo."

They found Hugo at the very back of the audience, his hands in his pockets as he toed pieces of straw. Mr. Derr stood as if he was a guard several feet away. Helen charged up and pulled Hugo's arm. A flash of anger crossed his features before Birdie moved beside Helen. His eyes softened. He motioned for them to follow him outside after receiving a curt nod from Mr. Derr.

"What are you going to do about Walter?" Helen demanded as they gathered a ways outside the tent. Adelle positioned herself next to Hugo.

"The Lyceum informed us he's to continue as the opening night lecturer." Hugo crossed his arms.

"He shouldn't be allowed near any of us after what he did to Flo." Helen rocked forward.

"About that, Helen." Hugo rubbed one hand from his nose to his chin. "Did Flo specifically name Walter as her attacker?" At that moment Walter's muted voice filled the silence.

Helen threw both hands up. "We all know it was Walter." She shook her finger at Hugo. "I warned all of you about him many times."

Hugo took a short breath as he turned towards Birdie. "You were there. Did Flo say Walter attacked her?"

A breeze swirled pieces of dried grass around her shoes. She knew to tell the truth. But she also knew doing so would further anger Helen.

"Flo couldn't speak." Birdie avoided looking at Helen. She tried to find comfort from the familiar peak of the tent, but tonight Walter's voice made that impossible.

Adelle grunted, making Birdie flinch.

"Thank you." Hugo pulled the chain to his pocket watch. "Because we have a difficult situation." Helen started to talk but Hugo held up his palm. "Walter claims he left right after his lecture. He called Mr.

James, our bureau manager, from the Picton Train Station." Hugo looked from Helen and then directly at Birdie. "He spent today filing official complaints against both Flo and me for breaking Westdale Chautauqua Lyceum rules."

Birdie gasped. Adelle looked as if she had swallowed a feather.

"Walter's full of hooey." Helen shook her head. "We saw him running from the tents long after his lecture." She started walking in circles muttering to herself. "And you know Flo might as well have said his name." She continued her pacing almost bumping into Adelle. "She cried out when I asked if it was Walter."

"Just ask Flo." Adelle flicked her too-long bangs away from her eyes.

"It's too soon to ask Flo." Birdie glared at Adelle.

Mr. Derr pushed the flap to the main tent open then motioned to Hugo.

"A circuit manager disappearing for a performance might warrant a complaint, but how could what happened to Flo be the same?" Helen stopped in front of Hugo in her full bearcat stance.

Hugo narrowed his red-rimmed eyes and looked more like a weasel than a bear. Birdie jerked her head towards the main tent at the telltale signs Walter was finishing his lecture. He had already banged the podium.

Mr. Derr started walking towards them.

"Is this Mr. James here tonight?" Birdie stepped between Helen and Hugo, breaking their stare down.

"He's meeting us in three days." Hugo wiped his face with his handkerchief, his forced stage face magically reappearing. "This is serious. Most likely I'll be put on probation. Flo could be fired." He pulled out his pocket watch and put it away. "I assume the Lyceum is arranging meetings as we speak."

"That's ludicrous. Fired for being attacked?" Helen's voice caused a few of the Anvil Choir boys to turn then look away.

"No one's been fired," Mr. Derr looked right at Hugo, "yet."

"That's a relief, Mr. Derr." Helen stepped back. "As you know, I warned all of you of Walter's unprofessional behavior."

"This matter is best handled by the Lyceum." Mr. Derr tapped Hugo's shoulder. "We need to get back inside to meet with a few of the town's leaders."

Hugo nodded then bent between Helen and Birdie. "Flo's consorting with a paying member of the audience was strictly forbidden," Hugo whispered, "as you both know." He then caught up with Mr. Derr.

Walter thanked the audience and the sounds of clapping filtered outside.

Birdie tugged at Helen. "Let's get to the boarding house." Glancing over her shoulder as they walked away Birdie saw Adelle stroll back into the main tent. Birdie turned to Helen who was well on her way down the street.

Birdie strode to keep up with Helen who sped through the dark spaces between the circles cast by the streetlamps. "Did Hugo explain where he was last night?"

"No." Helen faced Birdie. "Maybe we should file our own complaint with Mr. James. Hugo's the one who should be fired." She plunged ahead.

"None of this makes sense." Birdie wanted to tell Helen about the extra instrument cases, but she knew that it would only add to Helen's arsenal against Hugo. She decided to wait till she had a chance to confirm what she saw with Mary. Or maybe even Teddy since they had both been there at the Picton station.

"Now do you agree that Hugo's a windsucking crumpet?"

"A what?"

"A jerk"

A high-pitched giggle escaped from Birdie. She couldn't stop it.

Under the streetlamp, Helen's anger highlighted her cheeks, her entire face glowed.

"Honestly what could be funny now?"

"You. Me. My nerves." Birdie wiped her lips. She wished she had the audacity to tell Helen how radiant she looked right then.

"All I can say is Hugo's got dumb nerve."

"So does Adelle. What's *her* beef?"

Helen raised an eyebrow and Birdie had to suppress another nervous giggle. "Flo's rubbing off on you. Do you even know what that means?"

"Of course, I do. I'm not the same sap who auditioned."

"I have no idea what's gotten into Adelle. She's not one of my worries." Helen's offhand attitude towards Adelle relieved and awkwardly pleased Birdie.

"Her odd behavior is one of mine. She infuriates me."

"We each have our own battles, then."

They stopped in front of a lit-up brick row house with a wide front porch. Birdie squeezed Helen's free hand. "That we do."

"I hope Mary was right about the stew. I'm starving." Helen charged up the steps to their boarding house.

The Hudson Rooming House in Susquehanna was clean, comfortable, and familiar. The landlady welcomed them with a warm look, homemade stew, and freshly baked Snickerdoodles. Tonight, Birdie, Mary, and Flo shared a room. The girls had decided that it was best to forgo the room rotation for now. Flo became skittish unless with Birdie or Mary. Of course, Adelle acquiesced.

Birdie relaxed into an upholstered chair in their bedroom munching on cinnamon goodness. This room was much bigger, with three single beds, lace curtains, and crocheted bedspreads. All she needed was a glass of milk and she would feel like she was back at Willow Glenn. She scolded herself. With all her attention directed to Flo, she hadn't even thought of Lydia's miscarriage over the past few days. Birdie should try calling her again tomorrow. Surely the telephone connection from the Hudson Rooming House would be better since they were back in Pennsylvania.

Mary and Flo scuttled into the room. After dinner, Flo had wanted to take another bath and Mary had volunteered to guard the door. Birdie offered them the plate of cookies. Mary took one but Flo shook her head. She eased into the bed farthest from the door and covered herself with the bedspread. She turned away, curling into a ball. Birdie went over and rubbed her back.

"Thanks," Flo murmured.

Birdie leaned close. "I hope you can sleep better tonight."

Flo reached back and patted Birdie's hand.

Birdie pulled out her night shirt and beauty box from her suitcase. She whispered to Mary, "That almost seemed like our Flo."

Mary attempted a thin-lipped smile but her eyes looked sad.

Birdie rinsed her face at the washstand in the room. She dried with the soft cotton towel and noticed the tiny blue birds embroidered at the corner. Everything seemed better in Pennsylvania. She sat next to Mary on one of the beds.

"I've been meaning to ask you something," Birdie whispered. She looked over at Flo. Her body remained still; the only movement was her breathing.

"Did you see Hugo at the first-class car before he came up to us in Picton?"

"No. His whistling unnerved me." Mary gripped the edge of the bed. "The cheekiness of him just waltzing up the next morning. You know Teddy had to take care of everything."

"He did." Teddy had covered for Hugo that night, maybe he knew more.

"Did Teddy say where Hugo had been?"

Mary's eyes grew larger. "I'm not to tell."

"You can trust me." Birdie patted Mary's hands.

"It just makes me so mad." Mary glanced at Flo's blanket covered shape before she leaned back on the bed tucking one leg under. "Swear you won't tell anyone, especially not Helen."

Birdie crisscrossed across her chest.

Mary moved closer. "Hugo was making deals with some Canadian whiskey maker. He brought back hooch." Mary shook her head. "Teddy doesn't know how exactly, but he knows that's what he was doing last night."

Birdie nodded her head in slow motion. Breaking the law while working for the Chautauqua circuit seemed too risky, even for Hugo.

"Why would Hugo—?"

"To drink or sell," Mary replied. "Teddy says he's half-shot more than ever before."

"I've never seen him take a drink." Birdie searched Mary's face.

"Me neither." Mary looked down at her clasped hands. "But he must. Teddy doesn't lie."

Birdie agreed, she trusted Teddy and Mary. "You two have grown quite fond of each other."

Mary flushed from her collarbone to her cheeks. "He's a gem."

"Does he worry about losing his job?"

"No. Why?"

"The Lyceum rules. About not fraternizing with the talent." Birdie rubbed the back of her neck. She hoped the crick would go away tonight now she had her own bed.

"Oh that. Teddy says no one cares." Mary yawned. "Apparently those rules were written ages ago."

Birdie let out a long sigh. Another thing that Hugo hadn't been truthful with her about. Helen was right. Hugo continued to prove that he was a windsucking crumpet.

CHAPTER 17

Susquehanna, Pennsylvania

The Hudson Rooming House's telephone was out of service. Birdie asked Mary to sit with Flo during breakfast so she could hurry to the Susquehanna train station to telephone Lydia. Several birds flitted in and out of the sumac trees that lined the sidewalk. If only she had time to sit on a park bench to share her woes with her feathered friends.

Birdie paced outside of the telephone box waiting for a man to finish his call. How should she start her conversation with Lydia? She could ask about the family reunion, news about Aunt Edith or the latest gossip from the ladies' auxiliary. Birdie hoped Gerald would answer, so she could ask him about Lydia first. Finally, the man hung up the telephone and Birdie brushed past him.

She picked up the earpiece and smoothed her skirt, running her fingers along the waistband. She shook her head when the operator asked again.

"Hello. Whom do you wish to call?" The operator's tinny accent echoed in the earpiece.

Birdie cleared her throat. She wrapped the thin cord around her wrist.

"Ring 343 Walnut Street, West Chester, please."

"Hello."

"I'm putting through a call from Susquehanna." The operator clicked off.

"Gerald?"

"Bertha. How nice of you to telephone." Gerald's voice sounded muffled as if he was speaking in a tunnel. It seemed strained but maybe it was just the connection.

"Before you put Lydia on, how is she?"

"Yes dear. She'll be happy to hear your voice."

"But how is she really?"

"Every day is a new day." More than his voice was strained.

The guilt for not going home when he had telegrammed ate at her. Birdie leaned against the wooden frame, turning away from the morning buzz of a busy train station.

"Bertha?"

"Lydia. I'm in Susquehanna."

"I see." Lydia's monotone voice squeezed Birdie's heart. Birdie's carefully planned topics disappeared.

"I just wanted to call … how are you?" Birdie stumbled over her words. "I miss you."

"Yes, dear."

"Maybe you and Gerald can come to another show now that we're closer."

"We'll see."

"Are you resting and eating enough, Lydia?"

All Birdie could hear was rustling. Then she heard Lydia calling for Gerald as if she were far away. Birdie waited several moments for Gerald or Lydia to return.

"The other party has dropped," The operator said. "You owe forty-five cents."

Another failed attempt to talk with Lydia. Not every modern invention made life easier.

On her return to the Hudson Rooming House Birdie gave in to her need for respite in the nearby park. The telephone call to Lydia hadn't lasted near as long as she had planned. She slid her watch face upright and decided she'd allow ten minutes to soak in the fresh air, letting familiar birdsongs untangle her thoughts.

She meandered into the small garden that surrounded a white gazebo and situated herself on one of the wrought iron benches inside. She liked her view, facing the street, but still secluded by bushes and ornamental trees. Within minutes she had identified four different bird calls, a Baltimore Oriole, a Cedar Waxwing, an Indigo Bunting, and a Song Sparrow. She reached into her satchel for her Lifesavers. The cool mint calmed her nerves.

Birdie closed her eyes to discern more birds' calls. Her thoughts wandered back to her stunted conversation with Lydia, making her chest ache. She knew the loss of the baby was still raw, it had been less than two weeks now. She wished again she could have been in two places at once. She wanted to hug Lydia and rub her back like she did for Flo. Birdie couldn't change what had happened, but she also knew that having someone care could make a difference.

Cocking her head, Birdie detected a distinct flutelike call. It took her back to hiding in the woods near Willow Glenn with Edwin. While she was wishing, she yearned for him too. He knew how to comfort Lydia. When they were younger, he'd distract her with harmonizing familiar hymns or playing duets on the piano. Edwin's hugs had always calmed Birdie. She embraced herself as she mouthed a prayer for Lydia, then whistled back the Wood Thrush's clear song.

A familiar figure stood on the sidewalk peering in at the gazebo. Hugo. Any soothing from her bird friends vanished. Might as well confront him while her stomach was already in knots. Hugo appeared around one of the posts, his breathing heavy as if he had been running.

"I was hoping that was you, Birdie." Hugo inspected the gazebo. "Mary said you went to the station to make a call."

She kicked an acorn under the opposite bench. "I telephoned Lydia."

"And did you speak with Gerald, too?"

"Just briefly. Lydia's still quite distraught." She pressed her lips together.

"Oh, yes." He stepped closer, wiping his nose with his handkerchief. "To be expected."

"Hugo." Birdie leaned forward. "I need to discuss something with you."

"What is it this time, babe?" He hunkered down on the bench that faced away from the street, opposite of her.

She winced. Babe? Really?

"Where were you that night in Picton? You missed our performance and what happened afterwards without any explanation." She dove right in with her questions, even if his mischievous expression disarmed her.

"I had some personal business that became more complicated than I had planned." He leaned back, crossing an ankle over his knee. "It couldn't be helped."

"What business?"

He removed his hat, twirling it between his hands. "Why does it matter?"

She cleared her throat. This was harder than when she had rehearsed it in her mind. Direct confrontation was more Helen or Lydia's way.

"I saw you at the Picton station." She raised her eyes to meet his. "You loaded duplicate instrument cases into the first-class car."

He remained still, only the side of his mouth twitching. Then he replaced his hat. He started to talk but stopped himself a few times. She could hear two Northern Cardinals whistling back and forth behind them.

"I did it for you, babe," Hugo said in a hoarse whisper.

"You what?"

"I had an opportunity to make extra dough. I took it." He moved forward, so their knees touched. "I want to be in your league."

Birdie gritted her teeth. He was feeding her a line. She scrunched her eyes, hoping that created the fierce furrowed brow like Helen had mastered.

"What makes you think smuggling hooch would impress me?" He tried to speak but she held up her palm. "And I've asked you before, stop calling me babe." She folded her arms across her chest like she had seen Adelle do many times.

"Being mad doesn't suit you." A smug grin briefly crossed his face then changed to his congenial crowd-pleasing expression. "I doubt if you can understand all the complications around trying to win over a girl like you." He ran his hand through his hair. "I'm a rube, but I have aspirations to be someone like Gerald for you."

"Why me, Hugo?" That wasn't what Birdie had intended to ask. It popped out.

"Can't you see I adore you?" He opened his hands as if in question. "From the audition on, I've risked my job to impress you."

"But you hardly spend time with me. You don't really know me."

"I can't be seen with you. I've told you that." He sighed. "But that doesn't mean I don't want to spend more time with you once the circuit is over, just like I explained to Gerald."

"You seem to spend plenty of time with Adelle."

"That's different. We're old friends."

"Look at Teddy and Mary, they aren't concerned about some old-fashioned Lyceum rules." Birdie crossed her legs, turning away from him.

"I don't expect you to understand but Teddy's not a circuit manager." Hugo moved over to Birdie's bench and put his arm behind her. "And he's not being monitored by Walter."

Birdie looked up. He had endearing eyes, even if they were often bloodshot. "Why would Walter care about you?"

"We have history." He looked at his pocket watch then stood up.

Hugo grabbed both her hands, pulling her to her feet. He glanced over his shoulder at the street then pulled her deeper into the shadows of the gazebo. His lips pressed against hers with a soft urgency. His tongue pushed through her teeth and flicked the inside of her mouth. She pushed him away, her heart pounding. He tasted like the lager that Helen had bought for her in Picton.

"Have you been drinking beer?" His odor surrounded her.

"Of course not." He reached for her again. "It's only nine o'clock."

"No Hugo." She pushed away. He made her want to tell Mr. James about the smuggling. Perhaps she'd threaten him with that.

"How do you know what beer tastes like?" He flashed that smug look again but this time it stayed in his eyes.

"I, well, I've tasted it once." She could feel heat rising to her neck.

"Well, you're mistaken. I don't drink beer." He snapped his watch closed. "I've got to check that the tents are secure." He held out his hand to her. "You continue to surprise me."

She refused his hand. "We're both surprised then." How had he changed her questions about his smuggling to her drinking beer?

She stalked away on the gravel path leading to the sidewalk from the gazebo. Movement to her left caught Birdie's eye. Walter crossed the street, charging right towards them. Hairs at the nape of her neck stood attention. She glanced back at Hugo just as he recognized Walter, too. He sidestepped around her.

"What's going on here, Mr. Shubert?" Walter practically bumped Hugo with his protruding belly.

"Good morning, Walter." Hugo tipped his hat. "Are you headed to the tents or the station?"

"Why is Miss Stauffer alone with you?" He indicated to Birdie.

"I was perfecting the call of the Wood Thrush and Mr. Shubert stopped when he heard me." Birdie raised her chin. "Would you like to hear it as well?"

"I doubt that's all that was going on." He turned away from Birdie to speak directly at Hugo. "A smart man would have more discretion when their job is currently on the line." His face became spiteful. "You've been warned before." Walter stormed away down the street and turned at the corner towards the train station.

"That was clever about the bird call." Hugo wiped his face with his handkerchief again. "Quite the quick thinker."

"You bring out the worst in me." Birdie felt like she might throw up.

Hugo turned the opposite direction from Walter. "That's a compliment in my book."

Birdie didn't watch him walk away; she hurried towards the rooming house. What made Hugo think he could kiss her? She wiped her lips again. And that hooey about smuggling to impress her. She skidded up the curb. He was a windsucking cookie or crumpet or whatever Helen had called him. Hugo had evaded her questions and twisted their conversation away from him to about her. One thing was certain, she wouldn't let him kiss her again. She stopped at the corner. And what had Walter meant by Hugo being warned before?

Stomping up the brick steps to the Hudson Rooming House, Birdie flung open the screen door. Why had she not threatened to tell Mr. James? That would have made Hugo squirm. She had much to share with Helen, and it was going to be everything, even the extra instrument cases. When Birdie charged into the kitchen, it was obvious Mary and Flo had stopped their quiet conversation. They sat at one end of the long painted-wood table, their packed suitcases at their feet, eyes following Birdie as she took the steps two at a time.

Once in her room, Birdie stuffed her dresses, vanity case, and nightshirt into her suitcase, closing it with two snaps of the metal clasps. She stopped at the bureau's mirror for just enough time to tuck wayward wisps of hair under her cloche hat. Maybe Flo would feel up to giving her a trim tonight. She knocked on the room where Adelle and Helen had stayed. No one replied so she tried the knob, and it opened with a click.

"Helen?" Birdie glanced around the darkened bedroom.

"What are you doing sneaking around my room?" Adelle stood behind Birdie, holding her black vanity case, wearing her silk robe with her hair wrapped in a towel.

"Looking for Helen." Birdie sized up Adelle. Might as well get this over with too. "What's going on with you lately?" Birdie put a hand on her hip. "You haven't acknowledged what happened to Flo, you avoid the rest of us, and you're no help."

Adelle straightened her shoulders. "I don't owe you, of all people, any explanations."

"I'm not trying to pry." Birdie could see that Adelle's eyes were puffy as if she'd been crying.

"It's not your business, Miss Perfect Pitch." Adelle pushed past Birdie, dropped her vanity case on the bed, and grabbed the edge of the door. "Give me privacy."

"This isn't about me or you. It's for Flo." Birdie wanted to shake Adelle, instead she dodged the slamming door.

That hadn't gone as Birdie had planned. Birdie sucked in her cheeks as she clomped back down the stairs. Getting through Adelle's guarded exterior was going to take more than compassion, patience or even chocolate bribes. She'd have to figure out a new tactic.

Both Mary and Flo lowered their heads, as if they could hide that they had heard Adelle slam the door and maybe even more.

"What's for breakfast?" Birdie shifted to her singsong voice.

"Muffet's Shredded Wheat." Mary frowned then raised her eyebrow as a question.

"My favorite." Birdie placed a wheat square into a bowl, adding fresh milk. She stabbed the wheat biscuit with her spoon. "Have either of you seen Helen?"

"No. I thought you might run into her at the train station." Mary pushed herself away from the table. "I'm off to see if Teddy needs help."

"Of course." Birdie bit into crunchy cereal. It didn't taste as good as she had remembered. "We'll meet you at the station." She patted Flo's hand, but Flo stared off through the kitchen window towards the back garden.

Birdie and Flo were the last to arrive at the train station. At first Birdie didn't see Helen, but she recognized her blue Musketeer hat standing out among the men loading the trunks. Adelle stood a few steps from Mary. How had Adelle managed to beat them to the train station?

The steam and screeches announcing the train's arrival unsettled Birdie today. She assisted Flo up the metal stairs of their second-class car. Birdie chose an empty row mid-way back, and Flo sank into the seat closest to the window. After putting their things away on the brass shelf, Birdie reluctantly eased into the aisle seat. Mary sat across from them, and Adelle walked to the back of the car. Helen jumped on at the last minute and plopped down next to Mary. Birdie sucked in her cheeks; she'd have to wait again to share everything with Helen. If this morning's events were an indication of how things would be now that they were back in familiar Pennsylvania, she didn't want to be here. As the wheels clacked along, Birdie felt her new world unraveling, each clack brought them closer to Mr. James and the unknown of what would happen to Flo.

CHAPTER 18

Honesdale, Pennsylvania

Helen was so preoccupied over the next few days that Birdie felt certain she was avoiding her. Meanwhile, Birdie had to artfully brush off Hugo's attempts to get her alone which took extra diligence and energy she didn't have. Flo still hadn't volunteered the name of her assailant and being Flo's caretaker took every ounce of Birdie's patience. Birdie yearned for one night alone, with or without Helen. Worst of all, guilt snuck in late at night making Birdie question why she wasn't in West Chester trying to comfort Lydia instead.

Not surprisingly, The Versatile Quintet's performances were almost as depressing as Birdie's attitude. Hugo or the other circuit managers commented on it each night. Hugo had pleaded with the girls the day before to enliven their act and Adelle responded that he should take note that she played perfectly. Walter's grating voice after every performance of their opening act caused the girls to become fast change musicians. Helen even made a competition out of who could put their costumes away the quickest. "It's when things seem worst that you must not quit" became Birdie's inner chant.

The screeching of the train's brakes seemed to echo Birdie's apprehension about arriving in Honesdale. The expectation of when or if they'd be meeting with Mr. James hovered over the wooden train station. Birdie started what had become their arrival routine, helping Flo, still in her wide brimmed hat, off the train. The swelling on Flo's face had subsided, but the bruising seemed to have spread and yellowed. Helen and Mary carried everyone's personal items while Adelle took care of herself. Today, the overcast skies heavy with summer humidity didn't make things easier.

Despite the weather and their circumstances, the Honesdale train station had a hospitable appeal. Its two-tone green wooden slates allowed it to blend into the forest area behind it. Birdie had traveled to Honesdale with her family years before. There had been much hullaba-loo around some new locomotive engine at the time. It had been bright red, and Edwin had skipped around the station. Today townspeople swarmed around Hugo and the Anvil Choir as they unloaded the tents. What had become rote to her intrigued Honesdale.

"Let's get to our lodgings," Helen said in her take-charge voice. "We're staying at a boarding house on High Street." She marched off as if she knew Honesdale. The girls followed in line, and after several blocks it became clear Helen was right. Birdie marveled at how Helen always knew which direction to take.

Miss Jenkins's Rooming House, a two-story clapboard home with a wide porch, was surrounded by a chipped painted fence corralling dan-delions and dirt. The hand-lettered sign on a post by the hinged gate was missing letters. The gray clouds accumulating behind the house added to its ominous tone.

Helen looked towards the roof with missing shingles. "Hugo con-tinues to outdo himself with our accommodations."

"Maybe it's nicer inside." Mary opened the gate with timid fingers, stepped over two cats curled up on the steps and walked up to the front door. Helen followed, shaking her head. Birdie and Flo huddled on the little path. Birdie willed Flo to make one of her quips but Flo remained silent. Adelle stayed out on the sidewalk away from everyone.

"Hello." Mary called through the torn screen door.

There was no reply. "Anybody home?" Helen shouted.

"Hold your horses, I'm a comin'," yelled a high-pitched voice from inside. The rounded shape of a woman appeared through the mesh.

"Miss Jenkins? We're the talent from Westdale Chautauqua and have rented three rooms for the night." Helen held out a piece of paper.

"Your rooms aren't ready." She said through the closed screen. "I've had to clean them myself on account of my no-good help up and quittin'." She shifted to her other leg making her image closer to the screen. "Come back in a couple hours."

"Where can we leave our suitcases?" Helen asked.

The woman called over her shoulder. "Set them on the porch."

No one moved. Shaking a handkerchief from her pocket, Helen wiped her face and neck. Birdie peeled her dress from the backs of her thighs.

"We should keep our suitcases with us." Mary started down the steps, careful to not grasp the banister and stooped to pet a cat. "Maybe we can ask Hugo for a different place."

"I doubt Hugo will care about our lodging problems." Helen remained on the porch gripping her suitcase. "He has enough problems of his own."

"Let's figure it out over a cream soda," Birdie suggested. "We passed a pharmacy on our way here."

"Your treat." Adelle spun around, leading the trek back towards downtown with more gusto than they'd seen from her in days.

Helen hurried the others towards the pharmacy before the clouds let loose. Located at the corner of Park and Main streets, Peoples Pharmacy must have been Honesdale's most popular spot. Even with a long L-shaped counter, there were only three available stools. Adelle pounced for one while Birdie helped Flo get situated on another. Mary convinced a man drinking coffee to move over and motioned for Birdie to sit next to Flo.

"I need to talk with Helen, so you go ahead." Birdie nodded to Mary. "We'll keep watch for stools to open up."

Helen stared out the large shop window still gripping her suitcase. Birdie moved beside her, watching the wind blow leaves in little eddies around the sidewalk. Across the street stood an impressive three-story brick building with the words Hotel Wayne emblazoned near the rooftop.

"It would be nice to stay there." People milled about under the striped awning protecting the front entryway. A uniformed bellhop offered a couple a large black umbrella.

"We can't afford it." Helen seemed captivated by the hotel's activities. "Somehow our circuit is losing money. Hugo is cutting every corner he can."

"How do you know these things?"

"Let's just say Hugo isn't quiet when he's ranting." Helen said to the window.

Helen's innate knack of noticing important things continued to astound Birdie. Directions, the Chautauqua business, little nuances about people. It made Birdie wonder what else Helen knew that she wasn't sharing.

"Any idea when we'll see Mr. James?" Birdie turned towards Helen.

"I imagine Hugo's with him now."

"I wish we knew what will happen with Flo."

The expected rain came with gusto, falling at an angle as if their whole world had tilted on its side.

"About Hugo," Birdie said.

That distinct wet smell swirled around them when a few customers left.

"Do share." Helen turned her attention to Birdie.

"Open seats," Mary called.

"Later," Birdie whispered. "Not with the others."

Helen sank onto the first stool, so Birdie squeezed between her and Mary. The soda jerk appeared with his white creased paper hat, tapping his pencil on a pad. Birdie ordered a vanilla cream soda. One sip and she could be back at the West Chester Pharmacy, being scolded for spinning on the red covered stools. Helen asked for a cherry Coca-Cola.

Birdie leaned forward and saw Adelle whispering to Flo, both looked upset, their drinks untouched. Just as Birdie slipped off the stool to intervene, both girls wiped under their eyes. Adelle patted Flo's leg and reached for her soda glass. Birdie sat back down still wary of Adelle and her conflicting behaviors but felt relieved when she heard Flo slurping her Black Cow.

The cream was piled so high on Birdie's soda, it sloshed white foam down the sides of the glass when the jerk set it down. Using her finger to scoop the dripping white magic, Birdie let it fill her tastebuds and spirit. Helen's stool squeaked as she turned side to side while she chewed on the pink straw sticking out of her deep red soda. Their worries temporarily melted away as each of the girls, even Flo, took turns reminiscing about hometown soda shops. When it was time to go, Helen insisted she'd pay the tab.

A black Buick made shiny by the recent rain pulled up in front of Hotel Wayne. Birdie gasped when Gerald leaned out of the driver's side window and motioned to the bellhop. She inched backwards into the pharmacy as Lydia's hand reached for assistance and she rose from the passenger side. Dressed in a smart floral drop waist dress with a lace collar, Lydia looked too thin, their recent loss revealed in her unfocused stare. Helen's arm encircled Birdie's shoulders as they both watched Gerald place Lydia's hand through his arm and assist her into the hotel.

"Were you expecting Gerald and Lydia?" Helen whispered.

"Not here." Birdie couldn't pull her eyes away. "Come with me to greet them."

"All of us?" Helen nodded towards Flo, Mary, and Adelle who were outside admiring the hotel's ornate rooftop.

"Maybe not." Birdie suspected Lydia would say something judgmental about Flo.

"Hand me your suitcase." Helen wiggled her fingers. "I'll take it and the others back to the boarding house. You can meet us at the tents later." She led the others away from the hotel. Flo kept looking back towards Birdie. Adelle draped her arm around Flo's waist and together they followed Mary. The group looked like derelict travelers carrying their suitcases while dodging puddles. Helen mouthed "Good luck" over her shoulder.

Birdie crossed the street and walked up to the hotel entrance just as Gerald was coming back outside. He had his head bent and was putting on driving gloves.

"Gerald," Birdie said.

"Bertha." He wrapped her in one of his double-armed hugs, enveloping her in his familiar Black Cavendish and Brilliantine scent. It relieved her that Gerald hadn't changed. "We were hoping to surprise you at the show tonight."

"Oh, I'm surprised." It was a long drive from West Chester to here. Birdie wanted to stay outside with him but knew she should go see Lydia as soon as possible. "Is Lydia in the lobby?"

"She's in our room." He put his hand on her shoulder and leaned back. "Is that a new bob under your hat?"

"Yes sir." Heat creeped up Birdie's neck. She'd forgotten how much had happened since she last saw Lydia and Gerald.

"It suits you." He pulled off his driving gloves.

"Thank you." Birdie mocked a curtsey. "When did you get this fancy automobile?"

"Just before—ah, it arrived about a month ago. A Buick Model 48 Coupe." Gerald tapped the front fender with his gloves. "I had planned to do an errand, but I'd rather visit with you." He handed his car keys to the bellhop. "How about a glass of lemonade?" He held out his arm, indicating she should go inside.

"Shouldn't I see Lydia first?"

She followed him to two wingback chairs situated in a corner of the lobby.

"She's resting." He pulled his chair close. "I'd like this opportunity to speak with you alone."

Gerald only spoke to her without Lydia if they were planning Lydia's birthday or if it was serious. She edged into the paisley patterned chair clasping her hands. Gerald called a waiter over and ordered two lemonades. Any other summer day, Birdie would have delighted in a cold lemonade. Today her cream soda lay sweet and heavy in her stomach.

"What's wrong?" She'd only gotten a glimpse, but Lydia definitely was not her robust take-charge self.

Gerald chewed at the end of his unlit cigar. He placed it back in his pocket when a waiter arrived with two lemonades. The glasses gleamed with water droplets clinging to their sides. Birdie felt like one of those droplets, suspended in time. She almost asked her question again when Gerald finally spoke.

"I'm concerned about your sister." He gripped the arms of his chair as if to keep from heaving himself towards her. "She's having trouble pulling herself out of it this time." He stared over Birdie's head at a still-life painting centered on the wall as he spoke.

"I should have come right home when you telegrammed." Birdie leaned forward. "I was a fool to let Hugo call you for me." She covered her mouth with her hand, holding back the burning anger at her selfishness.

Gerald took a long drink and set his glass down. "That's not what I'm saying, Bertha." His eyes held hers. "I'm afraid even you couldn't have helped her."

"Oh Gerald, what do you mean?"

"She's despondent. She refuses Pastor Dickerson's counsel, pushes away the prescribed Pinkham Compound, and rejects any calls from her auxiliary luncheon friends." He eased back in his chair. "Neither Aunt Edith's pastries nor Uncle Bert's corny jokes reach her." He clenched his hands together. "I've exhausted all my ideas. Coming to see you was my last resort."

Birdie coughed, reached for her lemonade and the wet glass slipped from her fingers. Gerald righted it before much lemonade spilled on the table. "I'm so clumsy."

"You're just upset." He rested his elbows on his knees. "I'm hoping your show will engage her." His hands formed a steeple. "I suggested a trip to the ocean, but she declined. You know going to the Jersey shore is a treat for her. I was certain fresh clams, strolling on the boardwalks, and reading under the shade of a big striped umbrella would entice her." He released a Gerald-sized sigh. "But she still said no."

Birdie couldn't imagine Lydia turning down an offer to be at the shore; they had treasured going to Atlantic City for years. "Ask her again, you may have mentioned it too soon."

"I brought it up on our drive here." He eased back. "I had to beg her to come see you."

"Oh dear." Birdie patted Gerald's hand. Seeing Gerald out of sorts escalated Birdie's guilt about not going home after receiving his telegram. She'd have to find a way to help Lydia.

*   *   *

Birdie lightly rapped on room number 215. She leaned towards the door but didn't hear any movement. "Lydia?" She hesitated then knocked again. Birdie's hands shook as she inserted the room key Gerald had given her, turning it just as Lydia opened the door.

"Surprise," Birdie said. She saw a glimpse of a thin-lipped smile but when she looked again, Lydia's face had closed. The corners of her mouth turned down, not in a scowl, which Birdie had experienced many times, but a dejected frown Birdie had never seen.

Birdie's fervent embrace almost caused Lydia to trip over the entry-way rug. Their hug lasted longer than usual, Lydia patting and Birdie squeezing. Birdie leaned back, hiding collected tears with the back of her hand.

"It's kind of you to come," Lydia said, her voice lacking its usual command. She edged towards a wide window overlooking the street and lowered herself into one of the nearby upholstered chairs.

"How are you?" Birdie eased into the other chair, scooting it close so her knees almost touched Lydia's.

"Fine." Lydia rested her hands together in her lap.

"It's me. How are you, really?"

Lydia stared out the window as if searching the horizon, her eyes unfocused, her skin pale.

"Empty." Her voice barely a whisper.

"Oh, Lyd." Birdie enclosed Lydia's hands in her own. "I'm sorry I didn't come as soon as it happened."

"You couldn't have changed anything." Lydia continued to gaze outside. "No one could."

Sunshine burst through the overcast sky, spreading rays out as if in invitation. Lydia's shoulders hunched and it was as if her body folded in on itself. "It must be the Lord's will that Gerald and I will never ..."

"Don't say never." Birdie gripped her sister's cold hands. "You can try again."

"No, I'm done." Lydia pulled her hands free. "We have discussed it."

"Surely the doctors have some way."

"Enough." Lydia's familiar stern tone returned briefly. "You don't understand." She stood and walked away from the window.

The finality and implication of Lydia's words caught between them like the huge boulders in the rushing waters of the nearby Susquehanna River. Birdie almost recited the "Don't Quit" poem their mother had embroidered. It had become her own mantra lately, but she questioned how it would be received by Lydia at this time.

"Can I order you some hot tea from room service?" Birdie had to do something.

"How is your Chautauqua circuit?" Lydia pulled at the corner of the blanket covering the unmade bed. A curved indentation revealed where she had been resting.

"Good." Birdie had decided earlier not to tell Lydia what had happened to Flo. Or about Mr. James. "We're all a bit weary of doing the same act every night. I'm afraid it shows in our performances."

Lydia fixated on the rumples in the bed. She smoothed the bedspread several times.

Maybe Lydia hadn't heard her. "Traveling far and wide causes us to have a less than perfect act."

"Mediocracy is not acceptable," Lydia said with a flat tone, her dress emphasizing a waist as flat.

Birdie covered a choke with her hand, she felt powerless to the sadness that filled the room. She started chanting "when things go wrong, and they sometimes will, Don't Quit" to herself.

Lydia returned to the window. Birdie moved behind her, placing a light hand on Lydia's shoulder. They both gazed at the street below. Several people came out of the pharmacy with closed umbrellas.

Lydia brushed Birdie's hand from her shoulder and turned around.

"Would you like me to order something from room service?" Birdie asked again.

Lydia shook her head. "Are you enjoying Chautauqua?"

"Yes." It shocked Birdie that Lydia asked the same question again.

Lydia started to say something, then paused. After several seconds she said in a low voice, "The Lyceum pays you well, your performances should reflect that."

Birdie received Lydia's semi-scolding with secret relief. This was more like the older sister she knew. "What do you suggest we do?"

Lydia settled back into the upholstered chair, clasping her own hands.

Birdie squatted next to her chair. This might be a way to pull Lydia out of her melancholy. She'd taken charge of all their performances at the ladies' auxiliary luncheons.

"Do you have any tricks to enliven our act?"

Birdie's heart ached while she waited for Lydia's answer. She paused, knowing not to ask again.

Lydia replied as if talking to the rumpled pillows. "Change the order of your musical numbers." She went to the washstand and picked up the crystal water pitcher. Tiny rainbows scattered across the wall as she poured water into the glass basin. She dipped the corner of a linen towel into the water and blotted her face.

"Nifty. I'll tell the girls tonight." Lydia's eyebrow didn't even raise at Birdie's modern phrase. "Any other suggestions?" Birdie felt desperate. Maybe mentioning Lydia's favorite bachelor would get her engaged.

"I know *Hugo* would appreciate your help." Birdie looked sideways at Lydia who still held the towel to her cheek.

"Gerald's looking forward to the show tonight."

"No fainting this time." Birdie waved her hand in the air hoping Lydia would look at her. "I've grown since that awful Mount Carmel fainting performance."

Lydia sat on the edge of the bed, smoothing the bedspread again. Birdie didn't know how to help her.

"As a matter of fact, call time is soon."

Lydia smoothed the top of a pillow. "Don't be late on account of me."

Birdie had never seen Lydia so fastidious about bed covers. She wanted to stay longer but backed towards the door. "I can't wait to share your idea with the others."

Lydia leaned against the pillows. Birdie wished she could rub Lydia's back as she had with Flo. Instead, she sensed she wasn't needed. Or wanted.

"I'm sure you'll have other ideas after you've seen our show tonight." Birdie started to wave goodbye but pulled her hand back. "I'll see you soon, then."

Birdie stepped out to the hallway, pulling the door closed. It wasn't until she had reached the bottom step that she realized Lydia hadn't said a word about her Eton crop.

CHAPTER 19

Honesdale, Pennsylvania

Meandering along Main Street, Birdie relived her conversation with Lydia. She'd never experienced Lydia this disconsolate. Lydia had grieved their parents' and Edwin's passings, had been devastated after her earlier miscarriages, but had rallied stronger each time. Maybe Birdie expected too much, too soon.

She crossed Park Street and could see the welcoming canvas tip of the main tent peeking over the trees across the river. She stopped on the wooden bridge, letting the cool air and babbling water quiet her. Just as this river weathered floods, widened its banks, and survived winter storms Birdie knew that Lydia too would prevail. She removed her cloche, stealing a minute of the simple joy of wind mussing her hair.

Birdie strode into the tent with a renewed mindset. She hoped the others would welcome Lydia's idea of changing the order of some of the songs for tonight. Mr. James would be in the audience so it might be risky, but she knew they had to do something to give their act a boost.

Birdie's mood lightened more at the sight of Helen at the upright piano, her arm reaching down into the open casing.

"Want me to play some notes while you adjust the pin block?"

"Super. Play the C scale." Helen knocked the wood with her lever when she turned it. She pulled out a smaller one from her pocket.

"The A key is flat," Birdie said.

"I thought so too. Hit it again."

Birdie pressed the key several times while Helen tightened or loosened the strings with her lever. They both nodded when it sounded almost perfect. Helen sat down beside Birdie and played every note. Birdie cocked her head.

"It sounds better than it has in days." Birdie patted the top of the piano after replacing the lid.

"I figure we need everything in tip top shape for ole Mr. James."

"I wish we could be as easily tuned as a piano." Birdie sighed.

"Easy? I've been working on this all afternoon." Helen rolled her tools in a felt case and tied it with a string. "How was your visit with Lydia and Gerald?"

"It was hard." Birdie admitted. "Lydia is despondent and Gerald is at a loss. He can't figure a way to fix things for her. I've never seen either of them like this."

"I'm sorry." Helen patted Birdie's back. "I imagine it's hard to see your family in pain. Maybe what's needed is love, grace, and time."

"True." Birdie liked how Helen's cheeks gleamed rosily after working on the piano. "Lydia did offer a performance trick after much prodding. I think it might help rejuvenate our act."

"Do tell." Helen turned towards Birdie; their knees bumped which Birdie didn't mind.

"It's simple. We start with "Come Where the Lilies Bloom" and finish with the Patriotic Medley. Mixing things up will make it different for us, and hopefully more entertaining for our audience."

"Nifty idea." Helen played a few stanzas. "I should have thought of it."

"What?" Adelle asked. She must have snuck in while they were tuning the piano because she sat in the front row, with her ever-present newspaper on her lap.

"Open with our ending piece and close with the patriotic songs," Birdie said.

"Have you two lost your minds? Mr. James is here tonight." Adelle stood up.

"It won't be hard. Let's see what Mary and Flo think, before you can the idea, Adelle." Helen jumped off the platform, she held up her hand to Birdie.

"We never did anything like this last year." Adelle crossed her arms.

"Times are changing." Birdie took Helen's offered hand and they headed towards the dressing tent.

Birdie shared Lydia's idea with Mary and Flo as soon as she walked past the muslin curtain. Mary loved it and Flo nodded in agreement.

"You could lead us across the stage in a circle and then off for the finale." Mary mimicked marching with a trombone.

"I'll wrap up the last Sousa march from the piano and then you could add a finishing high C with the slide of your 'bone showing from side stage," Helen added.

"That sounds corny. Hugo will never approve," Adelle said.

"We don't have to ask for Hugo's permission. We're not adding new songs." Helen shook out her lacy dress.

"How will we open with our 'Lilies' song?" Mary asked.

"Adelle can lead us all on stage, we'll get in our positions and then Teddy can turn on the stage lights." Helen suggested.

"I don't like it." Adelle picked up her band hat.

"I do," Flo said.

The girls stopped what they were doing, each stared at Flo.

"And I don't want to ever wear this floppy hat again. No offense Mary." Flo flung it across the room.

"Good riddance," Mary giggled. Adelle huffed her way over to the mirror and tugged at the cowlick that often rose from the crown of her slick black hair.

Mary helped Flo use face powder and rouge to hide her bruises. Flo looked more like herself than she had in days. They were getting dressed into their lacy costumes when Teddy walked by and gave them the fifteen-minute warning. Mary dashed out to tell him about the order changes and Birdie could hear their hushed voices through the canvas walls.

"So, is Miss Jenkins's Boarding House nicer on the inside than the outside?" Birdie asked as she bent over to buckle her shoe.

"Barely," Helen said. "It's clean but old."

"It's disgusting." Adelle puckered her lips as she applied bright red rouge. "I plan to say something to Mr. James, if Hugo doesn't start booking better lodging."

Birdie hoped Flo would join in with one of her quips, but she sat on the edge of the trunk, picking at her fingernails. Maybe Flo still needed grace and time too.

"The good thing is we're the only ones staying there." Helen adjusted her feathered hairband. "We have four rooms among us."

"That's different," Birdie said.

"I suggested Flo take one by herself." Helen looked at Flo who kept her head bent. "But she wants to room with you."

"Fine by me." Birdie moved beside Flo and patted her shoulder.

Helen walked towards Birdie and Flo. "So, Adelle took the biggest bedroom and now everyone is happy." Adelle gave a swish of her narrow hips and left the dressing tent.

Teddy called five-minutes and Mary came back into the dressing tent. She motioned to the girls to gather around. Adelle joined the circle, sipping on a seltzer water.

"Teddy says Hugo's been put on probation. Mr. James is traveling with us for several days," Mary whispered.

"What does that mean for Hugo?" Adelle set the bottle down.

"I'm not sure. But it must be bad because Teddy is quite upset." Mary pulled at the collar of her lacy dress.

"Did Teddy say anything else?" Helen gave a slight nod towards Flo.

"Just that we need to do better than our best tonight." Mary shook her head.

"We can do that." Birdie clapped her hands. "It's good we switched up the order. Starting with our 'Lilies song' feels exciting."

Adelle shrugged her shoulders. "I don't like being the first one on stage."

"I'll go first, if you'd like." Birdie picked up her trombone. "I'm used to it and this time will be easy since I'm not marching."

Hugo started his introduction. His voice sounded strained. It was still loud but had lost its effervescence. As they lined up to go on stage, Birdie's nervousness returned. She hoped she hadn't made a mistake suggesting changing their routine when Mr. James, Gerald, and Lydia were all in the audience.

* * *

To everyone's relief, the Versatile Quintet's opening act went better than it had in days. Changing the order of the two numbers had made it fresh for the girls and that in turn filled the performance with new energy that the crowd reciprocated. It wasn't perfect: Birdie had sputtered during her bird call duet with Flo, but sputtering was better than fainting. The audience was on its feet clapping at the Patriotic finale when she held the High C for such a long time. It made her dizzy and her lips numb. But it was worth it.

As soon as their performance ended, the other girls headed to a local restaurant to celebrate. Birdie stayed in the dressing tent, putting the costumes away. She knew Gerald and Lydia would stay for the lecture and wanted to visit with them afterwards. She walked towards the mirror, accidentally kicking over Adelle's abandoned water, making the glass bottle spew across her shoes. "Doggone, Adelle," she whispered to herself.

Birdie had hoped to use this time to make a list of potential songs to add to their act. Since changing the order had been successful, maybe rotating a few new songs in would work some magic too. But as she sat tapping the paper with her pencil, everything but songs were coming into her mind. She blamed it on Walter's irksome voice.

Birdie met Gerald and Lydia once Walter finally finished. Lydia leaned against Gerald gazing off towards the side of the tent.

"Delightful performance, Bertha." Gerald clapped lightly. "I especially enjoyed the trombone theatrics at the end."

"Thank you." Birdie curtsied. "At least you got to see an entire performance this time."

They waited for comments from Lydia, but she remained quiet.

"Where's Hugo?" Gerald looked around the activity of the tent. Teddy and the Anvil Choir were cleaning up as the last few audience members strolled out.

"Ah, I believe he had to meet with some townspeople right after tonight's show." Birdie had no idea where Hugo was, but she suspected Mr. James would be right at his side. "What did you think of our show, Lydia?"

Lydia slowly turned her head towards Birdie and nodded.

"She loved it all, didn't you?" Gerald wrapped an arm around Lydia's waist, drawing her in. "Her foot tapped along with the Sousa numbers."

"We followed your advice. We moved 'Come Where the Lilies Bloom' to start us off and the Patriotic Medley as our finale." Birdie almost added something outrageous just to try to bring Lydia out of her melancholy.

"That's nice," Lydia said.

"The girls and Hugo appreciated your suggestion." Birdie hoped mentioning Hugo would rouse Lydia but it didn't. She couldn't help but remember their earlier conversation when all Lydia could talk about was Hugo.

"I'm tired, Gerald." Lydia looked lost.

Gerald asked Birdie to invite all the girls to breakfast tomorrow at their hotel. She knew they'd be delighted. She didn't want to think about eating anything from Miss Jenkins's Boarding House. Gerald added Hugo and Teddy to the invitation as they turned to go. Birdie hugged each of them, holding tighter than usual to Lydia. Gerald placed his hand at Lydia's lower back and Birdie stood at the tent's entrance watching him guide her away.

Birdie turned to see Helen standing between the benches. She trotted over and embraced her hard. Helen returned the hearty hug. Birdie felt an uneasy comfortableness that made her step away. Did she rely on Helen too much?

"I figured you'd want someone to walk you to our illustrious accommodations." Helen squeezed Birdie's fingers. Birdie wanted to hug Helen again but held back.

"It's nice of you to show me the way."

"Did Lydia like our performance?"

"I think so." Birdie sighed. "She's not herself." She started towards the exit. "No one is these days. Have you seen Hugo?"

"No sign of him or Mr. James." Helen waved to Teddy as they stepped outside. "I'm nervous for Flo. It's worse not knowing what the Lyceum has decided to do."

"I agree." Birdie leaned closer to Helen; the earlier rains made the night air cooler. "Why would they hold her to outdated contract rules when they know she was attacked? Hopefully, Hugo put in a good word for Flo."

"I wouldn't count on it." Helen walked along Main then turned left on High Street.

"Gerald's invited all of us to breakfast at Hotel Wayne tomorrow morning." Birdie looped her arm through Helen's matching her casual stride.

"Wonderful. I doubt if Miss Jenkins will provide more than day old bread and water." Helen snorted. "Wait till you see the place."

Birdie looked up at the stars. If only changing the order of things would make life easier for Lydia and Flo. She cast several wishes that turned into pleading prayers.

Helen was on the button about Miss Jenkins's Boarding House. The house had an odd odor, a combination of bleach mixed with mold. The stairs talked back with each step as Birdie followed Helen to the second floor. An open door with a dull light invited them to join the others gathered in Adelle's room. When Birdie sat next to Flo, her friend curled her arm around Birdie's as if to keep her from leaving. The face powder and rouge had done their job to cover the fading bruises but did nothing for what remained beneath the surface.

"Gerald's invited all of us to breakfast tomorrow at Hotel Wayne, nine o'clock sharp." Birdie announced. "Can you let Teddy know too?" Birdie nodded towards Mary who leaned against the headboard next to Adelle.

"And Hugo?" Mary asked.

"I guess." Birdie wasn't sure she wanted to include Hugo but couldn't bring herself to tell Mary tonight.

"Let's meet outside at 8:45," Helen said.

"Eight-thirty." Adelle flicked at the worn bedspread. "I don't want to stay in this shabby place any longer than necessary."

The girls seemed to hold a collective breath waiting for a clever remark from Flo.

"Breakfast together will give me a chance thank Lydia for her suggestion," Mary said after a bit. "Who knew changing the order of two numbers would make such a difference?"

"About that." Birdie gently removed herself from Flo's grip so she could look at each of the girls. "What if we prepared another song or monologue to perform every now and then, just to mix things up when needed?" She opened her hands, as if offering her question.

"In addition to what we perform now?" Mary cocked her head.

"Not in addition, as replacements." Birdie tucked a curl behind her ear.

"Anything we perform has to be approved by the circuit mangers, or I guess Mr. James." Adelle stood and smoothed out wrinkles from her side-draped satin dress. Flo stretched and moved towards the door.

"I agree with Birdie's suggestion that we have a few pieces in our repertoire that we can rotate in and out. Ones that have been practiced and approved." Helen stood up next to Birdie. "It could elevate our act."

"Red-hot idea." Flo leaned against the door frame, her pose making her look like one of the Vogue models despite what had happened. The girls directed their gaze towards Flo but she lowered her head causing her copper hair to cover her eyes.

"Let's discuss it more tomorrow, I'm done-in for tonight." Helen put her hand at Birdie's lower back, and they moved towards Flo.

"Good night." Adelle shooed them out of her room.

Once in their room Birdie eased onto the closest bed. The emotions of the day caught up with her causing a dull headache behind her eyes. Flo plopped onto the other bed and it made a scratchy squawk.

"This place is the pits." Flo bounced up and down several times causing the bed to play a squeaky tune. Birdie let Flo continue even though the noise made her headache worse. It was reassuring to see more than a glimpse of the old Flo.

"It appears clean." Birdie found her suitcase beside a small chair. She rummaged for her night shirt.

"It's a façade." Flo sat still. "Like Hugo."

Birdie jerked her head up. "What?"

Flo leaned back on the bed and drew her knees in, her colorful silk pajamas in bold contrast to the gray bedspread. "I saw him with those fake instrument cases at the Picton station." She rocked a bit. "Want to know what was in them?"

Birdie sank to the bed twisting her nightshirt in her hands. She should have thought to ask Flo before. She was injured but of course she could still see. Birdie nodded.

"Smuggled hooch."

Flo confirmed what Birdie knew from Mary and had more or less proved by Hugo's attempts at dodging the subject when she had confronted him in the park.

"You were awake when Mary told me what Teddy said about Hugo." Birdie released her grip on her nightshirt and laid it aside.

"Um-hum." Flo stretched her legs across the space between the two beds. "I had my suspicions before then."

Birdie turned her back and started to undress. It was as if a drum mallet pounded inside her forehead. She slipped into her nightshirt. "Me too. But I didn't want to believe them."

"It's all true."

Birdie nodded as she pulled back the bedcover and climbed in. The sheets smelled clean but were pilled, the mattress lumpy. "I asked Hugo about it in Susquehanna."

Flo's eyes widened. "I didn't think you had that in you." She looked like a cartoon raccoon with a one-eyed yellowed mask. "What line did he feed you this time?"

Bird swallowed, lowering her voice. "He said he did it for me."

"Hell's bells." Flo feigned surprise.

Birdie smoothed the top sheet's edging. "He claimed he needs more money to impress me."

"Or impress Gerald?" Flo pushed back her covers, lying flat on her back. "Nothing against you as a dame, but he's more interested in getting himself hired."

Birdie wondered if everyone saw that she was just a patsy for Hugo. Birdie rolled on her side, facing Flo. "Have you told anyone else?"

"You mean Helen?" Flo shook her head.

"Should we tell her?"

"You need to be straight with her."

Birdie rubbed her temples. "I'm glad you told me."

"I'm not good at keeping secrets."

Except the name of her attacker. Birdie almost asked but decided not to ruin Flo's mood. Tonight was the first time Flo had sounded somewhat like herself. Birdie stared up at the ceiling dotted with small water stains. They reminded her of Flo's bruises.

"How do you do it?"

"What?"

"Stay strong after what happened."

"Humph. I'm not all that." Flo turned towards the wall and curled her legs up. "I keep telling myself a dame doesn't quit because of a brute."

Birdie turned on her side, holding her hands under her head. It made her recall the "Don't Quit" poem, yet in "Flo'ism." What an odd twist of fate, Flo's need for Birdie had taught her so much.

"Sweet dreams."

"As if," Flo said. "I've still got Mr. James and the kooky Lyceum to worry about."

"Maybe the fact that he's taking his time is good." Birdie sighed.

Birdie went over what Flo had confirmed. Hugo had used identical instrument cases to smuggle in Canadian whiskey. Should she confront him again? She rolled to her other side. And Lydia. Would she get her spunk back? Part of Birdie wanted to go home to West Chester. It seemed consistent, calm, and comforting right now. But she would miss her friends and the circuit too much. Complicated as it was, she knew she was in the right place.

*   *   *

Breakfast at the Hotel Wayne was the bumblebee's knees. The group, minus Hugo—no one had seen him to offer Gerald's invitation—sat around a big oval table. Long windows on either side let in cheerful morning light. Gerald, in his most natural habitat, entertained everyone with engaging stories, questions, and comments. He generously persuaded each person to order what they wanted. Only Teddy needed extra nudging to order the hearty breakfast special. The coffee was hot, the cream especially sweet, and the orange juice fresh squeezed.

Looking around at her friends, Birdie wished she could bottle it all up to cherish again later. Across the table, even Lydia had perked up. She had always reveled playing her "role" as the Queen when Gerald held court, nodding at just the right time, and adding extra comments to Gerald's favorite stories.

Flo, to Birdie's right, was more animated than she had been since the attack. Perhaps losing the floppy hat and their discussion last night had helped. As everyone finished eating, Birdie decided she couldn't lose this opportunity to try and further engage her sister.

"Lydia, could you help us again?" Birdie leaned forward as all heads turned her way. "We'd like to rotate in some different songs or acts—to liven up our performance."

"Yes," Helen picked up Birdie's cue, "your idea to switch the order made such a positive difference last night."

"Teddy, time to excuse ourselves." Gerald scooted his chair back and patted Lydia's shoulder. "These ladies don't need us bumbling up their plans."

"Yes, sir." Teddy stood next to Gerald. His height exceeded Gerald's, but his girth was dwarfed. He looked like a wooden pencil next to a fountain pen. "Thank you for breakfast." His face beamed. "It was the best." Each of the girls all thanked Gerald too.

As Gerald and Teddy strolled away, Hugo appeared at the entrance to the hotel lobby. Gerald clapped Hugo on his back and the three of them stepped outside to the porch.

Flo raised her eyebrow and Helen patted Birdie's knee under the table. Lydia cleared her throat so Birdie turned her attention to her sister.

"Your act does need improving," Lydia said. This was just what Birdie anticipated, Lydia taking charge. "I suggest adding a Shakespeare monologue. They are highbrow and always appreciated with rural audiences." Lydia pushed her plate of unfinished omelet away.

"Which one do you suggest?" Mary tucked loose strands behind an ear and leaned forward.

"As Bertha can attest, Helena's speech from Act four of 'All's Well that Ends Well' always engages an audience." Lydia sat back; her eyes hooded as if she was reliving her own recitations.

"Thank you." Helen wrote something down in her notebook.

Lydia also listed several outdated songs. Only Helen and Birdie responded but thankfully the others let them. They seemed to sense this was what Lydia needed. Birdie knew she could trust her friends.

Mr. James came downstairs into the lobby, looking around for someone. He glanced out the front windows and went towards Hugo, Gerald, and Teddy, not even noticing the women seated around the table.

"I'm afraid it's time for us to leave for the station." Helen must have also seen Mr. James.

Birdie rose first. "Thanks for your helpful suggestions. We'll continue this discussion on the train."

"Of course." Lydia edged her chair back and Birdie reached to help. Lydia jerked away. "I'm not an invalid, Bertha," she whispered.

Helen waited nearby. "We appreciate your expertise."

"And please tell Gerald thank you again for the delicious breakfast," Mary added. "It's the best we've had all summer." Flo also nodded towards Lydia.

"Thank you but we can't miss our train." Adelle gave a slight curtsy and started towards the hotel's door.

"I'll catch up with you in a bit," Birdie said as the others left the table. She turned back to Lydia, searching her sister's eyes.

"Now Bertha. Don't get that look." Lydia dusted a piece of lint off Birdie's shoulder and straightened her collar.

"You worry me. You're not yourself." Birdie reached for Lydia's hands.

"I'm a Stauffer woman, Bertha. We're expected to endure." Lydia squeezed Birdie's hands, holding on. "It just took seeing you." It looked like tears in the corner of Lydia's eyes, but Birdie couldn't be sure.

"Thank you again for your help with our act. We needed you."

Lydia pulled her hands away staring outside. "I doubt that and appreciate your indulgence, just the same," she added after several minutes.

They stood side by side in the lobby, looking out the windows. Birdie stole a glance and Lydia had her vacant stare again. It was as if she had used up all her energy.

"Perhaps you and Gerald should go to the shore for a few days." Birdie patted her shoulder. "You've always found solace by the ocean."

Lydia turned to Birdie. "I haven't forgotten our agreement."

Birdie swallowed. Of course, Lydia hadn't. Birdie couldn't be farther from wanting to settle down with a West Chester bachelor now. She'd have to recruit Helen's help to figure out what to do.

"Have you made progress with Hugo?"

This was more like the Lydia Birdie knew. She didn't know if she was relieved or annoyed. Heat radiated up Birdie's neck recalling Hugo's kiss in Picton and his smuggling hooch. She imagined those weren't what Lydia would call progress. "It's complicated."

"Only if you make it so." She nudged Birdie forward. "Don't miss your train."

Birdie gave Lydia a full hug. She breathed in her lilac powder and held on a minute longer. Despite Lydia's ways, Birdie loved her. "Goodbye for now." Birdie walked towards the door.

"You bobbed your hair," Lydia said.

Birdie turned back around. "I wondered when you'd say something." She tilted her chin up. "I look sophisticated, don't I?"

"Not to me."

Birdie shook her head and waved back at Lydia. That was a move Lydia had done since she was a child. Make a parting comment when there wasn't time for a retort. She'd have Flo trim her hair tonight. She didn't want to lose its shape.

CHAPTER 20

Carbondale, Pennsylvania

The girls huddled close in the empty compartment they found on the train ride to Carbondale. To Birdie's amusement, none of Lydia's suggestions were listed in Helen's open notebook she balanced on her lap. Adelle started to argue about a song Mary suggested, but Helen encouraged them to create a list of songs first and then discuss which would work later. Even Flo had joined in with ideas and comments. The other girls shared reassured glances with each other, including Adelle. After some time, they had about ten songs that had been culled, discussed, and agreed upon.

"Now, what about monologues?" Helen crossed her legs, pen poised to jot down more ideas.

"I don't perform monologues." Adelle leaned back on the bench. "Count me out of this go around."

"I think we should stick with Helen's version of 'A Matter of Husbands'," Mary suggested. "It's funny, appropriate and a crowd-pleaser."

"And you have it timed perfectly." Birdie nodded her head in agreement. "Are you bored with it?"

"A little." Helen put her elbows on her knees and held her head in both her hands. Birdie loved when she sat like that. It was as if Helen's brain was too heavy with brilliant ideas.

"What if I joined you?" Flo said in a low voice. "I practically have it memorized, from night after night of hearing you yammer on."

Mary touched her fingertips together, as if in a flighty prayer. Helen turned her head towards Flo. "You'd do that?"

"Ab-so-lute-ly." Flo straightened her shoulders. "I've read the play, it's not that long. We could adapt it, and each play a part."

"Who'd play the earnest young wife?" Birdie asked.

"Helen, of course." Flo started to chortle. "I'm the only one in this bunch that could pull off the famous actress." She raised an eyebrow as if to encourage Helen to challenge her.

"Let's do it, Flo." Helen scooted closer. "We can practice this afternoon."

"And let's stick with the switched order of songs. It certainly worked last night," Mary added.

"I wish we had something new, more than just a song." Helen tapped the pen against her lips.

"I guess I could add different birds to our medley." Birdie glanced at the girls. "I know several more."

"I can play the saw," Adelle said from the far corner of the compartment.

"You're an old sow?" Flo mocked.

It was a relief to hear one of Flo's quips, but maybe not one that mean. Adelle's lips formed a thin line. "I can play musical numbers on the saw. With a bow."

"Does it sound pretty?" Mary moved closer to Birdie.

"I've heard the saw played before. It's eerily beautiful if done right." Helen nodded. She put her hand on her chin. "Especially if you played a more classical number." She scanned the list of songs.

"Do you have a musical saw here?" Birdie asked.

"Yes, I just need a bow." Adelle looked at Mary.

"I have the sheet music for many of these classical pieces." Helen looked up from the list.

"Anything you play on the piano; I can play on the saw." Adelle folded her arms across her chest. "I'd just need time to practice. And a bow."

"I only have one bow, Adelle." Mary shrugged her shoulders.

"Let's see if we can buy one in Carbondale." Helen nodded to Adelle.

"Suits me." Adelle leaned back into her corner. "As long as I don't have to foot the bill."

Birdie looked from Mary to Adelle, wondering what was going on between them. She turned to Flo and patted her leg. "It's great you offered to join Helen's monologue."

"Something needed to be done to make our performances better." She hit her forehead with her palm. "Why don't we add a jazz number?"

"I doubt the Lyceum would approve." Helen shook her head. "They only want classical music popularized and popular music dignified."

"They need to get with the times if they want to stay in business." Flo stretched her legs out. "'The Charleston's a loadstone."

Birdie nodded. "It is sophisticated."

"Good luck selling it to Mr. James." Helen pretended she was playing the jazz piece using her lap as her piano.

Mary jumped up to do a little jig just as the train slowed down. She tripped onto Flo's lap then eased back onto the bench. "I'm not a natural like you, Flo."

"You've always been a lousy hoofer, Mary." Flo turned towards the window.

Birdie followed Flo's gaze as the countryside turned into homes and the buildings of a small town. She offered Mary an apologetic look.

*　　*　　*

The Carbondale audience seemed smaller but enthusiastic. Flo was almost like her old self, making sarcastic comments about people in the crowd. The girls kept up their challenge to change out of their band costumes quickly before they had to hear much of Walter's lecture. His voice continued to irritate them, most of all Helen. Mary was always the fastest but that was because she had other reasons driving her, primarily one named Teddy.

"Let's find dinner before we go to the boarding house." Helen put her folded band pants into the costume trunk. "We passed a diner on our way from the train station. Hopefully it's still open."

"Good idea." Birdie added her band costume to the stack.

Helen had purchased a bow, approved by Adelle, in town earlier that day.

Birdie and Helen stood by the muslin curtain, ready to go, waiting on Adelle and Flo to finish primping. Flo was applying face make-up, dabbing, and looking into the mirror and Adelle was doing whatever it was she did that took so much time. Mary was with Teddy off stage. She spent every free moment with him these days. It made Birdie wistful in an odd way. She purposely hadn't been alone with Hugo since that morning in Susquehanna, which seemed like another lifetime ago.

A man cleared his throat on the other side of the curtain.

"Ladies, may we enter?"

Birdie flinched but before she regained her composure, Helen opened the curtain and Mr. James stood in the opening with Hugo right behind him. The men stepped into the middle of the dressing tent. Mary scooted in on their heels. Flo closed her vanity case with a loud click. The girls moved into a tight semi-circle around the two men.

"We need to speak with Miss Armstrong alone." Mr. James's black fedora sat atop his salt and pepper hair complementing his dark three-piece suit. Shiny black shoes pointed out from under his creased trousers.

"Whatever you have to say to me, you can say in front of my friends." Flo lifted her head higher. The bruising was hidden under her make-up. She looked equally tall and formidable.

"Uh Flo, it'll be better if the others leave." Hugo nodded to her while jiggling his watch chain in his pants pocket. His brown suit was wrinkled, his blue bow tie askew, and he needed a haircut.

"No sir," Flo answered. She narrowed her eyes at Hugo and faced Mr. James with a flat full-lipped smile.

Mr. James cleared his throat again. "Very well. The Lyceum has received a formal complaint against you, Miss Armstrong. We have just cause to believe you consorted with a paying audience member on July twentieth. This is a flagrant disregard of the Lyceum contract you signed." He remained stoic. "Do you deny this accusation?"

Flo took in a sharp breath. Moving closer, Mary slipped an arm around Flo's waist. Helen hit her thighs with closed fists. Birdie covered her mouth with her hand trying to hide her anger. It was as if he had Hoovered the air from the small tent. Only the acrid fumes lingered. Everyone knew that was the night Flo had been attacked.

"Miss Armstrong?" Mr. James stepped towards Flo.

Helen blocked him before anyone else could react. She was in her protective stance, legs planted firmly on the ground.

"Pardon me, Mr. James. Are you aware of what also happened *to* Miss Armstrong, that evening?"

"This is not your concern, Miss Wilcox." Mr. James removed his hat. "I'm addressing Miss Armstrong."

"I believe it is." She raised her chin a bit, her eyes dark and charged. "Wouldn't you agree that everyone's safety while under the Lyceum's employment is your concern?"

"That is altogether a different matter." He turned the fedora around in his hands. "First, I require an answer from Miss Armstrong." He shifted his body so he could look right at Flo.

Birdie had been so caught up watching Helen that she hadn't noticed that Adelle now stood beside Hugo. Birdie inched closer to Flo and squeezed her hand. If they were taking sides, she knew where she stood.

"Yes, I had dinner with a paying audience member on July twentieth." Flo said in a low voice. She crumpled slightly and her lip quivered.

"If I'd known we should file a complaint every time a circuit employee dined with the audience, we'd have hundreds of reports." Birdie blurted.

"What are you implying, Miss Stauffer?" Mr. James turned towards her. Behind him Hugo looked like he was about to explode. He vigorously shook his head at Birdie.

"We've seen Mr. Schubert have dinner with paying townspeople on many occasions," Helen added. "I've witnessed Mr. Grantham dining with different audience members almost every night."

"That's irrelevant unless you have something to report about the other Versatile Quintet members. Mr. Schubert and Mr. Grantham are under different contracts than the female talent." He took a loud breath in through his pointed nose and stared at Helen and Birdie.

Birdie's bravado left her. Helen remained silent too.

"The Lyceum requires me to enforce the rules, ladies," Mr. James continued in his direct, nasal voice. "Therefore, we have no other choice than to relieve Miss Armstrong of her contractual agreement. You are to leave the circuit tonight."

Birdie, Mary, and Helen responded at the same time. Helen protested with a loud "No" Birdie gasped, and Mary whispered, "That's not fair."

Tears trickled down Flo's cheeks and she did nothing to stop them. Birdie handed her a handkerchief, which she used to wipe off her make-up, exposing her bruised face. Mr. James hesitated then turned as if he was leaving. Hugo had both hands in his pockets, staring at the ground. Helen clapped her hands to get everyone's attention. Even Mr. James eased back around.

"You haven't addressed the other matter, Mr. James." Helen seemed unusually calm.

"I have. That's why we have the Lyceum rules." He stared at Flo. "If you adhere to the rules we've thoughtfully laid out, you will remain safe and secure."

"Did you notice the dwindling crowd tonight, Mr. James?" Helen's voice softened but her eyes remained dark. What was Helen doing? Birdie had never seen Helen acquiesce so easily. "We've been noting the decline for weeks."

"That's not your problem either." He took a step towards the opening.

"Ah, but it is." Helen stood in line with him. "No Chautauqua circuit, no pay for the Versatile Quintet. If you give me a moment, I'd like to discuss an enterprising idea I have with you."

Mr. James tilted his head and eyed Helen as if she had just offered a bribe. "Walk with me."

Helen glanced back at Birdie and winked. She went alongside Mr. James, their voices resonating off the sides of the canvas.

Birdie glared at Hugo. "Do something."

He bumped into Adelle as he turned towards Birdie. Hugo nudged Adelle away. She went over to the mirror, adjusting her hat as she surveyed the room.

"My hands are tied. I'm on probation." He blinked his eyes, softening his face.

"Be a leader. You're our circuit manager and hold some sway." Birdie mimicked Helen and put her hands on her hips and stood wide. "Ask Mr. James to put Flo on probation too."

He leaned close to her and whispered, "Meet me back here in an hour, babe. I can explain." His gaze lingered when he looked down at her.

Birdie frowned and shook her head with a quick no. She walked over to Flo. "Flo is staying with us tonight."

"Of course." He turned and faced Flo. "I'm sorry. Teddy will give you your final pay envelope tomorrow morning." He strode towards the exit. "We'll miss you."

Adelle looked at Flo, Mary, and Birdie. Then she followed Hugo. Birdie thought she heard Adelle call after him.

"This is all just bullshit." Flo rubbed her eyes with her knuckles.

"What is with everyone tonight?" Birdie put her hands on top of her head and paced around the trunk. "Helen sidles up to Mr. James. Hugo becomes milquetoast, and Adelle runs away." She had to do something to keep Flo with the Versatile Quintet if no one else would. "If I didn't know better, I'd think we were back in Canada."

"Helen has something up her sleeve," Mary whispered to stop Birdie's pacing.

"She does?" Birdie cocked her head. "What about Adelle?"

Mary shrugged. "Who can explain Adelle?"

"Give Adelle some grace." Flo wiped her cheeks and handed Birdie her handkerchief. "I suspect she has her own problems."

Birdie scratched her forehead.

"She's a peculiar duck," Flo released long sigh. "We all have our pasts to deal with in our own ways."

"I'll ask Teddy what else we can do." Mary shrugged.

"It's no use. I appreciate your attempts, but I think my swan has sung." Flo gathered her vanity case, pocketbook, and a few other items she had stored in the costume trunk. "I guess I'll suffer the consequences of my actions."

"It's not fair." Birdie wasn't ready to give up.

"How about supper?" Flo bundled up her things. "I'm hungrier than a grown grizzly bear."

"Only if you promise we make 'Save Flo' plans during dinner," Birdie said.

"All right, you hoot." Flo added her feathered headband to her bundle.

Birdie pushed back the muslin curtain.

Mary leaned towards Birdie. "Did Hugo whisper something to you?"

"He mumbled something about meeting back here in an hour." Birdie huffed. "Fat chance of that happening."

Flo stood by the exit surveying the dressing room. Her eyes seemed to pause at each familiar piece from the mirror to the trunks, to the stained canvas walls. Then she gave a firm salute and turned away.

Mary, Flo, and Birdie ended up in the restaurant inside Hotel Chellino, the only place in Carbondale still open and serving food. Seated at a square table by a window looking out onto Main Street, they didn't have the privacy Birdie had hoped for. Several local men stopped by their table to comment on their show, but the girls turned them away politely. Flo ordered fried chicken, green beans, and whipped potatoes. Mary asked for a roast pork loin with Waldorf salad and Birdie couldn't decide, so ordered the house special. At first they remained agitated by Flo's unreasonable penalty but soon Flo had switched the conversation to her rankings of their past boarding houses. She had both Mary and Birdie chortling by the time the food arrived.

Birdie gazed out the window as she blew on a spoonful of the Irish stew. The streetlights created a welcoming glow. It struck Birdie how all the townspeople were going on with their lives, planning to attend the next day's Chautauqua events, but to the girls at her table, their lives were forever changed by one incident. Birdie swallowed the hot stew, scalding the back of her throat. Nothing in life was predictable except for the changes living it brought.

"Hello, Birdie?" Mary nervously giggled.

"Sorry. Lost in my thoughts."

"I'm relieved you're no longer in a panic over me leaving." Flo balanced a dollop of whipped potatoes on a spoon and waved it with a flourish. "The way I see it, now I'm free. The first thing I'm gonna do when I get back to Brooklyn is find the swankiest juice joint."

"It just won't be the same without you." Mary pushed her plate of half-eaten dinner away.

"Dessert. On me." Flo waved to the waiter just as Helen appeared in the front doorway. Birdie beckoned to her.

"You've got two more weeks." Helen nodded to Flo and pulled out the empty chair next to Birdie. "But we've got to come up with a highbrow routine that features all five of our musical talents." She rubbed her hands together as if she had a pair of dice between them.

"Whoo-hoo." Flo jumped up and did her shimmy.

The waiter eyed Flo as he cleared away their dirty plates.

"We'll take your fanciest dessert." Flo tapped the waiter's shoulder with her empty spoon. Helen held back the dishes with Birdie's sourdough bread and the remainder of Mary's dinner.

"Level with me, Helen." Flo scooted her chair closer.

"I knew Mr. James would respond to money over vinegar." Helen buttered Birdie's leftover bread. "I told him we've been working on a special, classical piece that will attract larger crowds." She pointed the crust at Flo. "I insisted that you were instrumental in writing the complicated arrangement and that we couldn't do it without you." She paused to wipe her mouth with Birdie's napkin then added, "He agreed you could stay on for two weeks, then he'd make his final decision."

"That's the nicest thing anyone's done for me." Flo clasped hands against her heart.

"Don't thank me just yet." Helen ate a bite of Mary's salad. Birdie had become accustomed to Helen's atrocious table manners, but tonight Helen ate their leftovers with renewed gusto.

"Your probation comes with conditions." Helen pointed her fork at Flo. "You have to be chaperoned every night and—" she crunched the walnuts loudly—"we have to come up with a showpiece that will knock their socks, shoes, and pants off." She covered a burp with her hand.

"That's duck soup." Flo leaned over the table to awkwardly hug Helen.

Birdie couldn't believe Helen's gumption, but how she had really managed to sway Mr. James remained curious. Obviously, Helen hadn't eaten in front of him. Birdie turned towards the window and noticed

Adelle standing outside, looking right at them. Adelle raised her hand as if to wave, but awkwardly tucked her hair under her cloche instead.

"Just a minute." Birdie stood, pushed through the crowd at the door and crossed the street. She felt the others watching her. "Hey."

Adelle looked down and scuffed her shoe at the curb.

Birdie had charged outside to get explanations from Adelle. Seeing how she cowered, and recalling how Flo defended Adelle earlier, Birdie stopped herself. Maybe tonight Adelle deserved some grace too.

"Join us." She motioned towards the restaurant window, which with the glowing restaurant lights, gave a clear view of the others sitting around the table. The waiter had just set down a golden dessert and was handing out spoons.

"I don't know," Adelle murmured.

"Helen's brought good news." Birdie nudged Adelle towards the restaurant's door.

Once inside, Flo brought Adelle up to date on what Helen had arranged with Mr. James. The waiter followed with a chair and an extra spoon.

"I don't think any of the pieces we've selected will work." Helen spooned a big bite of the pineapple upside-down cake topped with pineapple sherbet. "We need something extraordinary."

"What about 'Lucia di Lammermoor?'" Mary suggested.

"It's a has been." Flo tapped her empty spoon against her temple.

"The quartet piece from Verdi's 'Rigoletto' is complex yet beautiful," Helen said. "But it's also been played by every symphony." She put her elbow on the table, holding her chin.

"What about 'It Had to Be You?'" Flo scooped up the last bite of the pineapple sherbet. "We'd be the first group to perform it on any circuit."

"We can't." Helen let her arms drop. "As I mentioned earlier, we've got to impress the Lyceum with a classical piece, no matter how outdated their thinking is."

"It needs to be unique, difficult to play, and highbrow." Birdie mused. She tried to think of different operas or symphonies that she had been to with Gerald and Lydia over the years. There were some that had moved her, but she couldn't recall names under this pressure.

"The most complicated classical piece I've played on the banjo came from a Russian composer." Adelle scooted her chair closer to the table. "I don't think it has a specific name, but it's an interlude from 'A Tale of Tsar Sultan.'"

"Who's the composer?" Mary asked.

"Rimsky-Korsakov." Adelle straightened her unused spoon. She looked around the table, paused at Birdie and gave her a slight nod. "I doubt if any whistler has attempted it."

"Are you talking about the part that's referred to as the 'Flight of the Bumblebee?'" Helen sat up. "It's a bit frantic and played at a fast tempo."

"That's it," Adelle said. "I've played it on the banjo with multiple players building off of each other."

A weighted silence fell on the table.

"You may have just found our piece, Adelle." Helen slapped the table making spoons rattle. "We could start slow, perhaps with Flo on the harp."

"And then I'd blend in on the violin, with a slight tempo increase." Mary nodded in agreement.

"And I could pick up the pace on the piano, then Birdie could join in." Helen was getting visibly excited. "And then you could finish on your banjo."

"I think Birdie should be the finale." Adelle raised her eyes. "If she can whistle at the fastest tempo of all of us, it would be something that's never been done."

All eyes centered on Birdie. She had no idea if she could whistle this music, but she wasn't about to disappoint her friends. Their camaraderie demolished her fears. "Of course, I'll give it a try."

"We'll have to purchase the sheet music." Helen tipped back in her chair. "Then I'll write an arrangement just for us."

Flo stood. The corners of her mouth twitched and she blinked several times. "I don't know how to thank you dames."

"I'd say this is just the Bumblebee's knees," Birdie said.

"Did our little bunny just say something modern?" Flo broke into giggles. "I'd call it the Bumblebee's lips."

Her high-pitched laughter spread so each of the girls joined in. Flo started naming other bee's body parts and soon they were all doubled over with laughter. The girls couldn't help but revel in Flo's release.

As they walked down Main Street and crossed the bridge over the river towards their boarding house, Birdie could see the peak of the main tent off in the distance. The canvas top appeared pink, reflecting the almost full moon. She wondered if Hugo sat in the dressing room waiting for her. She hoped so.

CHAPTER 21

Newton, New Jersey

"This is how you hold it." Adelle sat on a bench at the Carbondale train station with her skirt tucked around her thighs and the handle of a big wood saw squeezed between them. With her left hand she bent back the tip of the metal, the sharp teeth facing her and forming an "S" shape. She shook her foot a bit and then drew the bow across the smooth edge of the saw. An eerie silky sound came out.

The others watched, standing in front of her with their suitcases and instruments at their feet. Passersby gawked.

"Play a song." Helen bowed towards Adelle. "Something we know."

Adelle nodded and repositioned the handle of the saw. She bent it back then played the opening stanzas of "Auld Lang Syne."

Mary clapped her hands. "That's amazing. Can I try?"

Adelle moved over and showed Mary how to brace the saw handle between her legs. Then she stood up and helped bend the metal. "It's important to jiggle your legs." Mary placed the bow and pulled back. A long screech filled the platform.

Flo held her hands over her ears. "Make it stop."

"It's harder than it looks." Mary handed the saw back to Adelle.

"Anyone else dare to try?" Adelle looked from Helen to Birdie.

"I will." Birdie changed places with Mary. Helen looked down the track and back.

"Why'd you keep this hidden until now?" Flo asked.

"It's been in my suitcase all along." Adelle handed Birdie the saw.

Birdie had tucked her dress under each leg. She squeezed the handle between her thighs and picked up the bow in her right hand then paused. "Since I'm left-handed. Should I switch it?"

"If you want." Adelle held the bow while Birdie repositioned the saw.

She bent the saw back, wiggled her foot, placed the bow across the metal edge with her left hand. Flo covered her ears. Birdie pulled the bow backwards and a clear yet strange sound similar to what Adelle had played surrounded her. Adelle threw up her arms and Mary clapped.

Just then Mr. James and Hugo appeared further down the platform. Birdie pushed the saw towards Adelle, hastily straightening her dress. When the men arrived, Hugo stood off to the side, his face looked rough as if he'd been working outdoors too long.

"What's this?" Mr. James asked.

"Miss Rowley is a virtuoso on the musical saw." Helen nodded towards Adelle. "We're considering adding it to our act."

"Let's hear it." Hugo folded his arms across his chest.

"Not here, ladies." Mr. James looked around at the people gathering for the incoming train. "But I am intrigued. We had a gentleman duet act that played the saw on another circuit last year." He nodded to Adelle. "I'd like to hear you play once we're settled in Newton."

"Yes, sir." Adelle slipped the saw into a leather case and snapped the straps through the handle. She tucked it under her arm along with the bow.

The train entered the station with its whistle blaring. Steam clouds rolled around the engine when it came to a stop. Hugo followed a few steps behind Mr. James back to the first-class car. He looked like a trained mongrel with his rumpled suit and hunched shoulders. Birdie almost pitied him.

Once aboard Helen had Adelle sort through her sheet music. Together they chose an arrangement of Chopin's "Nocturne."

"Where did you learn to play the saw?" Birdie leaned across Helen to ask Adelle.

"At home. We use all sorts of things for instruments in West Virginia." Adelle pointed to the pages. "But we rarely played classical music. I learned that on my own."

"Playing the musical saw has become more popular." Helen put her sheet music away. "But it's usually men." She added, "I believe there are now saws made specifically for playing music."

"It's a thinner metal, so it's easier to play a wider range of notes." Adelle nodded. "No sharp teeth but expensive."

Birdie looked from Adelle to Helen. "It's haunting."

"You should try playing it again." Helen tapped her foot against the empty seat in front of her.

"I'd have to teach you." Adelle crossed her arms and lowered her chin to her sleeping-on-the-train position.

"We'll see." Birdie turned to the window. Each had developed their own train ride routine. Adelle sat in a bench's corner or in her own row reading a newspaper until she fell asleep. Mary sat with her hands clasped in her lap and could snooze wherever she landed. Flo sprawled out, she seemed to take up the most room of any bench or seat she shared. Helen alternated coaching one of them or sleeping with her head back, mouth open. Birdie preferred sitting by the window, watching the landscape glide by. She would invent stories about the people in the homes or farms that passed by, as she had done with Edwin as a child.

"We need to find a music store as soon as we get to Newton." Helen laid her head back. "Mr. James wants to know what piece Flo and I are working on." She ran her finger along one wing of her swallow brooch as if thinking of something or someone else. "You and Flo have gotten close."

"We have. She's surprised me." Birdie lowered her voice. "She's much smarter and caring than she lets on."

"If I didn't know better, I'd fear you prefer her company over mine." Helen's tone was carefree, but her eyes dark.

"Oh, you don't get off that easy." Birdie patted Helen's hand. "You're stuck as my best friend."

Helen hesitated; Birdie searched her face. The gold flecks in Helen's eyes flashed and then just as quickly disappeared. Helen turned back towards Flo and Birdie followed her gaze. Flo had her head against the window, her legs stretched across Mary's lap.

"That's good enough for today." Helen spoke in her quiet voice squeezing Birdie's hand, as if she was comforting a small child.

Birdie fought the urge to shake Helen and ask her to be more direct. At times Helen treated her like an equal and other times it was as if Helen was her big sister. Sometimes Birdie felt so close to Helen they practically shared the same thoughts and then Helen would say something that seemed mysterious. Birdie turned and took solace by gazing out the window.

*　*　*

Once in Newton, New Jersey, Helen turned into their familiar assertive leader. She gave Birdie the address to their accommodations and told her to take Adelle and all the suitcases there. Then she sent Mary to borrow a saw from Teddy and grabbed Flo to hunt for a store that sold sheet music. Mr. James had said that Flo required a chaperone and Helen decided today it would be her. Helen then instructed everyone to return to the tents by two o'clock, holding up two fingers for added emphasis.

Birdie tucked her own suitcase under one arm and picked up Helen's and Mary's. Adelle kept reorganizing her own suitcase and Flo's, picking one up and setting another down. By the time Adelle was ready, Helen and Flo were lost in the crowd of people leaving the station. Birdie glanced at the now crumpled paper with Helen's loopy handwriting that said Cochran House at Spring and Main. She figured finding Main Street couldn't be that difficult.

"Helen's always barking out orders," Adelle said to Birdie's back.

"She's a natural leader." Birdie waited for Adelle to catch up.

Adelle shrugged. "She doesn't have to be so bossy."

"True." Birdie slowed her pace.

"I'm surprised you're not defending Helen. You two are as close as a tick to a mutt."

Adelle's way of defining their relationship made Birdie shake her head. There was no doubt who Adelle would call the tick. When they reached Main Street Birdie turned right. Adelle set Flo's heavy suitcase down and flexed her hand. Birdie waited.

"Do you really think I can learn to play the musical saw?" Birdie started walking again.

"Oh, you master whatever you put your mind to." Adelle took a few more steps and then stopped, setting both suitcases down with a big sigh.

"Here, let me switch with you." Birdie handed Adelle one of the suitcases she had and lifted Flo's. "Goodness, does Flo travel with bricks?"

Adelle snickered. She matched Birdie's pace as they crossed another block. "You thought I was faking it."

"What song is easiest?" Birdie paused and looked at the buildings they had passed. They should be at the boarding house by now.

"'Down By the Old Mill Stream'."

It had been their signature closing piece when Birdie and Lydia performed at the women's auxiliary luncheons. "I'd rather play something more modern."

"Do you know where you're going?" Adelle turned and looked behind them.

"Helen said it's at the corner of Main and Spring." Birdie looked up at the street sign. "We're on Main Street."

Adelle plopped both suitcases down. Birdie released her three suitcases, rubbing her shoulder and wrist. They both looked up and down the block.

"What's the name of the boarding house?" Adelle shook her hand, requesting the piece of paper.

"Cochran House." Birdie searched for someone to ask directions. The only people she saw were three girls sitting on the stoop of a wide front porch, playing with their dolls. "I have no idea which direction."

"You could say that again." Adelle squatted on Flo's suitcase and put her head in her hands. "At least now I know something you're no good at," she mumbled as she crumpled the paper into a tight ball.

Birdie strolled towards the girls, who stopped their chattering and stared at her. "Hello. We're part of the Versatile Quintet, with Chautauqua. Could you direct us to the Cochran Boarding House?"

"You should ask for their mother," Adelle said in a low voice.

"Everyone knows the Cochran House *Hotel*." The taller girl came down the steps. "It's about ten blocks back, towards downtown." She pointed in the direction they had come.

"Are you certain there's not a boarding house also named Cochran House?" Birdie liked how the girl had fashioned her hair. Up close, she seemed older.

"Yes, ma'am. It's a hotel." She gawked at Birdie. "We've had our Chautauqua season tickets for months. It's the best thing that happens here all year."

Birdie nodded. "It is something special, isn't it?" She had been close to this girl's age when she saw her first Chautauqua performance at Mount Gretna. "What's your favorite part?"

"Birdie, we don't have time to lollygag." Adelle stood up.

"The theatre." The girl moved onto the sidewalk. "I'd be honored to walk you to the hotel." She looked back at the two younger girls who stood huddled on the porch. "Go inside and tell mama I'm helping these Chautauqua ladies."

"Thank you. I'm afraid we must be a bit lost." Birdie bent to pick up two suitcases.

"It's my pleasure." The girl reached for Flo's suitcase. "I can carry this one." She grimaced then carried it with both hands.

Birdie and the young girl chatted on their way back along Main Street. Her many questions about the travel and performing revived Birdie.

Adelle followed behind them several paces. Every now and then she moaned or complained that they walked too fast. Spring Street was two blocks past where they had turned right from the train station. The young girl pointed to a large quaint building, white with green striped awnings. The placard read Cochran House.

"We really appreciate your help." Birdie reached for Flo's suitcase.

"I can't wait to tell my girlfriends I met you." She clasped her hands.

"Come backstage after tonight's performance and I'll introduce you to the entire Versatile Quintet." Birdie winked.

The young girl walked backwards and then started running towards her home.

"Jeez." Adelle shook her head. "You are the sappiest person I know." She marched into the hotel and went up to the front desk.

* * *

When Birdie arrived inside the main tent at two o'clock, Helen sat at the piano with a pencil behind her ear, picking out notes and scribbling on sheet music. Squatting at the edge of the stage, Mary rubbed steel wool against a rusty, well-used saw. Flo lounged in the first row, filing her fingernails into rounded ovals.

"The Cochran House is a divine *hotel*." Adelle rushed in, stirring up pieces of straw with her heeled boots. "Modern, clean, and big beds." She placed her saw case on a chair by Flo. "And Miss Perfect Pitch has her own fan club."

"Nonsense, Adelle." Birdie dumped her satchel on the edge of the stage. "Just a local girl who loves Chautauqua."

"This is the best saw you could coax from Teddy?" Adelle held it away with her fingertips as if it were a dead mouse.

Mary handed the steel wool to Adelle. "He said this would make it like new."

Adelle pushed the saw towards Birdie. "Your first lesson is to clean this."

"I never should have volunteered." Birdie took the saw by the handle, holding the rusted blade upright.

"I didn't say it would be easy." Adelle dangled the steel wool in front of Birdie.

Birdie took it with a wry face and a can-do attitude. Maybe she had broken through with Adelle. She spent the next hour taking turns with Mary rubbing the rust off the saw. Adelle went to the edge of the stage to practice the Chopin piece. Flo took a short nap across the first-row chairs while Helen went back and forth between making notes on the new sheet music and offering unsolicited advice to Adelle.

Mr. James and Hugo stopped at the back of the tent, deep in conversation. Their voices disrupted the girls' afternoon camaraderie. Helen frantically waved, urging Flo to the piano. Birdie had to wake Flo, who jumped up, dropped her nail file, and leapt onto the platform.

Mr. James faced them, his body erect. The only thing that moved was a slight twitch of his mustache. Hugo turned away abruptly and left. Mr. James walked towards the platform; his eyes straight ahead but not focused on the girls. Flo sat next to Helen, playing random notes on the piano.

"Ladies." Mr. James nodded towards the group. "I believe one of you offered to play the musical saw for me."

Adelle had moved to the same front row chairs that Flo had just vacated. She positioned the saw between her legs, hiding the handle into the folds of her skirt with one graceful movement. Bending back the metal, she held the bow poised and looked up until she had Mr. James's attention. "Adelle Rowley playing Chopin's 'Nocturne.'"

When she started playing, the strains of Chopin's familiar piece filled the tent. Adelle pulled the bow, swaying, and the tent seemed to absorb and then echo the music. Birdie had heard this piece played by concert pianists, local orchestras, and on the gramophone, but it had never sounded like this. Watching Adelle was as mesmerizing as the music itself; she seemed to become the haunting notes with fluid movements of her legs, arms, and body. When she finished, she rested the saw across her knees and lifted her eyes to Mr. James.

All the other girls looked from Adelle to Mr. James, too. His face showed little expression. "Add it to the show tonight." He turned to Helen. "Are you ready to name your showstopper piece, Miss Wilcox?"

Helen blinked. Birdie could tell that Adelle's performance had moved her. Flo coughed behind her hand. Helen seemed lost and still didn't answer. Mr. James cleared his throat. Flo reached over Helen and picked up the sheet music. She strode over to stand in front of Mr. James, towering over him.

"We're still working out some kinks, but what we're arranging is from Nikolai Rimsky-Korsakov's famous opera, 'A Tale of Tsar Sultan'. It's commonly referred to as the 'Flight of the Bumblebee.'" Flo offered him the sheet music.

Mr. James's eyes looked up from Flo's shoes to the sheet music in her hands. Then his gazed turned to Helen, who had become alert when Flo announced the song. "And when will you be ready to audition this piece for me?"

"I'm not certain." Helen's voice sounded weak.

"I need an exact date."

Helen paused. "In one week then."

Birdie took in a quick breath. She had no idea how they'd manage that.

"Excellent." Mr. James nodded again to each of the girls. He walked down the same aisle from which he had arrived and disappeared.

No one said a word for several minutes, each waiting to hear him slam a screen door or something else to indicate he was gone. Birdie moved first. She leaned over Adelle to give her shoulders an awkward hug. Mary and Flo followed. They circled in front of Adelle, Mary with her hands clasped and Flo, still clutching the sheet music. Helen came off the platform and stood behind them.

"You were beyond fabulous." Mary clapped.

"The music encompassed you," Birdie said.

"The gnat's whistle if I ever heard one." Flo set the sheet music aside. "And you left old Sourpuss James speechless."

"He should have at least complimented your excellent performance." Mary eased next to Adelle.

Helen hadn't added comments. "And you, Flo," Birdie did a little sashay, but not with Flo's natural shimmy. "You were equally impressive."

"I showed him I knew my onions about arranging music." Flo looked over at Helen. The other girls followed her gaze.

"You both did great," Helen said flatly. "But we have a lot of work to do now that you told him the name of the piece."

"I didn't know what else to do." Flo picked up the pages, extending them towards Helen.

"And Flo's not the one who promised we'd have it ready in one week, either." Adelle slipped her saw and bow into its case. "I'm hungry. Anyone care to join me?"

Flo and Mary followed Adelle full of excited chatter. Helen went back to the piano and reshuffled the sheet music. She peered at the pages and rapped her pencil on the edge of the keys. Birdie slipped behind Helen, spellbound by the flurry of notes that covered the pages of music. They flew up and down each stanza, just like the haphazard flight of a bumblebee.

"That looks overwhelming." Birdie tapped the music. "It's going to be challenging to whistle that and breathe."

"The notes flow in succession." Helen put the pencil back behind her ear. "Listen." She played from the first two pages. Even at a normal pace it had a frantic intensity. Birdie could imagine how layering in the different instruments would make it more remarkable.

"Maybe I should start it on the trombone." Birdie sat down next to Helen. "Instead of whistling."

"Oh no. You don't get off that easy." Helen echoed Birdie's words from last night. "You can whistle this."

"I'm glad you think so." Birdie patted Helen's arm and saw that Helen still wore the green glass bracelet. It gave her confidence to question Helen. "What happened to you when Adelle played the musical saw?"

"I will keep the pace moving on the piano throughout the piece." Helen made another notation on a page. "That means I'll start it and then we can add the others." She focused on the music, but Birdie could see her eyes darting past the piano to the front row and then at the keys. She reached for Helen's wrist, resting her thumb on the bracelet.

"Helen."

Helen slowly turned towards Birdie. Helen's eyes were as green as the deepest part of the bay in Picton. "The way Adelle played that song reminded me of someone."

"Miss Briarwood?"

Helen nodded.

"Was she like a mother to you?"

"No, Pollyanna." Helen pulled her hand away and stacked the pages on the piano's music stand several times.

"I don't understand." Something tugged at the outer edges of Birdie's mind, but it was as if the idea kept slipping away. She wished Helen would just say what she meant.

"Never mind." Helen's eyes refocused on the music. "I've got to get this arranged and copied, so everyone can start practicing tomorrow."

"I wish you would be frank with me." Birdie pushed away from the piano. "I'm not a child."

"Sometimes you are." Helen played a few notes that mimicked their Northern Cardinal song. "But that's one of the things I like about you."

Birdie slid around on the bench so her back was to the piano. "I've shared everything with you."

"Have you?" Helen cocked her head. "Seems to me you've got some thoughts about Hugo that haven't been so forthcoming."

"I don't even know what I think about Hugo, so how could I share anything?" Birdie stood up; she had never told Helen about Hugo's smuggling in the duplicate instrument cases. Now certainly wasn't the time, especially since Helen must already know since she was so insightful. "Besides, this isn't about Hugo." Birdie stared at the stained canvas walls. She could hear Teddy or one of the other Anvil Choir boys moving things about.

"Can we continue this later?" Helen tapped the sheet music with her pencil. "I've got so much to do."

"Fine."

"Would you mind bringing me an apple so I can keep working?" Helen looked over her shoulder at Birdie.

"Sure." Birdie stood on the platform for a minute longer. Adelle wasn't the only hard nut in this group.

CHAPTER 22

Newton, New Jersey

The Newton audience was mesmerized by Adelle's musical saw rendition as much as the girls had been earlier that afternoon. The Versatile Quintet's entire performance reached the level they had achieved before the attack on Flo. The excitement around the potential show-stopper piece and adding Adelle's musical saw act revived more than what they did onstage, their camaraderie became complete. All five planned to meet for a late supper at the Cochran House Hotel's restaurant to talk through Helen's new arrangement. Adelle and Mary offered to go ahead to secure a table while Birdie waited on Helen to make last minute additions to the sheet music and for Flo to finish dressing.

Hugo's voice filled the dressing room with his rote introduction of Walter. When Walter stuttered during his opening lines of his lecture, Birdie glanced at Helen. She half-worried that Helen might do something to Walter one of these nights when they least expected. Helen stood over the trunk with a pencil poised in her hand. She didn't appear to have noticed, she tapped her foot to inner music, with a faraway look.

Walter stuttered again. Flo shrugged towards Birdie as she picked up her vanity case. Circling the dressing room, Birdie checked for misplaced costumes pieces and removed a feathered headpiece from the top of the mirror. Walter hiccupped several times. Helen picked up her music and Birdie slipped the headband into the trunk, closing it slowly.

The three had just walked through the muslin curtain when Walter stopped talking mid-sentence. Easing into the canvas walkway between the two tents, they could see Walter leaning on the podium, holding his head. Teddy pushed past the girls to the stage. Birdie gripped Helen's hand as Hugo and then Mr. James ran towards the podium. Teddy caught Walter just as he collapsed and with Hugo's help, lowered him to the stage floor. Flo paled almost to iridescent. None of the girls moved. Rustling and unsettled murmurs rose from the audience. Mr. James leaned into the microphone to ask for a doctor.

Soon there were several men on the platform surrounding Walter, who had been laid flat, only his protruding belly visible. Mr. James pulled Hugo aside, after which Hugo stood at the podium, offered an apology then announced that Chautauqua was finished for the evening in a calm voice. He used his forced show voice to thank the audience and invited them back for the next night's show. At first most of the audience stood to watch the mayhem surrounding the podium but Teddy and several of the Anvil Choir boys ushered people out.

Helen pulled Flo away and they went outside, but Birdie remained, her eyes fixed on the platform stage. As several men moved Walter onto a stretcher, Hugo glanced around and then left through a side flap. A breeze grazed the back of Birdie's neck, giving her shivers. Helen called for Birdie to follow them. Her legs moved forward but she kept looking back. She couldn't make out Walter for all the men crowded around.

Townspeople streamed by the three girls huddled together outside. Birdie caught bits of concerned conversations. Flo wrapped her fingers around Birdie's arm, as tight as she had the day after the attack. Helen stood a little apart, scanning the crowd as if looking for someone. No one spoke. Flo kept her chin bowed; color slowly returning to her cheeks. Once most of the audience had departed, Helen herded them forward.

"Where are we going?" Birdie resisted.

"To the restaurant." Helen went ahead. "Adelle and Mary are waiting."

"But what about Walter?"

"There's nothing we can do," Helen said over her shoulder.

Birdie clasped a hand over Flo's and together they followed Helen. Once at the Cochran House restaurant, they spotted Adelle and Mary seated at a table in the back. The room resembled a log cabin with heavy wood beams and low hanging lights. Much of the Chautauqua audience had ended up there as well. The place was dark, loud, and busy. People gawked as Helen led them single file through the restaurant.

"Is that poor man all right?" A woman asked.

A man grabbed Flo's arm as she passed his table. "Will we get a refund?"

Flo jerked away, backing into Birdie, her eyes frantic.

"I paid for a lecture and all I got was a variety show." Another man commented to his table, loud enough so everyone could hear.

Helen stopped. Her eyes rotated to each group who were now staring at the three of them stuck between the tables. "You'll have to take your complaints to the Chautauqua circuit managers." She reached for Flo's hand, pulling her towards their table. "We're just the female talent."

"Goodness sakes." Mary stood up. "What happened?" She patted the seat next to her for Flo.

"Walter fainted, well, collapsed as he started his lecture." Helen eased into a bench, scooting over to make room for Birdie.

Mary covered her mouth with both hands, slowly sitting back down.

"That explains the hostile crowd." Adelle shook her head.

Helen filled in what little else they knew about Walter's episode. The waiter dropped off their menus then darted away.

"Did Teddy go with Walter when they carried him out?" Mary asked.

"I don't know." Helen checked with Birdie, who shrugged.

"What about Hugo, did he take charge?" Adelle leaned forward on her elbows.

"Only after Mr. James gave him instructions." Helen snorted.

Should she tell the girls that she saw Hugo slip away? Birdie questioned exactly what she saw, so remained quiet.

"Is Walter going to live?" Mary blurted.

Helen sighed as she picked up a menu.

"He got what he deserved," Adelle huffed, glancing at Flo, who appeared green in the limited light.

Birdie wished she could order a lager. That warm numbness was just what she needed tonight. If she said it aloud, maybe she could lighten the mood. She glanced around the table, Helen looked beyond her menu, her eyes dark. Flo stared at her lap, and Mary watched the door. Only Adelle seemed to be reading the menu. Now wasn't the time for sappy humor. She settled on chamomile tea and creamed mushroom, the soup-of-the-day.

After everyone had ordered Helen tried to share her ideas about the "Flight of the Bumblebee" arrangement. She soon gave up—no one could think about music. The noise level came and went in waves, making conversation challenging. People kept stopping by their table asking questions. Helen tried to answer each with firm patience. Mary left to find Teddy before finishing her roast chicken dinner. Flo and Birdie each sipped their soup in silence. Adelle ate a full serving of shepherd's pie and ordered a slice of German Chocolate cake for dessert.

"Birdie, can we go up to our room now?" Flo's natural color hadn't returned.

Birdie wanted to stay with Helen, but someone had to stay with Flo. Most often that was her.

"Go on." Helen squeezed Birdie's hand. "We'll stop by the tents after Adelle finishes and bring back news."

"Let's skedaddle, Flo." Birdie's voice sounded as forced as she felt.

They walked into the lobby in silence. Birdie glanced around for Mary or Teddy. Maybe creamed mushroom soup hadn't been the best choice. Queasiness rode up the elevator with her to their fourth-floor hotel room.

"I need a bath." Flo lifted one of the white towels from the top of the dresser. "I shouldn't have insisted we both leave the restaurant so soon."

"It's all right." Birdie removed her hat. "I was more than ready."

"Do you think Walter will live?"

Birdie brushed her fingertips along the quilted floral bedspread. "Maybe Mary or Helen will come soon with some news."

Flo hesitated at the door. "I'd be lying if I said I liked him."

"I agree." Birdie caught Flo's gaze.

"You don't know the half of it." Flo closed the door and sank back onto a bed.

"What?" Birdie eased beside her.

"I really balled up this time." Flo crumpled forward, holding her head in both hands.

The insides of Birdie's cheeks felt dry and tasted sour.

"It wasn't him," Flo said in a low voice.

"Who?"

"Now Walter might die. And it's my fault everyone thinks it was him."

Birdie ran her fingers under her chin, gripping her own neck. "Who was it, Flo?"

"Does it matter? It just wasn't Walter."

Birdie swallowed bile. Hugo had been missing that night too. He and Walter had questionable history. Maybe he wanted Walter to take the blame.

"Was it Hugo?" It came out scratchy.

Flo sat still for what felt like several minutes. Then she rolled to her side, facing away.

"No."

Birdie let out the breath she had been holding.

"Hugo's a fried nudnik but he'd never do that."

"I shouldn't have asked." Birdie pulled her knees to her chest and held them with her arms, resting her chin. "Please tell me."

Several more moments passed then Flo started in a hushed voice, almost a whisper. "His name was Richard." She released a moaning sigh. "My university fella left me at the bar, zozzled—Canadian whisky packs a fistful." Flo looked sideways at Birdie. "Richard bought me more booze, then offered to walk me home. I couldn't find the stupid Red Maple Leaf, so ended up at the tents."

She wiped her face and sat up. "He didn't even look at me when he—" Flo's eyes lost their focus. "I tried to fight back but he must have been a boxer." She moved the small rug beside the bed with her foot. "He laughed when I said I'd report him to my circuit manager." She swallowed. "He said 'No one believes a floozy.'"

"Oh, Flo." Birdie rocked back and forth, balancing herself on the edge of the bed.

"When Helen was so set on blaming Walter, I just let her." Flo gestured with her hands wide. "But then tonight when Walter, you know." She dropped her head. "What if I caused him to die?"

"We don't know that yet."

"All of this is my fault." Flo held her face in her hands, sobbing.

Birdie held her hands tight around her legs to prevent herself from shaking Flo. Helen's hatred had been fueled by Flo's silence. Flo had led them all along.

"You despise me, don't you?" Flo leaned away from Birdie.

Birdie saw Flo heaped on the dirt and straw in Picton. Flo didn't deserve any of this.

"I don't, and—" Birdie released her grip. "You need to make this right." She put an arm around Flo's shoulder and whispered towards her ear, "especially with Helen."

"I will." Flo stood. "Tonight." She gathered her bath things and stood facing the door. "I don't deserve your kindness." She opened the door and left for the lavatory.

Birdie slowly changed into her nightshirt. After several minutes there was a light knock on the door. Had Flo forgotten something? Birdie absently opened the room door and Helen stood in the doorway with her hands at her sides, her hair mussed.

"Helen." Birdie embraced her tightly, breathing her in.

"Where's Flo?" Helen sank into the wingback chair positioned by the closet.

"Taking a bath."

"Walter's hospitalized, doctors suspect a stroke."

Birdie gasped. Helen reached for Birdie's hand, running her thumbs along Birdie's fingers.

Birdie gripped both her hands. She needed Helen. Something shifted as if a familiar yearning had become clear to her. Birdie bit her lower lip and looked right into Helen's calm green eyes.

Flo walked into the room with her hair wrapped up in a towel, dressed in her pajamas. Helen pulled her hands away into her own lap.

"What did you find out?" Flo clutched her things to her chest.

Helen told Flo what they suspected had happened to Walter. Birdie rested her palm on Helen's arm giving comfort and keeping their connection.

"I have to tell you something." Flo motioned and the three of them moved to the bed, sitting like sparrows on a wire.

Helen's body deflated as Flo shared a shortened version of what she had told Birdie about her attacker.

"Not Walter."

"No," Flo said. "I'm so sorry Helen. I'm worse than a cad." She pushed the towel off her head. "I took the easy way out and let you, along with everyone else, blame Walter."

Helen clung to the edge of the bed with both hands. "I didn't give you much of a chance to argue."

"There were many times I started to say something but chickened out." Flo stood up. "Neither of you need my kind of friendship." She began stuffing things into her suitcase.

"Stop," Birdie said. "You didn't choose to be attacked."

"Birdie's right." Helen leaned back on her elbows. Her skin glowed in the lamplight. "I imagine any of us might have done the same."

"I doubt that." Flo quietly closed the clasps on her suitcase. "Could I switch rooms with you, Helen?" She faced them, her high cheekbones pale, her damp hair unruly. "I'd like to be alone tonight."

"Are you sure?" Birdie asked, even though being with Helen was exactly what she wanted.

"Pos-i-tive-ly."

"Don't overthink this." Helen hugged Flo and then held her at arm's length. "As far as I'm concerned, I'm as much at fault as you."

"Is your middle name Grace?"

Helen half-laughed. "Now you're getting carried away."

"Are you certain being alone is best right now?" Birdie cocked her head, her eyes questioning. What Flo had shared was unforgettable.

"I have a lot to sort out." Flo embraced Birdie and whispered, "Thank you."

Flo left and Birdie pulled the door closed. She reached for Helen's clasped hands and stroked them both.

"You were more than kind."

"Are you implying that's not my usual way?" Helen's dimple tugged at her tired smile.

"I'm saying I'm relieved it's just us tonight." Birdie's voice went up an octave as her hand slid up Helen's arm.

Helen slowly faced Birdie. She turned Birdie's palm up, circling her fingertip from the pad over her wrist, towards the soft part of her inner elbow. Birdie couldn't shake the goosebumps Helen's touch created.

"What are you really saying?" Helen searched Birdie's face. "I don't want there to be any misunderstanding."

Birdie pulled Helen's hands, cupping them at her heart. Everything felt right.

"I need you." Birdie stepped closer so their noses almost touched. She looked at Helen's full lips. "I know this may be absurd timing, but I think I want *you*, Helen."

Birdie held her intense gaze, the desire between them almost visible. Helen tilted her head down towards Birdie, their foreheads touching. Birdie ached for Helen to kiss her. She wanted to know how Helen tasted. Were her lips soft or coarse? She closed her eyes and pursed her mouth, waiting.

Helen lightly stroked the back of Birdie's neck, causing the yearning to increase. "You take the lead, Birdie."

Birdie had little experience kissing anyone, man or woman. Her nerves threatened to overtake her desires. She wasn't going to lose what she felt towards Helen right now. She had done that too many times in the past. She let the "Don't Quit" poem push her forward, the irony that the words may not have been embroidered for this instance giving her added courage.

Opening her eyes, and her lips, Birdie kissed Helen lightly. Then kissed her again while she reached up to run her fingers through Helen's soft Marcel waves. Her heart pounded. Helen kissed her back with a slow encompassing embrace. Her Emeraude scent filled Birdie with a hunger that she still didn't completely understand.

"I, I don't know what to do next." Birdie pulled slightly back.

"Are you sure you want to continue?"

Birdie nodded.

Helen led her beside the bed and began to undress. Birdie had seen Helen remove her dress countless times, but this time was different. Birdie's eyes darted all over the room with occasional glances at Helen.

The floral upholstered chair made her recall sitting outside on the sunlit bench, right after they had first met. The curve below Helen's throat made a perfect crescent. Glancing at the braided rug on the floor, she thought of their tickle fit and how it felt to have Helen wiggle under her. A line of freckles zig-zagged down Helen's shoulders making Birdie want to follow them with her fingers. Looking in the mirror she remembered when Helen had called her Leatrice Joy. Birdie realized she had desired Helen from the start.

"Dollar for your thoughts?" Helen had climbed between the sheets and was propped against the plush pillows piled against the headboard. She patted the mattress beside her causing the silk strap of her slip to fall off one shoulder.

"Are you? Are we?" Birdie looked at Helen. "Lydia says it's a sin," she blurted feeling like an ignorant Pollyanna sap. She sank to the bed, hiding her face behind her hands.

"Oh, Birdie." Helen moved closer, rubbing circles around on her back. "Lydia is wrong." She tucked a bit of hair behind Birdie's ear and rested her finger on Birdie's cheek.

Helen tapped at her heart. "What I feel can't be a sin."

"But—"

"I'm not going to force this." Helen slowly exhaled. "It has to be your choice." She leaned back against the pillows, giving Birdie some space.

"How long have you known?" Birdie couldn't bring herself to say the words directly.

"Since I was old enough to know." Helen put her arms behind her head.

Birdie sat crisscross in the middle of the bed, her knee touching Helen's outstretched leg through the covers. "When I was around thirteen, my best friend, Rose often came home from school with me. One day some cute boy had flirted with her, so she asked if I knew how to kiss. I had no idea." Birdie wiped her hands flat on the sheets.

"We decided to practice. We sat on the porch swing and kissed. Twice." Birdie fidgeted, making the bed rattle. "It felt better than when I imagined kissing a boy." Birdie glanced at Helen, who was staring at the ceiling, her eyes darkening.

"Lydia sent Rose home and promptly washed my mouth out with soap. Her lecture about sin went on and on." Birdie uncrossed her legs and sidled up next to Helen.

Helen remained still, her arms behind her head. Had Birdie said too much? She liked how Helen's nose flared at the nostrils when she was angry. She loved how her eyes changed with her moods. She eased back and nestled her head against the enticing curve of Helen's underarm. As they lay together, the silence went from worrisome to comfortable. Birdie watched Helen's chest rise and fall with her breathing.

"I know now why my aunt doesn't like Lydia." Helen rolled on her side, her face a fraction from Birdie's. "She questioned my motives that day at the ladies' luncheon."

"I'm glad you're so persuasive."

Helen nodded. She looked like she was afraid. Birdie ran her fingertips along the dimple in Helen's right cheek.

"Did you have feelings for others after Rose?"

Birdie wasn't sure how to answer. She hadn't, not till she met Helen. But was it because she didn't have them or was it because she didn't think she should have them? She probably would never know.

"Only for you." Birdie reached for Helen's wrist, right below the sea glass bracelet. "I realize now you reminded me of Rose when we first met." They lay in contented silence for several moments, stroking each other's fingers, wrists, inner arms, shoulders. Birdie shivered, impatient for Helen's fingers to touch more.

"You deserve to know the full story about my swallow brooch." Helen's voice softened. "Miss Briarwood, Lillian, was my first real love. I started taking piano lessons from her when I was seventeen. She was several years older." Helen's eyes blinked. "We resisted what we both knew for over a year. I begged her to admit what we felt, and we shared several afternoons together." Helen turned her bracelet around her wrist. "Then she refused to teach me anymore. She hand-delivered the brooch and tearfully explained her fears that people would think she had unduly influenced me. She told me she'd wait for me once I had turned twenty." Helen clamped her eyes shut.

Birdie rubbed her fingers along the seams of the sheet, waiting.

"Two years later I went to her home on my birthday. Her mother slammed the door closed when she recognized me." Helen slowly opened her eyes "Months later I saw an advertisement for a choral concert featuring Lillian as the accompanist. I sat close to the front row, knowing she would see or at least sense me. Afterwards, I ran backstage only to watch as she embraced the lead soprano."

Birdie turned, cupping Helen's shoulder. "Did you talk to her, ask her?"

"No. It was quite obvious they were a couple." Helen ran her fingers through Birdie's short hair, tugging a few curls.

Moving close enough so she could feel Helen's breath on her face, Birdie knew nothing about what she was experiencing could be sinful.

"I love you, Birdie." Helen ran a finger along Birdie's cheek, swirling to her lips. "But we need to do this carefully."

Placing her hands on both sides of Helen's face, Birdie kissed her. They rolled over and kissed again. And again.

Laying face to face holding hands. Birdie revealed all she knew about Hugo. Then they talked more, sharing important, funny, and frivolous things interspersed with many kisses. After some time, Helen closed her eyes, her breathing slowed.

"Sweet dreams, sweet Helen." Birdie murmured. She reached for the blanket and pulled it over them, snuggling perfectly against the curve of Helen's body. She didn't want to ruin what they had by thinking too much, so concentrated on Helen's breathing. When she heard Helen's soft snores, she allowed her eyes to close too.

At a robin's greeting just before dawn, Birdie woke with her back nuzzled by Helen's body. Birdie lay still, soaking in Helen's scent and warmth. But soon her daylight thoughts made her squirm. She didn't want Flo or any of the others to find them like this. Birdie slipped out and climbed under the cold sheets of the other bed. She faced away from Helen and tried her best to figure out what she should do next.

CHAPTER 23

Leaving Newton, New Jersey

Helen was gone when Birdie woke the second time. Relief, then disappointment swept through her before she had stretched her arms. Birdie pushed away the stiff sheets and opened her suitcase. She ran her fingers along her own lips recalling Helen's kisses. A cold sensation brought doubts then nausea. Last night had been a big mistake. Birdie had let herself get caught up in the emotions of Walter fainting, Flo's revelations, and Helen's persuasion. She could not be "one of those women." She straightened and slowly rolled her head around, cracking her neck.

"Good morning." Helen charged in holding a cardboard box from a local pastry shop. "They didn't have maple iced ones, so I got cinnamon sugared instead." Helen's eyes were bright, her face shining. "I know how you're partial to Snickerdoodles." She placed the box on the dresser then hugged Birdie from behind.

"Thanks," Birdie murmured, her arms stiff at her side. She willed Helen to let go. She reached towards her open suitcase and Helen stepped back. Birdie balled up her navy dress, grabbed a plush towel, and started towards the door.

"You'll need this." Helen held out Birdie's leather vanity case by the handle. Their fingers touched in the exchange. Birdie jumped back as if electrified.

"I want to bathe before we catch the train." Birdie watched as she stepped over the threshold. "You can go ahead to the station if you'd like."

"I'm off to the tents. An inspiration for our new piece came to me last night. I can't wait to get it written down before we catch our ten-fifteen." Helen's voice had lost some of its buoyancy.

"Fine." Birdie stepped into the hallway, glancing up and down to see if any of the others had seen them. "I'll meet you at the station then."

"Birdie." Helen followed her into the hallway.

Birdie gestured that she had to use the lavatory and walked quickly away. She slipped into the ladies' lavatory and leaned against the door once it closed. Her heart drummed.

"When you're finished, come to the tents and practice with me." Helen said through the closed door. "I'll have your whistling part written out."

Birdie turned on the faucet in reply. She sensed Helen lingering on the other side of the door. Birdie opened the tin of citrus scented soap Helen had recently given her. How could Helen have felt so right last night and so wrong this morning? She swore she heard Lydia's voice above the running water, condemning her to hell or worse. She closed the new soap tin and found the sliver of Ivory from the bottom of her vanity case. Birdie scrubbed her face and arms hoping the hot water, washcloth, and soap would help her decide what to do.

Birdie was the last of the Versatile Quintet to arrive at the Newton train station. Knowing she owed Lydia and Gerald a letter she had spent the rest of her morning holding her pen, at a loss of what she could write to them. She'd start, then cross it all out—last night's events were the only thing present in her mind. Instead, she had written several notes to Helen, then shredded them all, wasting precious stationery.

Adelle stood away from the others gripping a crumpled newspaper in her crossed arms. Mary looked pale, wringing her hands, and pacing along the station platform. Birdie looked around and finally spotted Helen down the tracks near where the trunks and instruments were stacked. At first Birdie thought Helen had told the others about their clandestine night, but when she saw Flo huddled on a bench, holding her face, she realized Flo had told Adelle and Mary that Walter wasn't her attacker.

"Hey." Birdie touched Flo's arm.

Flo looked up with puffy red eyes. "All wet this morning."

Birdie patted Flo's back and then went alongside Mary.

"Have you heard any news about Walter?"

"Other than the bomb Flo dropped?" Mary gripped her hands together. "Why would she let us think it was Walter?" Mary searched behind Birdie and then started running towards the trunks. Birdie turned to see that Teddy and some of the Anvil Choir boys had appeared beside Helen. Mary's animated gestures and glances at Flo indicated that she was now sharing with Teddy what Flo had said. He listened with his hands at his sides then enveloped Mary in a long embrace.

Birdie stood off to the side, clutching her satchel and Daisy suitcase. She knew not to approach Adelle. As much as she wanted to know about Walter, Adelle's scowl and creased eyebrows clearly communicated that she'd have nothing to say to Birdie or anyone this morning.

The train was full of passengers and the girls had to find single seats next to strangers. It seemed fitting for this morning. Birdie found a window seat next to a women dressed in black. Mary settled next to a young boy who sat across from his parents. Adelle had walked all the way to the back of the car, Birdie had no idea if she kept going to the next car or found a seat. Flo sat across from Birdie's row next to a chatty young woman. Helen was the last to board. She slowly made her way down the aisle. She stopped when she got to Birdie's row but when Birdie turned to the window instead of acknowledging her nod, Helen went on towards the back of the car. Birdie heard Helen's voice asking if she could sit down. When Birdie looked over her shoulder, Helen was squeezed next to a man who took up more than his share of the seat.

Birdie found no comfort or make-believe stories from staring out the train's window. Her mind tussled with memories of her night alongside Helen and a strong feeling that it had all been wrong. She closed her eyes and soon her chin bobbed along with the movement of the train.

*　*　*

The Versatile Quintet's new routine now included extra practices in the morning and again in the afternoon before their normal nightly performance. They soon adjusted to what Flo had done, yet their familiar camaraderie that had so recently renewed showed signs of strain. Helen had written a beautiful yet challenging arrangement of the "Flight of the Bumblebee." She started on the piano, then Flo blended in with her harp, Mary came in on her violin and they picked up the pace together. Adelle blended in on her banjo, then Mary and Adelle increased the pace and played off each other as if they were two bumblebees flitting across wildflowers.

Helen had written a dramatic pause and then Birdie was to whistle the entire frantic phrase for several measures after which they'd all join her faster and faster for a climatic ending. Birdie struggled to whistle at the same pace as the others could play their instruments. She couldn't breathe and whistle without getting dizzy or spitting. She started to believe Lydia had been right. Birdie might have perfect pitch, but she wasn't talented enough to be a professional whistler. She knew she wouldn't be ready in the few days they had left. Her breathing was off and loud. Even Helen complained how she had to suck in so much air so often. No one understood how difficult this piece was for her.

Birdie also had to squeeze in time to learn the musical saw. Adelle was a strict and annoying teacher now that Teddy had finished cleaning up the saw he had leant them. She insisted that Birdie learn the basics, as if she was a beginning piano student before she'd allow Birdie to practice the Bach Concerto piece she had selected for their duet. There were far too many times Birdie had to refrain herself from swatting Adelle's turned back with the additional bow Helen had purchased.

"You can do it, Birdie." Helen played the specific measures on the piano and waited. Helen had persuaded Birdie to come early for this morning's practice of the "Flight of the Bumblebee." Birdie had agreed since she knew she needed the extra practice and she felt guilty that she had been avoiding Helen.

Birdie rubbed a finger across her swollen chapped lips. Helen only had to use her fingers to play the notes so fast and not her breath, cheeks, lips, and throat.

"I told you this piece was too hard to whistle. Let me play my part on the trombone."

"You can whistle this." Helen played the opening notes. "From the top."

Birdie felt like she was back in Lydia's parlor, Lydia sitting at the piano playing measures for Birdie to repeat. At least Helen didn't slap Birdie's knee with a folded fan when she made a mistake. Birdie tried whistling the stanza again but tripped up on the second measure. She slowed the pace and repeated the same mistake.

Helen raised her eyebrows and encouraged Birdie to try again with a slight nod. Birdie felt dizzy from the extra breathing it took to whistle and the confused yearnings she experienced whenever she was alone with Helen. Birdie took in another full breath and whistled a few measures much slower, but accurate this time.

"That's enough for now." Birdie sank to the edge of the piano bench. "I won't have anything left for when the others get here."

"You'll master it in the few days we have left." Helen patted her back. Birdie pulled away and moved off the bench. She looked over her shoulder to make certain none of the other girls had arrived yet. Helen moved her hands to her lap.

Birdie walked towards the dressing room. "I need my Vaseline." She had to explain her every move to Helen or she'd receive sullen stares or sagging shoulders. She wished they could go back to being best friends instead of having to cope with all this frustration, confusion, and discomfort.

As Birdie strode down the canvas walkway, she thought about all the changes that one night brought. Walter had been sent home, his left side immobile and his speech slurred. Mr. James had brought in a new lecturer, Mabel Walker Willebrand, who liked to hold court even more than Gerald. The other girls, especially Flo, clung to her every word. Mabel's lectures were intellectual like Walter's but also inspirational. Her words stirred up the audiences with her reading of "The Charge of the Light Brigade." There was something about Mabel that made Birdie uneasy. She wasn't sure if it was Mabel's delivery style or her mannerisms.

Birdie turned into the dressing tent and dug her Vaseline out of her vanity case. She leaned towards the mirror and made sure she had slathered the ointment on every part of her lips. When she heard footsteps on the straw, she turned towards the entryway, mentally preparing some new excuse to Helen about why they couldn't be alone together.

"Birdie." Hugo ducked into the dressing room, pulling the muslin curtain closed.

"Oh." She had to switch excuses.

Gripping her elbow, Hugo guided her towards the costume trunk and motioned for her to sit. "Mr. James treats me like a prisoner." He double checked their surroundings and then leaned in whispering. "I've missed you."

She tilted her head. His clear brown eyes reflected the morning light. His hair was neatly combed, and his skin seemed smoother. Today he looked quite handsome in a boyish, eager way.

"I, well." He stumbled over his words. She liked how he seemed to be nervous around her. It felt good to have someone made anxious by her instead of the other way around. "I wanted to thank you for whatever you said to Gerald." He lowered his voice. "And for what you didn't say." He squeezed her clasped hands briefly and then pulled his away. He looked around again. "But now I'm in a pickle." He paused as if waiting for her response. She raised an eyebrow, just like Flo.

"Gerald's asked for my resume. He'd like me to apply for a managerial position."

"That's what you wanted, right?" Birdie leaned closer. Hugo smelled like that new aftershave Teddy had started wearing, Aqua Velva.

"Yes. But now it's even more important that you not share with Gerald about my, ah, my …"

"Indiscretions?" Birdie filled in for him. This felt even better. She had something over him.

"That's one way to put it." He rubbed his hands. "But thanks, ba—I mean Birdie."

"You can call me babe."

He tried to raise an eyebrow but raised both.

"I don't know why I made such a big fuss before."

"You're like every dame I know. You change your mind with the weather."

"Take that back." She swatted at him.

"Huh?" He pulled her to her feet.

"I better not be like every dame you know." She put her hands on her hips in mock anger.

"You're absolutely not." He tipped her chin and ran his finger along her glistening lips. She was certain she felt a slight tingle. He pressed his lips to hers with gentle pressure.

She wrapped her hands at the back of his neck. "I'll be sure to cable Gerald that he should hire you."

"Excuse me." Mabel pushed the muslin curtain aside making the canvas crackle.

Hugo pushed Birdie away.

"Up to your old tricks, Shubert?" Mabel filled the dressing room.
Hugo recoiled. "What are you looking for Mrs. Willebrand?"

"You've got nothing I want." She turned. "But consider yourselves warned."

Birdie watched her bustle away. Walter had said something similar to Hugo. "What was that about?"

"Nothing," Hugo mumbled. "But I better make sure she's not on her way to tattle to Mr. James." He squeezed Birdie's elbow and strolled away, whistling his version of their Patriotic Medley.

Birdie paused. What was wrong with her?

CHAPTER 24

Salisbury, Maryland

Over the next three days, the additional practices, shows, train rides, and different towns ran together like late summer clouds. And with the room rotations back on schedule, Birdie had avoided alone time with Helen. She had convinced herself that they were just close girlfriends and that nothing between them had changed. Helen had been so engrossed in perfecting the "Flight of the Bumblebee" number that Birdie convinced herself that Helen hadn't noticed.

The night Hugo was their circuit manager, he slipped behind curtains or popped out of shadows to spend illicit minutes with Birdie. She welcomed his extra attention and it helped her avoid thinking about Helen. Having to be cautious of Mr. James, Mabel, and the others made each hasty rendezvous even more tantalizing. She was a little embarrassed yet also emboldened by what she allowed Hugo to do. His hands were adept at unfastening buttons or reaching under layers in their brief interludes. He seemed much more smooth, confident, and debonair when their encounters had to be quick. Of course, she hid everything from Helen. She mastered not thinking about what she was doing with Hugo and did her best to ignore his past behavior. Since being released from probation, he smelled, looked, and even kissed better.

Adelle had become quite the musical saw diva. When the previous night's audience gave her a standing ovation Adelle had announced that she no longer wanted a musical saw duet. "I'm quite fine by myself," she had told the others. Mary had squeezed Birdie's hand, offering comforting words. It wasn't like playing classical music on the saw was a personal desire, but Birdie had spent precious energy practicing the saw that she could have spent working on whistling Helen's arrangement.

That morning, after a short practice, Helen suggested the girls use the remainder of their time to either rest or perfect their own parts. She had looked right at Birdie when she said it. They all had. Birdie nodded, then left the platform before the others had put their instruments away. They had a ten-thirty departure for Salisbury, Maryland where Mr. James was meeting them for an early afternoon audition of the "Flight of the Bumblebee."

On her walk to the station, Hugo tugged Birdie into the shade of a large Balsam fir tree. The lower branches allowed for perfect cover.

"Look what came today." Hugo held tight to several folded pages.

She set her suitcase down, inhaling his overwhelming scent of Aqua Velva.

Hugo showed her Gerald's official job offer. "You're looking at the assistant manager of Willow Glenn Publishing."

When he lifted her up, a branch knocked off her cloche hat, causing them both to giggle as he lowered her into his arms. "That's just the bee's knees." She bent to pick up her hat and he playfully swatted her bottom with the letter.

Birdie had barely caught her breath when he pulled her close, his free hand popping the top two buttons on her coral blouse. "Not now, Hugo."

"Ah, come on babe." His brown eyes sparkled mischievously. "A fella needs a little something extra to celebrate."

"Later." She gathered up her gaping blouse. "Our train departs soon."

He pulled out his pocket watch. "Jeez." He turned, causing a branch to slap back, it's sap stuck to Birdie's arm. "Sorry babe, I can't be late."

Hugo pushed another branch out of his way. "If I didn't know better, I'd say you're bringing out the worst in me." She could hear him laughing as he trotted away.

She spent several minutes using the emergency sewing kit that Lydia had insisted she carry in her satchel to loosely attach the buttons. If Lydia knew why Birdie used the needle and thread, she'd pop her own buttons. While Birdie had been stitching and pricking her chest with the needle, she had heard the distinct back and forth calls and clicks of two Northern Cardinals. She ran the entire way to the train station.

Helen stood on the outside metal steps of the train car. The conductor was just blowing his whistle and its loud screech blended with her frantic shouts to Birdie.

"Hurry." Helen waved Birdie forward.

Birdie ran up to the stairs and handed her suitcase up to Helen. She started to pull herself up the stairs as the train lurched forward. If Helen hadn't grabbed Birdie's arm and hoisted, Birdie would have fallen off the steps. The force of the train coupled with Helen's strength pulled them together. Being this close to Helen made Birdie woozy. She clung to Helen and lingered in the security of her arms.

Helen glanced at Birdie's blouse. Birdie followed her gaze and realized that the top button was now gone. Helen handed Birdie her suitcase at chest level to help hide her gaping blouse. All eyes were on Birdie as Helen nudged her forward to their train. Flo sat next to Mabel Willebrand, who was by the window. Mary and Adelle sat across the aisle from them.

"We thought you were a goner, Birdie." Flo crossed her arms.

"Don't do that again." Mary waved her hand in front of her face like a fan. "You worried us."

"You cut it a little too close." Helen flumped down in the seat behind Flo and Mabel.

"Sorry." Birdie stood in the aisle, frowning. Mabel had insisted she'd travel with the girls instead of on her own schedule as Walter had done. There wasn't an open spot near any windows and the only vacant seats were beside Helen or way in the back next to a questionably dressed man.

"It smells like Teddy's new aftershave mixed with a Christmas tree." Mary looked past Birdie.

Birdie stretched to put her suitcase on the rack above their seats while holding her blouse closed with her other hand.

"We saw your acrobatics. Good thing Helen was there to save you." Flo winked. "And that you properly thanked her at the top of the steps."

"What does that mean?" Birdie took a step back.

"Never mind." Helen glared at Flo. "Sit down before you fall."

"I don't need you telling me what to do." Birdie gripped the luggage rack as the train jerked again. Flo leaned towards Mabel and whispered something behind her hand.

"Whatever you're gossiping about Flo, say it to my face." Birdie remained standing and tried to cross her arms, but the train's movement made it impossible.

"It's nothing to get defensive about." Mabel crossed her legs. "Some of the most talented women are sapphic."

"Oh my." Mary turned her head, her neck, and cheeks pinkening.

Adelle smirked as she lowered her folded newspaper. Birdie hadn't heard the word Mabel used but had sense enough to know she had compared Birdie to something bad.

"Let's discuss something useful." Helen leaned forward. "Mr. James is meeting us at one o'clock sharp to hear our progress with the 'Flight of the Bumblebee.'"

"I bet Pollyanna doesn't even know what sapphic means," Adelle said and Flo snickered.

Birdie slunk into the seat beside Helen and turned away. Birdie held her satchel against her chest and stared at her shoes.

"Flo. Have you forgotten why we're all working so hard to make the 'Flight of the Bumblebee' a success?" Helen's low voice commanded everyone's attention. She stood and offered Birdie the window seat. Birdie shook her head.

"No." Flo's face dropped a bit. She pulled her empty silver cigarette holder from behind her ear and twirled it across her slender fingers. "Can we just call it 'Our Flight?'"

"I like it." Mary's natural color had returned.

"It suits the piece." Helen nodded and continued her explanations about her arrangement's nuances. She reminded them that the tempo needed to build, and each girl had an important part.

Birdie studied the floor of the train. She wanted to know what the word Mabel used implied. It had to be unkind from the way the others reacted. She wished she could ask Helen.

After some time, the train's movement became smooth and mesmerizing. Mabel's chin rested on her ample chest and Birdie bet she hadn't looked out the window once. Adelle, still hidden behind her paper, lowered it and then jerked it up again. Birdie knew that soon she'd give in and fold the paper against the window for a flat pillow. Mary had her eyes closed and her head back against the seatback. She was the only one who could sleep like that and never snore. Flo had her head resting on Mabel's shoulder. Birdie's scan swept over to Helen who looked back with her soft green eyes.

Birdie averted her gaze. She didn't want Helen's sympathy. She studied the floor again. She had never noticed how tightly they laid the thin strips of wood. Each was grooved together, complete with little knots and imperfections. Shoes, boots, and heels had scuffed the wood in the spaces under the seats but there were also parts that were still varnished and almost untouched. Birdie glanced up into Helen's steady gaze.

Helen mouthed, "Quarter for your thoughts?" accompanied by a raised eyebrow.

Birdie looked down again as she pulled at a tiny bit of chapped skin on her lip. She cringed when Helen let out a loud sigh.

*   *   *

Birdie dropped her suitcase on the thick carpet of the Wicomico Hotel lobby. She released an audible breath of relief when Helen announced that night's room assignments. Mary was Birdie's roommate. Helen slapped her clipboard on the edge of the front desk, startling the clerk, who dropped the keys. Flo looped her arm through Helen's and pulled her towards the elevator. Helen remarked that they seemed to be booked in nicer places when Mr. James made the arrangements which brought a snort from Adelle. The three of them waited for the elevator, lined up as if they were waiting for autographs from a famous movie star. Birdie waited for Mary who lagged behind so she could talk with Teddy. Mabel was nowhere to be seen.

Birdie started tapping her foot. Between auditioning "Our Flight" with Mr. James and Mabel's comments on the train, she felt out of sorts. She glanced around the small but well-appointed hotel foyer. She'd have to ask Hugo why he had booked such mediocre places. She pulled the key from her pocket and put it back again. The desk clerk came from the back office and waved her over.

"Aren't you with the Chautauqua talent?" He held an envelope in his hand. "Can you give this to Miss Bertha Stauffer?" He extended his arm. Birdie recognized Lydia's precise lettering immediately.

"Absolutely." Birdie gave him a wide smile and took the envelope. He nodded to her and turned his back.

"You didn't have to wait for me, Birdie." Mary came up alongside her. "What's that?"

"A letter from Lydia." Birdie tucked it in her satchel.

"Any more mail for the Chautauqua talent?" Mary asked the desk clerk who shook his head no. Mary and Birdie walked towards the elevator. "I wish my sisters would write as often as Lydia."

Birdie pressed the button. "Everything all right with Teddy?"

A uniformed elevator operator opened the brass door and the girls stepped into the tiny space. Birdie showed him her key and they rode to the fifth floor. Mary started to answer but Birdie placed her hand on Mary's arm. She didn't want strangers listening in.

"Teddy shared Hugo's good news." Mary answered as soon as they started down the hall. "You must be so happy." Mary patted Birdie's hand.

"Working for Gerald is a great opportunity." Birdie noted the room numbers on brass plates attached to each door were increasing.

"And especially nice for you since he'll be close by." Mary giggled.

"We'll see about that." Birdie kept walking.

"I'd give anything for Teddy to live in Pittsburg."

"Lucky for you, Swarthmore College is only a train ride away."

"Teddy's hoping the Lyceum will promote him to circuit manager next summer."

Birdie stood before room number 528 and turned the key in the lock. They were greeted with bright shafts of light from two windows. The cream-colored bedding, black furniture along with the geometric artwork was the latest fashion.

"Isn't this place just the cat's meow?" Mary swirled around in the room with her arms outstretched, her suitcase almost hitting the black metal hat stand.

"Helen's right. We do stay in ritzier places when Mr. James does the booking." Birdie set her suitcase on the black lacquered chair next to one of the beds.

"Helen doesn't miss a thing." Mary started to unpack.

"Mary?" Birdie had her back turned. "What did Mabel mean? On the train?" Birdie fidgeted with the things in her suitcase.

"You mean a sapphic?" Mary's voice turned to a whisper.

"Yes." Birdie gripped her chiffon dress as she waited.

"It means sexual deviant."

"A what?" Birdie turned towards Mary, twisting the rose-colored clothing in her hands.

"Well, like pansies." Mary cocked her head. "Come on, even you can't be that dim."

"You mean Flo and Mabel think Helen and I are, are well—" Birdie could feel heat rise from her chest, spreading across her neck. The light in the room seemed to be shining right on her.

"We all did for a while." Mary opened her suitcase.

"You all did?" Birdie's heart beat as fast as a hummingbird's.

"Well, you and Helen are awfully close." Mary hung up her blouse. "And we all know who Helen prefers." She shook out her dress. "Flo thinks you might go both ways."

Birdie sank to the soft bed letting the duvet fold over her. The others had been talking about her being a sexual deviant. This was worse than she had even imagined.

"But don't misunderstand me." Mary interrupted Birdie's thoughts. "Of course, we all love Helen. She's the smartest pianist I've ever met." Mary slipped into her sky-blue chiffon drop waist dress. Flo had suggested they wear a pastel-colored dresses for today's audition with Mr. James.

Birdie nodded.

"It's part of being in the circuit." Mary sat next to Birdie, making the duvet sink further. "Thank goodness the guys aren't pansies." She giggled.

Birdie closed her eyes, turning away.

"You and Hugo have kissed, right?" Mary clasped her hands.

"Of course," Birdie murmured. So had she and Helen.

"I bet he proposes to you by Christmas." Mary jumped up. "And the Versatile Quintet can be bridesmaids in your wedding."

"Now you sound like Lydia." She shook out her rose-colored dress trying to remove the wrinkles she had just created.

"Aren't you going to read Lydia's letter?"

Birdie looked at her watch. "I will later. We need to get to the tents and Mr. James." She turned her back to Mary who zipped up her dress.

"Don't let what Mabel said upset you." Mary picked up her satchel.

"I won't." Birdie lied. "I'm worried enough about 'Our Flight.'" She dropped her Vaseline into her satchel. "I can't whistle it at the tempo Helen expects."

"I'm sure you will soon." Mary followed Birdie out of their room.

"If only." Birdie closed the door.

CHAPTER 25

Salisbury, Maryland

The others were already at the tent tuning their instruments when Birdie and Mary arrived. Helen's head popped from under the piano lid. Dressed in a mint-green dress, she looked like a Greek goddess. Helen whistled their Northern Cardinal greeting. Birdie searched in her satchel for her Vaseline. When the top of the piano slammed shut, she jumped and her heart played catch-up. Helen played the C scale, pounding each key with a pause. Birdie slathered the ointment on her chapped lips, rubbing them together as if holding onto her grimace.

Both Birdie and Helen looked towards the back of the tent when they heard Teddy and Hugo's voices. Mary waved Teddy forward, so he joined her on the platform. Together they set up four chairs spaced across the front of the stage. Helen sat at the piano running her fingers up and down the keys.

"Hey babe," Hugo whispered as he passed her, then motioned over his shoulder. Mr. James and another man walked several steps behind. Mabel centered herself in the front row. Her orange dress billowed around her taking up most of the bench which made Birdie think of Miss Muffet sitting on a tuffet. Oh, what Birdie would do for a spider.

Bright afternoon sunlight streamed onto the stage as a natural limelight. Flo situated herself in the first chair with her harp leaning between her legs. Flo's auburn hair shimmered against the pale goldenrod gown she wore. Her lips were painted in a perfect pink-colored bow like the night she had been attacked. Mary, in her light blue dress with a rhinestone brooch, sat next to Flo adjusting the strings on her violin. Adelle wore a lavender dress with a matching velvet head piece, nose up and eyes closed, her banjo resting on her lap. Helen sat at the upright piano beside the row of chairs. Birdie walked to the last chair. She should have made time to iron her rose chiffon dress. The other girls looked so professional and sophisticated. She felt like she was back at the audition with her outdated clothes and inexperience.

Mr. James, the other man, and Hugo sat to the left of Mabel. The other man's dark three-piece suit, thin black-tie, and stiff demeanor indicated he was from the Lyceum. Hugo straightened his bowtie, leaned back and then put his hands in his pockets.

Helen stepped forward and cleared her throat.

"Welcome." She spread out her arm and included all the girls. "The Versatile Quintet will play a custom arrangement of Nikolai Rimsky-Korsakov's interlude known as the 'Flight of the Bumblebee.'"

Mr. James nodded and Helen returned to the piano.

It began as planned, Helen opened the melody with slow and purposeful notes then increased the tempo with exaggerated movement of her slender fingers. After several measures, Flo played a complementary melody on her harp. She held her head high and her fingers moved quickly across the strings with flair. Mary blended in with the same melody on her violin, moving her upper body and her bow to the quickening cadence. Adelle joined in on her banjo and the melody clipped along. Mary and Adelle played the frantic music back and forth with precision, drama, and speed.

Birdie stood. Her knees felt like they might fold, so she moved to clutch the back of the chair. She licked her lips. Mary and Adelle paused on the same note in unison as planned. Birdie whistled the same melody but at a much slower pace. She could feel Helen's eyes urging her to whistle faster. She tried and skipped a few notes, spitting across the back of the chair. She couldn't take a deep enough breath.

Helen nodded and the others joined in at a much faster tempo. Birdie tried to keep up but only managed to whistle every third or fourth note. Maybe Mr. James and the others couldn't hear that she missed most of the final measures. The other instruments might be loud enough to cover her mistakes. By the end her head felt like it might burst from hyperventilating. Birdie sank into her chair, rubbing her cheeks in small circles.

Mr. James remained stoic with a hand cupping his chin. The other man stared straight ahead. Hugo fidgeted with his pocket watch chain. The girls waited in their seats. Birdie tried to see Helen's expression from the corner of her eye but couldn't make out if she was pleased or angry. Mr. James stroked his chin then leaned towards the other man. They spoke in hushed tones.

"Well." Mr. James stood. "It still needs work." He glanced at the man. "But we feel it should be added to the show."

"Thank you." Helen rose from the piano bench. "I'm sure with more practice it will be ready soon."

Mr. James crossed his arms. "Add it tonight."

"Tonight?" Birdie surprised herself by speaking aloud.

"Yes." Mr. James nodded towards her. "And you're the one who needs the most practice."

Birdie dropped her chin to her chest. "Yes sir." Splotchy heat moved along her neck to her face.

"Who wrote this arrangement?" The other man asked.

"I did," Helen said. "With assistance from Miss Armstrong."

"Of course." Mr. James started towards the back of the tent. He and the other man talked together and then turned, looking directly at Helen. Hugo followed them outside.

Birdie ran her finger across her swollen lips. It felt like that stupid bumblebee had stung them over and over. None of the others moved. She knew she hadn't been ready. Worse of all, she didn't know how to get better.

Teddy came in from the side stage slow-clapping his hands. "That was ab-so-lute-ly the berries." He shook his head. "I've never heard anything like it."

"I don't think Mr. James was quite as impressed." Helen pushed the piano bench in.

"They were." Teddy stood beside Mary. "Bosses just can't say it like me."

"Hugo wasn't impressed." Adelle set her banjo down.

"He's Mr. James's puppet." Mabel smoothed her dress. "You dames need to make a few changes for tonight's performance." She stood below the stage, right in front. "Lose the chairs and walk on stage in the dark." She motioned to Teddy. "You. Use a limelight to feature each player as they join the melody."

"Yes ma'am." Teddy nodded his head with big movements.

"And you." She moved right in front of Birdie. "Can you whistle at the same tempo as the others?"

Birdie felt a dozen eyes on her. "Not yet," she mumbled.

"It's obvious." She looked at Helen. "Reverse the order. End with the banjo."

Helen walked over to Birdie and put an arm across her shoulder. Birdie tensed. "Just until you figure out your breathing, okay?" Helen whispered.

"I told you I wasn't ready." Birdie said through gritted teeth. "And now everyone thinks I'm a failure." She knew it wasn't Helen's fault, but it was easier to blame her. "Maybe I should just sit out tonight's performance." Birdie ducked out from under Helen's arm.

"Not a chance." Helen reached for Birdie again but pulled back when Birdie stiffened. "You're part of the Versatile Quintet and a feature in 'Our Flight.'"

"Suit yourself." Birdie sensed that the others watched them. She stepped away. Mabel's mouth curled as if she had swallowed the spider.

"Let's take a break." Flo shook out her fingers.

"Great idea." Mary spoke with her high pitched extra cheery voice. "I saw a pharmacy on our way here."

"My treat," Flo announced. "As thanks to you hard working tomatoes."

Flo, Adelle, and Mary followed Mabel as she waddled towards the back of the tent. Mary turned around. "You two coming?"

"In a minute." Helen motioned for them to go on.

Birdie could feel Helen's eyes on her back.

"Wait for me." Birdie jumped off the platform and turned her ankle. It stung as she strode to catch up with the others.

"Birdie," Helen called.

Birdie kept walking, nursing her slight limp.

* * *

All during their late lunch at Buster's Pharmacy Birdie sensed Helen watching her from across the booth. Helen's eyes were hooded and dark. Guilt crept in, making Birdie's cream soda curdle. She hadn't meant to hurt Helen. Birdie wished Helen would forget their clandestine night at the Cochran House and understand that they had to be only friends.

Once the glasses had been cleared, the others talked about returning to the fancy hotel. Birdie excused herself to the ladies' lavatory, saying she'd meet them there. She lingered in the checkered pink lounge until she was certain they had all left. When she slipped outside there were only strangers. It relieved her that Helen must be already getting the unspoken message.

Birdie stopped at a small park that she and Mary had passed on their way to the tents. She eased onto a wooden bench that was surrounded by thick lilac bushes and rubbed her sore ankle. The fragrant blooms were gone but the clusters of wide leaves provided the seclusion she desired. She closed her eyes listening for familiar bird songs. Although it was a late summer afternoon, she didn't expect to hear many birds singing. Yet when it was so quiet, she couldn't help thinking that even her feathered friends had abandoned her. She stretched her legs long and watched as two girls played together across the park. The older one gave some sort of instructions. The look on the younger girl's face held pure adoration.

She rummaged through her satchel for Lydia's unopened letter. She wished she felt as excited about it as Mary did. Sliding her finger along the stiff paper to open the envelope she jerked her finger back. A tiny sliver of blood formed along the tip of her finger pad. She placed the stinging fingertip in her mouth.

The screech of a Blue Jay startled her. Its jeering call made her sit up straighter. When she was just learning to mimic bird songs, she had refused to copy it because it's song wasn't pretty. Edwin taught her that Blue Jays were one of the most intelligent birds. He insisted that she watch them at different times and listen intently. The Blue Jay did have a "whisper song," a series of clicks and brief liquid notes that was beautiful in a unique way. Birdie had learned from the *Birdcraft* book Edwin gave her that jays were also known to have tight family bonds. She looked up at the empty blue sky and thanked Edwin again for his proper admonishing.

She smoothed the delicate pages then held them up to her nose. The stationery smelled of lilacs and talcum powder, Lydia's signature scent. Birdie's stomach tightened. Had that scent always caused these feelings?

Bertha,

Gerald has offered Hugo a managerial job. It's imperative that you proceed with our plan and respond positively to Hugo's courting. He will be a suitable husband and I know you will find him so if you just get out of your own way. As summer is at its end, I trust you've gotten this notion of traveling out of your system and can now focus on what's most important.

Everyone asked for you at the Labor Day reunion and soon I ran out of excuses. Not much news other than Uncle Bert has taken ill and Cousin Andrew moved to Brooklyn in pursuit of some preposterous jazz career. Thank goodness you haven't gone that route.

Gerald sends his best. He's suggesting we get a dog and wants to know what breed you prefer. We all know I'd end up being the one responsible for it, so I insisted that it's up to me if we get one or not. Write soon,

Love Lydia

Birdie laughed aloud, causing the Blue Jays to squawk as they flew away. No jovial greeting, no rhetorical questions about Birdie, just straight to the point of what Lydia wanted. Birdie tried to find relief from the expected words Lydia had written, at least she seemed past her own grief. Folding the pages into her satchel, Birdie leaned to nurse her papercut, her sore ankle, and her bruised spirit.

*   *   *

Birdie arrived at the dressing tent just before six and partially hid behind the muslin curtain. Helen leaned against the trunk with a pencil tucked behind her ear looking over her notes. The evening sky filled the tent with golden hues and Helen absorbed the light that surrounded her. Birdie yearned to lean her head on Helen's shoulder, breathe in her scent, and stroke the back of her neck. Birdie shook her head. She squeezed her eyes, forcing herself to think of Hugo's thick hair, his brown eyes, how it felt when he kissed her. She swallowed. All she could muster for Hugo was a punch to her stomach.

Helen cleared her throat.

Birdie's eyes fluttered open. Helen had moved and now stood right before her.

"Helen."

"Where were you wandering this time?" Helen ran her fingertips along Birdie's arm. It felt as if a trail of butterflies followed Helen's touch.

"The others will be here any minute," Birdie whispered.

"You can't avoid me forever." Helen removed her hand yet stayed close. "We room together tomorrow night."

Flo's high-pitched laughter filled the canvas hallway. She eased past Birdie as Helen slid over to the mirror. Birdie gripped the edge of the muslin curtain.

"Move." Adelle charged into the dressing room past Birdie. Mary followed with a condolence pat on Birdie's arm.

"So, what's first?" Flo asked. They had discussed the order of their pieces at the Pharmacy but hadn't reached a consensus.

"I think we should open with the Patriotic Medley." Birdie's gaze found Helen. "It's better than the 'Lilies' piece."

"I agree." Helen held Birdie's stare.

"So, we wear our band costumes first?" Mary strolled over to where Helen had hung up the costumes.

"Yes." Helen held out a paper, her full attention still on Birdie. "I wrote out the order of our pieces here."

"Just because you wrote 'Our Flight's' arrangement doesn't give you carte blanche for our entire performance." Adelle snatched the page from Helen. "My musical saw piece should be the finale."

"Hooey." Flo flipped her hand above her head. "'Our Flight's' the finale and that's final."

"Then it should replace your harp and bird number. It's much more sophisticated and well-liked."

"Fine with me." Birdie pulled her eyes from Helen's and stepped into her band uniform pants. "I could use a break from the whistling."

"No." Helen took the page back from Adelle. "I'd like us to follow my plan for tonight."

"And Birdie is whistling *before* Flo in 'Our Flight?'" Adelle shook her band shirt as if ridding it of cobwebs.

"Yes." Helen turned away. "I'll start on the piano, then Birdie, Flo, then Mary, then it ends with you on the banjo. We'll take out the pause for now and all play the last forty-eight measures in unison."

"Shouldn't we run through it before going on stage?" Mary tilted her head towards Birdie. "It's a big change."

Birdie swatted the red feather in her band hat. "I can follow Helen's lead."

"That you can." Flo accentuated with a salty sashay.

Ever since Mabel had arrived, and Flo's probation had ended she had returned to her sassy self with more sting. Birdie secretly wished for the more subdued Flo and then scolded herself for even thinking that. She just wanted Flo to direct her quips at someone else.

CHAPTER 26

Leaving Salisbury, Maryland

The Versatile Quintet received an almost full standing ovation that night from the Salisbury audience despite their haphazard performance. "Our Flight" had impressed them with its fast tempo and Helen's arrangement. Birdie begrudgingly admitted to herself that it also might have had something to do with Adelle's banjo playing.

After the performance, the girls gathered in the dressing tent.

"What a fiasco." Mary pulled her costume over her head. "Adelle, why did you start our duet right after the Patriotic Medley?"

"Because Helen changed the order last minute." Adelle snapped her banjo case shut.

"The audience still swooned over 'Our Flight,'" Flo said.

"I can play it much faster." Adelle zipped up the side of her dress. "If Mary can too, we should finish with the two of us playing back and forth instead of all five of us." She looked directly at Birdie.

Helen concentrated on putting costumes away.

"I'd rather perform it as it is for the next several nights." Birdie gathered up the band hats, setting them inside the trunk. "What do you think, Helen?"

"Whatever the group wants." Helen's face was hidden behind the top of the trunk. Birdie frowned. It wasn't like Helen to give in so easily.

"It's settled then." Adelle brushed off her hands. "Mary and I will be the finale of 'Our Flight.'"

"Not so fast, Adelle." Birdie crossed her arms over her chest. She scrunched her brows at Flo, hoping for a "Flo-ism" as agreement. "Let's give tonight's order another chance now that we've tried it once."

"And risk the caliber of the show because one of you might be confused?" Adelle threw her hands up.

"Helen's the one who should decide." Flo pointed her cigarette holder at Helen like a magic wand.

"Can we decide over dinner?" Mary pushed the muslin curtain aside.

"And how." Flo strutted out. Mary then Adelle followed.

Flo poked her head around the muslin doorway. "Are you two coming?"

"We'll be right behind you." Birdie turned towards the costume trunk.

"Thank you." Helen lowered the lid and latched it closed.

"Adelle has become quite vain." Birdie rubbed her arms. "She doesn't get to change 'Our Flight' when it's your piece."

"None of this music is mine." Helen stood near Birdie. "It's just rearrangements of composer's pieces and even those are owned by the Chautauqua Lyceum."

"That's not fair."

"It's how the music industry works. I'm under contract with them so they own the rights."

"Well, at the least they should give you recognition in the programs." Birdie lowered her gaze to the straw covered dirt floor.

"That's not a fight we can take on just yet." Helen's fingertip touched the top of Birdie's hand. "But I treasure your belief in me."

All the nerves in Birdie's body tuned to Helen's touch. She couldn't deny that she wanted to wrap her arms around Helen, to tug at the fine strands of hair at the back of her neck. Eyes closed; Birdie willed those feelings away.

"Wooden nickel for your thoughts?" Helen whispered as she ran her fingers down Birdie's arm stopping at her wrist. Every hair on Birdie's arm stood up.

"You don't have one." Birdie's words were like sandpaper. It startled her. She swallowed and stepped away.

"For you, I may." Helen stepped into Birdie's space as if pulled by a magnet but refrained from touching her. Helen's voice lowered. "I'd like to know what you're thinking."

"Not now." Birdie's eyes went from the muslin curtain to the mirror, to the costume trunk, and back at her two-toned shoes.

"I won't wait forever." Helen squeezed Birdie's fingers and backed out of the dressing tent.

Birdie released the breath she had been holding in a whistle. She leaned against the costume trunk, turning her gaze to the mirror. A *woman* stared back at her. She took in the messy Eton crop, the high cheek bones, and pink swollen lips. This woman had something like confidence behind her hazel eyes, a sense of independence in the way she held her chin. Birdie ran her hands down her hips rubbing the rose chiffon between her fingers. She didn't look like Bertha Hintz Stauffer anymore. Maybe she didn't have to act like her either.

She should run after Helen and admit that every time she saw her it was as if hundreds of swallows took flight in her heart. Yet Birdie didn't move. She stuck to the trunk with Lydia and every other matron she knew clucking their tongues inside her head. She dug her fingernails into her palm. She knew she wasn't fooling anyone. She only posed as a modern woman. She was weak and worse; she had failed at being honest.

Birdie turned away from the mirror. She plucked a red hat feather sticking out of Flo's harp case. Maybe she should talk this over with Flo. Birdie ran her fingers along the feather, making the vanes open. Birdie had learned much from Flo's sassy ways. She smoothed the feather's vanes flat again. No, Flo idolized Mabel and together they couldn't be trusted. Birdie tossed the feather in the trunk and slammed it shut.

"What a pleasant surprise." Hugo strode into the dressing tent. "I knew you'd wait for me."

"I didn't." Birdie crossed her arms.

"Yet here you are." He reached for her forearms with both hands and pulled her to his chest. "All alone." His foul breath was hot and smelled of stale liquor. When had Hugo started drinking again? Or had he never stopped?

Birdie pushed him back and positioned herself behind the costume trunk.

"Babe?" Hugo cocked his head, blinking his long lashes at her. All she saw this time was his bloodshot eyes and splotchy cheeks. What had she done, encouraging him and worse, writing to Gerald to hire him?

"I—" She started to say she was sorry. Yet she wasn't. Birdie needed to tell Hugo the truth, or something close to it.

"Actually, I did stay hoping to see you."

"There's my babe." He put both hands on the trunk and leaned towards her.

"I'm not your babe. I never have been."

"Huh?"

Birdie put the strap of her satchel over her head. "I can't—No, I won't meet up with you anymore." Birdie took long strides towards the muslin curtain.

"But babe?" He followed her offering his frustration with open palms.

Birdie stopped him with her hand on his arm. "I'm not interested in whatever it was we started."

"You can't stop us. I have a job at Gerald's publishing firm."

"No longer my concern." Birdie stuck a hand on her hip. "We're through." She turned sharply and sashayed, as best she could, down the canvas hallway.

Being outside emboldened Birdie even more. She twirled around one of the heavy tent ropes stretched taut and almost tripped on the tent stake. Do modern women have to be graceful too? She giggled to herself, giddy with a little pride for realizing and telling Hugo the truth.

"Jeez Birdie, what kept you at the tents so long?" Flo charged up the hill, the night breeze blowing her skirt and hair forward. "You had me worried when Helen came to the restaurant alone."

Hugo strolled out of the main tent, his hands in his pockets. "Good night, ladies." He nodded his head and continued towards town.

"Oh." Flo scrunched her eyebrows together.

"It's not what it—" The words stuck in her throat. Birdie shook her head. "I'm not that." Birdie could feel Flo's bemused stare. She threw up her arms. "Oh, Flo."

"What's your beef?" Flo crossed her arms.

"You must have the wrong impression." Birdie stared at Flo's patent shoes.

"And what impression do I have?"

"I don't know." Birdie mumbled. Everything with Flo was a game. "That I'm a pushover."

"You're a sap, not a pushover." Flo's tone softened. "But you shouldn't be meeting up with Hugo. He's a cake-eater."

"A what?" If only Flo would speak English for once.

"Let's just say, he doesn't have your best interests at heart." Flo placed her hand on Birdie's shoulder. "I thought you and—" she avoided Birdie's eyes. "Oh, never mind." Flo put her other hand on Birdie's opposite shoulder, so she faced her and framed her. "Mabel tells me that each circuit season Hugo pursues a pretty dame. Don't let him dupe you."

Why were Flo and Mabel talking about Birdie behind her back? They reminded her how Lydia and her matronly friends gossiped about the younger, more modern women at the Auxiliary Luncheons.

"You're both just jealous." Birdie spit the last word. She turned out from under Flo's hands and stormed away.

"Now you're being loopy." Flo easily caught up with Birdie and stopped her with a curt tug. "Listen to me." She dropped her hand. "Like we've said before, Hugo is not as he appears. Talk with Helen. She's the one who has your best interests at heart. She's the one who cares for you."

Flo had no right to tell her what she should or shouldn't do. Helen must have told Flo some wild story. Birdie kicked a stone at Flo's patent leather toe.

"Bullshit."

"What?" Flo stepped back, her eyes wide.

"You heard me." Birdie strode away and raised her left hand like she'd seen Flo do many times. She flicked it with the best sense of disgust as she could muster.

"You're balled up, Birdie." Flo called after her. "And that means you're making a big mistake."

Birdie sped up. Flo baffled her. It was all jazzy words and innuendos. Birdie walked faster with her head down. This was her own fault. Nothing she said came out as what she thought. It was as if a goblin lived inside her head. Flo had cared enough to come looking for her. Yet Birdie had managed to anger Flo and that might lead to rumors.

Birdie ran into the hotel, took the carpeted steps two at a time, and charged into her shared room.

"We missed you at dinner." Mary sat on the edge of the closest twin bed.

Birdie opened her suitcase then shook out her cotton night gown.

"I've got some day-old cookies, if you're hungry." Mary offered a hanky wrapped parcel to Birdie.

Birdie shook her head and left for the lavatory. Mary's kindness made her feel even more mad at herself.

When she returned Mary was sitting up in her bed reading the latest *Vogue* magazine. "I'm glad you stood up to Adelle this evening. She thinks those standing ovations are only for her." Mary giggled a little.

Climbing into her bed, Birdie pulled the covers over her head. "Okay. I take the hint." Mary turned out her light. The room's silence felt cold and tight.

*　　*　　*

Birdie sat up straight. The room was dark, only a pale bit of light wavered across the geometric print of the wallpaper making it appear cinematic. She leaned against the headboard, massaging the dull ache in her stomach. What had startled her? The room was so quiet, she had to strain to hear Mary's breathing, yet her own heart was racing. Whatever it was, it was gone now. Birdie scooched down under the crisp sheets and pulled the cream-colored quilt to her chin.

Tomorrow night she'd be rooming alone with Helen. Birdie turned on her side away from Mary. How could she change their room rotation? She wiggled her toes and freed them from the covers. No matter how she looked at it, there wasn't a way unless she involved one of her other friends and she had stupidly pushed them away today. Well, not Adelle, no one pushes her. Birdie let out a long sigh. Adelle might be her answer. She had to somehow convince Adelle that they needed to room together. Birdie concentrated at the wallpaper for a long time, trying to put her worries into the different shapes. She fell asleep with a bitter taste in her mouth.

*　　*　　*

On the train ride to Staunton, Virginia, Birdie chose a seat next to a woman wearing a short-waisted jacket and matching skirt instead of sitting with any of her friends. By the time they arrived, she still hadn't mustered the courage to ask Adelle to help her. It was no use; she'd have to room alone with Helen and feign illness or something to avoid talking with her. As she followed her friends to their lodgings, she scolded herself. Helen was kind. Of course, she'd understand if Birdie told her she couldn't be more than friends. Birdie kicked a pebble that rolled down the sidewalk and bumped into the heel of a tall man who was ushered his family along. There were more people in Staunton than most towns they had visited.

When they turned onto Market Street, a multi-story brick building took up most of the block. Two white columns flanked the entrance, with Hotel Stonewall Jackson, in shiny gold letters at the front of the portico. Once inside, the hotel lobby was equally impressive with four tiered chandeliers and terrazzo floors. Mr. James had really outdone himself this time.

Helen stepped away from the front desk and motioned to the girls.

"This place is the lion's mane," Flo did an impromptu tap dance, the toes of her T-strapped pumps making beats against the marbled floor.

"It's brand new." Adelle flicked her newspaper, "They had a grand opening last month."

"Well, that might explain the fiasco with our rooms." Helen held out one key. "We have one room for the five of us."

"That doesn't make sense." Mary motioned around the large lobby. "There must be over fifty rooms here."

"One hundred rooms to be exact. And fifty more in the adjoining Hotel Virginia." Adelle nodded.

"Well, not all have been furnished and according to the desk clerk, 'the popularity of Chautauqua has pushed them beyond capacity.'" Helen dangled the single key. "I requested rollaway beds but we may not even get those."

Relief washed over Birdie. "Let's make it a slumber party with buttered popcorn."

"We're not schoolgirls." Adelle turned towards the front desk.

Teddy rushed up the group. "You're to be at the county courthouse in fifteen minutes."

"They only gave us one room." Mary pulled at Teddy's arm.

Teddy started gathering their suitcases. "We'll leave these with the concierge and sort it out later." He herded the girls towards the glass doors to the street. "Skiddoo, ladies, you can't be late to your own parade."

CHAPTER 27

Salem, New Jersey to Dover, Delaware

Over the next week, the Versatile Quintet's performance of "Our Flight" garnered standing ovations throughout most of the towns they visited. Word spread via gossip or local newspapers that this was the year to attend opening night at Westdale Chautauqua. Everyone improved with the tempo and the precision of their notes except Birdie. She lost sleep worrying about how to whistle and breathe at the tempo demanded. At least Hugo had heeded her request to leave her alone. And after that night at the Hotel Stonewall Jackson when they all five had to share one room, Helen had given her more space. Even Flo continued to be brisk and a bit chilly towards Birdie.

The internal storms that prevented Birdie from sleep became real thunderstorms at the Salem, New Jersey train station. Thick gray clouds streaked the morning sky, each layer a shade darker. Teddy seemed to be the only one in a jovial mood. He cajoled Flo and flirted with Mary. Birdie stayed back in the shadows next to Adelle. Helen was the last to arrive. The train blew into the station, its steam adding an even lower layer to the low-hanging clouds.

Birdie jumped on the train first to nab a window seat. She craved the distraction. Mary eased in next to her. Helen, then Flo went past them and settled several rows back. Adelle stood talking with Hugo before he turned towards the rear of the train. Mabel, who often joined the girls, boarded the first-class car today followed by Mr. James.

Birdie turned her gaze towards the inside of the train. "How's it going with Teddy?"

Mary clasped her hands in her lap. "My sisters want to meet him."

"That's a good thing, right?"

"Excuse me, I need to sit next to Birdie." Adelle stood over them with her hand on the back of Mary's seat.

Both Birdie and Mary looked up at Adelle. Her lips were drawn tight and she made a curt motion with her head, indicating that Mary should move.

"Oh. This looks serious." Mary winked at Birdie.

The last thing Birdie wanted was to hear a lecture from Adelle. "We were in the middle of a conversation." She placed her hand on Mary's arm. "You don't have to move."

Mary looked at Birdie with wide eyes. She stood up. "We can finish our chat later." She picked up her suitcase and struggled past Adelle towards the back of the car.

Birdie turned her head and said to the window. "Suit yourself."

Adelle fidgeted into her seat. Birdie stared out the window and watched as the wooden train station disappeared in slow motion. She closed her eyes. It wasn't until the train moved at a steady clacking pace that Adelle spoke.

"Hugo informed me that several Lyceum members will be in attendance tonight."

Birdie propped her head against the window.

"They are considering extending our circuit season." Adelle shifted forward.

Birdie kept her eyes closed.

"'Our Flight' has to be at its absolute best tonight."

Birdie sensed Adelle's concentrated stare. She could feel Adelle's breath moving the air by her head.

"I know you're awake." Adelle exhaled and sat back. "You're tapping your foot."

Maybe if Birdie gave into Adelle, the expected lecture would be shorter. Through squinted eyelids she saw that Adelle held a slim book on her lap. Her hands covered the gold lettering so that all Birdie could read was *Agnes Woodward*. Adelle's odd behavior made Birdie curious about this biography she held so tight.

"This is important." Adelle smoothed the cover of the book. That's when Birdie saw the second line of the title, *Whistling is an Art*. "I applied to this school last fall and completed their program." She opened the book and ran her finger down the Table of Contents. Birdie noticed penciled-in notes on the margins. "Their breathing techniques will be helpful." She flipped a few pages, stopping at page fourteen.

Birdie cocked her head, studying Adelle's face, her eyes focused on the book.

"Did you graduate?"

A glimpse of anger crossed Adelle's face. "That doesn't matter." Her composure returned. "This will help you improve your whistling."

"I think I'm managing." Birdie faced away. Rain splattered the window, blurring the passing landscapes.

"But you're not." Adelle tapped the book. "Follow this and you can match the pace set by the rest of us."

"Only if you tell me if you graduated."

"I don't have to tell you anything." She closed the book and gripped its edges.

"So, you agree that 'Our Flight' is fine as is?" Birdie fogged the window.

"No."

A raindrop hit the window and rolled downward, picking up other droplets on its way.

Adelle squirmed. "Look, I need the circuit season to be extended." She put her hand on Birdie's arm. "I need the job."

Birdie saw panic in Adelle's eyes. This wasn't about Agnes Woodward's School of Whistling.

Birdie patted Adelle's hand. "Let me see the book."

Adelle handed it to her. "Read lessons three through eight. And the breathing notes."

Birdie opened the book, skimming the title page.

"Did you live in Los Angeles?"

"Of course not. It was a correspondence course."

"A whistling correspondence course?" Birdie had no idea that was possible. "Why didn't you whistle as part of your audition?"

Adelle stared at the gentlemen's straw hat in the row in front of them. Birdie went back the book. She read several pages. This was a legitimate school. They listed proper whistling techniques and lip formations.

"She wouldn't certify me," Adelle said almost as a breath.

"Why not?"

"Miss Woodward said I failed the exams." Adelle pushed at her thumb's cuticle.

"Miss Woodward is a real person?"

Adelle reached for the book. "If you can't take this seriously, I don't want you to have it."

Birdie gripped the book. "I can learn something from it." She ran her finger along the page. "But why didn't you share this earlier?"

"You acted as if you knew everything, with your perfect pitch and all."

Birdie barely shook her head.

"But since you're still struggling with 'Our Flight,' I knew this could help all of us." Adelle nodded at the book.

Birdie tucked a loose bit of hair behind her ear and continued reading. Questions about Adelle's home life niggled at the back of her mind but not enough to take her away from the book. The mixture of music bars and words describing the types of whistles, lip placement, and breaths captured her interest.

Once the girls arrived at the Dover train station, the clouds that had followed them all morning released their hold. Helen started jogging first and the others followed, running the last few blocks thru the rain to their hotel. Birdie was the last to skip up the steps and she skidded into the lobby, bumping Adelle with her suitcase, who yipped like one of those lap dogs. Birdie shook off her cloche in the entryway and noticed that Mr. James had once again booked a nicer place than when Hugo had been in charge. The Hotel Richardson's arched windows fogged behind ornate damask curtains and the brass scones welcomed them with a bright glow.

Helen retrieved the room keys from the uniformed female front desk clerk and announced the room assignments. Tonight, Birdie would be alone with Helen. She hadn't known so didn't have time to finagle her way out of it this time. There were several hours before curtain call. She followed Helen down the hall with hesitant steps.

"What did Adelle want? I saw her make Mary switch seats." Helen took off her hat and cloak, hanging both on one of the door hooks. She fluffed her hair. Droplets from her rain-soaked cloak made little taps when they hit the hardwood floor.

Birdie hunched on the embroidered bench at the end of the bed in her wet clothes. She took off her lattice pump and rubbed her ankle. It had been sore ever since she leapt off the stage to avoid Helen. And for what? Now they were again alone in a hotel room.

"Did you hear that several bigwigs from the Lyceum are here for tonight's performance?" Helen continued as she hung up her clothes.

Birdie fidgeted on the bench. The coziness of this hotel room reminded her of what they had done together at the Cochran House. She kneaded her ankle harder.

"Cat grabbed your tongue?" Helen faced Birdie.

Birdie wanted to say something clever back but her mind was jumbled. Did she want to entice or discourage Helen? Each heartbeat willed her to reach out and stroke the hollow of Helen's creamy neck. Birdie tucked her hands under her arms, gripping the damp wool.

Helen eased closer. "You can trust me."

"I—" Birdie turned away. "Adelle gave me a book on whistling."

"That's swell but—?"

"She wants 'Our Flight' to be its best tonight." Birdie waved her hand. "Something about needing the circuit season to be extended."

"Can this book improve your pace?"

Everyone thought her whistling pace held them back.

"I'd like to find out." Birdie stood to go.

"We need to clear the air between us before you leave this room." Helen tugged at Birdie's damp sleeve.

"Now?"

"I need to know what you want, Birdie."

"I *want* to practice this breathing technique." She closed her eyes. "Can't we wait until after tonight's performance?"

"No."

"Oh, Helen." Birdie leaned over, hugging her own waist. "I'm a flim-flam inside. Sometimes I think I like Hugo's kisses." She paced to the windows. "And then I'd dream of you and our night—" Birdie slapped her own arms.

"You've kissed Hugo recently?"

"No. Yes. I did earlier, a few times."

Helen's eyes darkened and the crease between them deepened.

"I had to know." Birdie's words refused to say what she meant. "You know, if I liked him or not."

Helen seemed lost in her thoughts.

"How many times?"

"It doesn't matter. I told him last week we were through." Helen's focus on Hugo scared Birdie.

"It matters to me." Helen moved close, so their faces were less than an inch apart. Birdie fought the urge to tuck the loose wisps of Helen's hair behind her ear.

"What you're denying hurts." Helen tapped over her heart. "But what you're not telling me hurts worse." She put her felt wrapped tuning tools in her cloak's pocket. "You've had more than enough time to sort out your feelings."

Birdie hadn't intended to hurt Helen. "I'm sorry." She reached for Helen's hand and gripped her wrist, right above the dangling green glass bracelet.

"You can't undo what's done." Helen pulled away, rubbing her wrist as if it had been burned. She took her wet cloak off the hook and opened the door.

Birdie followed her. "I just need more time."

"Why? You overthink everything." She stepped into the hall.

Birdie held the doorframe as Helen walked away. Shame held her back. After several minutes, she closed the door and slumped down below it. Cold droplets from Helen's blue Musketeer hat dripped onto Birdie's head and down her neck. She squeezed her eyes as if she could erase all that had just happened. She wiped her nose with the back of her hand and pushed herself up.

Birdie went to the window. Rows of thin gray clouds piled across the sky. She walked to the bench and picked up her satchel, heavy with Adelle's book. Stupid "Our Flight." She sank back down on the embroidered bench and pulled out the book. She traced her finger along the pressed gold writing, *Whistling is an Art*. She owed it to Helen and the others to make that right first. Then she would find the perfect words or actions to show Helen exactly how she felt.

Cocooned in the safety of the plush hotel room, Birdie changed out of her wet clothes and arranged her things on the dresser. She washed her face, scrubbing until her cheeks burned. She sat on the bench rereading the whistling lessons and practiced the specific breathing techniques while whistling stanzas of "Our Flight" as she paced the perimeter of the room. She jotted down poetic lines of apology to

Helen. When the late afternoon clouds revealed blue sky, she claimed it as a good omen.

When she didn't find any of the others in the lobby, Birdie had to ask directions from the cheeky desk clerk. She questioned why she was trudging uphill when she knew most often the tents were set up down by a river or a park. It made her ankle throb but at least it gave her practice at deep breathing. She crested the hill, debating whether to turn back, just as the tip of the main tent peeked into her view. A hand painted street sign confirmed that it was at the end of Morris Street, just as the clerk had insisted. She heaved herself up the last bit and nodded to Teddy who was securing an extra rope to the main tent.

A loud wail interrupted her hike. It sounded like Helen. Birdie ran to the main tent, pushing the massive flap aside. Helen stood on stage banging the keys of the upright piano.

"What's your beef, Helen?" Adelle charged over from the dressing tent.

"This damn piano." Helen hit the top with her fist. "I've been trying to tune it for hours." She reached down with her arm and ended up putting her whole head inside. "It must have gotten wet." The enclosed piano muffled her voice.

Birdie stopped short of climbing on stage, her chest heaving.

"Well, hello." Adelle stood beside the piano, her hands on her hips. "Where have you been?"

Birdie bent over to catch her breath. Visions of Helen sprawled out under the piano faded away.

Helen stood at the piano and played the C scale. She shook her head.

"The G is sharp," Birdie offered.

"I know." Helen took out a different lever from her felt roll and propped the lid open.

"Did you use the whistling book?" Adelle rubbed her hands together as if she was about to roll lucky dice.

Helen peered inside the piano, one hand holding a long tool and the other gripping the lid's edge. "A string snapped."

Birdie still marveled that Helen knew how to tune and fix a piano. If only Birdie could use those levers to fix the harm she had caused.

"Whistle a few bars of 'Our Flight,'" demanded Adelle.

Birdie stepped up with her right leg, protecting her injured ankle. Adelle heaved Birdie onto the stage using both hands and she bumped the piano with her hip. The lever that held the top open clanked into the depths of the strings. The lid slammed closed with a loud pop.

"Open it." Helen pushed on the lid with her free hand.

Birdie pulled at the lid with her fingertips, it slipped and fell closed again. Helen exploded with a sharp yelp.

Adelle reached over, together she and Birdie held the lid up. Helen jerked her hand away. She bent over, holding her left fingers with her right hand.

"No, no, no." Helen moaned. Three of her fingers were splotchy and already swollen. Birdie could make out a purplish line just below the first knuckles.

"What have you done, Birdie?" Adelle screamed.

"We need to stop the swelling."

Teddy poked his head inside "What happened?"

"Get ice," Birdie called.

Birdie maneuvered Helen to the piano bench. She had never seen Helen so pale.

"Hold your fingers above your heart." Birdie eased Helen's elbow up. "It reduces the swelling." Birdie searched Helen's face. She wanted to blurt out that she loved her but with Adelle here she held back. Instead, she said, "I'm so, so sorry." She tried to tell Helen more with her eyes.

Adelle straightened the piano's lid, glaring in quiet accusation.

Teddy ran back in holding two chunks of ice. "The house next door had an ice box."

Helen remained on the piano bench with her arm over her head. Birdie used a handkerchief to wrap around the ice and held it against Helen's fingers. Mary and then Flo came up the aisle and stood before the platform. Adelle stood behind the piano next to Teddy. It was if they all held a collective breath.

"Who's hurt?" Hugo dashed in from the back of the tent.

"Birdie slammed the piano lid on Helen's fingers," Adelle hissed.

"She did not," Helen said.

Adelle disgusted Birdie.

"Let me see." Hugo stood over Helen.

Birdie lowered Helen's hand and unwrapped the handkerchief. Her three middle fingers looked like late summer purple carrots.

"Can you bend them?" Hugo opened and closed his own hand.

Helen's fingers quivered but only her pinky and thumb moved.

Hugo ran his hand through his hair. "Of all nights for this to happen."

"The Lyceum," whined Adelle as if she was the one hurt.

"Beat it Adelle, you're no help." Flo sat beside Helen.

"Helen needs a doctor." Birdie raised Helen's arm back up and the melting ice water trickled down both their arms.

"Who can play the piano tonight?" Hugo looked around at each girl.

No one offered. None of them came close to playing like Helen.

"Who knows the piano part of your routine?" Hugo insisted.

"I guess I can play the Patriotic Medley on the piano instead of my violin." Mary offered.

"First we need to get Helen to a doctor." Birdie's voice became louder. "Teddy, get the truck so we can take her into town."

"In a minute." Hugo looked at the others. "Who can play 'The Flight of the Bumblebee' on the piano?"

"I will." Adelle stepped forward. "I've played it on the piano to figure out the banjo chords."

"But can you play it like Helen?" Flo countered.

Helen cleared her throat. "It'll have to be good enough." She stared at her lap.

"I'll take Helen to the hospital," Teddy said as he and Mary eased Helen to her feet. Birdie held onto the damp handkerchief that enclosed Helen's fingers.

Hugo snapped his pocket watch closed. "You ladies have less than one hour to figure out how you're going to pull off the Versatile Quintet act without Helen."

"I'm going with Helen."

"No," Helen and Hugo said in unison.

"You need to stay and do your best performance tonight, Birdie." Helen gingerly pulled her injured hand away. Teddy helped her step off the platform.

"We all do." Adelle pushed Mary and Flo along. "Meet in the dressing room now."

"I want to be with you, only you." Birdie called after them, but Teddy and Helen were near the back of the tent.

"Come on, Birdie," demanded Adelle.

It took all of Birdie's will power to turn away from Helen. The verses of "Don't Quit" pounded in her mind. Birdie walked into a fray in the dressing room.

"And that's why I think I should play the piano for the entire act." Adelle retorted.

"Applesauce." Flo threw up her arms. "You're more of a mouse than a maestro, Adelle."

"Can anyone else repair the broken string?" Birdie slipped in next to Mary.

Each of the girls shook their heads. "Then maybe we shouldn't even use the piano tonight."

"We have to use it, you sap. It's on the stage." Adelle crossed her arms.

"We could play everything up an octave, to avoid that key," suggested Mary.

"Or down," offered Flo.

"Who's going to perform Helen's monologue with Flo?" Adelle asked.

"I can." Birdie nodded. "I have it memorized."

"Even Teddy does," Mary said.

"Teddy might liven up our act tonight." Flo shrugged.

"Come on Flo, be serious." Adelle rapped the top of the trunk. "We don't have time for your antics."

"We don't need a ninny bossing us around either." Flo strut over to the mirror and fluffed her hair.

"Let's go through the pieces in show order and figure them out one by one." Birdie grabbed her notebook and pen from her satchel. She turned around. It was as if she heard Helen saying, 'Atta girl.' She sent up a quick prayer for Helen.

"I'll lead us for the Patriotic Medley." Mary moved next to Birdie.

"I think we should only use the piano when absolutely necessary." Birdie wrote 'Patriotic Medley' on a blank page.

Adelle snatched the notebook from Birdie's hands. "We don't need your featherheaded ideas. Besides, this performance is obviously most important to me." She pulled a pencil from behind her ear. "We wouldn't be in this mess if you hadn't dropped the lid on Helen's fingers."

Heat rose up Birdie's neck and filled her face. "You're at fault too, Adelle."

"Enough." Mabel clapped her hands. When had she slithered into the dressing room? "Hand me the notebook." She held out her arm and wiggled her stubby fingers.

Adelle acquiesced and Mabel tore out a blank page. "Now follow me to the stage." She tossed the notebook towards the mirror. Flo scurried up alongside Mabel and the others followed them down the canvas hallway to the stage. Mabel dictated how they should perform their act without Helen and no one dared argue with her, except Adelle who was immediately reprimanded. To Birdie it was all noise. All she could think of was Helen.

That night's version of "Our Flight" featuring Mary and Adelle dueling with their violin and banjo, was well received. Adelle started it on the piano with such slow precision that even Birdie whistled at a faster pace. Mary played their "Lilies song" an octave higher while Flo and Birdie played an octave lower. It reminded everyone of what an integral part Helen had played in their performance. To Birdie's relief, the Lyceum men had stayed in their seats to hear Mabel's lecture.

Afterwards, Birdie rushed into the dressing tent. Maybe the hospital was farther away than she had realized. She heard Teddy and Mary whispering in the canvas walkway between the tents.

"Where's Helen?" Birdie stood in the doorway.

"Ah, she's—" Teddy wiped his hands on his pockets and looked away.

"Birdie, come with me." Mary averted her eyes as she guided them back into the dressing tent, pulling the muslin curtain closed.

Flo and Adelle were changing out of their costumes. Birdie hadn't noticed them earlier.

"How's Helen?" Adelle demanded.

Mary cleared her throat. "I'm not sure how to say this."

"Just tell us straight." Flo put her hands on her hips.

"Three fingers are broken. She can't play the piano for months." Mary's hands covered her mouth.

Birdie sobbed, sinking onto the costume trunk. Flo patted her back. Adelle dropped the stack of band hats she had gathered.

"Is she still at the hospital?" Birdie's voice went up two octaves as she leaned up.

"She's at the train station." Mary wrung her hands.

"Baloney." Flo tugged her dress over her head.

"What?" Birdie cried.

"Hugo appeared just after the doctor had cast her fingers. Teddy overheard them talking about going to the hotel to collect her things and then to the train station."

"Did Mr. James fire her?" Birdie almost screamed.

"Not that we know of." Mary shook her head.

Birdie pushed back the muslin curtain. "How long ago?"

Mary held up her hands in frustration.

"Something's not right." Flo moved beside Mary.

"Keep your voices down," Adelle said through gritted teeth.

Birdie flew out of the dressing tent. Flo, Mary, and then Adelle followed her outside.

"You're still in your costume." Adelle stood framed by the glowing tents.

Birdie ran down the hill. Gravity plus adrenaline propelling her. "I've got to stop her."

She bumped into a man as she ran up the steps into the train station. Charging out onto the platform, she dodged several other people leaving the station. The lights of a caboose flickered off down the track. Only the acidic smell lingered. She bent over to catch her breath and almost upchucked into the tracks below.

Once Birdie had steadied, she strode up and down the platform, checking every person, every bench with frantic urgency. She went back inside the station and circled the small waiting area. Helen wouldn't have just left without saying goodbye. She wasn't dramatic like Flo or Adelle. Birdie walked up to the closed ticket booth and tapped on the glass. A man looked up from his desk and pointed to the "Closed" sign.

"Please sir." Birdie rapped her knuckles against the glass, making them sting. "I need your help."

"We're closed miss." His muffled voice sounded deep and hollow. "Come back tomorrow." He turned away.

"Where was that train going?" She banged at the glass with her palms flat. "The one that just left." Her ragged breathing left a clouded circle on the window.

He picked up his jacket and cap. "Philadelphia."

Birdie leaned her forehead against the glass.

CHAPTER 28

Dover, Delaware to Chesterfield, Maryland

Birdie sagged into one of the benches inside the emptying train station. A janitor whistled bits of "Swing Low, Sweet Chariot" as he swept the lobby. His off-pitch melody pierced Birdie's ears as she replayed everything over and over in her mind, scolding herself for every mistake.

Both doors of the station opened wide, bringing in swirls of dried grass, leaves, and Flo. The janitor stopped whistling.

"Where is she?" Flo towered over Birdie.

"On the train that left just as I got here." Birdie stared at the chipped floor tiles.

"Hells bells." Flo walked around the empty station with her hands planted on her hips.

Birdie crossed her arms, hugging herself while she rocked back and forth on the bench.

Flo tugged at Birdie's sleeve. "This place is closing up." She pulled Birdie up and nudged her along until they stood outside. The doors clicked locked behind them.

Flo lit and then took a deep drag from her cigarette. Pinching the silver holder between her fingers, she blew a thin stream of smoke up towards the stars. "Helen's not a preening peacock, none of this makes sense."

"It's all my fault." Birdie sidled next to her, wishing she smoked too. "I let the piano lid fall and now her career, her life may be ruined."

"Poor little bunny. Adelle had a part in it all too."

"Why would Helen leave without talking to us first?" Birdie wiped her dripping nose with the back of her hand. She thought of Helen in her green cloak and royal blue Musketeer hat sunning on the bench in the Ladies Auxiliary Club's Garden. If only she could start over.

"There must be more to it." Flo took another long drag.

Birdie swallowed. "I need a smoke."

Flo raised her eyebrow and handed Birdie the slim cigarette holder. Birdie put it to her lips like she'd seen Flo do and sucked in. The crisp smoke singed the back of her throat, and she sputtered a cough. She cleared her throat and tried again, with a much shorter puff. The sensation soothed her in an uncomfortable way.

"Do you think Hugo told her to leave?" Flo's voice sounded raspy.

"That windsucking crumpet." Birdie pushed the cigarette holder back to Flo.

"Where did you hear that name?"

"Helen."

"Maybe she left you a note at the hotel." Flo tapped off the ashes.

Birdie crossed her fingers on both hands.

Flo put her arm loosely around Birdie's shoulder and offered her the cigarette again. "You haven't heard the last from her."

Birdie willed herself to be as certain as Flo as she took another puff.

* * *

The next hours blurred into days. There had been no note at the hotel, only Helen's damp Musketeer hat hanging on the back of the door. Birdie began a daily routine of inquiring for Helen at each hotel's front desk, train station office, and town's post office for mail or phone messages. She'd received another letter from Lydia, but nothing from Helen. She searched the local restaurants, the town squares, and the audience each night to no avail.

Birdie didn't have Helen's parents' full names, address nor phone number. She scolded herself for not asking for such simple information. Birdie went along with the now Versatile Quartet and performed their revised routine with the enthusiasm of a grub. Adelle became their unnatural leader and wheedled them into useless afternoon practices. Flo and even Mary complained, but Birdie participated with aloof indifference.

Soon Adelle's version of "Our Flight" became its own masterpiece and the audiences were oblivious that they were experiencing something different. At least Birdie had conquered her whistling and breathing problems. With the techniques learned from Miss Agnes Woodward's book, Birdie could match the pace of the others and had become quite a whistling sensation. Ironically, often it was she who the audiences gave standing ovations to. It made Birdie sad to think what "Our Flight" could have been if Helen was still there. It appeared as if the Lyceum board was impressed. Mabel shared rumors that their season would be extended into the winter months as Adelle hoped.

At first Birdie avoided Hugo and his attempts at attracting her attention seemed half-hearted anyways. Yet Flo's comment that maybe Hugo encouraged Helen to leave ate away at Birdie. After their performance the previous night, she had seen her chance to confront him. He was meandering alone just outside of the tents.

"Hugo."

He jiggled his watch chain as he shrugged his shoulders.

"Did you tell Helen to leave the circuit.?" Birdie grabbed his hand to stop the rattling of the chain. "That night after her fingers were broken."

"Me? Why would you think that?" His eyes darted around as he removed his hand from her grip.

"Because Helen wouldn't have left on her own without talking to us first." She felt like slapping him.

"Come on, now." He held up both palms and backed away. "I'm hurt that you'd blame me."

Hugo always managed to confuse her more with his answers. They'd probably never know the truth of what happened at the hospital until they heard from Helen. Birdie hoped it would be soon. She didn't know how much longer she could continue to live in this gray haze.

* * *

The bright morning sun greeted the girls at the Chesterfield, Maryland train station. Birdie was the last to board. Flo sat next to Mabel while Adelle held a curt discussion with Mary. Birdie sighed in relief as she ambled past all of them and found a vacant aisle seat near the back of the car. She set her satchel and suitcase on the window seat. Leaning her head back, she adjusted Helen's blue Musketeer hat and closed her eyes. The train lurched forward towards the next town, whatever it was. Birdie's mind went to Helen, where it did most every minute of every day. Helen's pert nose and flashing green eyes. Once the train's clacking had become rote, she reached into her satchel and pulled out her note paper. Birdie sat with her pen poised. She blinked. What could she write that would convince Helen to forgive her? She had started many letters over the past several days and each been torn, crushed, and tossed into the bottom of her satchel. She tapped the pen to her lips.

Her mind was like the mashed potatoes Lydia would attempt for holiday meals, stiff and starchy. Birdie recalled the number of times both she and Gerald had choked down those awful lumps to appease Lydia. She should write them too. She put her pen to the paper and traced the looped letters of "Dearest Helen" over and over until the pen scratched through the paper. She tore off the page and methodically tore it into thin strips.

Birdie released another long sigh and picked up her pen. She tapped her notebook and started to write about the changes of "Our Flight."

Her pen scribbled across the page with comments about their new routine, remarks about Adelle's quirky leadership, and quips from Flo. It was almost as if Helen sat beside her, them conspiring together.

"Scootch over." Flo appeared at her side.

Birdie looked up but didn't move.

"Fine." Flo pushed past her and set Birdie's suitcase on the floor under their seats.

Birdie closed her notebook and tucked her pen behind her ear.

"Another letter to Helen?"

Birdie nodded. "Trying to finish this one."

"In due time." Flo looked out the window.

Looking past Flo, Birdie noticed that the leaves had already turned to yellows, oranges, and brownish reds. It was as if autumn had rushed in over the past several days.

"Mabel says the Lyceum is adding a holiday tour." Flo faced Birdie.

"How is it that Mabel knows so much?"

"I think she's making whoopee with Mr. James."

Birdie guffawed. The vision of round Mabel embracing rigid Mr. James made Birdie's cheeks flush.

"It's good to hear your laugh." Flo twirled her cigarette holder across her knuckles.

"I wish you had thought of a different way." Birdie swatted Flo's hand. "Now that awful vision is stuck in my mind."

"I wouldn't put it past Mabel," Flo snorted. She continued to distract Birdie with more circuit gossip and her unsettling observations. They arrived at Seaford, Delaware and it too turned into just another town in her futile search for Helen. At least this time, Birdie posted a letter to Miss Helen Wilcox with only "Mount Airey, Philadelphia" as the address.

CHAPTER 29

Seaford, Delaware

M r. James strode into the dressing tent, his neck stiff, barely nodding to each of the four girls. They had just finished one of their "Applesauce drills" as Flo had adeptly named the afternoon rehearsals scheduled by Adelle. He clapped his hands as if beginning the tango. Birdie hid a snicker behind her hand. She couldn't get that picture of Mabel with Mr. James out of her head.

Mabel eased into the dressing tent doorway; arms folded as if blocking their escape.

"The Lyceum has decided to add a holiday Chautauqua tour. They are generously offering the Versatile Quartet to continue as opening talent," Mr. James announced.

"Thank you." Adelle's excitement made her voice sound forced. "We are most honored." She bowed. Mabel nodded in approval.

Giggles bubbled up. Birdie turned away towards the mirror, but Flo caught her look in the reflection. Flo hooted like an owl. Adelle gave them both her best schoolmarm's glare.

Mr. James continued without any acknowledgement of their antics or Adelle's flattery. "Each of you needs to sign these extended contracts." He extracted the familiar long sheets from his leather briefcase and handed them to Adelle. She distributed one to each of the girls then took hers to the costume trunk and signed it with a flourish.

"It says the weekly pay is five dollars less than what we make now." Mary read aloud.

"And we're to finish up in Boise, Maine on New Year's Eve?" Flo looked up from the contract. "That's hooey."

"The pay is more than generous considering it is a holiday tour." Mr. James stroked his chin.

"And trains run on New Year's Day." Adelle tapped the trunk with her pen.

For the umpteenth time Birdie wished Helen were here. She would negotiate with Mr. James to increase their pay and change the schedule.

"I need some time to consider this." Birdie said in a voice that sounded more like Lydia's than hers. Both Flo and Mary nodded in agreement.

"I'd be careful Miss Stauffer." Mr. James collected Adelle's signed contract. "Unless all four sign, it could change everything." He stood beside Mabel. "It would be a shame to cancel this opportunity for the others."

"A holiday tour means fewer performances, so less pay." Mabel fluffed her plump Marcell waves and gave Birdie a look that said any professional should have known that. "You would be foolish to not take this offer." She adjusted her short-waisted jacket and swaggered out of the dressing tent.

Mr. James looked at Mary, then Flo, and his eyes narrowed at Birdie. "You have until after tonight's show." He walked out with such purpose, that his shoes made loud clicks walking along the packed dirt and straw.

"Have you lost your mind, Birdie?" Adelle moved to prevent Birdie from leaving the dressing tent. "This is what we've all been working for." She raised her arms up in a big dramatic V. "It's what we all want."

"It isn't kosher to reduce our pay," Flo remarked.

"Teddy and I wanted to be home for Christmas." Mary turned away.

Birdie let their complaints linger before adding, "I'm not certain this is what I want, Adelle."

"Why let your wishy-washy ways interfere with our plans now?"

It felt like a slap. Birdie's over-thinking and flim-flam feelings were the reason Helen left. Did Adelle know somehow? Birdie's heart pounded like a bass drum.

"We shouldn't just settle for this," Mary demurred. Several tense minutes passed before anyone else spoke.

"We could refuse to sign until they at least increase our pay." Flo raised her head. "It's what Helen would do."

"They need all four of us to continue 'Our Flight's' success." Mary looked up at Flo.

Birdie put an arm across Mary's shoulder and another around Flo's waist. "Let's hold out until we get sixty-five dollars a week."

"That's baloney." Adelle stomped her foot. "It's more than we make now."

"And why not ask for more." Flo bumped hips with Birdie. "They're requiring us to work over Christmas and New Year's Eve."

"And 'Our Flight' has become quite a sensation, even in its current version." Mary picked up her unsigned contract.

Flo tapped Birdie with the tip of her silver cigarette holder. "Helen was right, you're not milquetoast."

"And I bet they offer Teddy a contract too, so at least we'll be together for the holidays." Mary clasped her hands together.

"Let's not count our money before its hatched." Birdie winked. She knew that Helen would appreciate their plan. "We need to convince Mr. James and the Lyceum first."

"And you'll all sign if you do?" Adelle looked each of them in the eye, stopping at Birdie.

"Ab-so-lute-ly," Flo said.

"Of course." Mary folded her contract. "The extra money will be nice."

"Birdie?"

"If they agree to our demands." Birdie raised her fist.

"Let's go talk with Mr. High Hat together." Flo stuffed her contract into her purse.

"Maybe I shouldn't have signed mine." Adelle pushed some hair behind her ear.

"You'll learn one of these days that haste makes paste," Mary giggled at her own saying.

Birdie rolled her contract into her satchel. A breeze of confidence flew through her. She could hear Helen's "Atta girl." Mary placed her arm through Birdie's as they walked outside.

"I've been meaning to ask," Birdie watched as Flo and Adelle took off towards the hotel. "How is it going with Teddy?"

"We're trying to figure out when he can come home with me." Mary squeezed Birdie's arm and let go.

"For the sisters' approval?"

"Yes." Mary wiped her hands on her skirt.

"He'll do fine." Birdie lifted her head when she recognized the sweet pitch of an American Redstart Warbler's call. She hadn't detected a bird's whistle in days. "He's such a charmer and a gentleman."

"But my sisters are so opinionated." Mary stopped next to Birdie and looked around. "No one is good enough."

Birdie started walking again. "Don't let them ruin your dreams. You and Teddy are perfect for each other." Was she thinking about Mary's sisters or her own?

"I wish I could be as confident as you." Mary huffed as they reached the top of the hill.

Birdie heard a Northern Cardinal's chirp from a nearby maple tree. She felt that catch in her heart as she did a full circle search for Helen.

"I'm more confident when telling others what to do."

Mary snickered at Birdie's full circle. "We all are."

Except for Helen. She was consistently confident and always encouraging. Birdie whistled her signature cardinal's call and looked around one more time before stepping through the open doors of the Morris Hotel.

Flo was flirting with the desk clerk and Adelle stood off to the side next to Hugo. He strolled over to Birdie as soon as she reached the lobby.

"Adelle tells me you're all here on business." Hugo held Birdie's elbow and turned her away from the others. "What's the beef?"

He had that old man liquor smell again. Birdie pulled her arm loose. "It's about the extended holiday circuit."

"What extended circuit?" Hugo looked down at her with sad bloodshot eyes.

"The Lyceum is offering the VQ a special holiday tour."

"Not me, I guess." Hugo put his hands in his pockets, jingling loose change. "And I just finished lunch with him at the hotel's restaurant."

"But you don't need to extend your contract. Don't you start at Willow Glenn Publishing when the circuit ends in two weeks?"

"Birdie. Get a wiggle on." Flo nodded towards Mary who was already walking towards the restaurant.

"I do, but—" Hugo reached to squeeze her arm.

Birdie swatted his hand away. She needed to share all she knew about Hugo with Gerald as soon as possible. She wouldn't allow Gerald to become another person that her hesitancy failed.

Mr. James sat alone at a rectangle table in the hotel's restaurant. The three women stood around the edge, across from him.

"Have you signed your contracts?" Mr. James looked up towards Flo.

Birdie realized then that they should have been more strategic about how they were going to make their demands. Flo cleared her throat and looked down at Birdie. Mary stared at the floor, her hands shaking.

"We, we think we should be paid more per week." A burning pain formed in Birdie's chest, making the words come out tinny.

"Is that so? Why?" Mr. James raised his shoulders as he leaned back in his chair.

"Well, with 'The Flight of the Bumblebee' such a success and the added tour over national holidays." Birdie fluttered her fingers in the air. "We deserve to be paid at least sixty-five dollars a week."

Mr. James took in a long breath through his pointed nose. He shook his head. "Maybe I'll just hire a different act to play the Bumblebee song instead of you ladies."

"But we've perfected 'Our Flight.'" Flo added putting her hands on her hips. "It's our piece."

Mr. James snorted. "It's not. The Lyceum owns the music."

Flo gasped and Mary gripped the back of one of the empty chairs at the table.

"Helen and I wrote the arrangement for us." Flo folded her arms across her chest. "This isn't fair," she said under her breath.

"Who owns the music isn't the issue." Birdie tried to change tact. "Why should we accept less pay than we're making now?"

"Because it's the only offer on the table." Mr. James opened his palms as if it wasn't his fault.

Flo leaned over the table. "You and I know that you could hire another act, but none of them have the talents we offer." She batted her eyelashes. Birdie had to stop Flo before she got them all in trouble.

"Enough." Birdie clapped her hands, causing Flo to jerk up.

Mr. James took his gaze away from Flo to Birdie. Mary and Flo also turned to look directly at her.

"We're to be onstage in less than an hour." Birdie had to find a way to get out from under this rock and Mr. James. "Perhaps we can discuss this again tomorrow?"

"I need a decision tonight."

"I don't know what I'm going to do."

Mr. James nodded. "I knew you'd be the one to fold first."

"Are you?" Flo's eyes pleaded with Birdie.

"I'm not," Birdie said to Flo. "What I'm saying is we're still under our current contract and need to perform our best tonight."

"She's right for once." Adelle had followed them and now moved closer to Mr. James.

"Just so we're clear. The contracts stand as written." Mr. James stood and buttoned his jacket.

"Clear as hooch," Flo muttered.

Birdie, Mary, and Flo turned away from the table and walked out of the restaurant. How had Helen made negotiating seem so easy? Birdie held her hands to her chest, pressing the pain away.

"I expect three signed contracts after tonight's performance," Mr. James called after them.

"How'd it go?" Hugo rushed up to Birdie with his best Cheshire cat grin.

"Scram, Hugo." Flo elbowed him away. "We don't need your gloating."

He glanced towards the restaurant but then scurried towards the hotel door. "You ladies better get to the tents for cast call."

"He's such a boob." Flo shook her head and corralled the girls together in the lobby. "That didn't go as planned."

"It's because we didn't have a plan." Birdie watched Hugo lumber down the steps.

"Or because Mr. James is so stubborn," Mary sighed.

"I told you it was a stupid idea." Adelle came up from behind them with her lips pinched tight.

"We needed a better approach." Birdie glanced at Flo. "Neither of ours was working."

"A broad has to use all her assets in negotiating." Flo shrugged and nodded to the bellman who held open the door to the hotel.

They walked towards the tents with no further discussion of their failed effort to be like Helen.

*   *   *

"Birdie, you have to sign it." Adelle practically moaned. They were the only two left in the dressing tent. Flo and Mary left to deliver their signed contracts to Mr. James. Weeks ago, Birdie would have relished making Adelle squirm but tonight she felt more empathy.

"You can be the Versatile Trio for this holiday tour. You don't need me."

"But we do. You heard Mr. James." Adelle counted off four fingers. "It's all of us or nothing."

"Maybe he made an idle threat, not an absolute." Birdie put her folded band pants on top of the stack.

"You're so selfish." Adelle boxed Birdie in near the mirror. Her stale breath swept against Birdie's face when she exclaimed "Why won't you sign?"

Lydia had also called Birdie selfish whenever she didn't get her way. "I don't owe you an explanation."

Adelle stood so close, Birdie could see the veins on her neck expand and contract.

Birdie frowned. "Why is extending the circuit season so important to you?"

"I don't owe you an explanation." Adelle mimicked Birdie in an off-pitch voice. After several seconds she added, "You'd never understand."

"Try me." Birdie scooted sideways to put more distance between them.

Adelle glanced at Birdie and for a brief second it seemed like she was going to share something. In the next second her face closed, and she shook her head. "I'm not falling for your insincere friendship." Adelle moved to the opposite side of the trunk. "Just sign it. It's not that much longer."

"I'm done with Chautauqua. I'm sorry if it upsets you."

Adelle knocked lightly on the trunk. "Nothing's been the same since Helen left."

"Truer words have never been spoken." Birdie walked around, keeping the trunk between them. "How about I teach you to whistle bird calls so you can do that piece with Flo instead of me?"

"You think I can whistle bird calls like you?"

"Even better. You have the Agnes Woodward training."

Adelle kicked the trunk. "I'd rather have you sign the contract."

"I didn't need any certificate to whistle those bird songs and neither do you." Birdie held Adelle's dark eyes. "It'll take extra practice on your part."

"I have no problem practicing. It's all of you who complain." Adelle pursed her lips as if she was silently whistling. She looked past Birdie and then extended her right hand. "Shake on it."

Birdie half-laughed, shaking Adelle's hand.

"You better start right away. Our summer circuit's over in two weeks."

Loud clapping and murmurs signaled that Mabel's speech was over. "I better go tell Mr. James I'm not signing his contract."

"What if he doesn't extend the circuit for the rest of us like he promised?" Adelle turned paler. "Or what if he fires you now?"

"He can't fire me for not extending a contract." Birdie said with more certainty than she felt. "And with three signed contracts, I'd think he has to extend the season."

"You better be right, Miss Perfect Pitch."

CHAPTER 30

Warrenton, Virginia

A few days later, Birdie sat on the bench outside the Crisfield, Maryland train station. She had hoped being outside would help change her mood, but the late summer humidity had different ideas. The air felt as dripping with melancholy as she did.

Mr. James had not liked her refusal to sign the extended contract. However, Mabel told them the Lyceum saw the extended season as a way to entice communities to book for next year and a way to recoup a percentage of this season's losses. She said the Lyceum was happy to have the Versatile Quartet become a Trio; it meant that much less paid in talent salaries and accommodations. Teddy was offered the circuit manager position, at his assistant's salary. He had eagerly agreed, telling Mary that it was the opportunity he had wanted. So, Mr. James' threats had been as hollow as his personality.

Birdie leaned forward to unstick her legs from the bench. The next train couldn't come soon enough. With the windows open, it had to be somewhat cooler. She could smell Hugo before he appeared beside her. She no longer denied that he was a drunk, but she had never mentioned it to his face either. It was one of many unspoken agreements between the two of them. Birdie felt no attraction to him, only pity. She felt oddly comfortable ever since she had told him they were not an item.

"Good morning, Hugo."

"Not so good in my books." Hugo sat next to her making the bench settle lower.

"Headache?" Birdie slowly turned her face towards him.

"What?" He took off his hat and raked his hand through his sweaty crown of hair. How had she ever found him handsome? "Well, that and Mr. James." He twirled his hat between his hands. "He's threatened to fire me."

The long-awaited whistle sounded, and Birdie turned her attention to the incoming train.

"I thought I might start at Willow Glenn Publishing but then Gerald would ask why I'm leaving the circuit early. Before you."

"He might." Today, on this train, she would write Gerald. She owed him the truth about Hugo. No more hiding behind social conventions or artificial relationships.

"I heard you didn't sign the extended contract." Hugo tapped her shoulder to bring her attention to him. "Mr. James is quite disconcerted by your show of independence."

"That's what happens when you count your turkeys before they hatch." She felt more confident than she had in days.

"I wouldn't be so smug." Hugo stood up as the train pulled alongside the platform and with it the glorious movement of air, even if it did burn her nostrils. His follow-up comment got lost in the sounds of screeching metal wheels on the metal track.

Birdie tugged at his arm. "What do you mean?"

"Look at what they've done to me." Hugo placed his hat back on his head and strolled away. Birdie brushed her hands as if to rid herself of his black cloud. Typical Hugo, to blame his problems on someone else.

Flo, Adelle, and Mary appeared on the platform. Birdie followed them up the steps into the train. She put her suitcase on the rack and reached over to release the latch to open the window.

"Flo, can you help me?" Birdie bit at the jagged edge of her broken fingernail. "This thing is stuck."

"That one's broken," said an elderly man seated across the aisle. "Several of 'em are jammed in this car." He nodded to the closed windows.

"I'm moving to another car." Adelle walked down the aisle and Flo followed. Mary found an aisle seat that was two rows behind the only open window, even if it was just a crack.

"Suit yourselves. You'll soon see the other cars are full." The man's wife fanned herself with a newspaper.

Birdie stayed in her seat near the open door. Maybe the conductor would keep it open during the trip. Sweat mixed with cheap perfumes and cigar smoke permeated the train. Her own perspiration pooled under her legs; her dress did nothing to help because it was already damp. Soon Adelle and Flo returned and found seats apart from one another. The train lurched forward and with the open door, Birdie felt a shaft of moving hot air filled with coal dust.

She leaned her head against the window and threads of moving air from around its seams offered her some relief. She thought again about how her indecisions had caused her to lose Helen and she was determined to not let it hamper her again.

Birdie had decided that today she would telephone Helen's parents, or at least try. It made no sense to be afraid to at least ask the operator for Mr. Wilcox of Mount Airy, Philadelphia. If they couldn't locate him, she'd be in a better place than second guessing herself. And if he did answer, maybe he'd tell her where Helen was or even better, Helen would come to the phone.

Birdie glanced a few rows back at Adelle, who was partially hidden by her daily newspaper. She was some odd bird. One minute Birdie's ally and the next her nemesis. Birdie searched for her Life Savers in the pocket of her satchel and she saw an unopened letter from Lydia. She slid her finger along the seal and pulled out scented stationery. After skimming most of it she crammed it back into its envelope and tossed it away. To think Lydia wanted them to perform at the Poconos Manor over the holidays. The last thing she needed was to be admonished by Lydia. She picked up her pen. Time to be honest with Gerald.

The townspeople of Warrenton, Virginia were crowded outside of the tiny brick train station. It made Birdie realize that even though she'd soon be finished with Chautauqua, there were people who had looked forward to this week all year. Maybe knowing that this would be one of her last parades made her participate with more enthusiasm. Or maybe this is what she had enjoyed the most, bringing music and joy to these rural towns.

She hopped up onto the back of the rusty pickup truck and straightened the ribbons adorning the sides. She waved to the people who lined Main Street and encouraged the children racing alongside their parade. She couldn't wait to share this with Helen in her next letter. Or maybe she'd tell her about the kids who cheered when Teddy and the boys unloaded the tents.

"These hooligans get worse with every town." Flo held her hands over her ears as another shout exploded when the Anvil Choir hoisted the first tent pole.

"They've been waiting for us all summer." Birdie blew kisses to several of the little girls crowded around the truck, causing a twittering of giggles.

"What's making you so chipper today?" Mary sat on the open tailgate of the truck and took one of the cold seltzer waters the driver offered.

Birdie joined her. "I guess I'm a bit nostalgic now that I know my season is ending." She took a swig of the cold bubbly water.

"We're going to miss you, Birdie." Mary swung her feet and hopped down. "Adelle is a better whistler than I thought, but she hasn't mastered your pitch."

"She's improving every day." Birdie surprised herself by standing up for Adelle. She had proven to be such a difficult student. Adelle's natural impertinence came out when Birdie tried to show her how to form her lips, breathe, and then whistle. No wonder Agnes Woodward hadn't awarded her a certificate.

"What are you going to do once you're home?" Mary asked as they followed Flo back towards town. Adelle followed way behind.

"It depends." Birdie knew she wanted to find Helen; she just didn't know how to start.

"On Hugo?" Mary said with a nudge.

"No." Surely Hugo had told Teddy, who had surely told Mary that they were through.

"Isn't he working for Gerald?"

"He starts in a week, I believe."

"Isn't that why you won't extend your contract?"

"No."

Mary raised an eyebrow and caught Birdie by the elbow. "Level with me."

"I'm not Hugo's gal and I'm definitely not going home because of him."

Mary covered her mouth. "Hugo told Teddy that one day you were a vamp and the next an icy mitt but we didn't believe him."

"What?" The gall of that man. Birdie charged ahead, staring at her feet. She was going to give Hugo a what for.

"Birdie. Watch out," Mary yelled.

Birdie stopped and looked straight ahead at the metal streetlamp that had almost given her a goose-egg. She couldn't manage all this drama. She was no Helen.

"Uh, thanks." Birdie edged around the pole and Flo caught up with her, leaving Mary to wait for Adelle.

"Helen always said you got lost in your thoughts, but I never saw it like that." Flo shook her head.

"Helen talked about me to you?" Birdie tugged at Flo's sleeve.

"Mostly in defense of your naiveté." Flo opened the door to the charming three-story hotel and waved Birdie ahead. "You're not the only one who misses her, Birdie."

"Any mail for Chautauqua talent?" Birdie asked her daily question at the front desk.

"Nothing today, ma'am." The desk clerk slid two keys across the smooth wooden top. "Your rooms are ready."

"Is there a private telephone I can use?" Birdie asked.

"Let's take Room Sixteen." Flo grabbed one of the keys. "A bath would do you good, buttercup." She held her nose.

"Yes ma'am. Follow me." The clerk nodded to Birdie.

"What's up?" Flo asked.

"I need to call uh, Lydia." Birdie fanned herself with her hand.

"You're going to be with her in a week." Flo playfully slapped Birdie's shoulder. "Why call now?"

"I, uh, to ask Gerald to pick me up at the West Chester station."

"Of course," mocked Adelle who appeared at the front desk. "Call Lydia." She twirled the other room key around her forefinger. Her pointed stare made Birdie think Adelle could read her intentions.

"Suit yourself." Flo flounced towards the stairs. "I get first dibs on the lavatory."

Birdie turned to follow the desk clerk. When she closed the accordion door on the cramped room, she agreed with Flo, she stank. That could wait. Fingers shaking, she ran them along the tiny wooden stand that held the telephone. She lifted the receiver.

"Please ring Mr. Wilcox, the architect, Mount Airey, Philadelphia," Birdie said in one breath. She jerked towards the door. Someone had brushed against it.

"Yes. I'll wait." She peered through a tiny crack and saw nothing but gold striped wallpaper.

She heard several clicks. The receiver became slippery in her palm. She hadn't planned what to say.

"This is Henry Wilcox." A baritone voice filled the receiver. Birdie pressed it to her ear.

Helen's father. The Grecian styled house Helen had stopped to point out to her loomed before Birdie's eyes. Static filled the line.

"Hello?" He asked.

Birdie couldn't find any words with her heart pounding.

"Helen, is that you?" His voice increased an octave, almost pleading. "Where are you?"

Birdie's chest burned as she clutched the earpiece. She covered her mouth with her other hand.

"Operator? There's no one there. The line's been disconnected." Mr. Willcox hung up.

Birdie let the receiver fall into its handle. She slid down the wall holding her head. Now what would she do?

* * *

Birdie's last bow ended with an extravagant curtsey, her arms spread wide and a catch in her throat. She already missed the musty smell of canvas mingled with popcorn and old straw and that exhilarating feeling only that performing on this stage could produce.

Had she really just whistled her last "Our Flight" with the Versatile Quartet? Their current arrangement still drew large crowds and enthusiastic applause. She followed the others to the dressing tent, slightly queasy with second thoughts about not extending her contract.

She rambled along the canvas walkway and absently pushed the muslin curtain open to Adelle, Mary, and Flo spaced around the costume trunk like statues in modern dresses. Flo's mischievous grin said more than their awkward placement.

"We wanted to send you off with something to remember us by," Mary said.

"But since you insisted on skipping out early, we had to make do on short notice," Flo added.

Adelle even wore a smile. Well, a half-smile. "We wouldn't have been as versatile without you."

Mary slid a wrapped rectangle across the trunk. Birdie carefully pulled away the crisp paper revealing a black photo album. Her fingers brushed the smooth cover as she opened it. Their group photo that Teddy had taken ages ago was centered between four corner holders glued to the first page. Beside it was written "The Versatile Quintet Chautauqua circuit 1924" in white ink.

Birdie took her time flipping through the book. The girls huddled around, pointing at the various photos with little notes written beside each. Adelle playing the musical saw, Teddy and the Anvil Choir hoisting the tent poles, and Hugo with his shirt sleeves rolled up. They all giggled at one of Flo charging up the stairs to a train station. Birdie traced her finger around the photo of Helen tuning the piano.

"Oh, my gracious." She wiped under her eyes.

"You've been a gem to us, little bunny." Flo hugged her. "Who's going to fall for my quips now?"

"Maybe you'll miss us when you look back over your Chautauqua summer." Mary draped her arm over Birdie's shoulder.

Birdie clutched the album to her chest. "Thank you." She nodded to each one of her friends.

Adelle tapped the album. "We've written our addresses in the back."

"Yeah. Don't forget us when you become famous," Flo said with a slap on Birdie's shoulder.

"*I* become famous? You're the ones continuing on with the circuit." Birdie blinked again.

"You're going places, Birdie." Mary bowed her head a bit. "Beyond the circuit world."

"I wish I was as certain."

"Let's not get all big-headed," Adelle said.

"Forever the killjoy, Adelle." Flo walked over putting both arms around Adelle's rigid frame. "That's what we love about you."

"I am going to miss each of you," Birdie said as much to herself as to them.

"We're celebrating with our own last supper," Flo announced. "There's this swanky diner on Main Street." She wiggled into her striped chiffon dress.

"Ab-so-lute-ly." Mary pulled her pastel dress over her head and folded it.

"This is just the bee's nose. Or the elephant's knees." Birdie watched the others.

"Such a sap." Flo applied mauve lipstick.

"I've already eaten a sandwich, but I'll come along." Adelle had changed and stood by the muslin curtain.

"You'll be wanting more once you smell this place." Flo turned back to Birdie who still stood clutching the photo album. "Skiddoo, Birdie."

Birdie placed the photo album in her satchel along with her vanity case, turning around in the dressing tent for one last look. As she removed Flo's headband from the top of the mirror, she caught a glimpse of herself. Her reflection looked more confident and worldly than she felt. She placed her costumes along with Flo's headband on top and closed the trunk.

CHAPTER 31

West Chester, Pennsylvania

As the train eased into the familiar West Chester station Birdie felt as if she'd been away longer than one summer. Gerald had predicted she'd mature over her Chautauqua journey but it wasn't until now that she fully realized her own transformation. She hoped Gerald, and especially Lydia, would be receptive to her metamorphosis.

Her hard-written letter telling Gerald all about Hugo sat unmailed in her satchel. Once she had re-read what she'd written, she had decided it would be better to tell him in person. Yet as she got closer to home, she became uncertain again. Was it her duty to tell Gerald that she believed Hugo to be a drunk, smuggler, and windsucking crumpet? Perhaps the most civil thing was to let Hugo start his job and prove himself to Gerald, good or bad.

The train screeched to a stop. As the people milling outside the brick station came into focus, that unwelcome burl clenched her stomach. Lydia stood on the platform, in a beige dress trimmed with black satin and matching torque hat. Birdie gathered her things and her remaining nerve.

"Come along Bertha." Lydia gave her a curt hug. "Gerald's waiting."

"It's wonderful to see you too." Birdie turned to follow Lydia, who barreled through the open doorway. With her satchel across her chest, her weathered suitcase in one hand and her trusty trombone in the other, Birdie struggled to keep up. It vexed her how easily she slipped back into her expected role. She stopped to straighten the blue Musketeer hat Helen had left behind, garnering more gumption as she tugged at its corners.

Gerald stood beside his sleek Buick, parked right at the front of the station's entrance just as Birdie had expected. He reached for her things and set them on the curb. She stepped into his wide embrace breathing in his signature scent of Cavendish tobacco mixed with Gerald. He held her at arm's length, as if surveying his prodigal daughter.

"You've become quite the sophisticated woman, my dear." He opened both their doors, put Birdie's things in the trunk and walked around to the driver's side. "I'm not sure West Chester is ready for you."

Birdie tucked in a smile as she slid into the back seat. "I am glad to be home." For now, she added to herself. Over the past few weeks, she had spent much time considering where to start her search for Helen, and decided it had to be a big city. She was finished with small-towns as much as she was finished with Chautauqua.

"The Poconos Manor manager is anxious to meet you." Lydia turned in her seat to face Birdie. "We have an appointment later this week."

"Uh, why are we meeting?" Birdie watched as the shops turned into reassuring brick row houses.

"Our performances there, of course." Lydia faced front. "As I said, he's quite impressed by your Chautauqua circuit experience."

"When is this performance?" Passing the Marshall Square Park gave Birdie a sense of comfortable melancholy.

"*Performances.* Over the holidays." Lydia stared straight ahead. "I explained it in my last letter." She glanced over her shoulder.

Birdie gripped the edge of the leather seat. She had read that letter. Then thrown it into her satchel. She had hoped by not responding, the idea would disappear. That was the old Birdie's thinking. She couldn't let Lydia maneuver her into things she didn't want to do any longer. Birdie cleared her throat as they passed Mosteller's Department Store.

"I did read your letter and I'm not—"

"Here we are. Home at last," Lydia announced in a louder than necessary voice.

Gerald hopped out and opened both passenger doors with a flourish. He assisted Lydia with an elbow boost and then offered his hand along with quiet advice to Birdie.

"Best to wait with your sophisticated ways till you've been home for several days," he half-whispered.

"I'll try." Birdie disagreed on the several days. She'd do her best to not upset Lydia this afternoon.

"I'm certain you'll want to rest after your travels." Lydia removed her hat after she opened the screen door. "We'll have a simple supper later."

Birdie stopped at the top step. A House Finch sang from the nearby crabapple trees. The welcoming porch called to her.

"I'm going to sit here awhile." Birdie dropped onto the padded porch swing and pushed her legs back until she balanced on her tip toes.

"Before you unpack?" Lydia cocked her head.

"Yes." Birdie released her feet, swaying back and forth.

"Gerald, place her things by the stairs." Lydia strode inside.

Gerald followed carrying the suitcase and trombone, shaking his head. Birdie delighted in the neighborhood reunion party. She identified and chatted with Black-capped Chickadees, Northern Cardinals, and a Brown-headed Nuthatch by the time Gerald stepped back outside.

"You've received several letters. And a package." Gerald handed Birdie a small box wrapped in brown paper. He shuffled the three letters several times then extended them to Birdie while scratching his temple, then he stepped away, closing the screen door with his fingertips.

Birdie stopped the porch swing. She set the letters aside on the seat and picked up the package. The lopsided "B" and unconnected "d" were unmistakable. She ran her pointer finger across the return address, a post office in Los Angeles, California. She peeled off the packing tape, unwrapping the paper, careful not to tear anything. Inside was an emerald silk box. She opened the lid to Helen's swallow brooch nestled on a cotton pillow. Birdie looked underneath and shook out the packing paper. No note. Just the beautiful, perfect pin. She smoothed the paper. Los Angeles? She squeezed the pin so the wings and pointed tails pressed against her palm, to make sure it was real.

Pushing off with her toes, she let the swing rock again. Birdie glanced at the letters in case any of them had a Los Angeles return address. One looked like a high school reunion notice, and the other two were from their West Chester Methodist Church. She started to tuck the brooch back in its silk cocoon and a crystal caught the afternoon light. She tilted the pin back and forth, causing reflected rainbows to dance across her lap and the porch. Birdie shook out the box, cotton, and wrappings, still no note. She pinned the swallows above her heart, took a full breath and went inside.

*   *   *

Birdie paused before opening the screen door the following morning. Visions of that March morning when she proposed auditioning for Chautauqua appeared as if she turned pages of a photo album. Coffee-soaked scones, blue and white china, and Gerald's Homburg hat. Older pictures came too, Uncle Bert teaching her the trombone, sitting on the swing with Rose, and learning to whistle with Edwin. Maybe one day Helen would be a part of her memories on this porch.

She pushed open the door and it hit the porch wall. "Good morning."

"Why must you slam the door, Bertha?" Lydia sipped her black coffee. "You're not living in a tent anymore."

"Good morning to you." Gerald turned the page of his newspaper. "The robins have already greeted the day."

"I'd forgotten how cozy my room is." Birdie had barely slept yet she felt the need to hide it from them. She had been up late writing to Helen and dreaming of California. She poured herself a cup of coffee, added cream and two sugar cubes. Not everything had changed.

"Is that a new brooch?" Lydia stared at the swallow pin Birdie had placed prominently over her left breast pocket.

"It is." Birdie touched a wing, then absently stirred her coffee. She sat down near Gerald.

"I'll see Hugo at the office today," Gerald remarked.

Birdie let out a long breath. Her truth-filled letter to Gerald was now stashed at the bottom of her cedar hope chest. The morning's nostalgia stuck in her throat. Finding a good time to speak privately with Gerald when Hugo had just started his job made things complicated.

"Don't frown." Lydia halfheartedly waved her hand but made direct eye contact with Birdie. "I'm certain Hugo will call on you soon."

Birdie had tried to forget her agreement with Lydia about choosing a bachelor before year end. Lydia now considered Hugo the chosen one. Birdie rubbed her arms. Making her new plans was proving to be quite challenging because she had to deal with old ones first.

"Please invite Hugo to dinner this Thursday." Lydia nodded towards Gerald.

Gerald glanced at Birdie.

"Perhaps we could wait a few more days?" Birdie turned to Lydia. "I'm quite tired from all my travels."

"Nonsense." Lydia brushed her hands together in that irritating way, indicating that discussion was over.

Birdie's foot started to tap.

"Now, we have much to do today, Bertha."

"*We* do?" Birdie moved to the edge of her seat.

"Aunt Edith is anxious to see you, we need to shop for a few groceries, and most important, go over the plans for our holiday show." Lydia picked up a piece of gingerbread and spread apple butter on a corner.

"I see." Birdie stirred her coffee again and set the spoon to the side of the delicate china cup. "I also have some errands of my own to do today." And they felt more important than anything on Lydia's list.

Gerald folded his newspaper. He took his time choosing his breakfast treat from the gingerbread and cinnamon rolls. Birdie sensed that he was waiting to watch what happened next.

"I can stop by Quality Market for you while I'm in town." Birdie selected a cinnamon roll and took a bite. "Do you have a list?"

"I'd prefer we went together." Lydia set her gingerbread on her saucer.

"It'll save us both time if I go myself." Birdie peered at Lydia over cream frosting. Her hand shook a tiny bit.

Lydia crossed her legs. Gerald leaned back in his wicker chair with a thick slice of gingerbread. Even the birds had paused their morning conversations. Birdie searched for her confidence out over the porch wall. Wisps of clouds rolled across the pale blue sky.

"Be back by two so we can rehearse, then conduct our afternoon visit." Lydia said with a firm voice.

"How about three? I need my hair trimmed."

Gerald's eyes went wide.

"I thought you were letting it grow out." Lydia's left eyebrow began to twitch.

Gerald looked at his watch, clearing his throat. "Time to get to the office." He brushed crumbs from his pants and rose. "Care to walk into town with me, Bertha?"

"Ab-so-lute-ly." Birdie jumped up and almost tipped the tray positioned on the wicker table. "Let me get my hat and satchel."

Birdie strode into the house, holding the screen door so it wouldn't slam. She could hear Lydia and Gerald's voices but not what they were saying. Probably for the best. She pulled the corners of Helen's hat down and straightened her pin in the entryway mirror.

"Do you have that grocery list?" Birdie extended her hand towards Lydia as she closed the screen door without a sound.

Lydia handed Birdie a slip of paper filled with her precise handwriting. "Don't let the butcher sell you the chuck roast from the case, ask for a fresh cut."

"Of course." Birdie started down the steps. Gerald kissed Lydia on her cheek and caught up with Birdie on their front sidewalk. They walked in uncomfortable silence away from 343 Walnut Street. Birdie had to tell Gerald what she knew about Hugo. Now.

Birdie grabbed Gerald's elbow as he turned the corner. "There's something I need to—"

"Let me offer some advice, Birdie."

She stopped. He had called her Birdie. "Yes?"

He pulled a cigar out of his breast pocket and hesitated before he put it unlit in his mouth. "Don't push all your newfangled ideas on us in the first day."

"Is it that obvious?"

A grin peeked around his cigar. "Tell me what you're thinking."

"Oh Gerald." Birdie clasped her hands. "I've discovered that there's more in this world than West Chester, Pennsylvania."

"I see." He started walking again and she strove to match his stride. "Am I correct that by more you don't mean the Pocono Manor?"

"Yes." Birdie stared at her kid leather pumps. "I don't want to quash Lydia's plans, but I just—" She kicked a pebble and it rolled under a pile of leaves.

"Tell her gently." He stepped towards street just as a black roadster rounded the corner. The driver honked and swung wide.

"Gerald." Birdie reached to steady him. "Are you all right?"

"Of course." He straightened his hat and crossed the street. "You've got to use finesse with Lydia."

"I'm not a natural like you." She thought she'd receive another sideways glance but he looked down instead.

"Lydia handles new ideas best if she thinks they're hers." Gerald turned onto High Street.

"I know." Birdie couldn't figure out how to make her own plans about Lydia because they weren't. Birdie had tussled with different scenarios so many times last night her head ached.

"If you share your plans with me, perhaps I can help convince Lydia." Gerald chewed on his cigar while staring at the new Mosteller's Department Store front window display.

"I need to work out some details first."

"Are you interested in California?"

Birdie's chin dropped.

"I saw the return address on your package."

Of course, he did.

"Lydia doesn't know about the package." Gerald answered anticipating her question. He put the cigar back in his front pocket. The tip was mangled.

"Yes. Maybe Los Angeles." Birdie said softly. He had no idea.

They stopped in front of Gerald's office building. "Then I think you should have this." He reached inside his jacket and pulled a slim envelope that looked as if it had been crushed. He hesitated before releasing it to her.

"Don't judge your sister too harsh."

Birdie saw that the envelope had been opened along the top seam.

"She loves you. She just struggles with how to show it." Gerald gave a half-hearted smile.

"What is it?" Birdie's fingers smoothed out the ivory card stock envelope.

He rubbed his face then placed a hand on her shoulder. "Talk with me before you say anything to Lydia." He buttoned his jacket back and looked off towards the granite office building before facing her again. "Promise me, Bertha?"

"Ah, yes." Birdie turned over the envelope. It was addressed to her. The return address said Agnes Woodward School of Whistling. She swallowed down her heartbeats.

"Look at me and say it." Gerald leaned close enough where she could smell the unsmoked tobacco of his cigar.

"I promise, Gerald."

"That's my girl." He tipped his Homburg and strode off.

Birdie's hands shook as she pulled out the single page. She glanced at the building where Gerald had disappeared then back at the letter.

September 15, 1924

Dear Miss Stauffer,

I have been following your performances with the circuit Chautauqua and am impressed with your artistic whistling abilities, especially 'The Flight of the Bumblebee' arrangement. You may have knowledge of our school; we offer courses in artistic whistling for young ladies. Agnes Woodward's Method of Whistling has become quite a current sensation.

She fidgeted with Helen's brooch. Could she be behind this? Birdie felt like she was riding the notes of "Our Flight." She gripped the letter with both hands to keep the words focused.

I would like to interview you for an opportunity to teach at our school. If you are hired, we can also discuss ways that I can promote your artistic whistling career. We are looking for a teacher to start in the January semester. Please telephone me once you receive this letter.

In warm regards,

Agnes Woodward

Director, Agnes Woodward School of Whistling

Los Angeles, California

Suite 521, 8th and Beacon Street

TRinity 8836

The outside world disappeared. Birdie twirled around and around in the middle of the sidewalk. A well-dressed man with a cane stopped so she wouldn't hit him. He shook his head then continued on his way.

Marshall Square Park was just down the block so Birdie floated to a bench to collect her thoughts. Cardinals chirped and chattered in the background while her mind struggled to sort through what this meant. Birdie opened the letter and mouthed the words over again. It was over a month since the letter was written. What if Miss Woodward had already hired someone else? No. Fate had determined she would move to California. Birdie closed her eyes, imaging life as a teacher with Helen in Los Angeles, but soon the awareness of what Lydia must have done screamed louder.

Lydia had opened her letter and then thrown it away. Gerald had retrieved it somehow. This was far worse than choosing a hairstyle or enticing potential bachelors. A robin's song echoed "Lydia lied. Lydia lied."

Birdie shook her head. Gerald had taken quite a risk giving her this letter. No wonder he had pleaded with her to talk with him first. Not judge her too harsh indeed. Birdie stood up. She owed Gerald much along with a huge dollop of thanks, plus she had to call Miss Woodward. She didn't have time to linger in the park.

CHAPTER 32

West Chester, Pennsylvania

Birdie's feet turned her towards the West Chester train station before she realized why—she couldn't call Miss Woodward from Lydia's home telephone. As she waited her turn for the public telephone just inside the station's office, Birdie wondered what Miss Woodward meant by an interview.

She reviewed several bird songs as her eyes followed travelers coming and going through the office's windows. There was always the recognizable Canary, but she decided to add Baltimore Oriole, Song Sparrow, and Meadowlark to show her range. Birdie silently urged the dapper businessman in front of her to hurry up his call. What if Miss Woodward asked her to whistle an aria or one of the songs that were printed in that book? She wished she had looked over the songs to have one ready. She crossed her arms and tapped her finger against her elbow. It sounded like the man closed his call with an "Atta boy" and Helen's encouragement filled Birdie. She knew she could do this as long as she didn't make any room for nerves.

The mustachioed clerk nodded that it was her turn. The letter shook in her fingers as she picked up the ear receiver from the telephone located near his desk and leaned in towards the mouthpiece.

"Please ring TRI 8836, Los Angeles, California."

"Yes ma'am."

Several clicks and crackles came across the line. It seemed to take forever for a connection.

"Agnes Woodward's School of Whistling, Verna speaking, how may I help you?"

"I wish to speak to Miss Woodward, please." Birdie turned her back to the three people in line, trying to quiet the station's mayhem.

"And who shall I say is calling?"

"Miss Bertha Stauffer, from West Chester, Pennsylvania."

"Ah yes, just one moment."

Muffled sounds came across the line. The loud screech of a train arriving filled the station along with billows of steam. How would Miss Woodward hear her whistling above the sounds of the trains, people, and the conductor's announcements. Birdie pressed her free hand against her chest to calm her inner chickadee.

"Miss Stauffer, I was beginning to think you had disappeared." A voice rich as velvet came on the line.

"I called as soon as I read your letter, Miss Woodward." If she only knew what had happened.

"I've told Verna we cannot trust the postal service. Telegraphing is much more reliable." She cleared her throat. "I assume this means you're interested in teaching at our school for young ladies?"

"Yes ma'am." Birdie tried her best to match Miss Woodward's professionalism.

"Do you have experience teaching?"

"Not officially, but I have taught a couple of ladies how to whistle bird songs and I've taught Sunday School for years."

"I see. And have you used the Whit-Cha?"

"Oh yes, it's a combination of the whip and chirp. I've used it for the Northern Mockingbird's song as well as others."

Miss Woodward continued with a series of questions about more whistling techniques, breath control, and songs Birdie had performed.

She asked Birdie to list the different bird songs she knew. Birdie's nervousness faded. It was if she shared ideas with a fellow whistler, almost a good friend.

"I'd like you to whistle your infamous 'The Flight of the Bumblebee' piece. You may warm up if necessary." The silence on the line that followed Miss Woodward's request rang with anticipation.

"Here?" Birdie's voice rose higher.

"Where are you? I've a trained ear for listening over long-distance lines."

"At the West Chester train station. It was the nearest public telephone."

"I see. Well, yes, you should be used to whistling in front of crowds. The folks at the train station may not be paying for a Chautauqua ticket, but they will appreciate your whistling all the same."

"Yes ma'am." Birdie buzzed her lips and whistled the Baltimore Oriole's song a few times to get her lips loosened up. Then she whistled their song of the Northern Cardinal for good luck. She sensed that the few people waiting in line to use the telephone stared at her back.

Setting the earpiece down, Birdie wrapped both hands around the mouthpiece and started whistling her part of "Our Flight." She tripped over the second measure, just as she had when she first learned it from Helen. Then she let the memories of the Chautauqua stage carry her and, flying into the frantic pace, she turned to face the small crowd that had gathered around her. When she finished, several people clapped and she caught a wink from the station clerk. She bowed, wiped off the telephone mouthpiece with her handkerchief and picked up the receiver.

"Magnificent. I hear people nearby appreciated it as much as I did," said Miss Woodward.

"Yes ma'am." The crowd that had gathered around Birdie dissipated and a conductor's call of "All Aboard" replaced her whistling.

"I'd like to offer you a position as teacher here at Agnes Woodward School of Whistling. I'll need you to start teaching in January but would like you to arrive at least the month before so we can be certain you understand my techniques and procedures. I can offer you seventy-five dollars a week plus room and board."

"I accept."

"Marvelous. Do you have any questions for me?"

"Ah, I am curious how you knew about me."

"A former student of mine, Miss Rowley."

"Adelle?"

"Yes. She mailed us newspaper clippings from several towns noting your success as a remarkable whistler."

"I'll, ah, have to thank her."

"I recommend a special notecard. Nothing expresses heartfelt gratitude as well as the written word." Miss Woodward must wear a strand of pearls of wisdom around her neck. "Anything else?"

The shock of Adelle recommendation jumbled Birdie's mind. "I'm certain I will have more questions once I arrive."

Miss Woodward laughed. "I imagine so. You do realize I'm asking you to travel to Los Angeles before the Christmas holidays?"

"Yes ma'am." Birdie would miss the traditional Stauffer Christmas Eve dinner. Maybe her acceptance had been too hasty.

"I trust your family will appreciate this unique opportunity. Once you have made your travel arrangements, please let us know."

"Of course. I am delighted to learn from you, Miss Woodward."

"Likewise."

Verna returned to the line and verified Birdie's address for a confirmation letter. She continued with a few more logistics and pleasantries, then it was over. Birdie hung up the receiver and skipped over to the station manager to pay her telephone charge.

"How much?" Birdie cocked her head.

"If you whistle my late wife's favorite bird, no charge," he said.

"I'd be happy to if I know it."

"American Barn Swallow."

Birdie cupped her swallow brooch from Helen and whistled the high-pitched short-sequenced song of a courting swallow several times.

"That's it exactly." The clerk squared his shoulders and stood taller as he motioned to the next person.

"Sir, I still need to pay." Birdie reached into her satchel. "My telephone call was all the way to California."

"Not today, Miss. You stick with your whistling." He waved her on with his cap.

* * *

Birdie shifted the box of groceries so she could see her watch and winced. It was just past three and 343 Walnut Street was still two blocks away. She hadn't meant to be late. She had spent a long time trying to track down Gerald. He wasn't at his office and no one seemed to know where he had gone. By the time she discovered that he was with a client, she was late for her hair appointment. The beautician had gossiped more than she trimmed but Birdie hadn't wanted to interrupt her in case that caused a slip with the scissors. She wished she had asked Flo to trim her hair before she had left. No one could style Birdie's bob like Flo.

She took the cement stairs two at a time and almost plowed into Lydia who stood at the screen door. Birdie felt like a mouse caught in a hawk's sights.

"You're late." Lydia held the screen door open.

"Here's what you ordered from Quality Market. Jennie asked about your knee." Birdie set the box on the kitchen table. "Did you hurt it?"

"Just a bit of arthritis." Lydia unwrapped and inspected the chuck roast before putting it in the ice box. She handed the grocery box back to Birdie. "Take the rest to the cellar."

When Birdie came back, she found Lydia seated at the piano.

"I want to rehearse some pieces for our Pocono Manor performances." Lydia ran her fingers across the keys in the C scale. The A key was sharp. "You didn't perform holiday tunes at Chautauqua, so I took the liberty of choosing the music."

"Lydia." The letter burned Birdie's leg through her dress's pocket.

Lydia leaned around on the piano bench. "Yes."

"The piano is out of tune." If only Lydia was half as talented as Helen.

"It's fine for today."

"I, well, when is the first performance at Poconos?"

"November twenty-fifth." Lydia cocked her head. "Why?"

"I just wanted to know how much rehearsal time we have." Why had she promised to wait and talk with Gerald first?

"Less than three weeks." Lydia's hands hovered over the keyboard. "That's why starting today is so important." She straightened the sheet music perched on the stand. "More important than a haircut." She muttered just loud enough.

Birdie placed her hand on Lydia's shoulder. "What was that?"

"I'd prefer if you grew your hair out. It's more becoming for a young lady."

"And I prefer to be a modern woman, not stuck in the past with a Grecian knot." Birdie stared at the back of Lydia's head. The tight bun of brunette hair shook.

"On second thought, I'm too tired to rehearse this late in the afternoon." Lydia reached for the music.

"Oh Lydia. I didn't mean to upset you." How did Lydia manage to make her apologize in times like these? Birdie was as angry at herself as she was with Lydia.

"Look over this music while I rest." Lydia handed the music sheets to Birdie. "We can discuss it after supper tonight." She swished out of the parlor.

Birdie stormed out to the porch, letting the screen door slam. She dropped the sheet music as she curled into a cushioned wicker chair. It didn't matter how much she had grown; Lydia was determined to keep them both prisoners of the past.

Gazing over the tops of the crabapple trees Birdie mulled over her dilemma with Lydia. What would Helen do in this situation? Helen had finessed Hugo many times and she had convinced Mr. James to let Flo be on probation then stay on the circuit. Helen was confident and prepared ahead. Ask questions as if you need their expertise. That had always worked with Lydia in the past, perhaps Birdie could try adding a bit of "honey" as Helen had taught her. Birdie absently whistled back a call to a Northern Cardinal. And of course, there was Helen's favorite tactic—always know what you want. That one was at the top of Birdie's mind.

CHAPTER 33

West Chester, Pennsylvania

The next day Gerald had out-of-town business so Birdie decided to switch her approach with Lydia. Defending her modern ways wasn't working and had proved exhausting. Maybe a day full of honey would convince Lydia that Birdie had matured. It meant she would have to stuff away her feelings about Lydia's betrayal. Birdie believed she could manage one day of being agreeable, delightful Birdie.

She dutifully ate toast with apple butter on the porch without spills and only whistled greetings to her bird friends when Lydia had gone inside. She dressed in the navy drop waist dress that Lydia suggested and followed cooking directions exactly as they made chicken noodle soup. When they visited Aunt Edith and Uncle Bert for lunch, she bit the insides of her cheeks when Lydia announced that they were performing at the Pocono Manor for the month of December. Birdie even stayed quiet so Lydia could tell exaggerated stories of her theatre days when they asked Birdie about the circuit.

Birdie allowed her sister to be in charge, in the limelight, and in her head. At their late afternoon rehearsal, it took all of Birdie's will power to go along with the sappy, boring arrangements that Lydia had chosen for their holiday performances. Right after supper, Birdie excused herself to her room because of a headache that crashed like waves across her forehead.

Laying on her back, rubbing her temples, Birdie counted the tiny cracks in her bedroom ceiling. She might have succeeded in making Lydia feel better, yet in doing so, she had lost herself. She turned on her side and traced the stiches of her quilted bedspread.

She wanted to move to California with Lydia's blessing. She wanted to be influenced by modern women like Miss Woodward, Flo, and especially Helen. Birdie released a long sigh. She wanted her problems with Lydia, Hugo, and Gerald to disappear with the wave of a magic ostrich feather.

A knock interrupted her musings.

"Yes." Birdie swung her legs around and sat up, a bit dizzy from the sudden movement.

Lydia opened the door and stood just inside Birdie's bedroom. "It's good to have you home today, Bertha."

Birdie nodded.

"I sense you're not excited about the arrangements I chose for our holiday performances." Lydia turned with her hand still holding the door. "Why don't you offer something different?"

Birdie raised her chin. "I'll see what I can do."

"Certainly, you learned a few tricks of the trade all those months on the circuit." Lydia closed the door behind her.

Birdie flopped back on her bed. She had played Lydia's game all day and all Lydia offered was to allow Birdie to make suggestions of holiday music arrangements. "Lydia's day" was over. Tomorrow Birdie would have her talk with Gerald and then confront Hugo since there appeared to be a shortage of magic ostrich feathers.

*   *   *

Birdie snuck out onto the porch before Lydia came downstairs to make the morning coffee. She wanted time in her sanctuary to review her day's plan. The porch swing swayed slightly as the sky filled with pinks and golds from the rising sun. A newspaper skidded across the cement, hitting the screen door. Birdie waved at Mr. Jones, who nodded and pedaled further down their block, flinging papers right and left. She whistled morning greetings to her feathered friends and eased onto the swing.

Birdie ticked off today's agenda on her fingers; first, secretly invite Gerald to lunch so they could have a serious talk about Lydia. She added another finger; she had to tell Gerald all she knew about Hugo too. She pushed back onto her toes, next she had to confront Hugo once again since he was such a windsucking crumpet. She released her hold so far back the chains clanked against each other. She'd uninvited him to dinner too. Birdie jumped off the swing into a little jig. Then she'd call Flo—it would be nice to share her news about Miss Woodward with a friend. She plopped into the cushion of the wicker chair. At some point, she'd have to share her moving plans with Lydia. Maybe they'd spend tomorrow looking for some suitable teacher outfits. Who was she kidding? Their shopping together days were over—for many reasons.

"Well look who got the early worm today." Gerald picked up the newspaper after he closed the screen door.

"Today's the first day of the rest of my life." Birdie pulled at Gerald's sleeve. "Can we meet for lunch?" She half-whispered.

He looked into her eyes briefly and then away. "Is this about what I gave you?"

The rich aroma of percolating coffee seeped through the screen door. Lydia would be outside soon.

"Yes."

"I'd rather wait longer." Gerald stepped out of her grip.

"I won't take no from you." Birdie crossed her arms. "It needs to be today."

He slapped his palm with the rolled newspaper. "Meet me at 12:30 at the Washington Hotel. It's on Chestnut, near Belmont."

Birdie nodded.

"Good morning." Lydia called through the screen door. "Shall I bring coffee and our breakfast to the porch? Or is it already too cold?"

"It's delightful outside." Birdie pushed herself up from the wicker chair with both arms. "Let me help you." Asking Gerald directly had gone more easily than she had expected. She carried the tray with coffee and cups while Lydia led the way with a walnut coffee cake. Today was off to a stellar start except for the storm clouds gathering to the north. She'd have to remember her umbrella when she went into town.

After breakfast, she hurried down the steps and picked up a stick running it along the neighbor's picket fence like she had as a child. Lydia had finagled Birdie into promising she'd help cook dinner in order to obtain "permission" to do her own errands. Knowing what else Lydia had done stayed on her mind, as if it was the chicken fat in the stock they had made yesterday, always floating to the top. The stick snapped in two so she tossed it into the gutter.

Birdie rehearsed her conversation with Hugo. She thought she had been clear in their past conversations, so today she'd be as direct as a speeding train. A flash from clashing clouds interrupted her thoughts. She glanced at the sky and picked up her pace. Miss Woodward had asked Birdie to move to Los Angeles by early December. It was as if God was using the weather to remind her of the urgency of her situation.

Birdie wondered if Flo had also heard from Helen. She glanced at the brooch pinned to the left collar of her cloak. She knew in her heart what it meant that Helen mailed it to her. But not having Helen's words to read over caused late night doubts.

Birdie ducked her head against the wind as she turned the corner to High Street. She couldn't believe her luck, there was Hugo just leaving Gerald's granite office building.

"Hugo," she called as she trotted up to him.

"What a pleasant surprise." Hugo took off his hat and ran fingers through his shortened, Brylcreemed hair. "I'm beginning to think our attraction is magnetic." He glanced around then pulled her into a quick embrace leaving greasy stains on the sleeve of her cloak.

Birdie stepped away. "Can you take a quick break?"

"I've got bank business." His eyes twinkled and the corner of his lip raised. "But since you're related to the boss, I imagine he'd allow a short dally."

She turned, walking with her head down and he followed her to the nearby Marshall Square Park. Birdie eased onto the same bench she had just days ago when she reread Agnes Woodward's letter. The euphoria of that moment empowered her. Hugo settled next to her.

"I need to be certain you understand that we are not an item." Birdie inched away from him.

"Aw, come on babe." He leaned back, spreading his arm along the back of the bench just enough to rest his fingertip on Birdie's shoulder. "You and I both know things are different now that I live here."

"I broke things off before." She raised her shoulders. "And we're still broken."

Hugo shook his head. The wind picked up, almost blowing her hat off.

"I'm at a loss, babe." He blinked his long lashes at her.

"Be honest with yourself. And me." Birdie stared at a broken oak leaf caught between her shoes. "You've never been as interested in me as you were in getting a job with Gerald." She stood brushing her hands together with wide strokes. "I am ab-so-lutely not your babe." She stared right into his brown bloodshot eyes. "And I do not want to be with you."

His eyes became glossy. "Lydia said you might be hesitant, but I never expected you to be cruel." Hugo lowered his head. Raindrops plinked against the bench.

He just confirmed her suspicions that he and Lydia had connived behind her back. "What does Lydia have to do with us?" A slap of thunder accentuated her question.

His reaction said "touché" but he continued. "You've stung me." He stood next to her. "I need to get to the bank before I get soaked."

"Listen to me, Hugo." Birdie raised her chin. "No matter what Lydia promised, I am not your girl."

He took a few steps, then faced her with his mischievous face back in place. "See you at supper tonight." He hurried away from her, the park, and down the street.

The impertinence of that man. She kicked a pile of acorns across the park's path. Maybe Flo could help. She dashed across the street and under the awning of the Washington Hotel just as the raindrops turned to sheets. The awning protected her from the rain but not from her anger. After several internal curses directed at Hugo, she stepped towards the doorway still steaming. She needed some good "Flo'ism" to get her past this outburst.

The desk clerk's eyebrow raised, but he led her to the phone closet with no pointed questions. Sitting in the velvet encased room brought back the times she had made futile phone calls to Lydia. Not that being present with her changed anything. What made Lydia think she could make promises to Hugo on her behalf?

Birdie tossed her hat on the bench and ruffled her hair, causing droplets to make darker spots on the purple velvet. Anticipation hovered over Birdie like her forgotten umbrella as she listened to the clicks of the operator making connections. It seemed like she had left her circuit friends years ago when it had only been days.

"Lincoln House Hotel, whom do you wish to speak with?" The desk clerk's tenor voice broke Birdie's musings.

"Miss Florence Armstrong with the Chautauqua circuit, please."

A long silence and then some scraping noises passed over the telephone line. Birdie tapped her foot against the wooden floor.

"Uh, Hello?"

"Mary."

"Oh, Birdie. What a pleasant surprise."

"How is the extended circuit? Is 'Our Flight' bringing in crowds?"

"It's not the same without you or Helen, to be honest." Mary must have covered the mouthpiece with her hand and lowered her voice. "Adelle can't whistle as well as you, no matter how hard she tries."

Melancholy draped Birdie like a lace shawl. She missed the Chautauqua stage. She really missed her friends.

"The hotel clerk said the call was for Flo, but I'm glad I took it."

"Me too." Birdie smoothed out a wrinkle in the velvet covered bench. "How's Teddy?"

"He proposed." Mary's voice got higher with her excitement.

"Atta girl. Spill the details."

"I wrote you over a page just yesterday."

"I can't wait for a letter now."

"Well, it was typical Teddy. He's such the romantic, he involved Flo and some of the Anvil Choir boys." Mary snickered. "After Mabel's lecture, Flo took me back to the main tent where a vase of daisies appeared center stage, and then he proposed."

"On one knee?"

"Yes. In front of the remaining crowd. We got a roaring ovation." Mary sounded so close. It was as if they were in a hotel room together recounting how it all had happened. Mary continued her story about the dinner that followed, layered with giggles and exclamations.

Birdie's mind went on a spiral of its own. Was she giving up on dreams of being married and raising a family, something that she had been taught to hope for all her life? She came back to the present when she realized Mary had asked a question.

"Ask again. Something crackled on the line."

"Will you be a bridesmaid?"

"Absolutely. I wouldn't miss it." Birdie hoped she hadn't just made an empty promise to her dear friend. "Give that beanpole a big hug from me."

"We all miss you. There's been no sparkle since you left."

Birdie's throat caught.

"I've rambled on too long. How are you? Did Hugo start his job with Gerald?" Mary spoke to someone in the distance. "I'm sorry. Adelle is calling, I've got to go. The Lyceum scheduled a special town-hall celebration for us."

"Of course." Birdie paused. "Give everyone my love."

"Did you want me to ask Flo something?"

"Oh. Yes, ask her to call me at Lydia's." When Flo called back they could schedule a time to have a long talk when Birdie could call from the train station.

"Bye for now." The phone clicked.

Bye, for who knows how long thought Birdie. A flash of reflected lights danced across the velvet and she stroked the cut crystals in her swallow pin. She tucked a damp curl behind her ear. She knew what she wanted. And even if it meant not living an old-fashioned dream, that was okay because that dream had never been hers.

CHAPTER 34

West Chester, Pennsylvania

The lobby of West Chester's Washington Hotel had been remodeled in the new geometric style that was popular from New York City. Just yesterday, Lydia had complained about the hotel's new décor when they visited Aunt Edith. The two women had clucked and crowed over the changes, commenting that it made the historic hotel look cheap and unrefined. Birdie was relieved that Gerald had suggested the Washington Hotel restaurant for their private lunch. After yesterday's snide remarks, she felt certain Lydia wouldn't appear.

Birdie waited in an upholstered chair shaped like a seashell and surveyed the lobby. She admired the symmetry from the sleek smooth walls to the geometric shapes in the chandeliers and tiled floor. She thought the black, white, and gold colors made it look sophisticated and modern. She shook her head recalling those two ladies spouting off about this hotel as if it belonged to them.

She turned the face of her watch and saw that it was half past twelve. Gerald should be striding through those glass doors any moment. She had to discuss how to confront Lydia about her betrayal, no matter how uncomfortable that made Gerald. And it was time to tell him what she knew about Hugo. Maybe then Gerald would uninvite him for supper tonight. She wanted to tell Gerald about her job with Miss Woodward and her excitement over moving to California. Maybe she should start with that first. She crossed her legs and leaned back. The tufted shell shape of the low back chair made it difficult. She inched forward and absently studied the interlocking triangle pattern on the floor. She shouldn't have promised Mary she'd be her bridesmaid. She may have created another difficult situation by trying to please a friend. She rubbed her toe following the floor's pattern chiding herself.

A dashing young man strolled past, overtly studying her. Rosy heat climbed up her neck into her cheeks. Gerald was officially late, which wasn't his style. She hoped he arrived before this young man found the nerve to approach her. Skirting unwanted advances wasn't her forte and she didn't want more practice right now. She needed what energy she had left to talk with Gerald. The man glanced at her from the fireplace, and she replied with a frown. Forget required social rules. She walked over to the front windows framed with brass arches to glance outside.

"Bertha." Gerald appeared in the doorway.

"I was beginning to fret you weren't coming."

The young man nodded to her as he walked past Gerald and outside.

"I had to wrap up a call from an irritated advertiser." He guided her into the restaurant located at the back of the lobby. It hadn't made the remodel list yet. Heavy tables and brocaded curtains reminded her of the décor at the West Chester Ladies Auxiliary Clubroom.

"Two for lunch," Gerald said to the head waiter.

Their usual camaraderie felt absent while they stared at their menus. Birdie set hers aside and watched the waiters arrange place settings at nearby tables.

Gerald cleared his throat. "Do you know what you want?"

"I'm hoping you'll order for me." She glanced at him then at her lap. "Like you've always done," she said in a softer tone.

"You're not too modern?"

A brief wisp of their friendship returned. "Not if it pleases the old man."

Gerald's shoulders shook with the low rumble of his laugh. "The lady will have the chicken croquettes with peas and I'll have the boiled ham and sauerkraut." He handed the menus to the poised waiter. "And two apple ciders."

Birdie blinked away the memory of drinking a lager with Helen, she needed to stay focused. "I have several things to discuss with you, Gerald."

"As do I." He leaned forward. "Normally, I'd let the lady go first but what I have to say is urgent, Bertha."

"But—"

"Please, hold your thoughts for now, I need your undivided attention."

The waiter set down two glasses of the amber cider.

"I regret giving you that letter. Forget you saw it." He shifted in his chair and ran his thumb down the condensation on the glass. "Please, for me as well as Lydia."

Birdie stared past Gerald, studying small rips in the gold trim of the brocade curtain right behind his head. When she turned her focus back, she noticed that his shoulders had sagged and he looked tired. She sipped the cider wishing it was a lager from Canada.

"I can't."

"Why not?" He leaned forward. "Lydia didn't want you to read it. I should have stood by her decision."

Birdie held both hands up. "I accepted the job at Agnes Woodward School of Whistling. In California."

Gerald fell back in his chair as if shoved by the wind from the morning's storm.

"Besides, I could never just forget that job offer, nor what Lydia did with it." Birdie sat up straighter. "She opened an official letter addressed to me, then threw it away."

"I know, I know." He rubbed his hands together and pleaded with his eyes. "But it was with the best intentions."

"How can you say that?" Birdie's tone rose with the volume of her voice. She had always considered Gerald her ally. Had she been mistaken? "Lydia doesn't know what's best for me." A couple nearby shifted in their seats as they glanced her way so she lowered her voice. "She never has."

Neither spoke as the waiter set down their plates.

"You don't understand what this means." Gerald spread his napkin across his lap. "Lydia will know I gave you the letter."

Gerald would have to do much to make amends with Lydia. Perhaps front row seats at the symphony concert, fancy dinners at the club, and even a jeweled bauble.

"I do sympathize, but that doesn't change what Lydia did." Birdie would not let Gerald's predicament change her mind. "I'm moving to Los Angeles to teach whistling. It's what *I* want to do."

He forked a bite of ham and strands of sauerkraut fell onto his napkinned lap. He chewed like his meal had turned into the letter. "When do you plan to tell Lydia?"

A waiter dropped a tray making Birdie jerk upright. "I'm not sure."

"At least promise me you'll wait a few weeks."

Should she tell him that Miss Woodward wanted her to be there as soon as possible? "I can't make any more promises that I can't keep."

"I wish you'd take time to consider what this means. For everyone."

"I have." She inched forward. Birdie had done what Lydia or Gerald expected her entire life. She couldn't let others deter her dreams any longer. "My mind's made up." Birdie placed a finger at her chin. "What if we said I received a second letter?"

Gerald brushed crumbs off the lapel of his jacket. "That might work. But it's dishonest." He rubbed his chin. "I can't lie to Lydia." He offered a sheepish I'm-practically-perfect look.

"I see." Birdie shifted in her chair. She and Lydia had told little white lies to each other most of their lives.

"What did you want to tell me?" Gerald took two big gulps of cider.

"Ah, I need to tell you what I've learned about Hugo."

"Go on." Gerald sat back with his hands steepled.

Birdie explained how Hugo had been on probation at the circuit, shifting in her seat as she described Mr. James' close watch of Hugo. She stared at the old-fashioned curtains again and told Gerald that Hugo often drank on the job yet hid it from most everyone. She paused.

Gerald pressed the tips of his fingers against each other, staring past Birdie.

She took a deep breath. "And he smuggled Canadian whiskey in duplicate instrument cases." Birdie moved some peas around with her fork. "He claimed it was to make money but I have no idea who he sold it to." She stabbed two peas. "For all know, he drank it himself." She let the fork clatter to her plate and looked up at Gerald.

He absently nodded.

"I realize I'm late telling you all of this. I tried writing you several times." Birdie reached for her glass. "I even have a letter written to you in my hope chest." She took a swallow then said, "I wish you'd uninvite Hugo for supper tonight."

"What?"

"Tell Hugo he's no longer welcome."

Gerald raised his eyebrow. "Why would I do that?"

"Because of what I just explained." She opened her hands. "And I've told Hugo we're through several times, but he won't listen." Birdie leaned back, crossing her legs. Had Gerald even listened to her list of Hugo's atrocities?

"Lydia likes Hugo."

"But now that you know he's a drunk, smuggler, and an unreliable manager I would expect you to change your mind. And Lydia's."

"Please, keep your voice down." Gerald sliced a bite of his boiled ham. "Accusing him of smuggling is serious. I doubt you know what you really saw."

"He practically admitted it to me." Was Gerald doubting her word too?

"I'll look into it." Gerald blotted his mouth with his napkin.

"Please Gerald." Birdie sank back into her chair. "At least tell him he shouldn't come for dinner tonight."

"I will not. It would upset Lydia and we both know I might be walking on cracked ice with her." He finished his last bits of ham in one bite. "You need to learn to confront whatever makes you uncomfortable, not avoid it."

"Just like you're doing with the decision to give me that letter."

"That's different and you know it."

"Only because it's a bird of a different color." Birdie crossed her arms.

Gerald stared at her. "Did they teach you impertinence on the circuit?"

"I'm sorry." She knew to stop pressing. "I just don't want to be around Hugo tonight."

"I'll help deflect conversations. It's just one dinner."

Birdie looked at his pale face, his tired eyes. He may have only heard every other word she said about Hugo. His mind appeared focused on his potential confrontation with Lydia.

"Of course." She cut into a croquette. A slight film had formed on the gravy. She scooped up a forkful of peas instead.

"So, tell me more about this whistling school." Gerald eased back into the upholstered chair. "Is the person who mailed your package from California related to the school?"

Birdie coughed up a few peas into her napkin and tucked it away. "The school is owned by Miss Agnes Woodward. She's quite famous and even developed her own technique for teaching whistling." She took a long drink of her cider, watching Gerald over the rim. A forced version of his take-charge smile had returned.

"And the package?"

The old Birdie considered ducking under the table. She cleared her throat. Gerald had said to confront whatever made her uncomfortable.

"It's a special gift from Helen."

"Oh?"

"She's become a very close, ah, friend."

"How close? Lydia doesn't like her."

It was as if a spirit flew through Birdie, cooling her embarrassment and emboldening her to tell Gerald the truth.

"I'm attracted to Helen." She swallowed. "I want time to get to know her better." It was as if the room shifted. She felt the same as if she had drunk several of those Canadian lagers.

Gerald's hands appeared frozen on top of his knees.

"This must be a phase, Bertha. You're impressed with her talent and sophistication." He wiped his hands with his napkin. "It'll pass, I assure you."

She debated whether she should just go along with Gerald's assessment. She touched the wings of the top swallow on Helen's brooch.

"It's not a whim."

Gerald's face became as white as the napkin he crumpled with his hands. "It can't run in a family, can it?"

"What?"

"Edwin." He spat his name along with a few bits of sauerkraut. "Lydia called him a sexual deviant." He pushed his chair back as if distancing himself from her. "Why else do you think he moved to Pittsburgh. He was no longer welcome in our home."

The realization hit Birdie like a roaring train. Edwin had been queer? Lydia had often claimed she never understood him. It was as if an old family photograph suddenly became transparent. Edwin had been Birdie's best ally and closest sibling. Maybe he had sensed something in her that she hadn't even known herself.

She closed her eyes, seeing Edwin strolling under their apple trees teaching her to whistle bird songs. They had an unspoken current between them, one that included uncomplicated acceptance and inside jokes. Birdie had always thought Lydia was jealous of their relationship, now she knew it was much more complicated. It made her sad to realize she should have written Edwin more when he moved away to Pittsburgh instead of siding with Lydia that he had inexplicably left them. Another betrayal and hidden truth from Lydia.

"Bertha." Gerald's voice had become husky.

Birdie opened her eyes, letting her memories of Edwin fade for now.

"You must be mistaken about this, this Helen."

"I am not."

Gerald shook his head. "You *will not* tell Lydia." He pushed his plate away. "She cannot know."

Birdie bit her lip.

"And you are not moving to Los Angeles either. Look what happened to your brother."

"You can't possibly think—" Birdie stopped herself as it became clear. Gerald thought Edwin got the flu and died because he was queer. She gripped the arm rests of the chair preparing to defend them both then slowly lifted her fingers instead. She couldn't change Gerald's or Lydia's outdated minds. She ran her hands up her arms, hugging herself. The hole that Edwin had left became bigger and more painful. Together they would have been a force against Lydia.

Two waiters laughed as they pulled the heavy curtains back from the large plate glass window. Rays of sunshine came through the clouds and shone on the dirty glasses and dishes of a nearby empty table.

Gerald looked at his wristwatch. "I'm late for an important meeting." Standing up he said, "Until we can talk privately again, are we clear that you will not tell Lydia anything?"

She looked up and barely nodded.

Gerald pulled his Homburg down over his drawn brow and strode towards the waiter. He handed him several bills then rushed out of the restaurant. Birdie sat at the table for several minutes. She remembered the day Edwin had left. She had stayed on the front porch until dusk, waiting for him to change his mind. Lydia had insisted Birdie was a fool that would catch a cold. She tapped her fingertips on the tablecloth. If only Edwin had been here today. He might have helped her devise a clever way to deliver her news to Gerald and Lydia.

Outside she was greeted by wet streets sparkling in the bright sunshine. She filled her lungs, hoping for some clean air but instead took in autumn's damp leaves, exhaust fumes, and mud. Birdie trudged off towards home knowing Lydia waited for her to assist with preparing Hugo's dinner. She angled her blue hat and took long strides. Gerald was right, she would confront whatever made her uncomfortable, even Lydia.

CHAPTER 35

Still West Chester, Pennsylvania

"Pick out the cherries one by one like I showed you." Lydia turned back towards the sink and rinsed freshly shucked ears of corn. "No one dumps the jar out in a heap."

Birdie scooped up the pile of maraschino cherries and plopped them back into the jar. Streams of pink liquid ran past her wrist to her elbow. Picking out a plump cherry she placed it at the edge of a pineapple ring. Silence was her best defense with Lydia this afternoon. Birdie chewed on a flattened cherry.

"Just arrange the fruit. I'll pour in the batter."

Birdie nodded to Lydia's back.

"You're very quiet this afternoon." Lydia slid a knife along the cob and bright yellow kernels tumbled onto the cutting board. "Are you daydreaming of Hugo?"

Birdie swallowed the cherry whole.

"No." Birdie covered her cough before she pressed another cherry into the pan.

"And why not? He's quite handsome, has a good job, and is educated." Lydia faced Birdie, holding the knife.

"He is." Another little white lie.

"And that's not good enough for you, I suppose." Lydia's left eyebrow twitched.

"That's not it." Birdie turned the cake pan around, admiring her creative arrangement of cherries and pineapple rings. "I'd rather not discuss it right now." If Lydia insisted on talking about Hugo's virtues, Birdie might burst with her anger over Lydia's betrayals. And that would make everyone uncomfortable. Birdie wiped her hands on her gingham yellow apron, making pink finger shaped streaks.

"When?" Lydia's waved the knife as if in the shape of a question mark before turning back towards the sink. "It's as if you forgot your promise."

Birdie tensed her shoulders and released them the way she had before going on stage.

"You'd never let me forget that." Birdie untied her apron and laid it across the back of the caned chair.

Lydia strode over and glared at the fruit arranged in the bottom of the cake pan. "You're supposed to make a symmetrical pattern with the cherries, not this mess." Her eyes bore into Birdie's. "Have you forgotten everything I've taught you?"

Birdie stroked her neck. There were so many things she wanted to say. She stared back and noticed gray hairs sprinkled in her sister's brunette eyebrows. Tiny crevices stretched out from the corners of her eyes.

"I find it modern and creative." Birdie took a few steps towards the doorway. "You can rearrange the fruit if you like."

"We barely have enough time to let it bake." Lydia slammed down her knife.

Birdie's eyes burned as she took two stairs at a time. Lydia was determined to have life her way. Nothing could change that. In her room, Birdie swiped the "Don't Quit" embroidered sampler off the wall and sent it clanking across the hardwood floor.

"What's going on?" Lydia called from the bottom of the stairs.

Birdie stood with her forehead against her bedroom door wishing Lydia was … she didn't know what at first. But as she cracked open the door, she realized she simply wished Lydia loved her.

"Bertha?"

Birdie could hear Lydia's foot stomp on the first stair.

"Everything's fine." She choked out before slamming her door shut.

* * *

From her spot on the half-wall along the front porch Birdie could see Gerald and Hugo walking up Walnut Street, their hats bobbing with conversation. Hugo cradled a small box along with a bouquet of white carnations. Aunt Edith had taught her that white carnations were given to women for good fortune. Had Hugo chosen those flowers because he knew their meaning or had they just been on sale?

Gerald came up the cement stairs first and tipped his hat to Birdie. He went inside, holding the screen door so it wouldn't slam shut.

"Hello, babe." Hugo trotted up the steps. "I brought you a peace offering." He held out the small cardboard box. "These are for the lady of the house." He held the flowers back.

Clearly the bouquet had been cheap. Birdie took the box and something inside moved. She peeled the folded flap open. A calico kitten mewed up at her. Birdie's eyes went from Hugo to the kitten and back to Hugo.

"A kitten as a peace offering?"

"Who can refuse a kitten?" He said hunching his shoulders.

"I can." She closed the flap and handed the box back.

"What?" He set the box and flowers on the wicker coffee table.

The kitten's paw tried to work the flap open. Hugo placed his hand on Birdie's upper arm, demanding her attention. "Let's start this morning's conversation over."

"Cats attack birds."

"I can take the kitten back."

"That's not it."

"You want the kitten?"

"No." Birdie lunged as the kitten darted out of the box. She picked it up, stroked its back and gently returned it to the box. She folded the flaps into each other, so they stayed shut.

"Return the kitten to its owners and leave, Hugo."

"Come on, babe." He leaned over the box and put his face close to hers. "I'm a swell guy once you give me a chance, a real chance." He paused, his lips near enough to hers she could smell the mint he must have chewed on his walk here.

She reared back and slapped his cheek. The box tumbled onto the porch floor. Popping out of the open box, the kitten skirted down the steps and into the bushes that lined the yard. Birdie stared at her stinging hand.

"Damn." Hugo backed away.

"Everything all right out there?" Gerald called through the open screen door. "We're filling the glasses just now."

"Yes sir," Hugo called. He rubbed his cheek. "That hurt."

"Get out."

"What will you tell Gerald? And Lydia."

"That you offer sincere apologies, but you suddenly felt very ill."

"Is that all?"

"Yes." Birdie held his gaze. She had already told Gerald what she knew about Hugo at lunch. And she still had her letter to Gerald if he acted as if he hadn't listened to her.

"Fine."

"And Hugo," Birdie scooped up the empty box and handed it to him. "As I stated many times before, we are through, finished, kaput."

"You haven't seen the last of me." He rambled down the steps rubbing his cheek as he strode away.

Birdie sank into the cushioned wicker chair cradling her head with both hands. Lydia held the screen door wide while Gerald came out carrying the silver tray with four glasses of lemonade.

"I know it's late in the season for lemonade, but Gerald tells me it's your favorite." Lydia looked around the porch. "Where's Hugo?"

"He wasn't feeling well so I sent him home." Birdie stared at her shoes. "Maybe it's catching, I feel sick myself."

Lydia reached to touch Birdie's forehead.

Birdie turned her face away. "I'm quite nauseous."

"I see." Lydia stepped back.

"Should you go upstairs and lie down?" Gerald set the tray on the low table next to the bouquet. He reached for Birdie as she stood on her own. It was clear he wanted her away as much as she did.

"Good night." Birdie murmured as she moved away, catching the screen door before it slammed. She stood just inside, listening.

"Wonder what that's all about," Lydia asked.

"I have no idea," Gerald replied.

Birdie started up the stairs. And Gerald claimed he never lied to Lydia.

Birdie lay with her head slightly propped up on her pillow. She hadn't faked being sick. Spasms of nausea came and went as the day played in her mind. She fiddled with the swallow brooch pinned to her collar. She missed Helen, who she knew cared for her. Was that even true? Helen still hadn't let Birdie know her address, hadn't written nor called. Birdie rolled to her side and curled her legs up to her chest. Here she was, disrupting all that she knew. She had challenged Gerald, pushed away Hugo, and was prepared to confront Lydia—all for a person who may not reciprocate the feelings Birdie held for her.

That she had committed this room to memory the night before she left for her first Chautauqua performance seemed ridiculous. Nothing felt comforting. Not her reading chair, with stuffing coming out at the seams. The Tiffany lamp never gave out enough light and the quilted bedspread was lumpy. The framed embroidered sampler lay bent and broken on the floor. Had her mother sewed that or was it another lie from Lydia? She rolled to her other side facing the window as the evening sky turned purple and dark.

Doubts crowded her mind when she needed to be certain and determined. Her mother hadn't seemed as demanding as Lydia as far as she could remember. Edwin had delighted in Birdie's every quirk. The fact that they were more alike than she had even realized made her melancholy. Flo, Mary, and even Adelle had befriended her and helped her grow. And Helen. She had a way of asking questions that made Birdie figure out what she wanted.

Birdie pretended Helen sat at the edge of her bed, rubbing Birdie's back with her slender fingers the way she had a few nights of their Chautauqua journey. She asked herself the questions she thought Helen might. Did Birdie want to leave West Chester? Yes, she nodded. Did she want to teach with Miss Woodward even if it meant upsetting Lydia. "Yes," she said aloud. Did she love Helen? Birdie rolled onto her back staring up at the ceiling. As she fingered the swallow pin, its crystals reflected tiny lights across the room. She began to question if she loved Helen or just the idea of Helen.

*　　*　　*

"Bertha. Wake up."

Birdie opened her eyes to the dark. She had dreamed someone called her name. She pulled the blanket over her exposed legs.

"Bertha." Gerald half whispered again through a crack of her open bedroom door.

Birdie propped up on her elbow. Squinting she could barely make out Gerald's fingers curled around the doorframe.

"What's wrong?" She swung her legs off the side of the bed.

"Someone insisted I wake you." He pushed the door open wider and stuck his head in.

"Here? At the house?"

"On the telephone."

"I'll be down in a sec."

Birdie grabbed her robe off the closet hook and slipped her arm into the quilted sleeve. She brushed past Gerald who stood in the hallway. His skinny bare legs and mussed hair conjured up a stork to Birdie. His arms were crossed against a loosely tied smoking jacket.

"I told her to telephone tomorrow morning. She rang again as soon as I hung up stating that it was tomorrow." He tightened his sash. "Inform her telephoning this late is completely unacceptable." His gruff voice didn't match his attire.

Birdie held back a snicker as she started down the carpeted stairs.

"I'm sorry she woke you. Please go back to sleep."

He muttered as he turned down the hallway.

It must be Flo. Birdie peered at the grandfather clock in the entryway on her way to the kitchen. It was around half past midnight. She picked up the earpiece from the marble-topped table.

"Flo?" She whispered.

"I woke a sleeping giant."

"It's after midnight here."

"Mary said to call you right away."

Birdie glanced around the hallway, up the stairs and into the kitchen.

"Hang on."

She tucked the earpiece under her arm, picked up the candlestick mouthpiece, scooched under the table and eased onto the floor. Facing the wall, she curled herself around the mouthpiece.

"I needed your advice, but I resolved that problem with a slap."

"Start at the beginning, you sap."

After a halting start, the stories of receiving Helen's brooch, Lydia hiding the letter with Miss Woodward's job offer, lunch with Gerald, and Hugo with the kitten flew out of her as if each had wings. Flo grunted and exclaimed at times but mostly listened. Birdie looked out to the porch wondering where the kitten had gone.

"I can't believe our little bunny socked Hugo."

"I hadn't planned to." Birdie opened and closed her palm.

"And the debacle with the letter. I knew I liked Gerald."

"I'm afraid to tell Lydia my plans."

"You don't owe that dame the why's behind your move."

Birdie peeked up the stairs and lowered her voice. "What if I move to Los Angeles and Helen doesn't want me?"

She could hear Flo taking a drag and pictured her manicured nails gripping her silver cigarette holder. Just the thought brought Birdie some comfort.

"I doubt that will happen, but what if it does? You've got a guaranteed job."

"But."

"You've got to start living your life, Birdie. Not Lydia's, not Hugo's, and maybe not Helen's."

"Have you heard from her?"

"No." Flo blew out another puff. "But she sent you that bird pin. It's a sign."

"I guess so."

"Maybe Helen left without saying goodbye because she wanted you to make up your own mind."

"That sounds like her."

"Birdie, remember—" Flo talked to someone in the background and then her voice became louder yet muffled, as if she held the mouthpiece too close. "You're not a dumb Dora anymore."

"Any chance you'd want to come with me?"

"Positively not. I can't get back to New York City fast enough."

"I hear Hollywood is where it's at."

"Not for this broad."

Where those footsteps on the stairs? Birdie climbed from under the table, looked up the stairs and down the hallway both ways. She slid back to her hiding place, pulling the cord tight so she faced away from the stairs.

"What's all that crackling?"

"Just checking the surroundings. I'm talking to you from under a table."

"Lydia can hear in her sleep?"

Birdie snorted. "You'll never believe this; Adelle's the one who told Miss Woodward about my whistling."

"Says you—that's over the edge."

"She mailed several newspaper articles about me."

"Adelle's more than a wet blanket."

"I wrote her a thank you note."

"You're such an old-fashioned sappy songbird." It sounded like Flo was tapping out her cigarette. "I'm not letting past events define me, perhaps Adelle isn't either."

"Oh Flo."

"I couldn't have gotten here without you."

"Says you." Birdie nervous giggled a bit as she shifted so her back sat against the wall.

"I've got to skedaddle, you jake?"

"Don't be a night owl." Birdie remembered Helen telling that to Flo the night she had been attacked.

"Quit worrying about Lydia. She's got Gerald."

Birdie nodded to the earpiece.

"Adore you." Flo made a kissing sound.

Birdie replaced the earpiece. "Miss you too, Flo."

Panes of muted light surrounded the uncut pineapple upside down cake drawing her to the kitchen. Cherries had been moved and placed symmetrically inside each pineapple ring. She selected a knife from the block and sliced a piece wide enough to include an entire ring. Placing the chunk of cake on a plate, she grabbed a bottle of milk from the icebox and walked to the porch.

She eased onto a cushioned chair, curled her legs under and pulled her robe tighter. A dose of Flo was just what she had needed. Balancing the plate on her lap, she ate a sticky cherry. Flo was right, she needed to start living her own—a weak mew broke her musing.

Birdie edged down the steps, squatted by the bushes, and clicked her tongue. The kitten trotted to her open hand, mewing, and shaking moisture from its matted fur. She scooped it up and carried it back to the wicker chair. She dribbled some milk on the edge of the plate and watched as the kitten's pink tongue took delicate licks of milk and then cake. Birdie pinched off a big chunk of cake and plopped it in her mouth. Together she and the kitten finished most of the milk then the cake wedge. She saved the pineapple ring for last. The kitten climbed into her lap, groomed itself before turning tiny circles and settling. Birdie closed her eyes as she stroked its soft fur. Her mind was made up. She would leave for Los Angeles tomorrow. Staying here only caused more tension between her, Lydia, and Gerald. Soon the kitten's purring lulled her to sleep.

CHAPTER 36

343 Walnut Street

"Bertha."

Birdie's eyes flew open. Where was she?

"Did you sleep on the porch?"

Birdie stretched her legs out straight. She felt a nudge from the kitten who must have moved behind her back sometime during the night.

"You better hope Mr. Jones didn't see you when he delivered the newspaper." Lydia leaned over the porch ledge, surveying the block. The sky had turned from deep purple to lavender gray on the horizon. Two Northern cardinals sang their high-pitched song back and forth to each other.

"Goodness. Whose is that" Lydia had directed her surveillance back to Birdie. The kitten stared up at Lydia with one eye open. It licked its paw and rubbed an ear.

"Hugo's idea of a gift."

"Isn't he thoughtful." Lydia picked up the kitten by its scruff cupping it in her hand.

"I'm returning it today." Birdie rolled her feet at her ankles. They were still waking up and the tingles felt like Lydia's hatpin pricks.

"You will not." Lydia put the kitten to her shoulder as if protecting an infant.

"Do you want it?"

"No, it's a gift for you."

"You know I don't like cats."

"Yes, but this is a kitten."

Birdie shook her head letting out a long audible breath.

"I'll mind it while you go clean up." Lydia sat on the edge of the other wicker chair. The kitten snuggled into the crook of her arm.

"I'm fine staying out here for now."

"Why must you protest everything I say, Bertha?"

Birdie watched as the sun eased its way over the neighbor's rooftop. Muted golden rays punctured the blue gray sky.

"Why did you open and throw away the letter from Agnes Woodward?" Birdie asked before refocusing her eyes at Lydia.

"What?" Lydia sputtered.

Birdie held her face still, her eyes holding Lydia's in concentration. The kitten jumped off Lydia's lap with a high-pitched squeak.

"How did you find out about the letter?"

"That's irrelevant." Birdie placed both feet firmly on the cold porch floor and leaned forward. "Why didn't you want me to read it?"

Lydia stood up. "You should never have seen it."

Birdie rose, widened her stance, and put her hands on her hips as she'd seen Helen do countless times. "Why Lydia?"

The kitten mewed and rubbed itself against her legs.

"It's not right for you."

"I accepted the teaching job at Miss Woodward's School of Whistling two days ago."

"You did no such thing." Lydia's volume increased. She stepped backwards.

"They want me in Los Angeles within the month."

"No." Lydia's knuckles flew to her hips.

"Good morning, ladies." Gerald called through the screen door.

Birdie and Lydia continued to hold their stances as if two roosters preparing to fight.

"There's no coffee." Gerald's complaint trailed off when he stepped onto the porch. "What's going on?"

"Bertha thinks she's moving to California." Lydia broke her stare, eyeing Gerald. "Somehow she saw that letter."

Gerald's colorless face spoke his guilt without opening his mouth.

"I should have burned it." Lydia's diction turned precise.

The kitten's meows became frantic. Birdie poured the last of the milk on the plate and set it on the concrete.

Lydia recoiled; her nose wrinkled with disgust. "You can't move away. You have a future here with Hugo."

"I've made no promises to him. Nor will I."

Lydia harrumphed as her left eyebrow started its tiny tremors.

"The job is not the only reason I want to move to California."

"Please stop, Bertha." Gerald stood right behind Lydia, holding tight to her shoulders.

"What other preposterous reason could you have?" Lydia stepped forward separating herself equally from Birdie and Gerald.

Birdie's voice remained calm. "I have my reasons." Flo was right, she didn't have to share everything she felt with Lydia. Knowing her feelings herself was enough. "Helen moved out there and I hope to meet up with her."

"I knew that flapper meant trouble the first time I met her." Lydia dismissed the idea with the wave of her hand. "I'll brew the coffee."

"I'm leaving today."

Lydia stopped as she held the screen door open, her back to the porch. Birdie raised her chin. Gerald's eyes remained glued on Lydia.

"What did you say?" Lydia asked the doorway.

"I'm taking a train to my future in Los Angeles. Today." Birdie was certain she heard "Atta girl" in the morning breeze.

"No."

"Lydia." Gerald reached for her.

"You can't just up and leave like that." Lydia turned towards Birdie; her skin had become a grayish color. "That woman must have coerced you."

Birdie clasped her hands. "This is *my* decision. Helen doesn't know I'm moving."

"We can find you another bachelor if Hugo isn't good enough for you." Lydia's eyes widened. "I can't believe you'd refuse marriage and throw away your future for some job."

"Those were never my dreams, Lydia." Birdie's heartbeat in her throat. "I'm doing this for me." Several tense minutes sat between them.

Lydia's lips curled as she spat her words at Birdie. "Fine by me."

Birdie started to reach for Lydia but stopped herself.

Lydia stormed into the house letting the screen door slam behind her. The kitten jumped and bolted down the steps into the bushes.

Gerald gave Birdie a quick I-was-afraid-this-would-happen look then followed Lydia inside, carefully shutting the screen door.

* * *

Birdie stood on the porch looking at the closed screen door, her over-stuffed Daisy suitcase in one hand and her trombone tucked under her arm. Her satchel, weighted with her *Birdcraft* book and scrapbook, hung low off her shoulder.

"Goodbye Lydia." She called to the house once again.

Only a few House Finches responded.

Birdie turned a full circle, her military-heeled shoes scraping the cement porch before she started down the cement steps. She stopped to look up at the porch of 343 Walnut Street one last time. She bit the insides of her cheeks to keep tears back. She could barely make out her sister's stoic silhouette from behind the parlor's lace curtains.

By the time she reached the end of the block she was out of breath, sweat dripping down the back of her crepe dress. She stood

the trombone case up, wiped her cheeks and neck with a handkerchief edged with flowers embroidered by Lydia then stuffed it back in
her traveling coat pocket. She gathered her things and continued past
Mosteller's Department Store towards the West Chester train station.

When she rounded the corner to Market Street, she could see
the recognizable puffs of steam billowing into the blue sky. Anxious
feelings roiled around her stomach as they had months ago, yet for different reasons. She had no idea how much a train ticket to Los Angeles
would cost nor how many days it would take to get there. She patted her satchel hoping her Chautauqua earnings were enough. Birdie
glanced at the station again and there was a familiar black Buick parked
right in front. Gerald stood by the driver's side, his arms folded, and an
unlit cigar tucked in the corner of his mouth.

"Birdie."

She breathed deeply, noting whiffs of burning steel, dirt, and
Brilliantine. He reached in his coat pocket and opened a packet full of
tickets.

"From here you take the coach at noon to Chicago's Union
Station." He folded down to the next ticket. "I booked you a single
room at the station's hotel then you'll be on a Pullman sleeper car that
leaves Chicago tomorrow at eight a.m. for your two-day journey to Los
Angeles."

"Oh Gerald." Birdie's words caught. "This, this is too much."

"Lydia would never forgive me if I let you go west without putting
you in a Pullman." He handed her the packet. "Besides much of this is
my fault." He looked down at his shoes and kicked a pebble aside.

"It's not, Gerald." Birdie touched his arm. "Neither of us should
have to live our lives dictated by Lydia."

"True, yet difficult." He looked directly at her. "I've promised to be
there for her until death parts us." He sighed. "And I love her."

Birdie swallowed. "What made you first fall for my sister?"

Gerald shielded his eyes from the noonday sun. "She made me laugh."

Birdie wiped the corners of each eye with her pointer fingers.

"You've helped me see that our lives are too precious to not accept those we love." He put his hands in his pockets. "Give her time, she'll come around."

Birdie caught her breath. "You'll take good care of her?"

"Ab-so-lute-ly." He mimicked Birdie's cadence. Wrapping her in an awkward one-armed hug, he crushed her trombone case against her leg.

"Telegraph me as soon as you arrive." He put his hand on her shoulder. "And write once you have an address."

"Yes sir."

"She named the kitten Pocono."

"Of course."

Birdie reached into her satchel and handed her letter explaining all she knew about Hugo to Gerald. "I should have mailed this to you weeks ago."

"We all have 'should haves' to live with." He gave her one of his sideways grins.

Birdie blinked her eyes several times. Gerald stepped away, easing himself into the driver's seat of his car. He waved his cigar out the widow as he pulled onto High Street.

Birdie walked through the arched brick entryway of the West Chester train station. She found a seat on a bench that faced the ticket booth and station office. She set her worn Daisy suitcase and her beat-up trombone case on the tiled floor. Birdie pulled back the sleeve of her traveling coat and twisted her watch around. Not quite two hours until her train to Chicago departed. Looking to her left, she could see the outside platform and watched as people hustled to their trains or sauntered off into the lobby. To her right, the doors to the front of the station stood guard. Every time they opened, she glanced, just to check who walked through.

Birdie waved to the station manager who had asked her whistle the barn swallow's song instead of paying for her long-distance telephone call just a few days ago. She wished he was in charge of telegraphs instead of the frowning clerk who made her wait while he shuffled papers around. After she finally got her travel details telegraphed to Miss Woodward she bought herself a seltzer water and a soft pretzel with brown mustard from the food cart vendor. She passed more time with people watching, dreaming of Los Angelos, and quiet whistling of Versatile Quintet tunes. When her train pulled up to the platform and a few passengers disembarked, she checked the train station's entrance doors once more.

At the conductor's first call, Birdie placed her satchel over her shoulder and adjusted her brooch. She hoisted her suitcase in one hand, trombone in the other, and stepped out to the platform. A breeze blew leaves and little bits of newspaper around her feet. When she climbed the stairs into the train car, the familiarity boosted her spirits. She lifted her suitcase to the brass rack above her head and placed her trombone under her seat. Settling next to the window she glanced outside to see only a few men who remained on the platform. As the train lurched to a start Birdie watched as the familiar brick buildings and streets of West Chester blurred into countryside. A single Barn Swallow glided with the wind and she pressed her cheek against the cool window looking for its mate. She tracked the bird as it flitted and dove by itself making wide circles against the blue sky.

Birdie adjusted her royal blue hat so she could lean her head against the seat back. It felt right to be starting the next chapter of her life alone on a train. She crossed her ankles and turned again to the window. She whistled her own arrangement of a Barn Swallow's song mixed with a Northern Cardinal, a Robin's greeting, and a bit of Birdie.

The End

Photo by Cindy Marsh

About the Author

The only constant in life is change—so after multiple doozies, **MELORA FERN** moved from Texas to North Carolina to become herself. Growing up a perpetual new kid she persevered by making-up stories and learned to hone that skill into writing fiction. As a recovering CPA, she now counts treasures and words discovered on her daily hikes. Turning the pages of her grandmother's Chautauqua scrapbook has opened infinite research rabbit-holes and ignited her debut historical fiction. In addition to all there is with writing, she enjoys her rescue cats, gardening, birds, and losing herself in novels of all genres.

Acknowledgments

This novel would not exist without the assistance of many, many people; some dead and most alive. I discovered much about myself, family, and friendship while writing this completely made-up story that is full of truths. I want to thank everyone in my flock—however, my memory can be flawed, so if I forgot to list your name, know that my heart is full of gratitude for you!

To all of you who helped me write this story into my own song—my appreciation is much more than these words:

To my "Northern Cardinals"—your loud distinctive call from the past, signifying hope, faithfulness, and love. I first acknowledge every person involved with the circuit Chautauquas, especially those with the Swarthmore Chautauqua where my grandmother performed 1925-27. Your influence was truly a building block of America and is still felt today. To the Haudenosaunee indigenous people whose word, language, culture, and land was appropriated, I give my heartfelt respect and sincere gratitude. To my grandmother, Verna: your own story sparked my curiosity just at the right time and I thank you for waiting to share it with me. To my mom, Laura Louise: your lifelong encouragement and enthusiasm allowed me to follow my dreams even when you lost the ability to recognize you were supporting me. To my dad, Frederick: your line edits, questions, and stoic cheering will forever be a part of my story. To Joanie: my dear writing buddy who died way-too-soon, the title is yours and I thank you for helping me bring it out.

To my "Barred Owls"—whose deep base calls signify wisdom, transformation, and insight—Vicki, Suzy, Alicia, Sang, Julia and the entire team at Sibylline Press Digital First, women "of a certain age," who support, encourage, and promote my debut novel—I thank you! Fred, Kate, Lisa, Culley, April, Mimi, and John, my manuscript workshop editors, I wouldn't be where I am without you, physically and literally. I truly appreciate your edits, challenges, discussions, and especially your own stories. Martha, Caroline, Helena, Shirin, Laura, and Camille—my Stanford CS and WFWA online workshop leaders— I learned and continue to learn much from your classes and notes. Each one of you has made me a better writer and the reason I can now claim I'm a published author!

To my "Song Sparrows"—your sweet songs signify productivity, creativity, and perseverance— my readers and writers groups: Shari, Gail, Cindy, Jim, Laura, Kendall, Sarah, Lily, DeAnna, Mary, Anna, Terri, and Lee Ann who added much to my novel with your suggestions, edits, comments, and especially your advocacy. This novel is better because of you.

To my "American Robins"—whose "cheerily-cheer-up" songs bring much joy, inspiration, and optimism into my life with your faithful support and encouragement: Jenn, Laurie, Kathy, Beth, Diane, Karen, Maggie, Sarah, Donna, Lori, Lee, Gayle, Cindy, and Anne. I appreciate each of you more than I let on.

And to my "Barn Swallows"—your twittering warble is music to my ears which gives me freedom, hope, home, and love. Emilee, Kyler, and Devin—thank you for becoming a part of my family, I love you for who you are and for who you love too. Sarah—you inspire me with your lively chatter, unique determination, and quirky sense of humor. Patrick—your whiteboarding expressions of love, goofy passion for living the fullest, and empathy for all keeps me going. Allie—what can I say? From reading the shitty first draft, to awesome editing advice on multiple drafts, to consulting/teaching/creating my media—Thank You barely covers my gratitude for all you have done to make my dream a reality. Love, love to each of you!

Reading Group Questions

1. *Whistling Women and Crowing Hens* is set in the 1920s but apart from the flapper era we often see in the media, did any parts of life in the 1920s portrayed here surprise you?

2. How much did you know about *Whistling Women and Crowing Hens* before picking it up? What surprised you the most?

3. What were the main themes or messages of the book and how did they relate to the story?

4. What character did you relate to most?

5. What were some of your favorite scenes from the book? Why did they stand out to you?

6. How, if at all, did *Whistling Women and Crowing Hens* relate to your own life? Did it evoke any memories or create any connections for you?

7. How did *Whistling Women and Crowing Hens* make you think or feel about a certain topic or issue? For example, pushing back against family wishes, using a solo journey to grow into yourself, or finding the line between society-determined paths or your own.

8. Are there any characters you wish you could have given advice to? What would you tell them?

9. How did you feel about the ending? Was it satisfying or did you want more?

Sibylline Press is proud to publish the brilliant work of women authors over 50. We are a woman-owned publishing company and, like our authors, represent women of a certain age.